Leah Fleming was born in Lancashire and is married with three sons and a daughter. She writes from an old farmhouse in the Yorkshire Dales and an olive grove in Crete.

Also by Leah Fleming

The Girl from World's End
The War Widows
Orphans of War
Mothers and Daughters
Remembrance Day
Winter's Children
The Captain's Daughter
The Girl Under the Olive Tree
The Postcard
The Last Pearl
Dancing at the Victory Café

Leah
FLEMING

The
Glovemaker's
Daughter

**SIMON &
SCHUSTER**

London · New York · Sydney · Toronto · New Delhi

A CBS COMPANY

First published in Great Britain by Simon & Schuster UK Ltd, 2017
A CBS COMPANY

1 3 5 7 9 10 8 6 4 2

Simon & Schuster UK Ltd
1st Floor
222 Gray's Inn Road
London WC1X 8HB

Simon & Schuster Australia, Sydney
Simon & Schuster India, New Delhi

www.simonandschuster.co.uk
www.simonandschuster.com.au
www.simonandschuster.co.in

A CIP catalogue record for this book
is available from the British Library

Hardback ISBN: 978-1-4711-4099-0
Australia Trade Paperback ISBN: 978-1-4711-4136-2
eBook ISBN: 978-1-4711-4101-0

Typeset in the UK by M Rules
Printed and bound by CPI Group (UK) Ltd, Croydon, CR0 4YY

Simon & Schuster UK Ltd are committed to sourcing paper
that is made from wood grown in sustainable forests and support
the Forest Stewardship Council, the leading international forest
certification organisation. Our books displaying the
FSC logo are printed on FSC certified paper.

AUTHOR'S NOTE

Anyone who knows Quaker history will be surprised that I have not used **thee** and **thou** as was common among Friends at that time.

For the purposes of clarity I have chosen to replace and reduce what would be their everyday parlance with the universal **you** except where its usage makes a significant point.

GOOD HOPE TOWNSHIP, PENNSYLVANIA

2014

He thought at first it was a trick of the light. It was far too early to be on site but sleep didn't come easy these past months since his retirement, so leaving his truck down the street to get some fresh air, Sam Storer made his way to the old chapel. That's when he saw the shadowy outline of someone in a long cloak which firmed up into a woman in one of those Amish bonnets, standing staring at the chapel walls, hugging a book or ledger close to her chest.

He called out, thinking she might be one of the volunteers from the Heritage Centre who liked dressing up in colonial costume, come to inspect the renovations to one of the oldest buildings in the township. He blinked again and she vanished.

What the hell was that? His instinct was to turn tail and head back down. He could feel the hairs on his neck rising, his heart thudding. Had he dreamed her up? What was it about this old place that drew her to be standing as if on guard? It was a face neither old nor young, just weary, with such burning eyes. Had he witnessed some strange slip of time into another era?

One thing was for certain: he'd tell no one, or there would be ghostbusters and cranks and it might slow up the job in hand. There had been enough debate about these renovations already. No one wanted the old place compromised. This Meeting House was not the original, but it was at least three hundred years old. The records were accurate enough and an extension was needed to accommodate their growing community. The team of willing volunteers was under his supervision, him being a bit of an expert on early colonial architecture. Each stone would be numbered and removed and then replaced carefully so as to keep the building authentic. It was going to be a tedious labour of love.

Sam smiled, thinking *if only these walls could talk*: all those years of meetings in silence, Quarterly and Preparatory gatherings, tearful confessions, joyful weddings and sad farewells.

It was later in the morning that a discovery was made that would change the whole nature of their alterations.

'Boss! Come and look at this,' called Dean, a volunteer, pointing at something in his hand that was wrapped in what looked like oilskin. 'It was hidden in the wall, tucked into these stones.'

Everyone gathered around to examine the outer surface covered in grit. Sam knew it was old and lifted it gently onto the bench. There was a leather thong around the cloth but one touch and it broke as he unwrapped the parcel, revealing a leather-bound book, foxed with age. His fingers trembled in case it fell to pieces in his hands.

'This will have to be preserved,' he said.

'Aren't we going to see what's inside?'

'No, better let some expert deal with it. It's as old as the building, I reckon.'

'How can you know that?'

Sam shrugged. 'Whoever it was wanted it to be kept for the future. Why take so much trouble to keep it safe within the wall?'

'It could be a treasure map or a time capsule,' Dean offered.

'Not in a Quaker church. They didn't go in for that sort of thing. It's probably an account book. It must go to the museum.'

'Suppose so.' Dean turned back to the task in hand. 'I wonder who put it there?'

'I wonder,' Sam replied, feeling protective of their find. Now was not the time to confess he'd seen it once already that morning, clasped in the arms of a ghost in a bonnet and cloak.

YORKSHIRE

2014

The forwarded letter was intriguing. Rachel Moorside picked up the outer envelope, curious as to why the local museum had re-addressed this to her. Who did she know in Pennsylvania?

To whom it may concern:
From The Historical Society of Good Hope.

During recent renovations to the Good Hope Friends Meeting House, a document was discovered within the walls, quite well preserved and dating from 1724. It is signed by one 'RT' and the early part of this account takes place in the West Riding of Yorkshire around the village of Windebank.

It is a unique insight for us into early colonial settlements, but it could also be important in tracing the families who came here from England to escape persecution. We would very much value any further information you may have on the Moorsides of Scarperton and their Quaker connection. If there are members of this family still extant perhaps they would be kind enough to shed light upon this person in order to add to her story. I enclose a copy of the journal for your perusal.

We look forward to hearing from you.
Yours
Dr Samuel Storer

Rachel sat back, shaking her head. Who was this Moorside, and how could they be connected to her? It was a common enough surname. There were no Quakers in her family as far as she knew; they were C of E to the core. She wasn't even sure where Windebank was; somewhere further up the dale.

There had been no time for delving into family history, being single with a business to run and having no immediate relatives with whom to share any finds. She was the end of the branch line but now, newly retired, she had to admit she was curious to know if this was indeed an ancestor.

Her parents were dead and her father's cousin was somewhere near York. They'd never been a close bunch, preferring to send cards at Christmas and turn up at funerals. But there was nothing like a bit of intriguing mystery to brighten up a dull Yorkshire day. She opened up the package and began to read.

An account of my journey from Yorkshire
to the province of Pennsylvania.
These be my true words.

R M T

In the year of our Lord
1725.

1

I like to think that my journey into this world began at first light in the fifth month of the year of our Lord 1666. From sea to moor to city, the early morning sun bathed the towers of York Minster with a touch of scarlet, mingled with the smoke rising from hovels and houses into a purple mist. High city walls warmed by weeks of hot weather soaked in more heat like embers and the stone walls of the York Castle gaol yawned at another day's onslaught.

There was no fanfare as the prison gates were opened and my parents stumbled out onto the cobbles with eyes no longer used to the brightness, out to the sharp early morning air in nostrils used to foul straw soaked with the stench of human waste.

The oatcakes and comforts pushed through the iron grilles had kept starvation from their bones but nothing more. My mother shivered, knowing there was a full sixty miles of walking to be done if they were to reach Windebank before my birthing began.

How did I survive such privations, quickening and twisting in her womb, keeping her from precious sleep? Perhaps in her dreams she was released from those walls to roam free out onto the moors around Windebank farm. Perhaps her dreams kept her full of hope and joy, as they have me on many such occasions.

'I will lift up mine eyes unto the hills,' she sighed. After six months' confinement, sixty miles was but a few footsteps with His help, no matter how harsh the terrain.

'Greetings, Sister,' said an old woman with a back arched like a bow, who shoved a parcel of bread and cheese into her hands. 'May the Lord strengthen thee for the road ahead.'

My father smiled as a sturdy walking stick was offered from a stranger in a tall hat, one of the York Friends who made it their duty to wait each morning in case one of their own should be released.

'Take these boots to guide thy steps in the right path,' said another, looking down with compassion at his bare feet, black with scabs and sores.

'Tha's got socks in there for both on thee. Dip thee feet in the horse trough and dry with this clout. Yer soles will be tough with walking barefoot. I'm a cobbler, I've seen worse than them,' offered another stranger.

'How can we repay you?' Mother said, her eyes blinking in the light.

'Keep the faith and happen one day it'll be your turn to be seeing to us in this place. Spend your first night off the road in a field barn, away from the town or you'll be taken for beggars and bog trotters and brought back to the constables. They's full o' tricks to catch us out.'

'Friends near Grassington will see you right. Have my cloak,' said the old woman. 'Yon rag'll not see you above five mile on the tops. It may be summer but there's rain in the air. It were a right gaudy sunrise.'

They scurried out of the mean, narrow streets, avoiding the morning waste chucked out into the gutters from high windows, out onto the stony tracks that criss-crossed the city, turning their backs on the massive towers of the Minster, over the river bridge and westwards as the sun rose behind them.

How different must have been that first forced march to York in winter over snowy tracks as punishment for marrying according to their conscience and not with the priest's command in a church. How fearfully Mother must have trembled at the thought of York castle gaol awaiting them. My grandfather, Justice Elliot Moorside, did not shirk his duty when his only son appeared before the local Justice. He begged him to see sense and not marry beneath his station to a lowly glove-maker. 'You shame us by this defiance. Surely one place is as good as another in the eye of the Lord?' he argued.

'Not in our light it is not. We have no truck with vows and ceremony. We choose to stand before our peers and await the Lord's will for both of us, not pay some hireling to babble his windy doctrines over us,' my father replied, still full of zeal at his new calling.

'I don't understand you. Have I not given you everything: education, fine clothes and the best of society, and now you throw this in my face?' The Justice shook his head in despair. How could a man who was not convinced of the truth ever understand why his son must abandon his Divinity studies to follow George Fox and his movement of Seekers?

'For all thy care I'm truly grateful, sir, but now I must think for myself and choose another gate to open. Be glad that I've found this path of righteousness and a companion to tread the way alongside me. In our suffering and witness is our heavenly joy.' With these words, father and son were parted forever.

But the foulness of the foetid straw, the dust and deprivation of the past months was not so heavenly; despite the scorching heat outside, the chill within struck at my father's chest causing him to shiver with fever. My mother hoped the open air would now cleanse his racking cough.

The father I have imagined was a tall man, stooped now by confinement under a roof that scarcely contained his inches. Soon he would stride out towards the dales and hills and stretch out again in health and vigour.

This man had walked across country for his calling, been beaten and bruised, battered and shamed but never unbowed. Prison, as I know only too well, is not for the faint-hearted.

My parents met at the Meeting House in Windebank when my mother returned from serving her apprenticeship to a glove-maker in Scarperton, afire with zeal from listening to this new preacher's words. Matthew Moorside was standing under a shaft of light as if pointed out to her, there and then. Their eyes met across the room and she knew that her place was by his side forever in this life. He, too was struck by the same lightning on seeing her in his congregation. The Lord had chosen well for them both. That is how it should be between Seekers.

My uncle Roger laughed at the sight of them and always called them two turtle doves. It was in his barn they were wed and it was in his farmstead they hoped that their child would be born. It would be good to rest up awhile and gather strength before the Lord called them on the next mission. If only her back didn't ache so much and her head was like feathers floating.

Their first good fortune on that journey home was when a carter of wool let them sit on the back of his load, among the soft oily fleeces and the scent of fresh clippings on the high ridge track toward Skipton. He dropped them off at a crossroads not far from the turn off north where they took water in the back yard of the inn and found another ride northwards. This was the Lord's work indeed, saving their legs for the rougher terrain.

'There's rain on the way,' the carter warned but the sky was blue and the skylarks were joyful in the air. They sat to devour the cheese and bread given for their sustenance by strangers. Then the heat overwhelmed them and they found some shade in a copse of small oak trees to take cover and hold each other for the first time in privacy for months.

'We will walk on until you tell me otherwise,' Matthew whispered. 'Your load is precious and the hills are high. Another day matters not after so long.' She looked into his blue eyes and found the strength within.

'Thee I love,' she mouthed.

'And likewise, Alice,' he kissed her parched, cracked lips. That was when I kicked and made them jump apart.

'I felt that too,' he laughed. 'What troublemaker is this who disturbs our peace?'

'A treasure not a troublemaker, a comfort and consolation not a trial, Matthew. The Lord has preserved it for His glory, of that I'm certain, to bring others out of doubting to the convincement of His truth. Time to be on the move while the light lasts,' Mother added, ever the practical one.

We took the drover's track, sheep scattering in all directions at the strangers' steps over the God-forsaken moor tops, bleak even in high summer. The curlews cried their lamentations as the first drops of rain began to fall. It was as if all the grime and dust, muck and dirt of York were being washed from them in this drenching. Alice lifted her face to the shower with relief.

No one but startled sheep watched as they stripped off their tattered clothes and let the rain soak through their shifts and wash their lice-infested hair. Three miles down the track they spied a fodder barn and crept inside to dry off their clothes and nestle in the dry dusty air, weary but content with this gift of a first day of freedom. They had the rest of their lives to enjoy together in service. No one would begrudge them a day of rest, but I was already making my bid for freedom.

Mother woke early, trying to get comfortable. There was a searing pain in her back that would not shift. She felt hungry and sick at the same time, anxious to be on the move. Outside it was pouring with rain, heavy, thundery rain and the clouds were full of more.

'We must get moving, I want to be at Windebank before nightfall,' she tugged at my father's sleeve but he turned on his side.

'What's the rush?' he muttered.

'I have pains,' she answered and he sat bolt upright, which set off a fit of coughing.

'We'll stop in Scarperton with friends. You can rest up there,' he replied, but she shook her head.

'No, I want to go to Roger and Margery. If we crack on we can make there.'

'Not in this rain, the path will be a quagmire.'

'Once I'm in the dale I know the high path. The sheep don't like their feet wet. They have ways to get out of the mire. Remember, you're the town boy, I'm a farmer's lass,' she teased.

There was always good humour between them; banter and teasing and good companionship, as there were always friendly arguments between Margery and her spouse, Roger. Couples had their own different ways of getting on.

Suffering had only tied them closer together in the conviction that they were about the Lord's work and under His protection.

They hurried on across strange paths, sensing the right direction, until with relief they saw a milepost and a crossroads that was familiar and welcome. They took water from a thatched hovel and a woman who stared at them first with suspicion and then with pity to be abroad on such a wild wet morning.

I fear the pain in Mother's back was getting worse and cutting her breath but there must be no stopping. If she thought about her weariness I would have been born on the open highway. Only the thought of my safety and a warm welcome, a posset of ale, a slice of salted ham and eggs or some crow pie by the hearth place kept her sliding forward on the slippery path. Father stifled his coughing, trying to guide her footsteps down the hillside into the next dale.

On high northern hills the weather beats hard on the rocks and grass and the wind bends the trees and flings branches into the air. This was no ordinary rain but a thunder flash that would send the becks into a spate and the rivers into swollen torrents. It was no time to be abroad but they dared not delay to take shelter.

Suddenly a gush of warm water poured between her legs to announce my arrival. They were still a mile or two off Windebank Farm, high among the wet grass and limestone rocks that lay like pavement slabs, a mile or two from the safety of a clean feather mattress and linen sheets and the services of Goodwife Ketley, the midwife of the village. A woman treads between life and death when she is giving birth and no mistake. They must push forward and she began to sing the Psalm again to cheer her flagging spirits. '*The Lord is My Shepherd, I shall not want . . .*' She stumbled and almost fell.

'What's amiss?' he asked but she forced a smile. There was no point in alarming him. Pains come whether or not there was anything prepared in the way of linen and binders. There was nothing to be done but lean on Matthew's arm as the heavens opened and the rain beat down upon them until they were sodden to the skin.

It would be madness to ford the stream for the quickest route; nothing left but a steep climb along the banks, the long way round. To be so close and yet so far was galling.

'I'm done in,' Mother gasped as a pain gripped her belly. 'Go and fetch help, I'm so tired.'

'Nay, lass, the last mile is always the longest. I go nowhere without you if I've to carry you myself. Come on . . . *"He will not suffer thy foot to be moved, He that keepeth thee will not slumber."'* In his fear my father often forgot to use the 'thou' as have I for many a year now.

'*Behold, He that keepeth Israel shall neither slumber or sleep,*' she mouthed, breathless.

'*The Lord is Thy keeper . . .*'

'*The Lord is thy shade upon thy right hand.*'

Then they saw the wisps of smoke out of the hearth chimney, the smell of a wood fire burning somewhere close by. Familiar buildings huddled together into the hillside and soon the stone house was visible where Roger and Margery would give them lodging.

They were safe. They were home. Tonight would be hard travail but there would be joy in the morning.

It was past dusk and the farmstead was shut up for the night when the barn hounds started up, waking the house with their racket. Nan, the maid, was quaking at the unexpected noise and reached for her broomstick, afeared for her life. Uncle Roger Windebank stumbled out of the drapes of the bedstead cursing, stubbing his toes and forgetting his holy ways in the search for a cudgel and his britches, too mean to light a candle stub.

'Who calls at such an ungodly hour,' cried my aunt Margery as she hid under the counterpane with a pillow over her head as if to drown out the banging. No one would blame her anxiety after years of alarums and unsettled sleep when Roundheads and Malignants roamed over the moors at all hours, skirmishes with swords and pistols bringing the wounded to their door seeking quarter. Now since the restoration of the King she hoped such disturbances were past.

She could hear Roger bellowing behind the door with the great oak studs and the bar secure across it. Curious, she lifted a sheep fleece over her shoulders and crept onto the upper landing.

'Open in the name of mercy, Roger . . . 'Tis thy brother-in-law, Matthew Moorside, and Alice. Her time is come and we can go no further in this storm!'

Margery shot down the stairs, 'Mercy on us! Get them inside . . . Nan, to the fire and the bellows . . . Blessed Saviour, open that door . . .'

The two of them stumbled in like drowned rats, ashen-faced and soaked to the skin, standing in a puddle of water on the stone flags. They trailed drips through the fresh strewn rushes as she hurried them into the houseplace where Nan was doing her best to beat up some flames and warmth.

'My waters have broken,' whispered Mother. 'And I have nothing but a few rags in this bundle.' She was trying not to cry with fear and exhaustion.

This was no time for sermons or questions. Father was coughing fit to burst and both of them looked like a bunch of bones covered with rags. Was this the handsome couple that had stood before the congregation and pledged their troth barely ten months ago?

Alice's delicate beauty was ruined, her skin grey from lack of sunlight, her eyes sunken into her cheeks but still with that glint of steely purpose that had brought her safe to the door. There was no gainsaying her when she had that look in her eye.

Margery had no time to dress with so much to be prepared. The front parlour would have to do for a lying in, but there was no bed in there yet and there was no fire. If only she had some notice of such a startling event.

Mother collapsed onto the flags in a faint and needed a warm restorative; a cordial of liquorice with honey must suffice. Old Dame Emmott's herb box was summoned from its shelf by the inglenook. Nan opened the blanket box and brought out an armful of spun sheets. Margery put back the finest in favour of patched ones. There was going to be a mess and Alice would not mind second best. She drew the tapestry screen to hide her modesty as they stripped her and Matthew went with the master to find dry clothes. Alice's shift was in holes and she smelt worse than the privy midden. A tub wash would have to wait. They must have hot water to bath the newborn.

Dame Emmott, Margery's old mother, now awakened by the noise, fussed and got in everyone's way but for once Margery was glad of her mother's counsel, being not yet blessed with children of her own, nor had she seen a human birthing before.

Being a Seeker barred her from such women's gatherings in the village, with all their birthings, up-sittings and gossipings. There was no point in sending for Goodwife Ketley, for she was in the pay of the local priest and dared not gainsay his will. They would have to manage as best they could and pray for the skills to see Alice safely through the delivery.

Feeling a useless onlooker, she watched Nan making sure her sister-in-law was dry and comfortable as she lay on the hearth rug, the thick pegged rag mat given as a bridal gift by friends in the faith. She tried to slide sips of berry tea through Alice's lips to warm her innards for the long work ahead. Praise the Lord, Nan, the maid, had seen some of her six brothers and sisters both in and out of this world. She was not afraid to examine Alice's private parts and feel her belly for signs of the birthing.

'Not long now, Mistress,' she smiled, but her eyes shone too bright, looking at Margery with concern.

'Take the rings from her fingers and loosen her laces to aid the passage,' offered the old dame. She was so forgetful these days.

'Nay, Mother, we Seekers wear no wedding bands or fancy lacings. She should deliver with ease.' Margery spoke more in hope than confidence, for Alice was far spent with travelling and chill. There was a fire on her brow as she began to moan, twisting her way through her pains while the onlookers banked up the fire and sponged her forehead.

'Where is Matthew?' Alice groaned, looking to the doorway in distress. 'He must not see my shame.' She need not have worried, for everyone knows birthing is women's work. My father was busy helping Roger secure the house against the storm. I have often wondered whether it is better men witness birthing for the labour that it is.

From somewhere deep inside herself my mother drew up her strength for one long last effort which saw my head crowned before she sank back again in exhaustion.

'Push on, Mistress! 'Tis nearly born . . . Push one more time and you shall see the bairn,' Nan shouted to raise her flagging spirit. There was a scream and a flurry as I burst forth all of a rush onto the waiting cloth, plump and purple like a newborn pup turning pink before their eyes. Margery felt the tears welling up, tears of relief and shock and envy as the storm raged outside and the thunder clapped over their heads.

They all took it well that I was a girl child, not male. Nan cleansed me in the warm water bowl, examining my body with care, cutting the cord with one of the meat knives and pressing the wound to stem the flow.

Dame Emmott bound my stomach with a binder and swaddled me with the torn sheet, lifting me up so my mother could see her trophy. Her eyes were glazed with tiredness and fever. I like to think she smiled at me but the effort of holding me was too much for her.

'Fetch the Masters! She needs physick,' said Nan sternly, reading the signs with alarm. Margery called through to the side door where the men were huddled waiting for news and Matthew limped to her side, kneeling down and whispering such affections in her ears as they all stood praying that the Lord would revive her shallow breathing.

I howled with such a lusty screeching that there was no fear of my early demise. It was as if I knew I would be robbed of her milk and comfort before the dawn rose, angry purple above the hillside.

There was no joy in Windebank that morning after all the night's turmoil but the storm abated and the ling thatch held on the old barn rooftops. The farm hands crept about their chores and Nan flushed the bathwater out of the door by mistake.

'Now you look what you've done,' shouted Dame Emmott. 'Now this lass'll roam far from the hearth . . . You must allus put girl washings into the fire to keep them at home.'

'But Mistress, we need the fire to warm the lady inside,' Nan protested, her cheeks flushed with shame.

'There's no warming Alice now,' whispered Margery, watching as the new mother slipped from them. It was as if all the stuffing so rudely pulled out of her left her body like an empty sack.

Roger wept, pacing outside while my poor father clung to the hearth, praying for a miracle. ''Tis all my fault for putting her through such an ordeal,' Matthew whispered. 'The jail was cold even in the summer heat and full of pestilence.'

'But the bairn is bonny and strong. Shall you name her after Alice?' said Margery.

'If it were a lad, it should have been called Joshua,' Roger interrupted. 'Have you seen the state of the walls outside? There're gaps enough to drive a coach and horses through. The drought has shrunk the stones and now the flood has swollen them, pushed them over. That lass'll be trouble and no mistake. Walls falling down's a bad omen, is that.'

'Shush, Roger,' said his wife as my father lifted me to the light and tried to smile.

'Her name is Rejoice. For all must face trials in this life before they find true joy. *Rejoice in the Lord always ...*' he whispered.

'That's a mighty burden of a name for a tiny mite,' sniffed Dame Emmott unimpressed, hoping her own name would be forthcoming.

'It must be so. Robbed as I am of my helpmeet, I will find comfort in this little soul. She'll be my companion in life now,' he sighed, kissing my mother's cold brow for the last time.

But it was not to be, for no sooner had her spirit departed through the open door than Matthew took such a fit of coughing and choking and being so swallowed up in his sorrow that no breath came from him, they lay together side by side in the cold parlour awaiting burial in the orchard croft among the apple trees.

Friends gathered to honour the martyrs and place them unmarked into the earth as was their custom. For this act of defiance was Roger fined one pound and ten shillings which he chose not to pay. The constable took away two fine milk cows to the value of three pounds ten shillings but Roger swallowed his fury at such self-seeking distraint.

I howled night and day until a wet nurse was found in the

village, one that would feed a Seeker child. I waxed strong as the warmth of summer returned, unaware of my loss.

To her surprise, Aunt Margery found grace and comfort in looking after me, I am told, so much so that she found herself at last with child and brought forth a son, Mallory, quickly followed by a daughter, Diligence. The once silent house was alive with the sounds of childish prattle and awash with swaddling bands and baby linen.

The Lord gives and the Lord takes. Blessed be the name of the Lord.

This is as true an account as I know, for I have no recollection of this, my first journey into the world, but it has affected all of my life. To be the child of a storm when all the walls fell down, a child born to sorrow, doomed to wander afar, whose coming robbed her parents of life, was a weary burden at times. Never to have known the comfort of a mother's arms has been a great sorrow to me.

Over the years I have pieced this account together from scraps gleaned from Roger, Margery, Nan and others. Each fragment is stitched with loving thread into a patchwork quilt of memories to treasure. In the bad times of my life I have wrapped these memories around me for comfort. They have warmed many a dungeon and dark place of the soul.

2

I was in my tenth year when the persecution of our people drew ever closer to home. The realisation that we were different from many of our neighbours in the village below was not some blinding flash of understanding but a gradual revelation, like the mist rolling up the hillside after rain to reveal a perfect day.

Windebank Farm lay hidden from view two miles from the township, set high on the fell facing south to catch the best of the weather. We were quite complete; our stone house was newly extended with rooms upstairs instead of a loft and a sturdy stone roof, a fine chimney breast that kept us warm in winter and a tall barn with great rafters that had stood for over a hundred years.

On the slopes facing south-west was a walled patch where Aunt Margery grew the herbs necessary for our survival: mint, tansy, rue, comfrey and many more green vegetables and sweet-smelling flowers to feed our bees. Our sheep grew long coats that were clipped in summer and we cleaned the fleece and spun the wool to knit into stockings and warm gloves. There were candles to be dipped and butter to be churned, fresh rushes to be gathered and little time for laiking about in the pastures but on the First Day of the week, which the worldly call Sunday, work was put aside for a meeting of believers, where we sat in silence until someone was moved to address the assembly.

Sometimes we sat a whole hour or more and nothing was said so it was hard to keep my mind from wandering or to stop Dilly from fidgeting. None of us had ever attended the church down in the village. Uncle Roger said there was nothing that the priest said that would speak to our spiritual condition.

I learnt then that every absence must be paid for and that is why Joseph Swinstey, the constable, came often to our door to collect a fine. When I saw his brown felt hat flapping up the track I hid up a tree out of sight. He never went away empty-handed, and that put Aunt Margery in a bad mood for days afterwards.

'Why does he have to take our cow?' I asked at the table.

'Because the Lord wills it,' she snapped, shutting her eyes as she spoke as if to rid the sight of it all.

'But why?' It has always been a fault of mine that I never know when to speak and when to be silent.

'You know well enough. Because we are Seekers after Truth, followers of Mr George Fox whom that false priest cannot abide, nor the fact that we don't attend sacraments or pay his tithes. He wants to make beggars of us to drive us back into his fold,' she argued, banging the broth into my bowl.

'Why does God need two houses here?' I was curious now.

'You ask too many questions for a girl, Rejoice,' she said. 'He bides in our barn when we wait on him, not in fancy buildings with graven images and coloured glass windows.'

Uncle Roger sipped his broth and tore a hunk of oatcake, waiting to make his own comments. 'I think he dwells wher-ever hearts are pure and simple, where love does His will.

Who's to say, Margery, that there are some even in the steeple-church who show His love ... We cannot judge or see what He sees.'

My uncle was like soft soap when it comes to shifting dirt, gentle in his admonitions, while my aunt was like pumice stone, scouring away at the surface until it is rubbed raw.

'Tis a pity my aunt and I walked together like two shoes of the wrong size. We rubbed against each other in the dairy, the kitchen and the hall. Why could I never do anything to her full satisfaction?

'You're a strange lass. May the Lord have mercy on us,' she sighed to any who would hear, whilst pointing out the one piece of beeswax I missed, dulling the polished table; the corner where my bunch of goose feathers did not reach the dust; the loose stitches of my glovemaking, uneven in the row that must be torn back and how the butter would not churn in the tub when I was in the dairy.

'Don't go answering all her questions. It only encourages her in waywardness, Roger. She's sharp enough as it is!' The air was chilly with her reproof. 'It's for thine own good, girl. If you're ever to make a good match with an equal then I want none to think I have shrunk from taming such a wayward nature. It would be a burden for poor Alice to have bred such a cussed child.'

I did not understand why the asking of questions was wrong but my champion had risen from the table to see to his farm boys.

'She can be as sour as the apples on the north side of the tree when the mood takes,' she chided and I wanted to rinse out her mouth with lye at these words. No child ever wants to be reminded that they are the cause of their parent's demise. It was hard to be the daughter of saints and to know whatever path I tread in this world I would throw only a pale shadow across it compared to them. How could I live up to their martyrdom, their holy devotion both to the higher calling as Seekers after Truth and the esteem they held for each other?

'Alas, there are many in this parish who cannot see the truth as it is revealed to us and prefer the old ways, both Papists and prayer-book followers at the steeple-church. They are blind to the inner light, but it costs us dear to disobey the church,' she added as if to soften her harshness, but the damage was done.

It has always troubled me to think about the sufferings of Friends when they are read out in Meeting and how I was robbed of a real parent's loving kindness. It's hard not to know of their tenderness. It is hard to be a mothered-on lamb and never to know your true kin.

Margery felt it her duty to educate me on all these matters, especially when we were hard at the scrubbing-down of the slaughtered sow, catching the blood in a bucket as it swung on the hook, boiling water to scrape off the bristles, preparing the skin for curing with saltpetre and my hands were raw with the mixture and effort.

This was the very time she chose to recite a litany of Friends' sacrifices, imprisonments, torture and exile; a sorrow that I know as well as any psalm. If I was lucky there was a snippet or two about my father; how he gave up his studies to follow his beliefs, how my mother could sew such fine doe-skin into embroidered gloves better than any in Christendom, her work sought after by the gentry of the district. How the lace-work and embroidery on the gauntlets was put away once she was convinced by Friends of the true light, in favour of making plainer gloves and wearing sober clothing as is our custom. For this she was dismissed and made to return to the farm.

The mother I have imagined needed no lace or ruffles to show off her fine bones and good breeding: her hair was like ripened wheat where mine is but damp straw, her eyes the colour of pewter whereas mine are like wet slate. Her gait was upright; nor did she slump in her grey cloak as I do to hide the buds growing out of my chest.

Sometimes I shut out my aunt's prattle and tried to picture my mother and father holding me proudly as they walked across the open fells, lifting me on their shoulders, laughing and singing; not lying stone cold in the parlour, unaware of my howling.

These pictures have chafed my mind like a scouring stone with knowing that I am all that is left of their sacrifice. I do not understand the ways of the Lord in saving such a wretch as I, a 'hoyden girl' of no consequence. What does He want of me?

Over and over Mistress Margery likes to salt my wounds with every detail of my unexpected coming. I turn my head from her inspection and mouth her words with my lips in mocking silence. I know that story off by heart. It hurts to be reminded that I am a burden left behind. Why did the Lord not complete his task and take me with them?

Then there is the burden of my name and the knowledge it was given with my father's dying breath. Grace, Faith, Hope and Charity, even Temperance, Soberness, Comfort or Patience maybe, but Rejoice is hardly a fitting name for one who was orphaned at birth. I blush with shame every time I am called to account for it. At least there was no public announcement, for Seekers do not hold with baptismal naming ceremonies.

When I look at Roger, my guardian, I try to see my mother in him but he has a ruddy face, sandy brows and red eyes that water often. His hands are like spades, rough but gentle. I have no image of my father. In my mind he walks tall and straight, the handsomest of men. Aunt Margery said I smile like my mother but have a stubbornness all my own that will be a life's work to curb.

I still do not understand why, when people see truth in different ways, there must be so much quarrelling and imprisonment and tell-tale spying in the district. Why could we not be allowed to get on with our lives in peace?

There was a clump of rosemary that sheltered beneath the orchard croft wall and nobody knew how it came to plant itself there, but it has always been my fancy that it is for remembrance of Alice and Matthew Moorside.

Sometimes I sat awhile when my spirit was low and stroked my fingers across the stem and sniffed the leaves, thinking about the two lovers buried within. They say the scent of rosemary feeds the soul with hope. From a tender age I tried to sense what they would wish of me, but no words came to my ears. It was hard to believe that I was ever anything but a nuisance, a motherless waif who did not quite fit in to Windebank farm, however hard Uncle Roger tried to include me.

Mall and Dilly had a place in their hearts that I did not, I feared. They had always done their duty by me, of that I had no qualms; but duty can be as chilly as bare feet on slate sometimes.

Mall walked the fields with his father, learning to rule the farm that would one day be his. Dilly sat close by her mother at their needlework, content to do her bidding while I looked on, further from the warmth and the light. Would it always be like this?

It was then that I prayed with fervour that one day I would find me a Matthew Moorside of my very own. It has ever been my opinion that true love in a marriage makes light everything that is heavy. How else can such sufferings as ours be borne?

3

Then came that fateful day when it was our turn to hold the gathering in the big barn. There were whispers across the dale that one of the 'Valiant Sixty', Mr Fox's trusty preachers, was in the district and many would want to hear him. My aunt ran hither and thither like a weaver's shuttle.

'If you've time to stand about, Joy Moorside, you've time to clean about. There's straw to be fetched and a floor to be swept. I don't want strangers to think we keep a rough house here and if I see thee at that book again there'll be trouble. How many times have I told thee no more skulking behind the door? Out into the barn with the besom and take Dilly. She's not too young to make use of her arms to further the Lord's will. Hearts to God and hands to work. Nan and me have a heap of pies to make, so shape thyself!'

However much I would be at my books, I dared not thwart her or she would stop my schooling altogether. Book learning was the joy of my life. I couldn't wait to rush through my chores to turn the next page and dive to the bottom of it. Reading came easy to me, whereas poor Mallory struggled to bark out his letters and Dilly would rather clean the hen coop than sit at a table. It did not matter how many miles we had to walk down to the schoolmaster's house in fog and hail, I was always first to be ready and eager to be off.

Uncle Roger was proud that I read off his accounts and copied them into his ledger with a fair hand. He said I was quick as a weasel with numbering and he patted my head with pleasure whilst my aunt shook hers with dismay.

'Don't encourage the lass in such vanity,' she sneered. 'What does it profit a girl to be a scholar and one that is so wilfully bent as this one?'

'Don't take on so,' he argued back. 'Joy is quick to catch on. Why should a girl not be a scholar? All are equal in the eyes of the Lord.'

I could have rushed over and knelt at his feet in gratitude but thought the better of it in case it gave Aunt Margery further cause against me. I decided to be extra diligent with the scrubbing.

The new slate roof over the barn was finished hurriedly but there were gaps that needed stuffing with moss to keep out the draughts. Planks of hard wood and hay bales made enough seating so there were seats for the older folk. We had hoped to remodel the house to make more rooms for sleeping aloft but what with the hearth tax and fines that are put upon all who will not attend the church, my uncle feared it would be foolhardy to spend on such an extravagance.

As we scurried about our chores I felt such a rush of excitement to think that our stone barn would be the centre of such a great stirring up of the Friends of Truth.

Dilly hovered round me like a buzzing bee and I wanted to shoo her away. She was such a fanciful child. When I told her a story about silver grey wolves roaming in the forest who try to catch little girls, she would not go kindling with me in the copse and when I told her about the hobgoblin who lives at the bottom of our well she wouldn't draw water and got a beating and I did feel so mean-spirited.

I don't know where these fancies came from. They bubbled up from nowhere. Sometimes I could make everyone laugh with my imaginings and then I'd be overcome with strange forebodings so fearsome that I daren't shut my eyes. I rode the nightmare shouting and screaming, waking the whole household with my racket and my aunt would take a strap to me but for Uncle staying her hand.

'The child is afeared. What ails thee?' he said half asleep, listening to my mutterings of half-remembered dreams of blood and death. How could I make sense of them?

'Spare the rod and spoil the child is what is written, Roger. She disturbs us all with her nonsense. We must bridle her wild spirit. There's work to do in the morning,' yawned my aunt, who never could understand my fears.

'True believers mustn't ponder over evil deeds of the imagination, Joy, but think on things of beauty and light. Go to sleep. Tomorrow is a big day for Windebank. Fret not, it will soon be sun-up.' His words must have comforted me for I slept in and woke to the bustle in the yard.

We were thronged with worshippers, strangers and Friends who had tramped half the night to gather on the First Day. There had been no bother from the steeple-house for many months but now there was a new incumbent, called Parson Protheroe, who was afire with indignation that half his congregation attended worship elsewhere. There were fears he might cause trouble in the district and demand his dues more fervently than the last priest who had been old and sick, enfeebled in mind and body.

I have never understood why Seekers were so reviled. We went about our lives in peace and charity, harming no man or woman. Nor could I understand why Constable Swinstey and his proxy, Morton, took such pleasure in robbing our fellowship.

Widow Bowlby had the very drapes ripped from her bed and all its covers when she lay in fever unable to defend herself. Tom Thwaite had his milk cow taken and his pig, and him with six small children to feed.

Ambrose Swinstey and his gang of rough boys pelted us with stones and called us names when we left the schoolmaster's house. Did he not know the priest would never allow any Dissenters' children to attend his charity school? Did they think they would stop us from gathering each First Day?

They might as well command the sun from shining or the tide from turning as to think they could stop us Seekers from following the Light of Truth as we see it. Sometimes I wanted to fling those rough boys into the dewpond and call them names, but our schoolmaster said that must not be our way of doing things.

'A soft answer turns away wrath,' he chided me. 'You childer are not empty pots to be filled with hatred and lies but fires to be lit, candles in the dark to shine out in the darkness.'

If it were not for Christopher Sampson, our schoolmaster, my week would be wearisome and without relief, but he opened his door every day to teach all those who were free to study for just a few pence. I don't know how he kept his household on the little that we brought in coinage. Uncle Roger tried to pay him in kind for the keeping of meeting house records, drawing up wills, accounts and certificates.

His wife, Isabel, helped us girls with samplers and stitchery. Without her tuition I would never have made my way in the world, but at that time I found it boring and frustrating.

When he read to us I found my eyes drawn to the fresh

darning in his dark stockings, where the colour of the mending did not match the faded rest. His britches were patched with loving kindness in neat stitches but nothing could disguise how threadbare their circumstances were. His legs were crooked, and Mall said you could drive a dog through them like a tunnel but that was cruel.

I sensed he suffered with rheumaticks but showed little of his discomfort to us. Sometimes when he bent to inspect our work I saw him wince and he gripped the board to steady himself.

Once he had been a man of the cloth, who became convinced of the Seekers' truth when it first came into these parts with Mr Fox. He lost his living in the steeple-house and now lived on his learning and the goodwill of others.

Our master could teach Latin but no one wanted to learn it from him. There must be a library of books within him. How could his head contain such knowledge, I wondered? He liked to linger after meeting for a warm brew of herbs and ale which Aunt Margery packed with honey and goose grease fortified with spirit to ease his chest.

We hovered as he sat warming himself, telling us tales of long ago: how he'd grown up in London and recalled the funeral of Queen Bess. How the great barge sailed down the river, attended by Lords and Ladies in black cloth. There was a procession to the big steeple-house and many lined the streets to get a last view of such an excellent monarch. He had seen two more kings on their thrones and the last one torn off it. Then Charles's son was returned to the land but I didn't understand why there was so much fighting in our district still.

'I'd like to travel abroad and see such sights,' I sighed, but my aunt tutted, shaking her head at me.

'There's enough mischief and misdoings in these moors, Rejoice. Be not giddy. Let your light shine on the darkness here, never mind gallivanting into strange parts out of curiosity. We don't have far to go to find our sorrows.'

I hated it when she called me by my full name. It set me apart from the others. I hoped that it would be forgotten in favour of Joy, which sits much softer on the tongue. Seeing my discomfort, Master Sampson tried to ease my blushes.

'You do well to have a curious mind, child. I may have travelled far in this life but let me tell you there's nothing to compare with the beauty of our purple hills and green dales, the glow of the stone walls at sunset and the rushing power of rivers and waterfalls. Here the air is clean and fresh, not foul with pestilence. They may be few of us but heaven is within these walls when we are forgathered to wait on the Lord.

'The prisons of London and Lancaster, York and Leeds are full of our Friends in Light. There may be wonder in foreign places but there is infamy and injustice too, so fret not young lass. Be wary what you wish for in life. I fear your turn will come to be a witness to trials and sufferings soon enough.'

We all fell silent at his warning and I shivered, suddenly sobered by the thought that I might have to share the fate of my mother and father. I turned to my posset cup with relief, letting the juice trickle down my throat, and prayed I'd have a brave heart for such suffering when it came.

Friends filled the track to Windebank. It promised to turn out a fine enough day for walking across hill and dale. Sitting in the draughts could be chilly but once the barn was packed tight with bodies amid the smell of cow byres and steaming dung, we soon warmed up.

It was my duty to see that Dilly didn't disturb the quiet with her wriggling and fidgeting. Soon she leaned her starched cap across my lap and sucked her thumb so my aunt couldn't see.

She found great comfort in her little secret and I hid her vice from prying eyes with my apron.

There was a brazier of logs burning by the door so that those who'd tramped the furthest could warm their hands and feet for a while but as usual on First Day, one of the constables watched the comings and goings from behind the great ash tree that marks the northernmost part of our farmstead.

The ash towered above the track, sheltering the farmstead from the worst the north wind can blow. I liked to watch its keys fluttering down at leaf fall when we played with them. To me this tree was a great giant that shielded our hall from the blast but not that day. We could all see Ambrose Swinstey with his father and Morton about their business, spying on our gathering as usual.

My uncle ran a great risk by holding a meeting in our barn for an act of worship which the authorities would call an unlawful Conventicle. Like many others he took each summons and fine with fortitude but on that fateful day, my aunt wore a pinched and worried look.

'How many more cows and sheep will we surrender, how many more twenty-pound fines must we bear before the constables come for my pewter and pottery, oats and stock to beggar the Windebanks for this disobedience?' she muttered under her breath.

Even I knew it was only a matter of time before Parson Protheroe in his zeal would have Uncle Roger before the Justice and sent to York Castle alongside half the men of this dale.

Joseph Swinstey was cunning. No matter how often we changed the time and the place of First Day worship, he knew where to come. I think he kept guard on certain cottages to follow the faithful of the township like a hound after a fox.

There were so many worshippers that day crowding the

barn door it would not shut. The yard was full and the visitors walked amongst us in silence. The men in their leather britches and high hats were no strangers to the dungeons and one bore a red weal across his cheeks where he had been lashed with a whip. His wife was standing by his side with worried eyes and sunken cheeks.

They sat as our guests and the meeting began as every other in watchful silence. The air was cold so I saw the breaths like vapour of those who were chilled by the fresh breeze outside.

One day perhaps if the Lord willed it would be wonderful to have our own meeting house with walls big enough to contain everyone, seats and shutters to keep out the chill, windows with glass, sure in the knowledge that all can freely worship as they choose; but that time was far off, I feared. Mr Fox had said many times that God doesn't dwell in temples of wood and stone, but in people's hearts; but I thought it was good to have a settled place to meet.

Suddenly there was a commotion outside, a stirring and shouting. 'Out Out. Everyone out of this barn!'

No one moved but Dilly stirred awake and I held her tight. 'What's afoot?' she asked, suddenly alert.

'Nothing, just Ambrose Swinstey's father at his mischief again,' I sighed.

'I demand the key to this building in the name of the King against this riotous assembly,' said the other constable, his eyes narrow with venom to have caught the meeting at worship again.

'The door is open and there is no key, as well you know,' said Uncle Roger. 'We do no harm. There is no riot here.'

'Out, out . . . Not another word, Roger Windebank. You are in enough trouble as it is. Have you not been warned time and time again against this unlawful gathering?'

The constable was red in the face and called in strangers I had never seen before to clear the barn. They pulled old Mary Thwaite off the bench as roughly as if she was a sack of ragged wool.

'Don't do that!' I screamed. Morton turned and eyed me with contempt.

'Shut your mouth, Joy Moorside or it will be the worse for you.'

Suddenly my heart was full of anger and I wanted to lash out. How dare he disturb our worship. 'The Lord sees all,' I cried. 'Watch your step, Master, or it will be the worse for thee!' I heard myself spit out strange words. 'The Lord sees all. His will is not thwarted. Watch thy step!'

'Shut thy gob, Rejoice!' warned my aunt, her eyes blazing with fear. 'Let him do his will. It is no matter.'

'But it's not fair,' I cried. 'There's no harm in this.'

'There must be great danger in this if simple folk are not allowed to think as they wish according to their truth,' whispered the Schoolmaster. 'Let me take your arm, for my leg is playing up again.' He guided me firmly out of the door where there was a line of soldiers waiting with stern faces. Men with hungry eyes that stared ahead, their ears deaf to pleas for mercy.

Swinstey picked out his neighbours as elders of the congregation, pushing them into a huddle apart from their wives and children and I could see Uncle Roger in the middle as they were herded like cattle away from us.

'What are you doing with them?' said Aunt Margery with a softness that belied her fear. Dilly started to cry and call for her father and I had to hold her back from running after him.

'They will go to the proper place of worship at the appointed hour and there the Parson will admonish them for leading simple people astray,' said Swinstey. 'You are a stubborn people. You heap coals of fire over yer own selves!'

No one protested but bowed their heads and turned towards the path of the arrested men. There was not a stave or dagger or implement of war amongst us but the air was afire with indignation and disappointment as the tall hats bobbed slowly out of sight.

I could see Ambrose Swinstey staring at me with a sour sickly grimace that would turn milk in the pail and I hated him in my heart.

'We have to follow them,' I whispered to my aunt but she was frozen to the spot.

'I will not go into that cursed place and listen to that impostor's prattle, that hireling priest on his wooden pulpit. There are folk here in need of succour and sustenance before their journey home. There are those who will wait for their husbands to return. My work is here. The Lord will protect His own.'

'But someone has to bear witness to what is said and done. I can go. They'll not notice me. I am not of age to be accused. Who will bother with a maid? Please ...' I cried, anxious to follow my uncle down the track to Windebank.

'Go if you must, but take care to take no part in the proceedings. Mind everything that is said and done, no more, no less.'

'Can I go?' Mall pleaded but Margery shook her head. 'I need thee here.'

I think both he and I grew six inches at those words.

I slid through the crowd like a knife in melted butter, crossing the track along the high road through the copse so I could catch up with the prisoners and enter the township along the little-used path that cuts across the drover's track, down past the Foss where the water rushes over the rocks, to a huddle of houses that nestle high above the riverbank, down the path to the cobbled square and the stone church with its square tower. My heart was thudding at the thought of entering a steeple-church but needs must when there was danger afoot.

I stood in awe at first of the high tower with slits in the wall like a castle turret and the stone walls, the windows coloured with glass and pictures, stone tombs lined with faceless statues. How could one ever think of truth when such distractions were all around to catch the eye? I crept though the door, hoping to be unnoticed, but folk notice strangers and some stared, pointing at me. 'That bairn's one of them.'

Now I knew what Peter felt when the cock crew thrice after he denied his Master. I huddled into my cloak, blushing with fear. Then the men were pushed roughly into a corner at the back of the church.

'Take off your hats!' barked the churchwarden but no one moved to obey him.

'I won't tell you again. This is the house of God,' shouted the parson from the pulpit.

'I doff my hat to no man but my Maker,' said Uncle Roger. Elias Morton took up a stick and knocked it off his head. 'This is not your assembly here, Windebank,' he yelled. 'Do your hat honour!'

The schoolmaster watched as his hat was torn from his head and stamped on but he said nothing. The priest rose up and began his tirade against the men assembled.

'Take heed! This is what happens when men take it into their own heads to defy the laws of the land and the authority of the Church of England, setting up assemblies under the pretence of an exercise of religion. Behold this unruly sect of people who call themselves Seekers, whose only purpose is to overturn majesty, overturn ministry, overturn all our good practices. What say you to them?

'These are men who deny all authority but their own, deny the common courtesies of hat honour, disturbing the priest in his pulpit, denying his good offices, withholding what is his due in tithes; who gather in public places to the annoyance of all. What say you to these charges?'

This short stocky man with blazing eyes was whipping up a frenzy of noddings and starings as the assembly began to stir and call for punishment.

'They are yours to deal with as you think fit,' he added, wiping his brow. 'For they have sore vexed my patience with their murmurings and housecreeping. I will have none of them in this parish.'

'Aye, aye,' shouted two men who left where they were standing and started to knock their neighbours about the ears. 'Out, out,' screamed the mob turning angry, pushing the men out of doors down the churchyard path.

I tried to get out with the crush but being small and insignificant I could only wait, edging my way through as best I could to see what was happening.

It was as if my nightmare returned. These were neighbours of our village, faces known; hands shaken over deals at market now beating down upon defenceless men. What was happening?

Uncle Roger was beaten to the ground and kicked. All I could see was a confusion of men with sticks and staves beating the visiting preacher, beating, beating and I was crying out when I saw what was done to our schoolmaster Sampson. He lay prostrate, his head covered in blood as they beat upon him. In my dreams for many years after I still see those sticks beating like drums about his head and the blood on the stones.

'Stop! These are your neighbours,' I screamed. 'Why do you deal like this? What have they done to deserve such? Stop this. Oh please stop hurting them.'

No one listened to me but a rough woman held my arms and pulled at my hair, bending my head back. I ripped her kirtle with my hand and tore away.

Then the black crow priest marched through us with a gleam of triumph in his dark eyes. 'Enough ... I think these Friends have learned a lesson for today better than any sermon. Go back to your wretched congregation and warn them that this is what we think of your message. There will be no more meetings out of sight. I will post a watch at the barn against any further defiance. Be ye assured I will make it my business to destroy this pestilent sect from our town. Get up and go home. I want to see every one of you in church on Sunday.'

The men staggered bruised and battered but one lay on the ground unmoving.

'Pull him up,' shouted the priest, pointing at Christopher Sampson. They started to lift him but he fell back.

The crowd fell back, silent, watchful as Uncle Roger and farmer Brindle bent over him tenderly. The rest helped carry him carefully across the cobbles under the lych gate and down to the schoolmaster's house. I followed behind with his blood-stained hat, my heart dark with curses, not looking back for fear I would turn on that black crow and earn a beating.

Uncle Roger turned to me and whispered. 'Go quickly for Mistress Sampson, send for Margery and her box of herbs. Hurry, Joy ...'

It was hard to run uphill when I was weary, frightened and alone. It started to rain hard and I was soaked by the time I reached the safety of the ash tree, tears running down my cheeks, tears of relief, of fear and shame and shock, I know not which. I delivered the message and sank down in the empty barn as the congregation rushed down to Windebank to see for themselves.

Then my parents were no longer alone in the orchard. There was another grave dug by their side. Our schoolmaster did not wake up from his beating but lay for days until his heart stopped. There was no justice on this earth for him and no one was charged with his murder but I record here every act of violence I saw on that day and the names of those present were etched into my heart for eternity. The loss of him was grievous to us all and now there was no one to teach lettering and ciphering but myself.

The Lord was not mocked. A week later in the torrential rain that turned every track to mud and the beck into a raging torrent, Elias Morton lost his footing when hurrying to see if our barn was secure. His body was found down stream and my warnings of his fate did not go unheeded in these parts but there was no pity in my soul. His drowning troubled me not a jot.

The loss of my teacher was another matter and I could not swallow any food for days. Everything stuck in my throat, making me sick. I kept seeing the sight of him lying in his own blood, helpless against the fury of his neighbours. What harm had he done any of them other than to bring the light of knowledge into the minds of little children? What was there about our lessons that demanded his life?

That was the first time it dawned upon me that the world was unfair, that rain and suffering fell upon the just and unjust alike in equal measure and also that in those strange dreams I had foreseen it all. Thankfully I was still too young to understand why the gift had been bestowed. That would come in the fullness of time.

4

Looking back to that time nothing was the same after the parson's attack on us. As months stretched into years we grew used to having a regular watch set over our barn to prevent any further meetings there. In winter it was not the weather for standing sentinel on cobble stones with the east wind rushing through the yard nor for us to meet on the fell tops in the hollow of the great rock.

There was a falling off of visitors, stunned by the death of Kit Sampson and the harshness of those we had thought our neighbours, although sometimes it was possible for Friends to sneak up unnoticed. Quiet meetings were held under cover of darkness, out of sight of the constables, but more than five adults in a house and we would be accused of riotous assembly.

Joseph Swinstey was not eager to stand in the muck of our farmyard while the farm hands bustled around and we hurried past him to the dairy, pretending he wasn't there. He sent young Will Carr as a replacement for Elias Morton.

It was not easy to ignore him for he was built like a bullock. At first there were no warming possets of ale, hunks of oatcakes and crumbling cheese handed out in his direction, until my aunt weakened at Uncle Roger's command.

'The lad knows no better. He's under orders but since he is in spiritual darkness, let's show him the hospitality of Friends.' My uncle limped for the rest of his life from the beating that he received at the hands of the priest's men, but he bore no grudges.

It was my job to offer the young man warm cordial and havercake which he wolfed down like a hungry dog. It was hard for him to refuse such generosity and I could see his cheeks flushing every time I danced past him.

I was growing out of my kirtles and boots, filling out my bodices and shifts in all directions and took delight in his discomfort, tossing my head like a frisky colt, pretending I had not noticed his admiration.

Being at the beck and call of others did not sit easily on me and having few social companions outside the family was a constant itch. The Carrs were great farmers in the district. Had they been of our persuasion perhaps I would have eyed him with more sympathy. I daresay Will was just a son doing the bidding of his father, as I must fetch and carry, spin and sew and work for my keep here.

'It's good training for your position,' Aunt Margery said whenever I baulked at her orders. 'One day you will thank me for training you up to be a helpmeet to some master. When you have a cradle full of noise and bother to wake you of a night, you'll happen train up a maid to serve you. What I order is for your own good, Rejoice. Obedience is the first rule of humility.'

Obedience was an itch I always scratched raw. I was restless, straining at a leash of my own making. There was not even any respite in walking down to Windebank for lessons with the schoolmaster now. It made the days longer and darker up here.

Sometimes Dilly and I were sent down with a basket of

pasties and oatcakes for his poor widow. She sat by her meagre fire making lace to sell and we watched her twist the bobbins into such intricate patterns. We could not buy such trimmings from her basket. Seekers even then favoured plain apparel with stiff linen collars and cuffs and very little fancy work, to set us apart from worldly people, I suppose.

Isabel Sampson had promised to continue to teach us our stitchery but it was proper lessons I wanted to learn and no one had offered to replace the master. I dreaded passing the lych gate where that picture of him lying on the ground with his head stove in and the death pallor on his face flashed into my eyes. My uncle fretted that his barn was shut against the Friends but my aunt seemed relieved.

'You were spared prison because of the schoolmaster's death. It will be hard enough paying the fines again. What will become of us if you aren't here to guide us?'

'Tush and nonsense! You'll manage fine with Mall and the farm hands. If I am called to make sacrifices in this world for rewards in the next, it's only what the Apostles suffered for their faith. We must do likewise . . .'

'That's fine talking but how will I manage without thee?' There were tears in her eyes and a furrow across her brow. For all the starch in her collar my aunt looked to her husband in every matter. They bickered and shouted like snapping puppies but underneath there was a great fondness one for the other that puzzled me.

'Men and maids are made for mischief,' warned my aunt whenever the girls in the dairy were fooling with the farm hands but the affection between husband and wife, that tenderness of concern, was something from which children are apart, I fear.

It was a strange time, sometimes yearning for the warmth

of her mothering concern, yet other times wanting to lash out in response to her words with defiance. I was neither child nor maid but some half-changeling, betwixt and between; a stranger amongst all that was familiar and known. What was it that had changed me so?

I was musing on all this one afternoon when Dilly and I walked back along the ridge. We stopped to see the landslide where Constable Morton had met his end and I pondered on the warning, spoken in the heat of anger, that I had given him: 'Watch thy step.'

Was it possible by my very words I had caused his death? By wishing hard, was something so? Would I be thought a witch for having spoken them?

As we climbed the track another thought came into my head, a notion from nowhere which stuck in my mind, a silly bold idea and it wouldn't go away. Dilly was picking the last of the black spice from the hedgerow, bushes that stretched across the field walls waiting to be garnered.

We stopped to test them but the frost had shrivelled them to nothing. They'd been kissed now by the devil and were dangerous to eat. I felt a branch arch over and touch me, staying my progress, and a voice in my head.

'Think on, Joy, there's schooling to be done. Feed my lambs . . .' I spun round, expecting to see Christopher Sampson puffing up the hill behind us, but there was no one, just his voice in my ear. 'Feed my lambs in the barn.' It troubled me greatly enough not to want to sup my broth or finish my platter that evening.

'She's sickening for something again,' sighed my aunt. 'I hope you don't have notions about Will Carr, all this moping at my table. What ails thee now?'

Out it all tumbled about Elias Morton and the warning about

the voice on the blackberry path and the idea growing in my head to keep a school in the barn.

'No one can begrudge the children some learning,' smiled Uncle Roger. Mallory bent his head down and sulked. Dilly jumped up and down wanting to be the teacher.

'What do you know?' snapped Mall.

'I can teach letters and ciphering. We can read scripture and practise what the schoolmaster told us. I heard his voice. I have to do it.'

'You're daft in the head,' he snapped back.

'No, I'm not!'

'Enough!' Uncle Roger banged his wooden platter on the table. 'The lass'll do the Lord's work in our barn until He provides another Master.'

'She's got her chores to do, Roger.'

'I'll fit them in and Nan can help me teach sewing if you will spare her,' I added, pleading with my best smile.

'It breaks my heart to see my poor sister's smile in this bairn, all sweetness and light one minute and cunning the next. She winds you up like spun yarn around a bobbin, Roger Windebank. It'll all end in tears if we open up the barn against the Parson.'

'It's my barn and my farm. We are free to teach school on a weekday. No one has spoken against that,' he answered.

'Just you wait. You won't be happy until you've beggared the lot of us. I'm sure the Lord in His mercy does not wish us to tempt providence,' she snapped back and Mall looked hopeful.

'I have spoken on the matter, good wife and there's an end on it!' My uncle had the last word and Mall kicked me under the table but my legs were longer and I kicked him back so hard he winced and gave me one of his scowls that made me laugh.

'If the wind catches your face like that it'll stick,' I teased.

'I don't care,' he replied. 'Don't expect me to come to your lessons.'

'When you can read and write and number as well as the lass, then I'll give you leave to skip a page,' said Uncle Roger, winking in my direction. 'If the Lord is to bless us in the field and in the basket, we have to do our bit to promote honest trading and good practice. How can a lazy lummock who can't read or write his name, or work out a sum of money make much profit?'

And so it came to pass that Widow Sampson left her cottage with horn books, slate boards and primers. We set out the benches as for a meeting, convincing young Will Carr that school lessons in the week were not breaking the Sabbath ban. Even the Parson could not expect a watch to be kept every night of the week.

If some of the parents gathered with us after lessons to sit a while in silence then who could say it was or was not Divine worship?

There was just a trickle of pupils at first from Windebank; children of the faithful who could be spared: Tom and Barbary Middleton, Jennet and Sam Brindle from Middle Beck Farm. Widow Sampson left me to work with Dilly and Nan who wanted to read Scripture portions.

On wild tempestuous days when the branches swirled about and broke and the river overran its banks, no one braved the journey and we sat at our studies, or at least I sat, hoping to pursue my reading until my aunt called me in to see to my chores.

After a week of terrible storms it was First Day again and Joseph Swinstey called to check there was no one in the barn. I made to slip past him.

'None of that! No worship here,' he shouted.

'It's just First Day school,' I put on my sweetest smile and bobbed a bow. 'Just Dilly and Mall and me at our studies.' My cheeks were afire with cunning.

'Well be sharp about it,' he snapped. 'It's an idle wind is this, one as goes through you not round you.' He made his pleasantries hoping for some hot broth.

'Why do we have to go to lessons?' whispered Mall, pulling away to be after his father.

'Stand by,' I ordered.' You'll see. Do as I say. Just act normal and shut the door.

On the First Day there was just the three of us, sitting as we did at meeting in silence, reading our portion of scripture. By the next sevennight word passed round and the Middletons and Brindles brought their children. Two sevennights later there was a bench full of infants, some just toddling, content to waddle around the barn.

Their parents gathered in the chill outside in silence as we sat for an hour, not in study at all, but soon the cat was out of the bag and more Friends gathered and the constable began to complain. He flung open the door to find us sitting in a circle, as we were trained from when we were small infants to wait on the Lord as if we were grown-ups at meeting.

'This is no schoolroom,' he declared. 'What's going on?'

Mall pointed to the Bible. 'We aren't doing anything wrong.' I tried my false smile but it was wasted on him. 'Just reading practice,' I lied.

'Why, you sly minx! You can't fool me. This is no study lesson. Wait until the authorities hear about this! Out you come now, all of you!' he barked.

This was not the time to argue with him. The point was made, the defiance noted. It was time to leave meekly.

'Well done, lass. I'm that proud of thee. Your parents would be proud to see they've bred a stubborny mare,' said my uncle and I glowed with pride at his praise.

The next sevennight they were all lined up against us; Swinstey, Carr and their hangers-on waiting to bar the door but we were already hidden behind the straw to thwart them.

The other children were turned away from the barn but we had managed six of us meeting in defiance on a bench, each sitting fearful at this second act of disobedience.

My heart was thumping, knowing I was the instigator of this act, old enough now to be accountable for my crime but still not of age under the law.

Once again we were hauled out and set down before the constables and warned. This time I bowed my head and said nothing, passing through them meekly.

We tried one more time to defeat the law by assembling children to hold a meeting but the Parson came up on horseback to see us for himself. Dilly huddled into my lap as we sat in silence, not daring to look up.

'What is this mischief?' yelled the black crow. 'Who has put them up to such rebellion?'

'Rejoice Moorside. She's trouble indeed, sir. Yon maid over there.' Swinstey jabbed a finger in my direction.

'Well! What have you to say for yourself, girl?' he spat as he marched up to inspect me more closely. He smelt of stale ale and tobacco. I refused to give him my eye.

'Suffer the little children to come unto me' I whispered with a muffled voice.

'What, what say you?' he grabbed my arm and yanked me up. I was puffed up now with righteous indignation.

'Jesus said, *suffer the little children to come unto me, for of such is the Kingdom of Heaven.* These are not my words but our Lord's.

Children must also wait on the Lord on First Day.' The words came from somewhere out of my head.

'Enough!' he spat, turning to face the onlookers. 'This is a disgrace that your wayward daughter should rule over a household. Where does it say that in scripture, tell me that, farmer. Like father like lass, another windbag from Windybank, is it?' he laughed.

'Sadly she is no daughter of mine but the daughter of the martyrs, Matthew and Alice Moorside and kin to the Justice at Scarperton Hall. She has taken upon herself to teach our childer that lately were robbed of their schoolmaster, Christopher Sampson, struck down by a violent act, as well thee knows.' Roger was standing by my side full square against that horrible man.

'Don't you thou and thee me!' snapped the Parson. 'Have you no respect for your betters, no respect for a man in holy orders? I can see where she gets her defiance from if this is your attitude.'

'Are our childer to be denied a schooling?' My uncle stood his ground.

'This is not schooling but a devious way to hold a conventicle, yet another illegal assembly. Out of my way ... you've been warned too many times,' the Parson roared.

'But they are minors,' said my uncle. 'They do no harm. Rejoice is right to quote the scripture. Would you disobey our Lord and forbid them to come to him?'

'Who are you to argue with the church's law? These minors are making a mockery of the law of the land and must be punished, minors or not. If they wish to worship there is only one dedicated place as well you know. Let them attend service each week or face a fine. As for this forward lass ...' He sniffed, looking me up and down. 'I'm sure Justice Moorside must be informed of her arrogant behaviour. If you cannot control this troublesome wench then he must. I have heard enough of your ranting. Now it's time to stop this once and for all. Out, all of you! You were warned, but are too proud to listen. Now you must be taught a lesson.'

This time we were rudely herded into the yard while the constables went about their sorry business, smashing up the benches into kindling sticks, piling up the chairs and straw into a bonfire. How can grown men behave so wickedly? Will Carr bent his head and obeyed the orders but I sensed his heart wasn't in it.

The tears rolled down my cheeks. This was all my doing. Was it false pride that made me think I was cleverer than the might of the powers against us? I was only trying to be true to the voice in my head. Now that obedience had led to trouble and I was cast down in shame and confusion.

I could not bear to watch as they set the tinder alight within the barn until it roared like a furnace and the walls cracked with the heat and the beams crumbled, the slates crashed down and all Uncle Roger's hard work came to nought. Yet into my heart the flames lit a spark that burned into a rage and the words rose up, whipped by the smoke and stench and heat.

'You can't stop a fire. You can burn our barns and our houses but you can't stop the Lord's will. Seekers cannot be cowed or beaten into submission. The Spirit of the Lord will rebuild this place, this I know. God is not mocked. If you will not let children worship, then be thee warned. The children of the Lord will rise up against you and take you where thou wouldst rather not go. Memories are long in these parts.' I was beside myself in fury.

'Shut the hussy up for me. She's bewitched with her own vainglory. I will have her examined and whipped,' said the priest as he watched the flames engulfing our ancient barn.

'I beg you, spare the lass. She is young and quick to speak. I will admonish her,' pleaded my aunt, dragging me away.

'She will go before the Justice on the morrow. He will deal with her impertinence forthwith and that's an end on it.' The Parson mounted his horse and rode away as we stood watching the flames devour the barn in silence.

'Now look what you've done,' shouted Margery. 'Get her out of my sight. I cannot bear to look on such cockiness. We take thee in out of the goodness of our hearts and this is what it comes to! Shame on you!'

'Enough, Margery, you're upset. The girl followed her conscience. She is her mother's daughter. Be proud of her conviction.' My uncle tried to calm her anger but none of us was thinking aright as we pumped the water up into pails and tried to douse the flames from catching any other building alight.

I needed no one to tell me that this was all my fault as I lay on my mattress in the loft peering out on the starry night. There would be a hard frost for my journey tomorrow to Scarperton. The barn fire was dying but the flame of rebellion in me was well alight. I had tried and failed but Uncle Roger's voice in my head was clear. 'Trying's all that matters, Joy. Hold fast to what is true and you'll not go far wrong.'

Yet I could see that look of frustration on Aunt Margery's brow. Now they would have to find a secret meeting place and it was too cold for gathering outdoors in the hills. 'No more of such giddy capers, milady. You can't defy the parson. This one's not soft in the head. He knows all the tricks and now he's brought the Justice on our heads. What is he going to make of thee? Happen he'll learn that where Rejoice appears, trouble soon follows . . .'

*

I lay awake all night listening to the creatures of the dark about their business, the mice scrambling and scratching in the walls, the hoot of the tawny owl, the smoky fumes wafting from the barn and the restless stamping of the horses in the stable.

Where would I be sleeping on the morrow? Would the Justice be sending me to York Castle or to a House of Correction? Suddenly the fire of my bold action was doused by a bucket of icy water. I was to be turned out of the safety of Windebank farmstead, out of the only place I had ever known as home into a strange world of danger, and I was sore afraid.

Had I known then that this journey was but the beginning of an exile that would last a lifetime, I don't think my head would have slipped so easily onto the mattress; but youth brings comforts of its own and the grass in the far pasture is always sweeter than the croft by the door.

5

As soon as it grew light I drew back the casement shutters early to scan the sky. There was a shepherd's warning cluster of crimson clouds rising from the east, a promise of more wild weather to come. This was no morn to be venturing into foreign lands and yet . . .

When you have never been above five mile from your homestead, it is a fearsome prospect to journey abroad. We sometimes went to market, or to hear a visiting Friend preaching from his fellside pulpit, but Scarperton was over hill and dale, a full ten mile or more, with a river dividing us. This was punishment indeed and yet, if I was honest, there was a flutter of excitement at the thought of such an adventure too.

How strange that my secret wish to travel afar was being granted, albeit not of my choosing and under the cloud of admonishment. But any flicker of curiosity was snuffed out by the prospect of standing before Justice Moorside: stranger, judge and grandfather. What would he want with me? Would I be banished from the county, put into bondage or transported across the seas?

At that moment I wanted nothing more than to be about my daily chores within this houseplace, seeing to the farm hands' breakfast porridge, sweeping up, stirring the gruel pot, getting under Aunt Margery's feet, setting up everything in the dairy; all the familiar duties of a farmer's daughter. This would be a day like no other in my young life.

Before me on the carved oak chest was a clean shift, my stomacher and bodice and best woollen skirt, new knitted stockings, thick petticoats, my best jacket with freshly starched collar and cuffs and my thick cloak.

My hair must be braided tight under my linen hood, plain style. It felt like First Day, not a workaday. Everything else would go in the wooden kist with the leather straps on the pony; my parents' hand Bible, the rest of my second-best shifts and collars, under-skirts and bodices and the precious books given to me by Friend Sampson for the instruction of children in reading.

'Master Kit would want you to carry on the good work among the poor children,' she said, patting my hand with encouragement. 'May the Lord go with thee.'

Then there was my sewing kit and needle pricks and Bessie, the wooden Bartle baby that had been my constant companion all my life.

'She's too old for babbies now,' teased Mall, watching my packing, full of envy. 'Dilly should be having it.'

'Dilly has her own babby to play with,' I snapped, not ready to yield up my wooden companion. 'Cecily goes where I go.'

'Joy needs a baby!' Mall shouted, lifting Cissie out of the kist and throwing her in the air.

'Give it here!' I screamed and chased him, trying to snatch her away from his grasp but he clung on. 'She's mine! Give her to me.'

'No!' he yelled. Mallory Moorside could be so stubborn but so could I.

'I'll count to three and if thee don't ... One ... Two ...
Three ...' The rage just burst through my bones and I grabbed
his hair until he yelled and punched me and I punched him
in the belly and winded him and there was an almighty howl.
Cissie was bashed against the wall and her head cracked and
split. That shook us both with horror so that my blood-curdling
scream had everyone rushing from the cobbled yard to see who
was being murdered.

Mall was crying, holding tufts of his hair in his hand and I
was howling for my broken Cissie, inconsolable. It was a sorry
sight for Uncle Roger, who burst out laughing.

'That's what comes of warfaring. Just look at the two of
you, winded, wounded and the poor innocent babby destroyed
beyond hope. I hope thee's proud of theesen. Is this to be our
last memory of you leaving Windebank, Joy? Is this how I must
recall you in years to come, clothes all awry, red-eyed with fury
and tears; a girl born for trouble indeed?'

That set me up snivelling and sobbing and in need of comfort. Dilly sat down beside me and sucked her thumb and that
got Mistress Margery huffing and puffing and threatening bitter
aloes on her fingertips.

'Friends do not fight each other with fisticuffs. Friends forgive each other's shortcomings. Friends make peace before they
bid farewell,' said Uncle Roger. His face was grim but his eyes
were sparkling. 'Give each other your hands in peace and we'll
say no more on t' matter.'

I could have strangled my cousin there and then but for
the sake of the day, I swallowed my bile and reached my hand
vaguely in his direction. He bowed his head and grasped it
but neither of us said anything and I could feel the tickle of
his torn hair still in his palm. It must have really hurt, but he
did start it.

'That's better. Let that be a lesson to you both. Don't start what thee can't finish. Besides, we want your last hours to be pleasant, not tearful and Mistress Margery has something of interest to take with you,' said Uncle Roger as he tousled my head with affection.

My dear uncle was ever my ally, oil to my mistress's vinegar. How I was going to miss the comfort of this gentle giant.

My aunt was holding out a soft linen bag. 'This will be proof of thy birthright, proof you be the daughter of Matthew Moorside and here is something only the Judge himself will recognise.' She shoved the package in my hand. It smelt of dried lavender and crushed tansy flowers. I fingered it, unsure.

Inside was a pair of the most exquisite gloves I have ever seen; creamy calfskin gauntlets with lacework cuffs of gold thread with spangles and decorated motifs of velveteen, highly beaded into intricate patterns and the letter M scrolled and embossed for all to see. I had never seen objects of such beauty before. 'Whose are these?' I asked hardly daring to touch them.

'They were sent in secret to Alice by Millicent Moorside; her own wedding gloves, sent as a token of her wish to be reconciled with her son and his bride before the lady died. The Justice was bitter with disappointment at his son's betrayal but a mother will always bleed for her son and never could accept the estrangement. She sought to send this token as objects of friendship and beauty. What were we to do?

'They were both in prison and by the time she returned . . . well you know the rest. Friends do not display such extravagances. We don't have the worldly ceremonies where fancy dresses and finery like these are on show.'

'They're beautiful,' I smiled, feeling the long tapered fingers and the stitching.

'They've been packed away for safe keeping but alas, your

mother never got to see them and I almost forgot we had them until now. Justice Moorside will recognise their significance, for he must have given them to his young bride many years ago,' said my aunt with a sigh.

I traced the patterns with reverence, seeing the skill that created such embroidery and design. The gloves were for display not use, bridal tokens, speaking as they did of another time and another world of elegance and wealth. The colours were as bright as the day they were finished, like a rainbow of jewels in my hands. How I yearned to put my fingers inside and feel the soft skin's caress.

'I will take care of them,' I whispered, suddenly feeling grown-up again.

'Don't go making idols of them, Joy. Think on, they are but tokens of something no jewels or baubles can buy. Don't go hankering after worldly decoration either, it will only disappoint,' came her warning.

I swallowed my fascination and stuffed them back into the bag, sinking them deep into my travel chest, hiding my sighs, but the enormity of my going was overtaking me fast. 'I don't want to go, Aunt,' I croaked, feeling tears dripping down my cheeks. 'Let me stay a while longer.'

'Don't take on so, girl. The Justice has sent for you and we must render unto Caesar what is Caesar's and to God what is His alone. 'Tis the Lord's will that thee stand witness to our cause within his walls. Remember who is your father. We will hear of thy witness and rejoice. It is not so far a journey to Scarperton . . .' My uncle hugged me and I smelt the warm smoky smell of his jerkin in my nostrils. Margery patted me on the shoulder.

'You're a troublesome lass at times but I'll miss your smile, for I see Alice in your eyes . . . Now let's be having thee on the way before I start blubberin' mesen,' she said.

'Thanks kindly, Aunt,' I snivelled.

'What for now?'

'For giving me a home, teaching me to honour the truth and showing mercy on my weaknesses. I will write, I promise, if parchment can be spared. Perhaps we will visit each other someday and I can return here ...' Why was parting such a painful sorrow? Why did I feel as if the end of my world was nigh?

'Don't make promises you cannot keep, lass,' said Aunt Margery with sharpness but her eyes were full of concern. 'Be about the Lord's work and that'll please us all and honour thy parents' memory, right enough. And think on ... Honour the Lord and He will honour thee in all things. You will find their worldly town ways different from ours, happen. They are all steeple-house goers. It'll be hard to hold fast to what is seemly, I fear, in such places.'

Uncle Roger mounted his horse to escort us down the track for a mile or two. The young constable rode behind us, keeping his distance. Nan followed behind me, sniffling and weeping to be leaving Windebank after so many years, but I could not travel without a chaperon. My hood was pulled hard over my head like a blinkered pony about its business, plodding forward, not looking back to what once was but sniffing the embers of the ruined barn.

This was the only way I could manage our leave-taking. *Don't look back*, whispered the voice in my heart. *Forward is the only way now.* Yet with each step I could feel the tug of pain at such a forced departure.

At the far crossroads it was time for us all to part company, to dismount for one last embrace. It was here that Uncle Roger, his eyes brim-full of tears, pressed a purse of coins into my palm with a smile. 'To pay the fines, if the need arises,' he whispered.

'Write us a letter to say how it goes. May you always walk in the light of truth and be a beacon in the darkness, Joy. Fare thee well wherever the good Lord takes thee.' That got us blubbering all over again.

'Tell Dilly I will dress her a new babby out of scraps,' I said. My little cousin had run away from us as we mounted, refusing to make a fare-thee-well, only too aware that our world was topsy turvy. She would be hiding up in the loft out of sight.

Young Will Carr, ruddy cheeked and fresh faced rode to the fore and led us slowly down the track, out of the wide open dale with the stone walls stretching like ropes across the hills, one behind the other, trudging along in silence. My heart was thumping with terror at the thought of what lay before us, dark woods and bridges, unfamiliar faces and the old man waiting in fury at Scarperton Hall. What would I say to him? What would he make of me? Would I be confined to the dungeons like my parents?

Yet as I rode forth, there was a surge of curiosity as I gazed across the unfamiliar territory, past clumps of stone houses and byres, over the packhorse bridges, moving ever southwards towards our destination. My new life was about to begin, and with it the certainty that however far I travelled, part of my heart would ever be buried by the rosemary bush in the orchard croft at Windebank Farm. One day, I vowed, I would return and I prayed it would be soon.

GOOD HOPE

2014

Sam was pleased to report a welcome email from Rachel Moorside in Yorkshire which arrived in time to be shared at the scheduled monthly progress meeting for the renovations. He had also heard from the paper conservator in Philadelphia, who'd been recommended to them by the Foundation of the American Institute for Conservation online. She was as excited as they were at this find but urged caution in trying to read through any more before the pages were prepared and restored fully.

'It's a miracle it was as well preserved as it was, given it was at the mercy of damp, stone, changes in temperature and humidity. The binding has taken most of the punishment but the pages are cockled with dampness and needed straightening,' she advised.

Sam was impatient to read more from this mysterious woman's feathery handwriting but he knew they must be patient as her story was revealed. He read out the email from Rachel and printed off the photos to hand round.

Dear Dr Storer

Thank you for your intriguing letter which was passed to me by the Curator of our local museum. I'm afraid I know very little about the Quaker connection to our family, if indeed there is one.

My distant cousin, Marcus, assures me that the Moorsides have been in Yorkshire 'since Adam were a lad' and held some positions of importance during the Stuart reigns in the 1600s. He is looking into a connection in the Judiciary as he once saw a pair of fine white gloves that were said to belong to a judge in the family.

Your letter was most opportune as I have recently retired and will have more time for further researches on your behalf. It all sounds very interesting and it would be helpful for me to have more copies of your discovery so I can follow up any leads when they become available.

I have made a visit to Windebank. The layout is little changed from Joy's time but I was disappointed to see that the village mostly consists of empty holiday cottages and the old meeting house is now a private home.

A Quaker friend of mine lent me Besse's Book of Sufferings for the Yorkshire District, *written in the time of persecution, where I found the names of Matthew Moorside and his wife, Alice. This confirms that they were sent to York jail for four years for marrying outside the church but were released and later died. The early parish records were lost.*

Please feel free to email me at the above address if you have any further leads for me to follow. I have attached some photos of Windebank Chapel and local scenes. It is a beautiful part of our county and was filmed many years ago in the drama series All Creatures Great and Small *which I know is popular all over the world. The Quaker movement was born out of such a territory as ours.*

Best Wishes
Rachel Moorside

6

My nostrils told me we were coming into habitation; the air smelt foul, not like a farmyard hum. On the outskirts of Scarperton I could just see the ruins of the old castle with broken walls and turrets from the bombardments of the Royalist army. The street was cluttered with wagons, beasts and stalls, crowded with strangers about their business, not even looking up to watch us pass by.

I had never seen so many people in one place except at prayer in one of the mountain worship meetings when Friends from near and far gathered to see George Fox who came into our district to preach the New Way.

Nor had I seen such gaudy apparel: soldiers in uniform, women in bright cloaks and hoods whose scarlet petticoats swished in the mud, carrying baskets full of trimmings and lace while flags and signs fluttered over the doorways. Children were running barefoot in the chill and mire, wild like puppies in the wind.

It was as if the whole world was gathering in noisome chatter, yelling their wares across the banter of costermongers and the clack of wheels, the snorting of horses in the frosty air. The sounds of a town were indeed strange to my ears and the speed of men rushing hither and thither, faces down, was most unfriendly.

I was glad that Nan rode close by me as we followed Will Carr who was waving and nodding to strangers in a fashion that surprised me. Had he been introduced to so many unknown faces? He was pretending that we were none of his charge, embarrassed to be in the company of such plain folk as us.

Then we crossed yet another river bridge and came out above the town on the other side. Would this journey ever end? I thought of my poor mother and their sixty-mile trek home. No wonder I was born all of a rush after such an experience. My seat was sore and bruised, my stomach rumbling with hunger, for the oatcake and cheese were long eaten up.

Then we turned through a great gate and up a long lane lined with trees towards a house standing set back in a park, the size of which I had never seen before; a house of grey stone with many windows with small panes, a buttressed tower in the corner like an old keep.

Will pointed to the path leading round the back by the side of the building to the cobbled stone yard and stables. This was an entrance more in keeping with our station.

'In my Father's house are many mansions,' said the Bible. Was Heaven full of such dwellings? Windebank Farm would fit many times into this stone palace. Was this my grandfather's house? Suddenly I felt so small and afraid, so out of place in such a vastness while men in livery rushed to take the horses from us. Would Justice Elliott Moorside see a likeness of his son in me?

'We'll report to the court house,' said Will as he dismounted, leaving us to get down as best we could. The tired little steed, muddy and sweating, was led away by a groom.

Just the name 'court house' made me shiver. The very words were fearful to me. Was I to follow in my parents' footsteps and on to York Castle Goal? Nan stepped quickly to my side, seeing the look of terror in my eyes.

'Fret not, Joy, you've done nought wrong in the eye of the Lord but worship in thine own way,' she whispered. 'All shall be well.'

I wished that I had her confidence. There was no comfort in her words for me.

We were ushered towards a large barn door that opened into a stone-walled room with arching rafters and a stone floor upon which stood a table of oak, the biggest I had ever seen, and a carved chair with a high back all coiled with wooden leaves. The arms were scrolled, the ends like knotted fists that frightened me. The room was empty. I felt like a small pea in a cask.

We stood clutching each other for comfort, not knowing what to expect. 'Wait there,' said Will Carr, who looked as flummoxed as we.

This was a sorrowful place and in my mind's eye there were flashes of frightened men and women dragged before that awesome chair in fear of their lives. Was this where my own mother and father were brought to hear the charges of their Mittimus and know their fate?

Yet it was but an old barn, plain as many in the district, plain like our meeting house at Windebank where we worshipped each First Day, with the rough stones, bare walls and benches I knew so well.

Suddenly it was no longer so fearsome to me, for the Lord was tempering the wind to the shorn lamb. Now there was only Justice Moorside to face and his mighty voice calling me to account for my stubbornness. How should I, a mere maid, answer his accusations? What would he look like?

We waited and waited, sitting huddled on the bench with the chest of possessions close by my feet. My stomach was rumbling with hunger and Nan fished into her skirts to bring out a fresh apple from the apple loft. It smelt of home comforts and the morning picking them from the apple orchard where I was always so content, knowing my parents were lying close by. I was far from their protection now.

Nan could always be relied upon for treats with a little something to soothe my endless hunger. She had been forced to leave her place just to hold my apron strings and see me settled safely.

Never was I more grateful than now for her thoughtful gesture; dear Nan who was fitted for Heaven early in a way I would never be. This journey would not have helped her cough that brought her low each year before spring came again. Why did I spell trouble for everyone I met?

Suddenly we heard the barking of dogs and horses' hooves, the bustle of servants outside and the rattle of wheels as if the whole courtyard was alive with the entrance of soldiers, huntsmen and coachmen all at the same time.

My right foot jumped up and down as it does when I am afeared. I shivered in my thick cloak as if there was a chill wind blowing through the hall. The Justice was here, and punishment was at hand.

'Stop your chittering, Joy Moorside,' I muttered, summoning all my strength to sit calm and upright opposite the chair, my eyes following its carved curvings like a river. Remember who you are: daughter of martyrs, maid of the high dales. What was it Nan had said? *All shall be well with you.* I bent my head in prayer and refused to budge when the door was flung open and a gruff voice barked above me.

'Well, bring forth the culprit.' It was a rich northern voice, deep with phlegm. 'Rejoice Moorside ... what a damn silly name for a wench.'

I sat forward, not moving, not wanting to face my foe.

'Stand up, lass, when you're spoken to. Let's have a look at this dissenting baggage.'

All he could see were the backs of our large hats and hunched shoulders. 'Look at me, damn it!' he yelled.

I turned to face the voice, expecting a tall figure to dwarf me, a man built like a barn door just like my uncle Roger. To my shock he was but a barrel on legs with white hair tied back; a man not a foot above my head, dressed in hunting leathers and high boots, who smelled of horses and sweat, splashed with mud. I could scarce contain my surprise and bowed my head.

'So this is the slip of a missy, the house creeper who defied the constables and the priest to hold conventicles in the barn!' he laughed, staring at me closely.

'I didn't hold services, sir. We don't hold with chantings and steeple-house prayer books. I was just teaching ...' Out the words spilled like peas from a sack: me and my big mouth holding forth as usual.

'So it speaks at last! Bold and forward like all of these ranting Quakers. And not above thirteen by the size of her,' he added.

'Fifteen come fifth month,' I replied, looking straight above his head with defiance.

'Look at me when I am speaking, the cheek of it! Rejoice indeed ... whoever gave you such a name?' he said.

'My father, Matthew Moorside, on his death bed.' I stared up at him, watching his expressionless eyes blink as that blessed name reached his ears. There was no mistaking those same slate-grey eyes as mine own.

His cheeks flushed as if I had spoken of a curse. There was hesitation now in his guarded reply. 'So it's true what I was told, then.' He turned to his henchman. 'This is my own flesh and blood before me. I thought never to see such in my lifetime. Why, even in death these people chose to make an exhibition of their faith by picking such pious outbursts for their offspring's names. It beats me why they make show of stubbornness. I wager this maid is not baptised either. Getting children to defy the authorities, indeed!'

'No one made me teach school. If the priest had not let his men kill our teacher Friend Sampson there would have been no necessity for anyone to take up his primers and horn books. I bore witness to their devilment and how they cracked his head with cudgels when we were taken to the steeple-house—'

'Enough of the theeing and thouing ... Do you know to whom you speak?'

'Aye, to Justice Moorside, my grandfather as I am told, and I must tell you that the priest Protheroe did not stop those evil men from their deed.'

I was not going to be distracted from my witness by his interruption. I was afire with indignation but Nan was quivering and tugging at my sleeve end.

'The priest did not assault the man, I am told. Do not bear false witness,' said my judge.

'One word from him and they would have ceased their work,' I argued back. 'We were about our business in peace. Why is that so wrong of us?'

'Enough of this nonsense! You are a very forward lass to speak of your betters in such fashion. I take it then that they have taught you to read scripture and make letters?' He sighed, shaking his head. 'This is what comes of educating children above their station.'

'Aye, I can read, write, cipher and make accounts. I can spin and knit, sew and make cheese,' I replied with pride, unaware that he was mocking me. Then I recalled the gloves in my kist. 'I have proof of my parentage, here in my box ...' I bent down to open the straps but his voice boomed over me.

'Enough! I need no proof of your parentage. One look at you and I see my son in all his spitting arrogance; the same jutting chin and fierce eye. What are we to do with such defiance?' he sighed again, wiping his brow with a lace-edged kerchief.

'But I have something to show you. Mistress Windebank said to be sure and show—'

'There you go a-prattling again, all the manners of a cottar child, not a Moorside but educated to be a ranting Quaker ... By Jove!' he sat down in the big carved chair with the table between us, staring at me as if I was some piece of pig muck.

'We don't rant, we preach the holy Word,' I answered meekly.

'Do you not know when to speak and when to be silent, baggage? I should have you put in the stocks for your impudence, or send you to the House of Correction to teach you obedience, but now you are here and I see you have spirit and courage with your waywardness ... Oh heck! I suppose you know no better. What can a lass learn in a farmyard up the dale but coarseness? Perhaps it would be best to keep you close at hand for a while and see how you shape up under strict instruction. Send for Dame Priscilla this minute, she'll happen sort you out...' He wiped his forehead with a kerchief. 'I'm too old for bothering with troublesome wenches who don't know their place.' He leaned back in the chair, seeming relieved with his decision.

'Would you prefer that I return back from whence I came?' I offered, smiling, hoping to charm this barrel of gunpowder who was hissing in my direction but all I did was light the fuse of his temper.

'I've not summoned you all this way to let you meander back to that den of dissention, theeing and thouing to all and sundry. Any fool can see you are wilfully bent but now that I've had a gawp at you I see there's something in there worth training up. But be it understood that I'll not stomach any Quaking nonsense from you under my roof!' he bellowed, standing up. 'Where's that bloody woman got to?'

My heart was thumping in my chest but I stood up none the less. 'Sir, I have to follow the truth as I have been taught. I know no other way.'

'Not another word, baggage, your rough voice grates on my ears. You will do as you are bid in this household or it will be beaten into you. I am sick and tired of you Quakers standing before me with hats aloft as if you were my equal. You think you alone have the right path to glory. Here you will repent of your former ways and learn that there are other paths to follow,' he shouted, his cheeks flushed with fury. 'I am sick of seeing sour maids dragged before me, dressed in torn rags displaying their nakedness for all to see in the streets of this town, flaunt-ing their bodies to the whip as if they were martyrs. It's time you were brought to heel like a disobedient hound. Where is that wretched woman?'

He turned to the open door impatiently as a woman scurried through, dressed in black, the keys on her chatelaine clanking with the rush. 'What ails you, Master?' she panted.

'This is Dame Priscilla Foxup, she will find you a suitable place in the household to teach you your manners.' Turning their backs on us in a huddle of concern, they whispered out of earshot. The woman kept flashing glances over her shoulder as if she could not believe this unexpected addition to her house-hold. Her hands were twisted with frustration. I don't think she was pleased at all. Then she slowly walked around me like a farmer eyeing a heifer for sale.

'You will shape her coat according to our cut, Mistress,' my grandfather ordered. 'It must be of our fashioning, not hers. She's a Moorside when all is said and done. Let's hope it's not too late to undo some of the nonsense that's been drummed into her silly head. Whatever it takes, Priscilla, whatever it takes . . .'

The woman eyed me with suspicion, taking in my stature and face. Her eyes were cold and forbidding but perhaps that was because she was taken unawares. 'She's straight backed, plain spoken but I see the Moorside look. I see young Matt and a little of poor Millicent,' she nodded turning to me with a sigh. 'You are fortunate, young woman, to be the object of such charity and concern. I hope you will repay the Master with obedience and loyalty. The maid, I presume, goes back to the farmyard. I want sole charge of this lass,' she added with hands clasped, awaiting instructions. 'Tell the farmer that we will deal with her in the household according to her rank,' she ordered, looking at Nan with disdain.

'Yes, Ma'am,' said Nan, bobbing a curtsy, and turned to me. 'I'll tell them thee is well looked after. Master Roger will write you, I'm sure, and Diligence when she knows her letters. May the Lord be your guide and consolation.' Then she hugged me and whispered, 'Take heed, Joy, of this worldly company, for you can't touch pitch tar without it leaving some mark.' I was crying and clinging to her. Why must she leave me here amongst strangers?

'That's enough fussing,' said Dame Foxup, pulling us apart. 'Anyone would think you're being sent to prison, not given a chance to rise above your station.'

Nan bobbed again, sniffing as we said our farewells. I stood watching her walk slowly from the hall, concerned about her journey. Why did I not run after her? My legs betrayed me, rooted firm to the spot.

'Surely she must not walk back to Windebank in this weather?' I asked, turning to them both for reassurance.

'The Constable will escort her back home in due course. There will be some oatcake and broth in the kitchen. Have no concern. 'Tis good that you care for your servant, Missy.'

'She's not my servant. She belongs to my uncle and aunt. We are friends and equals.'

I felt a sharp clip on my ear from an iron fist.

'You will learn to speak when you are spoken to in this house. Everyone has their place and no one is too high or low not to feel the back of my hand. Do you understand, Rejoice?' snapped the Dame. Tears stung my eyes but I held them back.

'She can get rid of that name for a start. Surely it is shortened into something less formidable. Speak up, lass,' said the Justice, patting my arm. 'Dame Priscilla barks only for your best interest.'

'My cousins called me, Joy, sir.' I replied, suddenly feeling overwhelmed with homesickness at what I had lost forever.

'That's not much better, but more in keeping for nobbut a maid. Miss Joy will do for now, until we think of something better for your baptism,' he replied.

This was neither the time nor the place to argue about christenings in the steeple-house. Baptism was a sacrament that I could not endure if I was to stay faithful to my beliefs. He meant well, this little man with the barrel chest and warm eyes but of my new instructress, Mistress Foxup, I was not so sure. There was a glint of ice in those flecked eyes. My arrival here was not of her choosing and there was no warmth in her welcome at all. I would have to watch my step with her.

7

It was hard not to be impressed by the grandeur of such a dwelling as we made our entrance through the back door, through
the kitchen hall, past tables and sideboards where girls slumped
over their pounding bowls, looking at me with curiosity. I had
never seen such a mound of food; birds of all sizes hanging from
hooks, eggs, pastries and fancy sweetmeats in the making.

'Are there many guests in the house?' I asked, hoping not
to be boxed on the ears for my enquiry. There must be many
mouths to feed here.

'This is nought but the Yuletide preparations. I like to be
ahead for the festivities,' said Mistress Foxup, inspecting each
girl in turn as she went about her business.

'Yule?' I questioned, not understanding the significance.

'The Christ–Mass feasting for the Twelve Days ...' she said
with impatience.

'What are they?' I was curious now. How could such a
holy time be the cause for such excess? Christmas was a time
of soberness and quiet reflection, a full working day. In my
mind a warning bell rang of mention of such pagan ceremonies
amongst worldly folk.

'Surely you have made merry at Yule? Alas, it was banned

for many a year by Cromwell's miserable mob, but since King Charles's return, God rest his soul, why everyone celebrates with enthusiasm, making up for all those years lost,' she replied.

What was there to say? I bowed my head and swallowed the reply, knowing that it would mean another clip around the head. Never in my whole life had I celebrated such ceremonies or pagan feasts. We were set apart from such antics.

'Don't look so pained. Christmas tide is no punishment. A Moorside must learn how to keep a good table at such a time, to entertain company and give the season its due, I say.'

Had she not realised that I was nobody of rank, I thought, but said nothing.

'We make the best Christmas pie in the district and the richest mince puddings. A new dish for every day of the feast with only the best trimmings. You will learn what goes with what and how to lay a fine table. Mary and Bess will show you how,' Dame Priscilla replied.

'We ate in simple fashion at Windebank,' I offered, not daring to raise my eyes in pride or relish the delicious aromas coming from the spice box.

'So I gather from the size of you, but that was then and this is now,' she snapped. 'Justice Moorside in his wisdom has chosen to honour his family's charitable name by taking you into his household. You, of course are expected to repay such with obedience, respect and deference to his wishes at all times. What better time to start but at Yuletide. We will order a suitable gown to be made in haste and a hood befitting your elevated station. You will take your place at his table and learn from me. Now what do you say to such generosity?'

'Are you the Mistress of the house?' I asked in innocence, not sure how this woman stood in the household.

'I am the keeper of the house in all matters domestic,' she

said with head held high. *But you would be mistress of this place*, I thought as I watched her cheeks flush with pride.

'Beg pardon, Mistress. All this is strange to me,' I offered. 'Forgive my ignorance. I am but a poor country lass, unused to worldly matters.'

'Why is it that everything that comes out of your mouth sounds like a pious sermon? There will be no more theeing and thouing under this roof, do you hear? You will learn quickly or feel the back of my hand until you do. A show of gratitude would be a start. All I've seen so far is a sour face, a stubborn will and a sharp tongue. You have a lot to learn, my girl, and quick if the Master is not to be disappointed.'

We carried on up the back stairs to the great hall at the front of the house, a room panelled and well furnished with fine chairs and tables, a great hearth and walls full of portraits. Faces peered down at me from ruffs, their eyes following me around the room; ladies and gentlemen bedecked in fancy furbelows, silks and satins and jewels, such gaudy hangings and ornaments. There were no plain collars and cuffs, no sober clothes on these gentlefolk.

Living in Scarperton Hall would be taking me away from the only world I had ever known. If my father knew my fate he would not rest easy in his eternal sleep. This was everything he had chosen to deny. If only I could run away, but disobedience would mean being sent to the House of Correction, to the cold dungeons of despair. I was not strong enough in my faith yet to face such suffering.

Better to conform outwardly but hold my faith tight within, where no one could reach my spiritual heart. I must be firm and resist the temptation to enjoy the trappings of finery and gentility. If they wanted gratitude then they would get the right words but not necessarily with the right sentiments. I must dissemble and learn to deceive further if I was to survive. My heart sank at such thoughts, but what else could I do?

The next days were spent helping oversee the cleaning and Yule preparations. There were to be visitors from afar. It appeared that my grandfather's brother, Ned, who died at the battle of Naseby, had family who were distant cousins to me. They visited every year at this time so there were many chambers to air and clean and make ready.

It was my job to flick the goose quill brush around the surfaces and see that the arks and bed hangings were polished and mended. The maids were to do the rough work. I was to be Dame Priscilla's spy. They giggled and stared at me and did little work until I knelt down to show them just how to scour the corners of each chamber with vigour and ruthlessness. Aunt Margery would be proud of me. It all took longer than expected and Mistress Foxup was in a bad mood when she caught me on the floor with them. I was taken aside and told that a Moorside was above such menial work.

Instead I was taken to the seamstress who measured me for the gown and waistcoat with full sleeves and a lace collar trim. I did suggest that my fine trimmed collar would do but they laughed and said the rough linen would show up the sheen of the brocade.

'Master Elliot does not want to see a Puritan at his table. You are a fortunate lass, indeed, to be honoured with such luxuries, what is wrong with you? You will wear the hood to church.'

Never in my life have I worn bone lacework. I have seen it made and sold but not to adorn the shoulders of a Quaker girl. It was indecent. Never in my life had I attended a church service but this was not the time to argue or refuse. Dame Priscilla was much distracted by the news that her son, Miles, was returning from his studies at the university. His name dripped from her tongue at every opportunity; how he was the brightest of scholars at the grammar school, the handsomest of men at the college, the kindest of sons to his widowed mother and the paragon of all virtues. I disliked him already for not being real.

'My father was at the side of young Master Ned when he fell in battle, Master Elliot has taken care of me and my boy since then. He has treated Miles like his heir, having such disappointment in his own children. The Master suffered many misfortunes and reversals after the late King was executed. Since the Stuarts returned to the throne the Master's fortunes have revived, Praise the Lord! You are thrice blessed in such a benefactor for he has overlooked your father's desertion in favour of your upkeep. Never forget that, Missy.'

She would never call me by my given name nor by Joy either. I was Miss, Missy, lass, girl or worse. My room was a small chamber off the turn of the stairs, skirted round with oak panels with diamond panes in the windows and a bed hung with crewel-work drapes. I had all the necessary offices but when I opened the casement I saw only the grey stone walls of the court house and the yard below. How I missed the wild hills and the moors of Windebank Farm. It was not easy to settle in such a confined space as Scarperton Hall.

And then came one of those monthly curses daughters of Eve must endure. I was glad that Nan had explained their purpose and what I must do to hide them from view. How the blood would come and go with the moon as long as I was pure and undefiled. I hid my cloths at first but then took them to be boiled in the laundry vat where the old woman barely lifted her eyes at my request.

This meant that I was now considered old enough to wed and bear children but how that was achieved I knew not, except how the bull goes to the cow in season. This was something I must ask of Nan if ever I saw her again. Mistress Priscilla would not allow such an impudent question.

It was hard to fathom her ways. In my grandfather's presence she smiled and appeared kind, patting my shoulder, but on the stairs she berated me for slouching, for not sitting upright, for having a rough accent to my words or eating too heartily at the table.

'It is my duty to make a silken purse out of this farm-bred pig's ear,' she laughed in front of Mary and Bess in the kitchen. I pretended not to hear but my cheeks rouged up with dismay. I never let her see she was making my misery worse. Didn't anyone guess how awkward it was for me to find myself in this gaudy prison, being watched for every fault and peccadillo? I bent my head but made no show of outward discomfort.

This was the first of many times when I learned the art of retreating into silence, to let things glide over the surface as if I was unruffled by cruel words, giving me an air of infuriating calm that belied the confusion within. It has stood me in good stead over the years.

She was waiting for a show of temper, a show of pride in answering her back. I would never give her the satisfaction of a response. Instead I asked Bess to show me how to mould the raised piecrust ready for the filling, ignoring the jibes as if I were deaf.

If Miles Foxup was anything like his mother then my troubles would be doubled. Was it not enough to have to celebrate Christ's birth in giddy fashion, feasting and dancing with strangers as the worldly do? Now there was a cartload of holly, ivy and greenery to deck around the walls and tables.

Only the scent of the strips of rosemary gave me comfort. The scent between my fingers took me back to the apple

orchard of Windebank and my parents' grave. It was painful to
know I was dishonouring their memory just by being here. I
sat many a night in the darkness, praying that the Lord in His
Mercy would forgive my weakness and find me a way out of
this trial.

Then came a long-awaited letter from Uncle Roger with
news of all I loved far up the dale.

*Parson Protheroe hath been removed from his hired living. The
new incumbent turns a blind eye to our meetings away from
the village but still demands his tithes and fines none the less.
The days speed on here. Mallory doth work alongside me like a
man for all his tender years and will have no more of learning.
Diligence hath taken to her horn book and lettering but is
learning lace making from Widow Sampson. The Mistress
asked to remind you that you must be a shining light of industry
and piety in yon worldly place. Away with vain fancies, she
entreats but what doth the Justice make of the gloves you
brought?*

*We hope ere long to visit with thee. Thy loving Friend and
Uncle, Roger Windebank.*

I hugged the letter to my chest, re-reading it many times for
consolation. As for the gloves they were still tight packed in
my kist. The Justice had no desire to inspect them and I had
no desire to bring them out. They were safely packaged with
herbs, out of sight.

I wondered whether to show them to the seamstress who
came to fit the new gown on my shoulders. It was a summer sky
blue, of a heavy shiny cloth that swished when I turned about
but was cut low across my breast and needed a collar. I ought to
be grateful and excited to be wearing such finery but in truth,

I was scared to put on such a vainglorious gown. It did not sit right upon my shoulders for I was aware of acres of bare flesh and how my new bosoms lifted out of my corset.

Mabel Ackroyd, the embroiderer, who spent all her days sewing beads into intricate patterns down the front of dresses and gloves for hours and hours, said it looked fine on me and set off my colouring. Sometimes I sat with her to watch the skill of it all. She made such fancy work that my fingers ached to copy her. My efforts were hopeless, being all thumbs but it was soothing work.

It was she who told me that it was the custom to give gifts at Yuletide, in gratitude to servants for all their endeavours in the household. What could I give, having no money of my own? Then I recalled Uncle Roger's gift tucked safe away in case of fines. Perhaps I should use some of that to purchase small mindings for Mary and Bess, and Mabel too? I would have to ask the Mistress what was expected of me.

It was only right to show gratitude for my keep, yet to spend Roger's coins did not seem fair. Still, there was no other way. I would have to ask permission to venture into Scarperton to the High Street and find some tokens, as there was little time to make anything up myself.

'You have left it late to purchase gifts, Missy,' said Mistress Priscilla, sniffing as if I was a bad smell under her nose. 'But I myself will take the horses into town beside you and supervise some suitable tokens. Ribbons are always welcomed by the girls for decking their tired gowns. I hope your new gown has growing room, you look a leggy lass to me and such a lucky one to have found favour with your kin. You must give your grandfather something to show your gratitude,' she added.

I nodded and retreated back to my chamber in despair. What did one give a man who everything in this world? I was taught that true gifts are of the spirit: love, kindness, sacrifice, charity to all in need. None of those could you buy on a costermonger's stall in the market place.

These gifts didn't matter when you ran free over the fells, jumped across the becks and sat in the cottages of Friends who had nothing of show but a few sticks of furniture yet had hearts a big as pressed cheeses. Here I was a wild bird caught in a snare at the whim of the fowler. Above or below stairs I did not fit in with my homespun ways and rough tongue.

Sometimes when I met my grandfather on the stairs, he would stop and look at me as if trying to place me. He had forgotten I was under his roof, staring to think of my name, perhaps.

'Hah ... er. You are so like ...' then he sighed and hurried on. I was the last link with his children, with his wife, Millicent, his daughter, Maria. Perhaps I reminded him of them and for a second he thought they were still alive and well and he was young again. He had gathered in that which was lost, ensnared the wild creature to protect it from harm. I was sure he meant well but there was no warmth or consideration of my welfare. I was just another bothersome maid to feed and clothe and keep under control. No one looked on me with compassion, they were too busy preparing for this cursed Yuletide.

'*Better is the life of the poor man in his cottage than delicate fare in another man's house,*' I sighed to myself as I climbed the stairs, and '*better a dry crust and quietness therein than a house full of sacrifices with strife.*'

There was a small room filled from floor to ceiling with books, mostly in Latin that I couldn't read. It was a good place to hide when I felt low in spirit. There was a smell to the leather and the must that was strangely comforting. I fingered the books lovingly, knowing that these were the very books that fed my father's mind. I felt closest to him in this room and imagined him sitting at his studies cramming his head with knowledge that one day he would use to argue his case against heretics and Divines.

There was no portrait of my father within the house, on the walls of the hall or stairs. When I made a comment to Dame Priscilla she snorted with contempt.

'Your father, Master Matthew, lost his place in this household when he defied his father so his portrait was removed I know not where. That is why you should kneel down in gratitude to this gracious man who's shown such preference to an inferior. Not many men would be so generous. It is up to you to find a gift to honour his kindness,' she added.

How many times was I to be reminded of this? What could I give a man who had everything, a man who had lost his sons and his future name? What could I give that would make him notice me? Perhaps I would find inspiration in Scarperton.

'You're not leaving this house in that attire!' shouted Dame Priscilla as she eyed me up and down. 'Take off that ridiculous black hat. You look like a farmer's wife up from the country with her butter.'

'It's what I wear when the weather is rough,' I explained, seeing the sleet blowing from the windowpane. It was wet and slushy outside after a fall of snow. What better than my plain cloak and felt hat to protect my clean linen cap.

'No Moorside lady goes out looking like a servant. Have we not taught you anything these past few days? What will Goodwife Ackroyd think when you go for your fitting? There is a fine hood you can borrow and pattens for your shoes. Take off those old boots too.' She was in no mood to hear my plea but perhaps I could appeal to her thrift.

'I would dearly love to display my finery but it is wet and I would not want to spoil them or make more laundry work when there's so much work to be done.' I smiled meekly, hoping she would be placated. 'A tall hat with a brim makes good sense.'

'Take it off and there's an end on t' matter. We are the main folk in these parts and you will dress accordingly, sleet or no.'

I was not used to wearing pattens for I preferred thick leather boots with strong soles to grip the rough earth. What a fuss and palaver for a trip into the market town. The streets of Scarperton were thronged with folk, heads bent about their business. No one would notice what I was wearing in this driving sleet, I smarted, trying to edge my way down the slippery path in my pattens.

In my head was a list of ribbons to buy. I would have preferred to give the girls a broadsheet or tract, something to stir their souls rather than their vanity, but few of them could read. Besides, they would look askance at such a plain gift. I was not intending to buy Mistress Foxup anything. I scarce knew her.

We lingered over the trinket stalls and the packmen with open cases full of a rainbow of dangling ribbons. Costermongers were shouting their wares across the street above the cackle of geese and fowls in their pens. There was no one to greet in this crowd, not one known face to wave to but my eyes caught the tower of the church at the top of the street. It would be my fate to stand within that building in the pew to hear the windy doctrines and incantations of some hireling priest. There was no escape from attending service with my grandfather. It was expected of me.

A panic of breathlessness flooded over me at the thought of such a betrayal. I turned my eyes skyward and prayed for deliverance as I turned to catch up the Mistress as she strode ahead.

It was with a mind full of anxieties that I stepped forward and slipped on the slush sending my legs one way and my body the other, landing in an ungainly heap on the wet ground. There was a burning pain in my ankle as I tried to rise, blushing to have caused a spectacle of myself. The Dame turned round to see what the fuss was about and stormed to my side.

'What now! Can't I leave you two minutes and you get into trouble. Get up,' she said, yanking me to my feet, but the pain was fierce.

'I can't . . . it hurts so.' I cried, hoping no one thought I was some drunken drab. The crowd gathered round us to gawp at my plight.

'Let me through,' boomed a deep voice. 'I will see to the maid.' A man in a long black cloak and cavalier hat with a tattered feather knelt down to examine me.

'Fear not, I am Doctor Titus Cranke, at your service, ladies. I will make a full examination and see what ails it.' He smiled with the brightest coal black eyes as he fingered my ankle carefully.

'Alas, 'tis a rupture of the membranes. But the angels were hovering over you, for I have just the appliance awaiting in my caravan to see you home. Dora!' he yelled. 'Beloved, fetch the splints for this poor creature. Give her comfort in her hour of need . . .'

A woman's face peered out from the tattered flap of a caravan wagon dripping with pots and pans and wooden boxes. A tired black mule was feeding from a nose bag and two ragged children peeped out of the flap as she hurried to his side.

The woman's purple cloak, splattered and stained, smelt of many roads travelled and nights spent under the stars as a blanket. Her hair was the colour of sea coal, twisted into a tiny cap that had never seen a tub of lye soap.

The Mistress took one look at the pair of them and jumped to my rescue. 'We have no need of your splints or any such service. There is no need for fuss. The groom will get her home. Really, Miss. Can I not take you anywhere?'

'But it hurts and I can't move my leg,' I croaked, not wanting to bear any weight on my foot, hoping for sympathy where there was none.

'Your daughter's had a fright, Mistress. What she needs is a tincture of herbs to soothe the pain, a restorative. It is our good fortune to have many such in our boxes to sell on the stall. Titus, dear heart, fetch the jug and the liniment oil to wrap a poultice on the swelling. Of just such a restorative did my Lord Busby of Brackenfoot partake, he who was bed-ridden and laid low for weeks. One drop on his lips and he was up and dancing. Come try before you buy,' she smiled with a crinkly wild-eyed sweetness, offering me the liquid to my lips.

I hesitated, already feeling dizzy with the pain and the crowd and the foul air of body odours around me, odours not yet familiar to me. The doctor in his swirling cloak hovered over me like a great crow, with fire-water breath as he brought the splints with straps. 'You're in luck, for these are my very last pair. Truly the angels must protect you, young lady.'

'And who might you be, offering poisons and restraints to a silly lass?' snapped Priscilla in my defence.

'Fret not, madam,' said the doctor. 'I studied medicinal arts for many years and have travelled far and near with my beloved here, offering my services to high and low as the Good Lord doth present.' The Mistress sniffed, unconvinced.

'He speaks the truth, for he is known throughout the length and breadth of the north country. Hal will testify here,' said the woman, pointing to a little boy who bowed his head. 'And Holderness; his name testifies to his birthplace and who knows where the next will be named,' she laughed, patting her swollen belly for all to see. 'The girl looks pale and needs to be indoors before the chill aggravates her bones further.'

'Never you mind what she looks like. Miss Moorside has no further need of your services. We can strap up her ankle easy enough with a kerchief. Be on your way.' The Dame was all for dismissing them. The splints did look sturdier though. How would I find the cart home without strong arms and support?

'A comfrey poultice is what she needs, hot and cold bathing to stir the blood.' The doctor was not so easily shaken off. Then the church bell boomed for the noon hour.

'Look at the time, and not a step nearer your fitting,' sighed my Mistress. 'No point in dawdling ... Where to find young John but the ale house, if I'm not mistaken.'

'Let us do the honour of at least escorting you back. The splint will hold her up if I strap it tight,' the doctor said as he made to put it on.

'Don't you dare touch a hair of her without the Master's say-so,' my defender cried. 'I'll do it myself to save time and money. I'm sure you mean well but we have our own physician.'

'And might I be acquainted with his name?' asked Doctor Cranke, turning those burning black eyes in my direction.

'That's none of your business,' replied my guardian. 'There, that'll do for now.'

'Might I suggest,' said his wife, bending down to examine the straps, 'a little tighter might be more efficacious.' She pulled on the buckles and patted the leg, making me wince but it did feel firmer.

'The little miss has such neat ankles and firm bones. They will heal soon enough. But a powder would lessen the shock,' she insisted.

'How much?' said the Dame.

'Three pence a dose,' Dora Cranke smiled, holding out her hand.

'That's a mighty price for a little powder,' sniffed the Dame but she dipped in her hand in her leather pouch just the same.

'The splints will be a shilling,' smiled the wife.

'Oh, no! That's all you're getting from us. You can collect the splints. I'm not foiling out for them and all,' came her swift response.

'In that case, Mistress, we'll follow you back in our caravan,' said the man, swishing off his hat into a mocking bow.

We were a slow lumbering trail of wagons homeward bound; John the carter with Priscilla, her face set tight with fury and I, sitting bolt upright, soaked through, with the clanking caravan jingling behind us. Not only was the excursion a disaster but someone had stolen all the ribbons I purchased whilst I was prostrate on the ground. And now there was nothing but an empty purse and nothing to show for it.

'You don't move until the swelling goes down,' said my escort as he helped me down. 'I am not called Doctor Marvel's Miracles for nothing. Rest costs nothing but it is hard to come by in this busy age we live in. Comings and goings, comings and goings is the ruination of many a constitution, I say and I should know for I would be martyr to the ague if it were not for Dora's wonderful physicks.'

On arrival in the yard I was carried off into the kitchen with much fussing, sat on a bench with my splints for all to see. All I wanted was to get out of the sodden skirt and petticoats and silly hood that soaked through into my braided hair. My head was throbbing and my ankle heavy and sore with the tight strapping.

'Can we give them some broth for their troubles?' I whispered. 'The children look frozen through.'

'Master Elliot does not encourage callers and bog trotters to the kitchen door,' the Dame replied. 'We'll never get rid of them touting cure-alls and pills to the silly girls. They are not slow to make profit from your misfortune.'

'But the splint does help, I'm sure,' I pleaded. 'I'll pay for it myself, and for soup.'

'So there's money in your purse after all?' she snapped.

'A little gift from my uncle, Roger,' I replied, knowing I had wasted one full coin already.

'Suit yourself. If you want go encouraging mountebanks and quacks; all pills and potions and nonsense. Anyone can see he's no more than a rogue in a cloak, all airs and no graces ... give them an inch and they'll be back for more.'

I brought out the last of my coins and offered payment for the loan of the splint but Dora shook her head.

'For the season's sake, from you we ask no payment but the broth for the poor children. It will warm their bones.'

'Where do you sleep on such sharp nights as these?' It would be cold in the wagon, with few comforts.

'There is always a barn or a room. We do the Lord's work. He is merciful and there are friends ...' Dora smiled, taking the wooden bowls.

My ears pricked up at the word, friend. 'You are Seekers, Friends of the Truth,' I whispered.

'All the world's our friend,' winked the Doctor, sniffing the broth with relish, not understanding my hint, sadly. 'We set up our stall at Scarperton each Yuletide, Halifax at Easter and all the feasts between. Doctor Cranke's Marvellous Miracle Medicines: nothing too small or large for us to cure. I have testimonies for all to see. You must all come and visit, bring your friends. We have remedies for warts and skin itches, stomach pain and back ache and things that worry pretty maids ...'

he was looking at Bess and Mary who were flushing scarlet at his attention.

'Take the broth to Halifax and Holderness before it goes cold and some oatcake too,' I said.

'A merry Yule to one and all,' he replied, doffing his hat again. 'And to you, young Mistress, a speedy healing of your bones. Send the man with the splint when you are finished. May all your wishes be granted . . .'

'Are they still hanging around?' The Dame bustled back. 'See them off with the dogs if they are not gone in half an hour and rinse those bowls when they are finished,' she ordered. 'This jaunt hath set us back a whole day and nothing to show but expense!' she added.

How quick I was to seize the moment. Praise be to God for those Crankes and the rough streets of Scarperton. Now I couldn't walk nor venture forth to the church or partake in any of the junketings of Yule. I would spend the season untrammelled by all the frivolity, secure in my chamber out of harm's way, sure of my piety and proud of my strength. Oh, that life was so simple. Does not pride come before a fall?

8

It seemed forever dark on those days when I was confined to my chamber. The sky was heavy with snow feathers, the light poor and the wind rattled down the fireplace chimney, moaning as if catching the gloom of my mood.

The Yule preparations below stairs went on apace without my reluctant efforts. Bess brought up a bowl of water and comfrey oil to bathe the swollen ankle. There were no broken bones and in truth I could bear a little weight but nothing would induce me to endure their festive ceremonies even if I must feign discomfort and act a cripple.

One morning my grandfather popped his head round the chamber door, muttering below his breath words I couldn't hear. It was as if he had almost forgotten my existence and made an effort just to see if I was still in residence. 'Rest, rest the leg or you'll miss the dancing...' was all I could catch as he sped away as quickly as he arrived.

From my window seat I could see the comings and goings of a coach and four horses, the clatter of new arrivals racing up the stairs, the bustle of chests being lifted and faces I didn't recognise making for the warmth of the kitchen. The laughter of children along the passageway cheered my solitary gloom.

The guests had arrived, the nephew and his family from Ripon way.

I was curious to see just who these distant cousins might resemble but nervous to be in such grand company. It was time to put down my mending and make an effort to receive them, time to braid up my hair and join the assembly at the given time. Dame Priscilla was not impressed with my efforts.

'Let your hair down, lass, for a change, some curling irons would soften the edges into curls which are all the fashion, I'm told. If you can hobble to the dining chamber we can find a stool to rest the foot. Our guests will want to meet their new-found cousin. Come, shape yourself. No starched caps at Yule. It's a time for lace and frills. You're a maid, not a matron yet,' she laughed. 'I'm sure Master Thomas will be eager to meet someone of his own age. He's quite the young man now, the same age as my Miles.'

'Has your son arrived home?' I said, seeing a look of agitation flit across her furrowed brow.

'By and by ... Tomorrow, happen. The tracks will be trodden ice and the weather's fast closing in, poor lad: all this way to be with his mother. I'll not settle until he is safe under my roof. He'll travel with company, other scholars and travellers for safety's sake, but that is no warranty on these wild highways. May the Lord deliver him who is the only joy left in my life,' she sighed.

'Indeed,' I nodded, moved by the softening of her tight drawn features at the thought of his arrival. To be loved and waited upon, to be welcomed and gathered in was something strange to me. There was a flash on my inner eye as I saw him racing forward through the snow to be at her side and I knew he would be unharmed.

'He will come safely, I know it,' I smiled with certainty.

'My but you're a funny wench. Where do you get such notions? But thank you for your comfort. Now wipe your hands and face, put on your new dress and smarten yourself up.'

The moment of intimacy was past like an open door soon slammed shut. It was time to face the Moorside family for an inspection. How could I not be found wanting?

The new gown took some putting on, layer by layer. I felt strangely changed by the feel of it around me, as if I was becoming a new creature, lifted from the air as it swirled and swished at my feet. There was no time to make a fancy lace-work collar to cover my bare neck so my best collar had been edged with threaded blue ribbon to match the material, nothing too elaborate.

My plain cap did in fact look out of place so I unwound my braids and wound some of the same ribbon through to good enough effect, I thought. Wearing such fancy clothes did not sit easy on my soul but I steeled myself to be gracious and bow to the season as little as I could. No one would expect a cripple to dance and jest and race about. I could sit quietly and observe the proceedings from a corner.

It was as much as I could do to hobble with a stick whilst managing the fullness of the skirt on the stairs, my feet pinched in borrowed slippers. It was like walking in a cage but I must put in an appearance for courtesy's sake.

The assembled group were already at table and eyed me with interest. 'So this is Matt's lass, the Quaker girl?' said a tall man in fancy brocade with ribbons at the knees of his britches and long wig.

'Why, she's just like Aunt Millie's portrait, fair with the Moorside chin,' laughed a round lady bedecked with so much lace at neck and cuff. I feared it would be stained with gravy by the end of the dinner. I was always told I took after my mother,

Alice, not my father's side. I tried to smile and hobble and grimace all at the same time so no one would be in any doubt that I was here only to sit and be inspected.

'Now then, lass, this is your Uncle Royston and his spouse, Kitty,' shouted my grandfather from his seat at the head of the table. 'And these are all their pups, Eliza, Ned, Dolly and big Thomas. Meet your cousin, Rejoice.' They bobbed and guffawed at the sound of my name. Thomas towered over me and bowed.

I should be used to the amused titterings by now. Worldly folk have no concept of name-giving, preferring always to name their offspring after relatives. Seekers do things always for a purpose, but it would be casting bread before swine to explain.

'I am called Joy, for short,' I replied, trying to bob a curtsey without success.

'Well that's not much better, is it?' cackled Aunty Kitty, looking at me as if I was a prize heifer. 'These Dissenters and their terrible names . . . I knew a servant once called Humility and she was the most cussed girl I knew! They make fools of themselves, giving their sproutings such ghastly names.'

'Shush, my dear. I'm sure Joy had no choice in the matter,' said Royston, looking at me with concern but his wife was having none of it.

'I hope when you are wed, Thomas, you will not make a fool of us but name your children from the family vault: Edward, Millicent or even Katherine,' she grinned, pleased with herself. Her voice was loud and rough on the ears.

Thomas blushed to his roots, staring at me, then dropping his eyes with embarrassment.

Such taunts slid from me like raindrops down window panes.

Well, I thought meanly, whatever Moorside good looks there were, I was the recipient of them. These cousins may have had family names but they all had horse features: bulging eyes and wide mouths with forward teeth.

Poor Thomas had the build of a carthorse, lumbering and slow, plump-breasted like a stuffed fowl and his fair eyebrows melted into his sandy face. His thighs bulged over his chair like cushions. We were placed side by side and the dinner was brought forth in all its wanton waste: guinea fowl and perch, a stuffed bird and raised pie, custards and a bowl of medlars with ripe cheese.

I sat straight, recalling the Dame's instructions not to slouch and to use my knife neatly, to pick daintily and say thank you for such a delicious meal as if I meant it; but it was all sticking in my throat. It was wearisome listening to the talk of people I didn't know, nodding and smiling where it was appropriate whilst Thomas wolfed down everything on his plate with a noisy relish and slurped his sack. He talked with his mouth full about horses and guns and the land they owned to the east across the great Pennine hills. When I smiled at him he blushed and stammered.

'It's grand to see the young ones getting on so well,' said my grandfather, pointing in our direction. 'Perhaps we'll have some singing and dancing this evening. I don't suppose Quakers do much of that,' he added. 'It's all trembling and theeing and thouing. You should have heard her at it, but we put a stop to that, didn't we, young Trouble?' He was drunk with wine and high spirits to have what was left of his family around him, I supposed. I made no reply to his teasing. If only it was possible just to sit out this agony without a yawn or a belch, hiding out of view and letting them get on with their card games like some stranger in a foreign country who knew not the language.

Later Aunt Kitty made for the spinet so the young girls could jig about to the music. Thomas joined in to please them, clumping about like a dobbin horse without any sense of the timing. Grandfather was snoring in his chair, oblivious to the noise and I wanted to creep out of the room unnoticed. This was the longest I'd been in his company since my arrival and still we had not had one profitable conversation, one nod of friendship between us. Why had he brought me under his roof? Twelve whole days of this to endure; how would my spirit survive such an attack?

I thought of the Crankes holed up in some barn with those poor children, Hal and his brother. I imagined Master Miles Foxup riding through the storm to be with his mother. I prayed that all travellers would come safely through this night to their loved ones and that the Lord in His Mercy would look on my righteous deception for a few days more.

On the eve of Christmas there was a heaving of cartloads of greenery into the hall and the setting up of a huge hoop wrapped around with ivy, yew and holly berries to be hung from the rafters. 'What's this for?' I said from my perch at the top of the wide oak stairs. I was in all innocence of such a custom.

'It's the kissin' bunch, Miss,' giggled Mary, bobbing a curtsey.

'I don't understand, what kissing?' I was puzzled.

'Every house has one, for dancing with the lads, for forfeits and games. We kiss until there's no berries left. It's a right laugh when all the boys come in to the hall for their Christmas boxes. You'll see what giddy times we have, laikin' about.'

No, I won't be a party to such flummery and wickedness, I decided. No wonder it was said at meeting that more maids were undone in the twelve days of Christmas than at any other time of the year. When men and maids met in darkness there came mischief and I wanted no part of it.

The very thought of Thomas's blubbery lips seeking my own to kiss made me feel sick. I was too young for such silliness and yet in my new blue gown with my hair down and the pretty ribbons I had not stopped my good foot from tapping up and down to the spinet music. Temptation was nigh and I must be strong.

It was time to take myself off to my chamber with a quill to write a long letter to Windebank. How I missed the simple warmth of their fireside, the gentle Nan and even Aunt Margery's nagging tongue. I must explain away this new life here. How I had not been sent for correction and how I was doing my best to uphold their teachings. I was confined to my room and would take no further part in the Yuletide frivolities but sit in quietness. In my mind everything was planned. Hah, how are the mighty fallen!

I told them about the kindness of Titus Cranke and how they travelled from town to town and could they furnish me with the names of good Friends who might help them find lodgings? I scratched in tiny letters all round the precious page, not wasting an inch and sealed it with borrowed wax that was warmed up for me. It would be sent when the post boy next called.

To Aunt Margery and Nan I said that so far there was not one tar stain on my conscience. They need have no worries for my honour or my steadfast hold of true doctrine. Little did I know that temptation was already standing in the yard; my cruel fate was close by ready to laugh away all my pious intentions.

From the window perch I could see there was a horse, tired and sweating, a mudstained rider wrapped in a riding cloak, his head covered in a broad-brimmed hat. Miles Foxup was home for Yule at last and I was curious, putting away my quill pen to inspect this new arrival for myself.

No words can describe the sight of him standing at the

bottom of the stairs, nor the effect his presence stirred within me. He was not what I expected from so plain a mother. It was the eyes I noticed first, deep set, fierce as flint. I'd never seen such eyes on a man. The power of such a gaze burned like a dart of fire in my belly.

He was like no other man I had ever seen at the meeting house. There was nothing gentle or sacred in his appraisal of me. He whipped off his hat and bowed to reveal a mop of chestnut curls looped with leather into a bunch at his neck.

'Ah, so this is Troublesome Moorside, the Quakerling ... at your service. I've heard you were brought here under sufferance to be the new mistress of Scarperton Hall. Miles Foxup bids you a merry Yule!' he laughed, throwing down his riding gauntlets with a flourish. There was no witty riposte in my mouth, only a silly girl's tongue-tied confusion, saved by Dame Priscilla rushing in to greet her son.

'Miles, at last! Praise be, you are returned to me in safety. The girl said you would be,' she smiled, looking up at me puzzled. He eyed me again with one brow raised in a question. 'But I see you two have already met. Let me give you a hug, son.'

'Don't touch me yet, my arse is still glued to the saddle. I must smell of a dozen inns and stable yards not fit to house a dog. I'll not be seen until I am scrubbed clean of the mud in a tub. Let me look at you, mother ... a little rounder in the rump, I see. Let's boil some water for the tub and you can scrub my back,' he laughed again as all the women fluttered around him like chattering pigeons.

'Nay lad, bathing's dangerous in this weather. 'Tis not the season for such risk taking. I have clean linen prepared and a warm fire in the grate. Come and tell me all your news ... It's so grand to have you by my side.' Her face melted with delight, flushed with joy at the sight of her own flesh and blood.

Suddenly envy consumed me, raw envy that I had never known such a loving of father and son or mother and daughter. I limped back to my chamber flushed and stirred by the handsome man who mocked me with his quizzical interest.

How could just one look from a stranger's countenance make me feel homespun and plain, a silly maid with no refinements or learning to match his own? I wanted to throw the letter on the fire but could not waste paper or sealing wax.

The Lord was not mocked and I must humble myself in asking for strength to withstand such strange lustful thoughts. If only I could walk back up the dale, but for once the ache in my leg was real. There was another wound in my spirit that defied my understanding. Something was happening to me and I needed a safe corner to hide in, something to busy my unquiet mind. Now was a time for spinning, feeling the soothing oils of the rolls of wool in my fingers, the treadle to rock my restless foot. Sorrow and doubt always fled my heart when my fingers were busy.

I burrowed in my kist to find a needle stick and some spun wool. My fingers found the package tucked away and I lifted out the precious gloves, sniffed the scent of lavender oil, fingered the silver lace and pearly beads and rubbed them against my cheeks.

These gloves were mementos of a bygone age. I hoped my grandfather would receive them with pleasure, knowing the love in which they had once been given to his wife and to her daughter-in-law, my mother.

I peered out of my window only to see Miles striding across the yard to his mother's cottage. Something made him turn round and catch my eye. He smiled and bowed mockingly as I darted back, puce-faced with fury to have been caught spying.

If only I could pace through the park and sniff the wind off the moors, ride on horseback and get myself back to Windebank to the world I knew. I would be safe there. This was Satan's country and I was afraid.

The next morning I hid in my chamber, making a fuss that my ankle had flared up again and could not bear any weight. All the household made for the stone church as was their custom on a holy day. I laced up the splints to convince myself that the injury was still painful.

The Master was put out that I was not making an effort and no doubt suspected my disobedience but such was the bustle and excitement of the little cousins that I was soon forgotten. Only the servants in the kitchen hall were allowed to stay at home to prepare the feast day pies and roasts and I was determined to offer help. I felt more at home there than among the fine glasses and pewter plates, the napkins and finger bowls of the dining table.

There was enough food on the boards to feed the whole of Windebank for a sevennight. I sat myself to help with some herb chopping, happy to be doing something useful.

There was a fluttering in the dovecote at Miles Foxup's return. The girls were blethering on and on about his fine manners and university ways. ' I can't wait to get him under the kissin' bough,' whispered Bess.

'The old Dame'll box your ears if you carry on wi' him,' warned Mary. 'Beg pardon, Miss,' she said, thinking I might tell tales on them. I moved the stool closer to hear more.

'She has great plans for him. They say he will go abroad as a tutor to some young gentleman or go into the church, but not before I've had a go at him,' Bess chuckled again.

'Shut yer gob, Bessie Bullock, what'll our Joy think of such smutty talk?'

She turned in my direction but I pretended to be absorbed in my chore, reciting a psalm.

'I'd watch yer step. The old Dame means a good match for him. He's her golden egg that must hatch forth some shiny brass to keep her in her old age,' Mary warned.

'She's not old,' snapped Bess.

'She's well above forty summers,' Mary replied.

'Who cares? Yule is but once a year and I mean to get me a taste of him.' Bess was still yammering, trying to draw me into their gossip. 'Don't you think he's a tasty dish to set before the king, Miss Joy?' Both pairs of eyes flashed in my direction, hoping for a response.

'I had not noticed,' I lied, hoping they would not see my neck flush red.

'Look, she's got a pink rash at the thought of him!' they teased. 'Now you just watch your step with the likes of him. He likes to pick the first apple off the tree, I've heard,' said Mary, staring at me which only made things worse.

'You have to watch his hands, Miss, they do roam where they should not, given a pretty smile,' Bess added. 'Over hills and dales and in between,' she mouthed but her hands made plain just where such places on the body might be. It was hard not to be shocked and curious at the same time.

'Now stop that, our Bessie. This poor lass knows nought of the ways of men. A pretty girl like you must not be alone with such a black rover. He'll be all over you like the pox, making inroads up your petticoats in no time,' Mary warned, lifting her skirts lewdly. 'Don't let him storm your ramparts, put the drawbridge up on his ardour if you see his battering ram ready for action or there'll be trouble swelling in your belly.'

'Stop this! This is filthy talk not fit for such a holy day,' I stood up to leave. 'You do Master Miles an injustice to be so

lewd. He is a scholar and will be a man of the cloth in no time
or a schoolmaster . . . I will not hear another word.'

'Hark to the preacher. They are the worst, believe me,' said
Bess with a stern face. 'Ask little Prudence Billing why she can
no longer call herself a maid but sells her milk as a wet nurse.
Scholars come and go and sew their seeds in byres, hedgerows,
lofts and alehouses. Master Miles will be no different from the
rest, I reckon.

'They like to take their pleasure from silly misses foolish
enough to believe their pretty words and lies. Don't take on so,
we mean no harm, just a bit of fun for the season. There's no
wrong in that nor in giving Master Thomas a bit of encouragement. He looks as if he could pack a few acres into his trousers.'

I would hear no more of this ribaldry. 'You forget yourselves.
I was taught to judge by the fruits of the spirit alone; kindness
of heart, courage, joy and not outward appearance,' I snapped
back.

'There she goes again on her tub stool! Who cares a fig for
such virtues when there is Yuletide fun and games. 'Tis only for
twelve days and then it's back to the grindstone and the gruel.
Once a year we're all equals in singing and dancing . . . Loosen
your laces, young lady, before you are old and withered on the
branch. Then you can be as sober and pious as you like for no
one heeds a crone. You're only young the once, the bloom on
those cheeks won't last forever in these harsh hills. Tomorrow
we may be stricken with plague boils or the pox but tonight is
for kissing and dancing. 'Tis not much to ask of life, a few days
of feasting . . .' Bess turned to her spit and Mary rushed into the
cold buttery leaving me standing there, confused, humiliated
and uncertain.

Why did they call me pretty and in bloom? How hard it was
to see myself as others saw me. I caught my reflection in the

silver platter that graced the table on special occasions. My eyes were bright, my lips rose pink and cheeks flushed with anger. No one had called me pretty before.

Seekers never looked for outward beauty but for sacredness within. The true spirit of man or woman lay in their deeds and in the goodness of a heart, that piece of our bodies divinely touch by the hand of God.

I hobbled up the stairs to view the portrait of Millicent Moorside with renewed interest. She wore a silvery grey gown that caressed her shoulders. Her face was fringed with ringlets. Her features were firm with bold eyes that followed me as I tried to walk away. Did I really look like this lady? If only I had a mirror glass . . .

Vanity, vanity, all is vanity, saith the Lord. The warning rang in my head like a bell. This was temptation and I must resist, a time of testing to see if my convincement was real. Now was the time to stand firm against the enemy within.

9

Once again I found myself seated at the feast table next to Thomas, finding his conversation dull and stilted. The parson had preached too long a sermon for the day and Uncle Royston had fallen asleep which amused the little girls greatly. Everyone was ravenous for the feast to begin but not before the Christmas candle was admired as it burned in the window and the smoking Yule log that graced the hearth, kindled from last year's embers.

'The light of the world is come unto our darkness,' I offered but everyone looked at me as if I had said a rude word. It was a waste of good tallow, I thought but said nothing more. We feasted on a stuffed goose, partridges and chickens, thick sauces and fruits washed down with mulled ale caudle, plum porridge and frumenty. Dish after dish appeared for the table until I felt sick.

Then the servants came up one by one and I dished out fresh ribbons and trinkets from the basket Dame Priscilla had left for us. There were wooden hoops and tops for the Moorside girls, a lace kerchief and posy of herbs for Aunt Kitty who looked pleased as she took her place near the hearth. There was a bunch of fine velvet ribbon for me, much to my surprise.

I waited until everyone was occupied with their own presents before producing my own gift. I wanted to have my Grandfather to myself but he was sitting by the hearth in his big chair, smoking his tobacco pipe and staring into the flames. For the first time I saw he was an old man with lines furrowed across his brow, sleepy with a surfeit of food and wine.

'I've brought these for you,' I whispered. 'I thought you would want them back.'

'What's this, more gifts?' he said, fumbling with the purse string. He pulled out the gloves and then stared up at me as if I was someone else. 'What the deuce!'

'It's my gift to you,' I whispered. 'I thought them rightfully yours. They've been kept secure as fresh as the day they were made. I hope you like them.'

'What the blazes do you mean by this?' he shouted, bringing Aunt Kitty to his side.

'They're wedding gloves, Elliot, beautiful ones. Where did you come by these, child?' She was looking at me for a second with suspicion, fingering them with envy.

'Don't touch them!' The Master snatched them back. 'Those were Millie's gloves, given as a gift on our wedding day. What the devil is this girl doing with her gloves?' he snapped looking up with fury, his hand shaking them in my face.

'The Mistress, my grandmother, sent them to my father for his bride on her wedding day as a token of reconciliation. I told you of them in the Courthouse.' I stuttered.

'She did what?' His curiosity was fired up now and everyone in the room stood like statues to watch the drama unfolding.

'I was told they were a gift, a token of her forgiving my parents' marriage,' I repeated loudly as if to a deaf man.

'And you have the affrontery to shove them in my face, young lady?' he exploded.

'Remember, sir I brought them to prove that I was indeed your kin.' I answered, trembling to see his fists crushing the gloves in anger and grief.

'And she did this behind my back ... without my consent? How dare the baggage disobey my command! Our son was dead to us the moment he denied his calling,' he looked up at his audience, seeking for sympathy. 'Who can find an honest woman?'

'Now then, Uncle Elliot, don't take on, 'tis but a misunderstanding. The girl meant no harm,' said Royston coming to my rescue, seeing the agitation on the Master's face.

'I don't care what the minx meant. I am greatly offended: coming into my house at my expense, taking my charitable hospitality and then throwing these in my face. You chose ill to show me them,' he shouted, his spittle spraying into my face. He turned away in disgust, staring into the fire.

'If it eases your mind,' I offered, shaking my head, 'my parents never received them.' I hoped to give him consolation but the gesture was in vain. 'They were in prison in York Gaol by the time they arrived.'

'I know where they went,' he said dismissively..

'Perhaps she just wanted to be reunited with them. I gather she was ill and not long for this life. It was perhaps her way ...' I pleaded. 'They, too, were not long in following her to the grave. There was no time to show them and my Aunt Margery Windebank put them away for safe keeping as proof.'

'Proof of what? How do I know you have not stolen them? This is some trick to make me soften towards your cause or disobey my stern command to withhold blessing on my errant son. I have no wish to be reminded of that time. Take them out of my sight!'

'I only thought to please you, sir,' I cried.

'Well you thought wrong. I am much displeased that you should taunt me with them,' he snapped and shook the gloves in the air. 'Keep them, they are nothing to me and you are nothing to me now. Trying to weaken my resolve, indeed.'

I was sobbing now. I did not care who saw my tears. 'But they were given in love and gratitude. I did not mean to harm you,' I pleaded.

'They were given in weakness. I want nothing more of them or you, you ungrateful puppy.'

For a second I thought he was going to fling them into the flames and I reached forward to snatch them before they fell into the ashes. I knelt on the floor and clutched them to my chest in panic.

'As God is my witness I meant no offence,' I whispered.

'And this is the wench I thought we could train up from her humble station to be amongst us as an heir. In time she would wed Thomas, over there, to keep the name growing in the district; a comfort to me in old age so that this house would be full of young Moorsides. But what do I get in return? Impudence, betrayal and ingratitude from a girl who knows not her place!'

I could hardly breathe with the shame and injustice of his words and the knowledge that I had almost sworn an oath that was forbidden amongst the Seekers.

'Enough now, Uncle Elliot, words have been spoken that can't be undone here. I'm sure the girl meant no harm, just misguided in her innocence. We have to forgive her lowly station. How was she to know your feelings?' said Royston, edging me away from the hearth. 'Come, don't take on, lass. Let him stew awhile in his own juice. It's the sack talking. His wits are befuddled. Let him sleep off his choleric humour.'

It was as if from the far corners of the room, from the dark recesses and the flickering dimness of the gathering gloom of a

December afternoon, a blackness engulfed me, voices receded and an icy blast of past grief and hurt was flooding over me so I could hardly hobble out of his presence, blinded by tears.

What had been given in love had been thrown back in my face. What I assumed would give comfort had only given distress; the burden of my mistake left me helpless under its weight. I stumbled and fell but Thomas rushed to my side and gave me his arm to lean on.

'Don't worry, he will come to when he is sober,' he whispered.

There were no words I could utter now to make everything joyous again. 'Let me be, I'll manage,' I said, shaking my arm away from him. I wanted nothing more to do with any of them.

'You're in no fit state to be going upstairs,' he insisted but his kindness only irritated me further. 'I can walk unaided,' I snapped, wanting at least some semblance of dignity. 'Thank you, sir.'

'Please call me Tom, cousin,' he offered with a smile.

'Thank you, Thomas, but it appears I am no relative of this house. Our Master has made that plain enough. Please let me be.'

The steps up to my chamber were like climbing the highest peak of Penyghent into a stiff wind. Oh to be free to climb the fells and shout into the wind and blow all this anger and hurt away! Never had I felt so alone or so desolate. How could something seem so right yet come out so wrong? How could I stay in a place where I was no longer welcome?

I had not chosen to come here of my free will. What was to stop me heading out northwards back from whence I came without hindrance? What was all that about marriage to Thomas? Was it the wild fancies of his fevered brain or had that been his plan in his bringing me under his roof to serve his own purposes?

I could no more contemplate wedding that lump of lard, kindly as he was. Was I some pawn piece in the Master's game, to be shoved hither and thither at his will? If he could reject my gloves so easily then surely I was free now to walk my own way? If only it were easy for a girl to choose her own path in life.

I knew enough of life to see that Mallory would have choices that Diligence would never be offered; parents must have their say in whom their daughters wed. Seekers must wait on the Lord's will to guide them to a suitable helpmeet. We did not marry worldly men, but one amongst our own meeting. A couple must be vetted for sincerity and convincement. To marry out of the meeting was to be shunned and banished from their fellowship. I was not ready to marry anyone, not even a Moorside relative, not without that spark of recognition that my parents discovered in each other.

I sat in the dusk with no candle lit, enveloped in my dark thoughts, half listening to the thud of feet in the hall and a fiddle playing tunes, laughter and merriment. I held the golden gloves for comfort for there was love and forgiveness and understanding stitched into them. The soothing scent of lavender tinged my senses with hope. I would never be parted from them again. They were my gloves now.

That night I dreamt a strange dream. I was standing by a broad blue river, the like of which I had never seen in this district. It stretched for miles and miles in both directions. There was a green field and wooden house made of boards and huge trees with broad leaves. I was standing with other company whose faces were misted over with a veil of cloud but we were at ease with one another and I was wearing the golden gauntlets. Then I unpeeled them and gave them to a girl with dark braids but her face was unclear as we embraced and I put them in her hand.

She took them with a cry and hugged me as I stepped on the water. It carried me far from that shore, I think. I woke with wet cheeks, strangely comforted, smiling, wishing I could return into that fair country.

Were they now mine to give as I pleased? Millicent Moorside had meant those gloves for her son and his heirs. They would not be offered to Master Elliot ever again and the matter would lie heavy between us. We would never speak of it.

His spirit was mean and racked with guilt about my father's death. He was too old to change his ways. Now he was trying to trap me into doing his will, as he had forced my father to make his choice.

Perhaps my future lay not in Scarperton Hall nor in Windebank but somewhere by that big river far away. How I would find such a river was beyond my understanding.

Next morning I was wakened by Aunt Kitty, peering down at me. She had come to my chamber early. Her face was pinched and her brows knitted into a furrow.

'So you slept, then? Thomas was quite concerned for you. I told him girls of your age can sleep the clock round if left to their own devices. I just wanted to make plain that Uncle Elliot was talking out of his boots last evening. I hope you understand that he's an old man disappointed by grief and misfortune. He will mellow given time, when the drink is off him.'

I rubbed the sleep out of my eyes, wondering why she looked so agitated. 'I think I understand better than I did before why he brought me here,' I said.

'And that's another thing, forget all that nonsense about marrying your cousin. Whatever silly notions he has put in your head on that score, they are out of the question. Thomas is spoken for, an arrangement made years ago with the Bellamys of Brimingthorpe Hall. As if we would condone an old man's fancy of marrying two cousins, indeed! You are hardly a suitable bride for a gentleman: a hill farmer's dairymaid. It is unthinkable he should make such presumptions.

'I have a half mind to remove us all from this hall immediately so no further contact can be made. I'm sorry if he has given you a false hope, my dear. Men are so hopeless at these matters. You do understand?' she said, standing back as I sat up.

'Oh yes, I understand,' I smiled, trying not to show my relief.

'So you see, I think it better all round if you keep out of Elliot's sight for a few days. I've arranged for you to dine with Dame Priscilla at a different time. The children can join you for games but not Thomas. It's better for his sake to keep you apart, for I fear he has taken a strong fancy to you and that must go no further.

'The Mummers are coming tonight to give their play and we must all be present, so if you could keep with the servants and help Dame Priscilla, I think that would do the trick. I hope my words don't spoil your Yule . . .' she paused, eyeing me carefully.

'It's not that you aren't presentable, but there is still the whiff of the farmyard about your manners and accent. There's been enough misunderstandings already. If you want me to take the gloves I can try him again at some other time,' she offered, seeing them on my pillow. 'They are very beautiful.'

'No, thank you,' I was quick to reply. 'They don't belong here now.'

She looked at me again. 'But they belong in this family.'

'Yes, they'll stay in my family to be passed on as I see fit,' I said.

'I see,' she snapped, not seeing at all.

'And fret not about my welfare, Aunt. Yule is not important

to me. What I have learned here is how easily our good intentions can be misconstrued, however well meant. The Master owes me an apology, but I do not seek one. He is proud and stubborn, just as I am and in that we are kin indeed. I think my father must have been the same. Did you ever meet him?' I asked, hoping for some comfort from her recollections.

'I do remember one meeting but I was very new to the family. He was a great scholar but I recall him jumping a gate like no other rider as if he was flying through the air. He had a good pair of feet at the dancing and he was as handsome as he was wise. No wonder his father has never gotten over the loss of his company,' she sighed, and made for the door.

'That's why I will do everything in my power to see that dear Thomas makes the right choice in harmony with our own desires. No one understood why Matthew gave up all his advantages to join a bunch of penniless preachers. I don't think Aunt Millicent ever recovered, but she must be obedient to her husband in this matter, irksome as it was and still is. Are you sure I can't take those gloves for you?'

'No, thank you,' I insisted. 'I had a dream last night that Grandmother came to comfort me. She wants me to hold them for her,' I smiled.

'You're a strange girl, Joy. Thomas is a noble young fellow and not at all suited to your temperament. I hope you're not too disappointed at this news.' She made to pat my hand but I withdrew it quickly.

'Not at all, Aunt, for I'm far too young to be considered for such an elevated position, I'm sure. I must wait on the Lord's will for my intended. He will appoint my husband in the fullness of time.'

'No more of this priggish Quaker talk.' Aunt Kitty raised her hand with alarm. 'I have heard how the women have a forward manner in decision-making and count themselves equals with their men ...'

'Before God, all are equal in His sight, high and low, bond and free, male and female. My parents died for that truth. I will not betray them in plighting my troth with an unbeliever, however elevated his position,' I replied, not caring how it sounded.

'So you think my son is not worthy of your hand?' My aunt looked shocked.

'That decision is in the hands of the Lord. *"Be ye not yoked to unbelievers"*, the Bible reads. I'll not marry to please my grandfather's will or to assuage his guilt and loss of heirs. I came here with nothing and I will go with nothing. If he wants his name to live on it will live on in your offspring well enough. He will have to be content with that honour. Everything has its price, I'm thinking. He wants things to be as they were but that can never be so and he knows it in his heart.'

'You are very certain in your judgements, young lady, and as harsh as he is. I'd watch your step,' she said, wagging her finger in my direction. 'There's many a lesson to learn in life before anyone can be so sure ... You're two of a stubborn kind. Elliot's met his match in you and no mistake. But don't be so above yourself in these matters. Youth has little wisdom. I can quote too and in my book, "Pride cometh before a fall". I bid you good morning.' She slammed the door, unused to being thwarted. Good riddance, I thought with all the arrogance my youth could muster.

I was in no mood for the St Stephen's day Mummerings and antics but I would not be hidden away just to please the Master's sensitivities. I brushed out my hair and left the back to fall to my waist, I dressed with care and pinched my cheeks. I threw off the splints for I had no need of them now and made my way down to join the revels, hovering in the candlelight, uncertain what was going on. I had never seen theatricals before and was a little afraid.

Yule has its own fragrance of spices and ale, the scents of the garlands of leaves, the smoke from the great block of wood in the hearth, roasting meats and tobacco pipes, the freshly strewed rushes on the floor.

Through the door tumbled a rush of dancing men with blackened faces and strange robes, tattered like the feathers of an old crow. 'We bid thee greetings. It is our delight to dance and sing and tell an ancient tale.' They waved to everyone, being but local men dressed in disguise. Everyone was laughing and cheering as they swirled around in their black rags, banging drums and frightening the children.

They say that people in these parts have danced these jigs since before Christ walked upon this earth, when darkness reigned over us all. I was greatly afeared by the look of them, stepping back from the noise only to tread hard on the foot of Miles Foxup standing close behind me.

'Hey up, little Miss Quaker! This is no place for a Puritan maid,' he teased. 'Not so Puritan, I see by the toss of those golden locks and the colour of your low cut gown. What have we here but a pretty peach ripe for the plucking.'

I ignored him but the heat rose to my cheeks and my heart beat a little faster. How dare he make such suggestions! What Bess had said was true enough, then. No gentleman in the making would talk to me like that. Yet a part of me was flattered that my change of dress and hair was noticed, that the blue shimmered in the candlelight.

His mother was staring from her perch by the door. I made to walk away with head held high whilst Mary and Bess with their gaggle of girls skittered across the room to drag him under the kissing ring. He was their willing prisoner and kissed them all in turn to much cheering and guffawing which I thought demeaning. I turned from the scene to find Thomas hovering in the shadows, beckoning me to his side.

'Will you be my partner for the dancing?' he smiled, his cheeks pink with hope and eagerness.

'Thank you, no,' I replied. 'Your mother would be displeased and I have caused enough offence. I don't think my ankle is up to the strain,' I lied, not wanting to hurt his feelings. The thought of his big feet crushing my toes made me wince. 'I will sit with you awhile,' I said, smiling sweetly, knowing how that would aggravate Aunt Kitty.

There was a bit of me feeling mean and mischievous tonight. Perhaps this festive season did make you forget sorrows and disappointments for a few hours. No harm could come of that, surely?

We sat together watching the Mummer's play unfolding before us; how the dragon was slain by good Saint George; the antics of the doctor and the Turkey man, the battles and sword fights, the cheers when it was all over. Even grandfather was enjoying the spectacle from his throne by the fire. I did not dare venture into his presence, wanting no repeat of yesterday's humiliation.

The servants feasted from the big table in the kitchen hall, slices of cold pie and meats, trenchers of bread, fruit and curd and raisin tarts, a great dish of frumenty and bowl of wassail punch which warmed my throat and loosened my limbs so the ache in my leg no longer throbbed and the ache in my heart was forgotten.

Everyone pushed and jostled for their share of the feast, high and low together for a change. Then they pushed back the table for the fiddler to strike up his tunes as a thunder of stamping, dancing feet beat out the drum in the dancing jigs.

There was no time to slide away and soon I was caught up in the circle of the carolling dance. 'Here we come a-wassailing . . .' round and round we swung, under and over, linking arms; girls in one circle and the men in the other, swinging round and moving on.

I have to admit I kept Miles Foxup in view. I knew where he was in the circle and the point where we must link arms but the music stopped just in time and I didn't know whether to be relieved or furious. To my surprise I did not step out of the ring but waited as eagerly as the next for the next jig to begin, breathless and defiant.

I sensed poor Thomas watching from the doorway knowing I preferred servants' company to his own.

The kitchen was where I felt most at home. Since Elliot had made plain I was no longer his protégée and Aunt Kitty said there was no taking the farmyard out of me, I might as well be true to form. Tonight I would do as I pleased.

To my chagrin it was a dance in pairs and I had no knowledge of such steps so I made to leave the circle but a hand grabbed my own. I turned in protest to see Miles smiling down at me. Something inside made me stand and return to the circle, seeing the pained look on Bess's face as she was making for him too.

Who was this stranger within myself; this headstrong lass with feet like wings, shaking hair like a wanton and forgetting her half-way rank within this household? It was Yule and a time for all to be equal after all.

Dancing did strange things to my resolve when the measure was fast and strong arms whirled me round like a top. My eyes grew bolder as I stared at my partner when he swung me round. My heart was thundering in my chest, not with exertion but with a curious wilder beat that I didn't understand. My bosoms rose and fell as my kerchief slid away. I hardly noticed how much of my flesh I was exposing. It was the touch of his jacket on my bare arm, the warmth of his fingers gripping mine; all I cared for was the very moment I was living now.

There was laughter bubbling up from my throat. In that moment there was joy and youth. I was pretty and desired, the centre of attention and envied for my partner; this wonderful adventure was so new. How could I know that it was only the potent brew in the wassail cup that was altering my understanding, firing me up with strange lustful thoughts of being kissed and caressed, or was there more? I danced like a silly wanton whose befuddled wits did not see where such danger might lie.

Miles whispered in my ear, 'The young mistress is not so straight-laced now, I see. She shows promise and gives permission. Is it time she be taught a lesson in the ways of love, in the ways a maid should be obedient to a man?'

'You talk gibberish,' I laughed, too proud to show my ignorance of his meaning. 'I have had lessons enough in obedience in this house.' The room was spinning now.

'Then let me teach you other delights that your grandfather, the Justice, will never speak of, nor that clodhopping cousin who dribbles with desire at the sight of you. Come away into the yard and I will show you ways to please a man.' Those flinty eyes sparkled, his eyebrow raised and at last I fumbled through the hazy fug to his real meaning.

'Stop there!' My voice was raised enough to cause a stir. 'Don't insult me any further. I'm not one of your taproom drabs to use as you please. You forget yourself, Miles Foxup!' I pulled myself away, shocked to have raised my voice so others could hear. Suddenly the place was chilly.

'There you go again, Miss Sobersides. I meant no offence, just testing the thickness of the ice for cracks,' he smirked, turning round for support. 'I see the Quakers have frozen thee well enough. Thine honour is safe with me.' He was mocking our speech.

'Thy conversation was not that of a scholar, sir. The maids' stories of thee are true enough,' I replied. Two can play at that game.

'Take no notice of gossips. They are all far gone in lewd boasting,' he snapped. 'I don't have to force myself on anyone, but I'm sorry to trouble you.' He was looking discomforted, especially as his mother came into the room to search him out. 'Shall we start again?'

I shook my head. 'It's late, my leg aches, people are staring at us, staring at me, thinking I am one of your Yuletide conquests. You've done me a great service in reminding me of my calling,' I bowed stiffly. 'I bid thee goodnight.'

'But Joy . . .' he called after me as the servants parted like the Red Sea before me in silence.

I stumbled on up the stairs, feeling sick and silly. Once more I had shamed myself in public. Mary and Bess were staring grimfaced at the drama unfolding. The family were at cards in the hall and looked up briefly. I was trying to slide away unnoticed but Eliza and Dolly broke the tableau by rushing to greet me. 'Come and play cards with us,' they shouted in unison, their faces eager. How I envied their innocence, their certainty of station. 'Joy can come and play, can't she?'

Aunt Kitty was quick off the mark. 'Joy is tired. She needs her rest. There's been enough excitement for one night. I think the Yule cup has gone to her head.'

I curtsied and crept upstairs, with aching heart and spinning head.

If only Miles had left me alone and not made me dance . . . It was all his fault.

If only grandfather had accepted those precious gloves ... It was all his fault too.

If only Thomas would stop making eyes at me. If only my Aunt was not so superior ... if only. I could make a hundred excuses why I behaved so shamelessly but there was one blinding truth. I was tempted and found wanting.

'If you dip your fingers in pitch tar it will stain.' I thought of Nan's warning words. I was proud and defiant and this was what came of it. I wept into my pillow and knelt by the bedpost to beg forgiveness. 'Lord, take this temptation from me,' I pleaded. 'I have learned my lesson. Show me the way out of here and I will honour thy ways forever.'

My dreams were full of Miles's blazing eyes and dancing with him in circles. I woke to the worst headache of my young life.

10

The household slept in late after all the roistering of the night before. The platters and pewter were cleared, the stone flags swept and sanded and the dogs snuffled through the rushes for the scraps. There was the smell of oven bread baking ready.

Today was the day of the hunt so the horses were tacked and groomed ready for the chase and the stirrup cup was warming by the grate.

At least the house would be quiet, I thought as I crept down to the kitchen to make myself useful to the household. No one looked up to greet me. Bess was clattering pots with a face on her like sore feet. The Mistress huffed and puffed, ignoring my offers of help. I dare not even ask if her son was close by, not that it was any of my business.

There would be a house full of hunters and families; farmers and gentry folk. There would be more feasting and drinking to prepare. This Yule season was hard work for the servants. No wonder there was extra help drafted in to the kitchen. Aunt Kitty had said that the Cliffords were on the move but perhaps the Lady Anne Clifford's former entourage and distant kin in the castle might call in for a caudle and light refreshment with the Justice as they had done when she was alive. The house must be kept in readiness for such an honour. It was made plain that I would not be welcome at such a reception.

All I wanted to do was to find some chore to busy my fingers and keep my mind from its dizzy wanderings. Then I thought about the splints that were now cast off. It was time to return them to the Crankes; a walk in the fresh air would clear my head and strengthen my ankle.

'I can't spare anyone to escort you,' said Dame Priscilla on hearing my suggestion. 'But it would help if you were to take a basket of food for our old servants who live in the alms-house. They will be expecting some gifts from the hall. The Crankes can wait. I suppose I could spare one of the boys,' she sighed, packing some pie and meats into a linen napkin. 'They can have a little plum porridge. Just for our old women, mind, don't go feeding the others. Widow Medley, Widow Robinson and Old Peg are our responsibility.' Then we both saw Miles leaning on the doorway watching the packing. He had heard everything.

'Let me escort her,' he said. 'I could do with a good walk.'

'Nay, son, you are wanted here for the hunt,' his mother replied, looking up at him with alarm.

'What for? You know I hate all that jumping walls. The kitchen is women's work and I have books to collect from the Parson for my studies,' he insisted.

I could see the look of hesitation on her face. This was the last thing she wanted, but I could not walk unescorted.

'Well just there and back and be sharp about it,' she snapped. 'This is most irregular but needs must ... Wrap up well, son, for the air is chilly.'

Funny how she was concerned for him but not for me, I mused. He was the last person I wanted for company but no matter. In His wisdom the Lord was putting us together so I would redeem myself after last night's shaming: another test to prove my mettle.

There was a fluster of busyness, collecting the baskets and stuffing extra food out of the sight of the Mistress. I wanted the Crankes to have some of the leftovers too.

We walked down the pathway in silence. I wore my thick cloak and my tall hat over my cap. I wanted to look as plain as possible.

'It was the ale talking last night,' he said, breaking the chill between us. 'I am sorry if I offended you.'

"Tis no matter,' I replied, head held high. 'It is what is expected from worldly men. That is why Seekers shun this season with such vehemence.'

'That is their loss,' he said. 'In the darkest point of the year, we need light and fun to cheer us through the winter solstice.'

'That's just pagan superstition.'

'You misunderstand. The candle is lit for the coming of Christ, the light of the world. His coming promises new light and spring. That's the rub of the matter.'

I watched his breath puff like smoke before him in the chill air.

'Then why must we have all the excesses and foolishness? Drink makes fools of us all . . . It made a fool of me.' I argued.

'There you go again, talking from your pulpit. Why are you so priggish? No one forced you to drink so much strong punch, but merriment and bright colours suit you.'

'It is so demeaning to be judged by appearance alone,' I snapped.

'You've a lot to learn, Joy Moorside. We're young and need some lightness in our daily grind. The skies are grey enough here, the rain falls hard and the nights are long. That's enough to sink anyone's spirits. Why dress like the weather?'

'Speak for yourself,' I replied, not wanting to carry this argument further, for some of his words were reasonable enough. 'I was taught that jesting and merriment grieves the Holy Spirit. We have a truth to proclaim.'

'I don't see that at all. Didn't Jesus himself enjoy the wedding at Cana when he turned the water into wine? There has to be a bit of levity to balance the serious with the frivolous, heavy and light. Our drudgery needs some honey to sweeten the taste,' he added, looking at me for some sign of agreement.

'We can have our reward in heaven, there is sweetness enough then,' I said.

'There's no arguing with you, is there? You are always so . . . so sure of the truth.'

'I am a Seeker. Our way is right,' I said, shaking my head with sadness at his words.

'How can you be so certain? Have you no doubts that others may also have answers different to your own?' He was not going to give in.

'Doubts are for the faint-hearted. We are taught to believe in our convictions and see them to the end no matter what the cost. That's why my father left this house. I have to be true to his sacrifice.'

'I think you are too severe. I have many doubts,' he confided. 'Too many doubts ever to enter the church and that will break my mother's heart.'

'It is no loss, a hireling priest is no occupation of honour,' I replied.

He stopped and looked at me again. 'You are a pious know-all. Such ugliness does not suit you . . .'

'And you are a pompous unbeliever . . .'

We walked in silence after that. There was nothing else to say but the bitterness of his words was as bile in my mouth, acid and burning and hard to swallow. There was no meeting of minds with this man. The walk had gone quickly and we were soon on the path into Scarperton where the church and the stone almshouses clustered around the top of the high street. He nodded and went toward the parsonage while I made for the gate through into the cluster of little cottages where my food could be distributed.

'I shall be here at the noon bell to escort you back,' he said raising his hat.

I nodded and turned away. Why did people not think as we thought?

I was greeted at the doorway by the warden of the houses who peered in my basket with interest and pointed me in the direction of the widows. Not one of them was at home so I left the gift with the warden and trusted all would be fairly distributed. Now there was time enough to go in search of the Cranke family.

The town was bustling with stalls and shows. I was glad to be dressed like any other country girl but strode out in search of their caravan. I did not have to look far. They had set out their stall with a raised flap of cloth over a table. There were bunches of dried herbs, boxes of strange stones, pastilles and ointments. The doctor was shouting out his wares to the crowds passing by.

'Come buy my heart's delight, made to ease an old man's ticker. Up and doing for those in need of a pick-me-up! I have Balm of Gilead for sleepless nights. Don't be shy, come buy, loosen your purse strings and try! I've cures for chilblains and corns, warts and all. I draw teeth so fast you don't know they're gone, not a thing will you feel or your coin is returned. Trust none but Titus Cranke, sometime doctor to the highest in the land!' Then he spotted me in the throng and waved.

'Behold, the tender maid who last week fell amongst you and see she walks unaided by the help of my splints. See they are in her hand, another miracle of healing. Welcome, your presence is timely,' he added. 'Dora, dear heart, the lady is returned. You're good for business, everyone likes to see a pretty face.'

'How now, dear heart, why it's the lady from the hall.' Dora sprang from the back of the caravan. I thrust the package into her hand. 'Thank you for the loan of the splints and here is some Yule pie for the children. Where are Hal and his brother?'

'No longer with us,' she smiled.

'Oh no, what's happened?' I could still see those pale little faces peering out of the back of their van.

'They have gone home for the winter, praise God! It is too cruel a time for them to travel. After Twelfth Night we'll be on our way. I think the good citizens are all but spent up now.'

'When will you return? I can visit your children, if you like, and see that they are well cared for,' I offered, glad to be of help.

'Oh no, they are well placed. It will only disturb them to have visitors. In spring we'll return. I see your ankle is healed but your heart is not so easily mended, I fear,' she said, looking over my shoulder.

How does she guess all the past day's troubles? The woman was smiling and winked at me and I turned around to see Miles standing behind me.

'There you are,' he said, raising his hat. 'I thought I might find you at the fair. You didn't stay long with your old ladies.'

'None of them was at home and I wanted to return these,' I snapped at him, blushing as I spoke, showing him the splints.

The black eyes of Dora Cranke missed nothing. 'I see where your trouble lies, Mistress, but no matter, all will be as it will be, given time. A Merry Yule to you both,' she called out as we walked away.

'What're you doing with those two charlatans?' Miles asked, but I shrugged my shoulders.

'Returning a kindness with some Christmas pie for their children,' I replied, tired of his snide remarks. The Crankes were good people, parents who were farming their children out so they might be safe from the bad weather to come. 'They have little ones to feed; two boys called Halifax and Holderness, not above four or five years old. I wish I knew where they were lodging them. I thought they were dead when she mentioned it first. I hope the good doctor knows what he's doing.'

'He's no doctor, little more than a pedlar selling coloured water and hedgerow cures,' said Miles, striding ahead as if he was finding my company awkward.

'They helped me walk again,' I argued.

'They could see you coming, a well-dressed young lady with a full purse.'

'That's not fair. Why do you see the worst in their motives?' I said, wanting to have the last word on the matter.

'There are hundreds of roadside hawkers peddling their wares to the gullible and ignorant. If he were a real doctor he'd have a fine house and be settled with his family around him. It stands to reason,' he replied.

'Not to me it doesn't. There're hundreds of good Seekers of all ranks who roam the highways to proclaim the good news of love and forgiveness. He is doing the Lord's work. That is reward in itself to the righteous,' I argued. Miles Foxup was not going to dismiss the Crankes like that.

'As you wish, you seem to know best on all matters spiritual. There's no arguing with you,' he sighed, clearly bored with the subject.

We walked back, one in front of the other, making no more attempts at conversation. I stared up at the skeletons of bare trees arching over the paths, at the stone cottages with turf roofs and the blue smoke spiralling up into the chill morning. Then Scarperton Hall came into view.

There was nothing more to say to Miles Foxup. I ought to feel relieved but all I felt was miserable. He could have been a friend but now he was my foe.

The thought of spending winter shut up in this stone prison being neither servant nor family made my heart sink. Now I could walk I would be expected to attend the steeple-house services with the household. There had to be another way to live than this.

I could hear Nan's words in my head; 'A burning log soon cools away from the heat of the fire.' Seekers needed each other for company and fervour. My light was dimming fast. I needed spiritual company and a congregation of other believers before I succumbed to temptation again.

It was not as if anyone here cared one way or another how I lived as long as I was obedient to their wishes. Suddenly my heart leapt with excitement. I was answerable only to God and He would want me out of here. There must be a way, a secret way if I had the courage to take it without delay.

Why hadn't I seen it before? My mind was spinning with resolve. I would not stay another minute in a house where I wasn't wanted and among worldly people. I would do as my father had done and make my own way in the world.

I hugged my secret with glee and limped a lot, saying the walk had strained my ankle yet again. It was easy to sit at the spinning wheel with bent head not wanting to draw attention while a hundred ideas flashed around my head.

Only the stuff that I had brought into the house would be taken with me, no blue gowns and ribbons, lace-trimmed collars and stockings; just the honest clothes of a country woman.

There was a little of Uncle Roger's gift left. I would spin the wool and earn my bread here taking only what was due when the time came. Everything would have to fit into a knapsack that could be carried.

Yet my dreams were haunted by fears. What if I was taken for a vagrant, a loose woman or worse? The safety of other company on the road was my first task until I found a safe haven among Quakers. I needed a disguise in case of a hue and cry that the heir of Justice Moorside had absconded from his custody.

Steady the sinews, I prayed. 'The Lord is with thee. He will direct thy path in all things.' He would not give me this instruction if it were not His command to find a true community of believers or that somewhere out there I would find my heart's desire as my parents had done all those years ago. Somewhere my life's companion was waiting for my coming. I was not running from the hard way but running towards a stiffer challenge which would take all the strength and trust I could muster. But if I were wrong, what then? My courage failed for a second. What fate might befall a single maid with no escort?

For the first time in weeks I felt calm within, a sense of peace that this journey would have the Lord's own blessing. Only a few days were left until the final festivities on Twelfth Night and then the revels would be over for another year, the house would go back to hard work and plain porridge and I would be gone.

I have often found that when a right decision is made then all things work towards that end. The Ripon Moorsides suddenly upped and left the house in a flurry of noise and packing. My grandfather took to his bed with coughs and sneezes and demanded his housekeeper be at his beck and call. Her son disappeared back to his college on horseback without even so much as a nod in my direction and I was furious to be ignored. What could I expect when I had sulked in my chamber away from the noise and roisterings below stairs.

The hall was quiet and empty, nothing to do but clear away and get back to the chores. Even the gossip in the kitchen fell silent when I entered the buttery. My little flirtation with Miles Foxup was not forgotten. There was nothing but a sense of duty keeping me here but mingled with it were memories of rejection and humiliation. No one would miss my going and a sense of urgency flooded over me.

The fair and the travellers would soon be gone from the town. They would travel in safety as a band on the wild roads, finding shelter in bad weather. I needed to be among their womenfolk, rough though they might be. I would be travelling light; every inch of my sack must earn its keep: a clean shift, stockings, collars, my precious gloves double wrapped for safety at the bottom of the bag and enough food to see me through the first day's journey. I must be plain and invisible, blend in with my escort and trust in the Lord's providence.

That last night under my grandfather's roof I knelt by the sturdy oak posts of my bed and prayed hard. *Find me good company*, I pleaded, *and a safe passage. Guide me to where I am needed next.* Needless to say I tossed and turned all night at the enormity of my disobedience in leaving without permission. The note I wrote was brief, asking for forgiveness in rejecting the Judge's hospitality in favour of finding my own way and hoping he would feel relieved not to have the burden of my care. I promised to bring honour to his name.

What else was there to say? It was not fair to confess I found his house cold and unwelcoming and his rejection of my gift humiliating or that I did not fit into its grandeur.

Before first light I woke and dressed silently, layer upon layer, careful to take nothing that had been given here. I slipped into the buttery for cheese and oatcake that I knew could be spared, a lump of kettle cake and pie. This food would have to see me through for many miles. The coins in my purse would not last long on this bold adventure.

It was a crisp winter morning, the sun rising in a lemony lavender sky, weak and chill. I was glad of my coney mittens and muffler, thick cloak and all my petticoats covering my legs. With each firm stride I felt my body warming and cheeks flushing. No looking back on the house and the comfort of a feather bed, I thought, but striding forward to catch the travellers packing up in the town.

My first disappointment was the sight of the quiet empty streets with no wagons and carts and stalls. All was as if they had never been, just one wagon at the end of the corner, by the ale house with the sign of the black horse hanging from the door. I was too late!

Drawing closer with relief I recognised the familiar covered wagon of the doctor, with its pots and pans but no horse and no signs of life. Perhaps it was not too late. I stood by the wagon, hope rising in my chest but there was no sign of them as the morning street began to fill up with carts and townsfolk. It was not like the doctor to leave his goods unguarded. I could hear arguing through the open door of the ale house, deep voices raised and coming my way.

''Tis all a mistake, landlord!' the sonorous tones of Doctor Cranke boomed as they spilled out onto the street.

'Nowt of sort. You was out to diddle me of my dues and no mistake! The mule is mine now. There's charges for seeing to him.' The landlord in his leather apron and arms folded was barring the door.

'And you shall have every penny. Dora will fetch you one of our copper pans as recompense,' smiled the doctor, unaware of my presence. Dora was scuttling into the wagon at his command.

'I've pots enough to line from one beam to another. It's silver I'm after, all my dues for stable and hay and those mutton chops and all the ale you've drunk these past weeks. You can push your bloody lotions and potions all the way to London, you cheating thieves.'

'Steady on, landlord, we can come to some arrangement,' argued the good doctor. This was my cue to step into view and come to their rescue.

'Can I help?' I smiled, revealing my face to them. The couple looked shocked to see me standing in the half light. 'What's the problem?'

'Nothing, nothing, my dear,' said the doctor, raising his hat. 'A little misunderstanding, that's all. The sales were poorer and what with the children's keep we are embarrassed.'

'You drank all your sales and more besides, don't listen to him, Miss,' said the landlord, eyeing my sober garments.

'Oh Titus, we're ruined! What is to become of our poor children – and another on the way? This always happens to us. We try to be kind and look we are misunderstood, charged for more than we agreed,' wept Dora, flinging herself on the ground in distress.

'I can help,' I said, ferreting into my person for my hidden purse. 'I can lend you some coins. 'How much do you owe?'

'They owe me five shillings . . . a crown and not a penny less.'

'No, no we cannot take your charity,' replied the doctor, barring my arm. The landlord snatched the coins and bit them to test their metal. He turned away, no longer interested.

'How can we ever thank you for your charity?' Dora pressed herself upon me; her breath smelt of stale ale.

'Look upon this as a payment for services rendered,' I replied. With one stroke my problem was solved too. 'May I ride with you?'

'You are leaving here? Whatever for?' she said, staring hard to understand.

'I am not who you think . . . Just a farm girl who must make her own way in the world, under God's orders. I cannot travel alone.'

'Indeed not, Miss, but this is very humble transport. You'd better to take the coach. We've no money for inns or lodgings as you can see,' said Titus, bowing low. 'We would be delighted to be of assistance but we make towards Leeds.'

'Then to Leeds I will go.' In my eagerness to leave I would not have cared if he had been going south, north or any direction. 'I've no money now for fancy coaches but will be of service as you see fit. I am looking to find Friends, Seekers of the True Light. They will take care of us.'

We must have looked a jolly caravan plodding slowly eastwards towards the sun rising over the hills. My heart was full with relief that I had rescued them and they had rescued me. In my youthful innocence I thought our troubles would be few and there would be Godly signposts showing me every step on this new adventure in trust. That such an impulsive decision to take this road to freedom would have its own joys and discomforts I was soon to find out.

GOOD HOPE

2014

Hi Rachel

Thanks for your email and those photos. I think we have something really interesting going on with our combined research. We are building up quite a picture of her life in Yorkshire.

You say that Scarperton Hall is now a boutique hotel and you found the tombstone of Joy's grandfather, Elliot Moorside, in the parish Church. I have been Googling Scarperton and its district; such a beautiful place and very historic. I hope you can follow these extracts as they are copied for us to read. All that 'thee-ing and thou-ing' can seem a bit excessive but it's how they spoke to each other, I'm told.

She really is quite a character, don't you think?

The paper restorers are positive that they can rescue all the pages so I have to be patient. I think this is the most exciting thing that has happened in Good Hope for years. The local newspaper is full of it.

Best wishes

Sam

11

Even after so many wanderings, I can recall every detail of that first fateful journey across wild rolling Yorkshire country, following the River Aire down from high peaks whipped by every wind; seeing fine views in every direction, slithering on lower slopes between snowy passes. It was a zigzag of icy tracks in the depths of winter with only the warmth of righteous indignation and the fire of Titus's warm potions to stop my fingers and toes from blackening with frost.

What a relief to see we were not alone, for the tracks were well trodden with fellow travellers: packmen carrying fleeces of wool, pedlars with burdens on their backs, soldiers from the wars returning, journeymen in search of work and servants in need of hire. There were rougher men in gangs, roaring boys with staves and ragged coats who eyed our wagon with interest until they saw we had nothing but pots and pans. My meagre supply of food was soon exhausted and what we ate came from the forage pot. The doctor had his pistol at the ready and Dora a long knife of Sheffield steel that glinted when unsheathed. This couple knew how to take care of themselves.

Now and then we caught up with a carriage and four struggling to stay upright and Titus would hang around at the inn to sell the last of his remedies for chilblains and colds. If these sales were good we would pay for refuge in the stables in the warm hay; if not we found a high wall for shelter, piled on all the sheepskins over our frozen bodies and huddled together for warmth. That was when temptation came in my dreams of feather mattresses and Bessie's stews, tantalising smells wafted under my nose and I woke shivering and hungry.

If only it was a straight path to the town, but the Crankes were determined to milk every coin from the smaller out-of-the-way villages and townships past scattered farmsteads with far-flung barns that gave us shelter. We set out the stall sometimes at dusk after a long day on the road. Buyers crept under cover of darkness for fear of the priest. I saw to the old mule, finding water and oats while Dora sold love potions, snail juice and cough syrups from the crockpots.

That's when I learned that there were many remedies to relieve women of their monthly burdens, tinctures of wild poppy and greased balls of herbs. Dora laughed when she told me her goodwife's rescue remedy for emptying the contents of a tired womb. Here was I thinking that tansy was a useful flavouring for stale food and a deterrent for biting fleas and other pests. I was too young to see how desperate these farm women were to rid themselves of unwanted children. I didn't understand why she stuffed padding under her skirts to make people think she was with child when she was not.

It was a pity that whatever money was made was soon consumed in the ale house. Titus had a great thirst after a day on the road. I knew I was becoming a burden to them and offered them the last of my coins in way of recompense. These were gratefully received and quickly spent.

There were few greens and herbs to gather from which to make fresh stock and sometimes to my enduring shame we were reduced to stealing from barns and byres, hiding by the milk cow and calf to pull milk from her teats into a bucket for our gruel.

Soon all my clothes were exhausted, torn and encrusted with muck, my cheeks roughed from the chapping winds and my hands raw and coarse, my stockings in holes and my boots leaked. We looked like all the other bog trotters on the moor, little more than animals foraging for food and shelter where we could and my heart was laid low with tiredness.

My freedom was coming at a high price. The town where I would find my own community of Friends was fast slipping over the horizon and I had outstayed my welcome, being no more than another mouth to feed. No wonder they had offloaded their children.

When Titus was full of ale he became quarrelsome and noisy. He and Dora would fight and use vile language, the like of which made me blush. Sober they were kindness itself but fired with spirit they became strangers. I learned a new vocabulary in their company. One that when pushed I am still inclined to blurt out, to my eternal shame.

Sometimes in the morning they woke and poked me in the ribs to rise up and see to the chores so they could lie abed and make up their quarrel. I soon learned how it is between a man and a woman and that he was no different to the cock with his hens or the bull in a field of cows.

So it was true what Bess had whispered in the kitchen, that they that marry for love with no money had merry nights but poor days. When they were about their lusty business they did not care sometimes if I was aside them or not, such were their carryings on. This brought me much embarrassment and confusion. I was not sure I wanted to be infected with the disease of amorous love after all.

When I opened my legs to receive a man I wanted some

clean sheets and a full belly and the light of the Lord's blessing over our heads, not some scrabbling in the straw.

The coarseness of their couplings troubled my dreams. This journey was not how I had imagined. Perhaps I had chosen the wrong path after all.

'When do we reach the big town?' I whispered to Dora while we were searching for snails hidden in the crevices of walls and hedgerows. Spring was at last in sight, the hours of daylight pulling out and the sun warmed my face and itching sores. At least there would be a pot of warm broth to feast on tonight, but Titus had other ideas.

He grabbed the pail from us, ignoring my question. 'We don't go into Leeds without fresh stock. Off you go for fresh shoots, fennel, hart's tongue and liverwort to pack onto the snails. We can leave them over night to cleanse themselves and with the last of our syrup we can let their juice down into the liquid. If we're lucky I can squeeze enough to fill the empty vials. Then you can shell the snails. Nothing must be wasted. In smoky towns they need our snail juice to cure the lung troubles. There'll be rich pickings.'

There was comfort in the meanderings now; even the sight of a steeple-house cheered me. Every bridge we crossed was bringing me nearer my goal, every market cross and thatched roof brought more customers, but the constable stood around at nightfall to shove us out of town, out of sight. I sensed the journey was coming to its natural end and I would not be sorry to leave their company.

They were not the friends I hoped for, sharing truths and godly concerns, but the friends I needed to survive: cunning, worldly wise, foragers, thieves and tough skinned, these protectors. The Lord had chosen them wisely, I suppose, but at the time all I could see were their faults.

My belly had long forgotten the taste of good food, my clothes hung from me and my hair was lank and itchy. How could I make my way looking like a beggar? At least a beggar maid was invisible, untouchable. Sometimes we were shouted away and threatened with staves. There was safety in numbers. I ought to have been grateful, but one morning my faith in them was utterly destroyed.

I can still feel the lurch in my stomach when I caught sight of Dora ferreting in my knapsack thinking I was out of sight. I had spent hours searching for the docks to make us pudding with the one egg we had found by the roadside. It was to be a special treat. She turned, waving my golden gloves in the air.

'Who's a sneaky thief, then?' she winked. 'These are worth a pretty penny. Look at the quality. Fine ladies' gloves'll fetch gold at Leeds market . . . Titus! Come and see what little miss pious has been hiding all these weeks!'

'Put them back!' I yelled. 'They are not for sale.'

'Not for sale! After us nearly starving to death and keeping a roof over your head, sharing every last penny with you and you tell me these are not for sale?' Dora's eyes flashed like flints. Her claws were out for a fight. 'These will set us all up in comfort for weeks. Look, gold wire lace-work and seed pearls. You sneaky girly, no wonder you wanted to leave Scarperton in such a hurry. I bet there was a hue and cry after you skedaddled from the hall and here's us thinking you were such a pious little Puritan.'

I lurched over to snatch them but she was too quick for me, waving them over my head. 'Put them back. Dora. They belong to me . . .'

'Pull the other leg, and you a farmer's maid? You snatched them from the old lady in the hall. I could have the constable on you,' she threatened.

'And I could have the constables on you for watering down medicines and selling stuff to ladies to rid them of their bairns,' I snapped back, still trying to get the gloves.

'They're no ladies but whores, bawds and strumpets who need rid of the fruits of their lusts. Come on . . . share and share alike.'

'No! They're not for sale, ever. They were a gift . . .' I began.

'I don't believe it,' she stood firm.

'Look at the letters on the embroidery. M for Moorside and E for Elliot, on the cuff for my grandfather, the Justice and M, for Millicent, his wife who gave them to my mother. This's all I have left of them. See, read,' I pointed, knowing full well she knew not one letter.

'Why were you so happy to leave, then? M is a common letter.' Titus was seeking to catch me out. 'So you steal some gloves; none of us is perfect but how else do we survive?'

'I thought you were a doctor,' I replied, suddenly exhausted.

'And we thought you were Miss Trembling Quaker, whiter than white. Come on, think what a price these will fetch. You owe it to us,' he said, his eyes hard and menacing now. Suddenly my anger flared up like a firecracker.

'If you do not put those gloves back, I swear on the bones of my martyred parents, I'll curse thee so hard you'll never walk again! The first man I cursed went feet first into a swollen river. The next was removed from his living. Touch them not for they are precious in my sight, never to be worn. They belong to my family.' My voice was deep and throaty, hard like the calling of a disobedient dog. I was rigid with determination. 'This is my last warning.'

Something in my threat must have touched a fear in them. 'Calm down, no one will touch your blessed gauntlets. Starve if you want to but you go not another mile with us if that's your attitude. You have learned much from us, ungrateful wench!'

'Ah yes, to cheat and lie and steal. I gave you every coin in my purse. I have earned my keep and starved to keep his lordship here in ale and cakes. I'll go no further with you. Give me my sack,' I stood as Dora flung gloves and sack onto the track.

'Why, you ungrateful cow, too good for us now, are we? Lucky for you we're in striking distance of the town. Without our aid you'd have been selling your body up against a wall every night and begging me for tansy balls to clear your troubles,' Dora shouted for all to hear.

'And for that I will be grateful but to steal from one another is so uncharitable.' I was in tears now. How would I make the town before nightfall when I knew not a step of the way?

'Hop back on the wagon,' Dora called seeing my distress. 'Don't be so proud.' I shook my head as I walked behind them, sniffling and weary. I kept up the sulk for a mile until I stumbled and fell and lay face in the mud, utterly forlorn. When Titus picked me up and plonked me back amongst them, I did not resist. What could I do but sit hugging my bag, staring out at the trail behind us wondering if I could ever trust them again?

'When will you go back for Hal and Holderness?' I asked, more out of politeness than interest.

'Who?' Dora looked at me strangely and then made a big sigh. 'Would you want a child on this road in all weathers? When summer comes, happen that's the time to see them. They don't mind.'

But I minded. If I had parents of my own in the world I would travel the seas over with them by my side, not leave them to strangers. I did not understand the ways of worldly men. I do now.

I sat in silence, dangling my legs behind, lost in thought and the sudden realisation I had sworn an oath before them on the bones of my parents. I was no longer a Friend of light but a child of darkness, no better than they were in their ignorance. I was lost in a mire of my own making and was sore afraid.

We parted company at the edge of the town bridge. To my disappointment the river was grey and narrow and not the big river of flowing water of my dream. There was a ruined Abbey and many tracks to take. I waved them on their way with relief in sure hope that our paths would never cross again in life, but the Lord had other plans on that score, as I will come to later.

If there was a hiring fair I would find work, perhaps, but not in the state I was in. I made my way to the riverbank to wash the filth from my face and hands and unpick the one coin I had sewn for safety into the side of my cloak. With it I might last a few more days, change my collar and cap and make myself presentable to Friends as the daughter of sufferers and prisoners. No one knew me in Leeds. My new life was beginning.

As I sat disconsolate there was a flash of blue kingfisher skimming over the water. How many times had I seen the bird at work in Windebank along the water's edge in that other country where I was carefree and innocent. How I longed for that time to come again. Now I felt soiled and no amount of scrubbing and fresh clothing would wipe the pitch tar stains from deep in my soul.

Why had I run away without permission? I had not even written to Uncle Roger about my intentions. He would be thinking the worst of me. What would become of me here? I resolved to write a letter of explanation to them when I was settled.

Who might show me the next step of the way? Only the

Lord in His wisdom could light a path out of this darkness. My heart was heavy with shame and my eyes were blinded with tears. I was too weary to turn back north so it was time to head towards the town in faith.

'Courage is thy sturdy staff.' I tried to mouth Uncle Roger's words. Courage would keep me on the track for I was too proud to admit defeat.

Everywhere I looked there were clumps of stone cottages leaning against each other with broad windows and low thatched roofs, lines of tenters with cloth stretching across the open field like bands of broad ribbon. I joined a straggle of carts and wagons behind a drover's herd of oxen with dogs barking. There were jaggers carrying bales of cloth, farm tumbrels with cheeses piled in the back and not a known face among them.

I followed behind, trying not to show my fear as we walked into the town lined with buildings, carts and coaches. In the centre was the Moot Hall. Looking upwards to admire such a sight, my eye was drawn to three poles on which were stuck the heads of three men, little more than skulls now picked clean by wind and rain but terrible none the less to someone who had never even been to a hanging.

No one else gave this warning a second glance but my eyes kept darting back to the poles. Who were these men, traitors or believers? What fearful place had I come to?

Where could I find a change of cap? At that moment I would have given anything to catch up with the Crankes and join their company. Where would I lay my head this night? Better to turn back and head for the hills in daylight, I thought, but something stopped me, some inner assurance, some guiding light that I have never been able to explain, pushing one foot in front of the other, past the dreadful pikes and the Moot Hall onwards.

In the corner of my eye I spied a haberdasher's stall off the Briggate where there was a display of collars and cuffs, lace work and ribbons. I lingered deep in contemplation as if I was buying the crown jewels, not the cheapest plainest collar, turning my cloak inside out to hide the worst of its dirt.

'Up from the country for the market?' said the woman who eyed my clothes, missing nothing.

'I am that and in need of hiring,' I said quickly, glad to make conversation with a human voice again. 'This is a bigger place than I thought.'

'There's allus work here for those who can shift themselves,' she replied. 'Go and stand at the hiring corner and be sharp about it for the best jobs is gone well before noon. What's your work?'

'Farm work,' I said. 'But I can spin and sew, teach childer . . . anything.'

'Not much call for farm work here, lass,' she answered. 'This is a cloth town, carding, spinning, dyeing is the trades. You'd best go for a servant but mind the men as stares at you too long. Let the women do the choosing. You look plain enough not to cause any bother. The mistress is the one who'll see if you suit her. Answer plain and speak up when spoken to. Stand up tall and pinch yer cheeks to show yer bloom. They don't want sickly maids. Good luck, lass. I hope to see you again when you've got some wages to spend,' she said as I turned to where she was pointing.

'I thank thee for thy kindness,' I replied, eager to be on my way to where the market stalls were laid out in the distant field, wondering if the Crankes would be setting up but there was no sign of their wagon, only stalls of butter and cheese and barrels. This was not the main market day.

Would there be anyone looking to hire? My heart sank

when I reached the corner for there was no queue, only a lone man standing on a stool addressing the passers-by waving some papers in the air; a tall thin man of middling years trying to out-shout the clamour of the stallholders selling their ware.

'Woe to you, sinners and back-biters! Repent, for the day of the Lord is nigh, when all shall be called to judgement!'

'Cut it out, preacher! We've heard it all before! If I want a sermon I'll go to a priest ... Bugger off, I've got butter to sell before noon,' yelled the nearest costermonger. 'Go somewhere else!'

The man was undeterred. 'Repent, for the Lord sees all thy sinning whether thou givest full measure on thy scale. He is not mocked ... Come and take heed and rejoice, for the time is upon us.'

Someone threw the contents of a piss pot out of the casement above in his direction but it caught me by mistake and I stepped back in horror as my new collar was drenched 'Oh no!' I cried. 'Not my new cap too!'

He saw my distress and stepped off his stool. 'A thousand pardons, young lady. Thee hath taken my punishment. How cold are the hearts of men when it comes to salvation. What retribution they will suffer if they seek not the truth? Rejoice in the truth.' His voice was deep and strong and his eyes afire with indignation.

How strange to hear my name called out. Was this a sign? I was trying to wipe off the dousing. 'Rejoice is my given name, sir. I have travelled far to find work and follow the inner light of truth as revealed to us by George Fox.'

'Have thee, indeed?' he replied, staring hard into my face. 'From whence have you come?'

'Many a weary mile from Scarperton, sir, over the high dales from Windebank. Now I find no one at the hiring corner and my only collar is ruined,' I said, feeling the tears of frustration welling up.

'So the Lord hath brought thee to the hiring corner but not on the right day. He hath brought thee to where you are sore needed. Come with me. I know where there is work enough to fill thy days. Come, have no fear, thy journey is over. He hath guided thy path to my door. My name is Zephaniah Webster. This is my third-day preaching corner. Do you have a letter of introduction with you? Have your parents given consent that you are free to take work?'

His questions were coming thick and fast but I was in no mood to follow him.

I shook my head. 'My uncle can vouchsafe for me. We have had hard times and our meeting house was burnt to the ground. 'Tis a long story. My parents, Matthew and Alice Moorside, were prisoners and sufferers but I see there're no hirings today so how can I find work?'

'Come with me, my wife is in sore need of help. We will find work for you if you are willing,' he said.

'But I do not know thee,' I said, bending my head. How could I just walk off with a stranger down the street? Was it safe to trust his words? He looked a man of substance with a fine woollen jacket and britches; his stock was white and crisp, his face unmarked and his hands clean and he wore no wig but a tall black hat.

'Ask any in this town if Zephaniah Webster, the cloth merchant, keeps his word.'

'Do you know of this man?' I asked, looking up at the man who had dowsed me in piss.

'Aye, lass, 'tis the owd windbag Quaker, Zeph Webster who stands on street corners calling to all and sundry, deafening the trade and waking me of a morn! He's been up before the Justice more times than I've had hot pasties and gives the Parson an ear-bashing whenever he passes, but he'll not cheat at the cloth market and his tokens are good copper. If Webster says he'll find work for you then he'll do it, silly old wazzock.' The man nodded. 'He can't help his funny beliefs.'

'Sir,' I said turning back to him. 'I am trusting thou art an honest man.'

'And I am trusting that thee is who thee says thee is, for there's many claiming to be Friends of the Truth who are in paid employ of the constables as informers.'

As we walked he told me how persecuted the meetings were in Leeds, that many had suffered for their faith as we had done.

'My poor wife is sick after childbirth. We have many young children, a business to keep going and markets to attend. My word is my bond, as I trust yours is too, Rejoice Moorside?'

Could it be so easy? Had I found true Seekers and employment at a stroke? Was this a sign of blessing on all my enterprise? After the long journey, had I found my spiritual home at long last?

Nevertheless as we walked I was taking note of every street and turning so if need be I could make my way back to safety should this all turn out wrong: right, left, over the grey river bridge the other side to stone houses leaning together holding each other upright.

There were more fields of cloth stretched on tenter posts, waving in the breeze.

'I know nothing of cloth making,' I offered, fearing he would find me unfit for service after all.

'Nor should thee, lass, being delivered to us for quite another purpose. Thee will be my dear wife's right arm and her body in all things. She does not like to lie abed but the strength has left her legs. Thee will suit her, being plain and sturdy enough . . . it's not far now.'

And thus I came into the employment of clothier Zeph Webster as servant, nursemaid to his eight children and legs and right arm of his wife, Tabitha, who ruled her kingdom from behind the drapes of their four-poster bed. Another adventure was begun.

12

The house of Zephaniah Webster was by the riverbank and had nothing of the quiet grandeur of Scarperton Hall, being both workplace and dwelling and close to the cloth market where their broadcloth was sold. It was a sturdy stone building with flagged floors that hummed to the spinning wheel and clacked with weaver's looms, back and forth all day. Most of all it swarmed with children's chatter. But once a month the house was silenced when the Fellowship of Friends gathered for a meeting under cover of darkness.

My mistress had borne ten children, two living only a few days and their latest son, Will, did not look long for this life. No wonder she was worn out with travail but she made her wishes plain enough so that the household ran to her command.

For weeks after that first arrival I did not raise my head from clearing, washing and rounding up the brood as they tumbled out of every nook and cranny like noisy puppies. That they came in twos like peas out of a pod was a strange marvel; Abraham and Abner, Tamsin and Susanna, Hiram and Hepzibah, then Mercy whose sister did not survive and little Will who lay swaddled in the cradle with such a yellow face and no mind to suck.

Tabitha Webster struggled to lift herself even to do the

necessaries; her right leg was so stiff and swollen she could scarce lift it off the bed but with a stick beating down on the wooden rafters she could bring me scurrying up to do her will. She was a stickler for laundry and linen being pressed and folded to her satisfaction and that her children wore clean linen each day.

I tried a comfrey poultice on her leg to ease the swelling all to no avail. I offered every restorative we used on the farm but nothing would shift the bad humour within the flesh. None of old Dame Emmott's receipts had any effect either.

The Master went about his business, buying and selling cloth, overseeing his own weavers and spinners and apprentices. He sat long into the night with a candle, busy about his accounts; sometimes I found him still asleep in the morn with candle grease dripped all over the pages of his ledger.

It was good to feel useful but there were times when exhaustion overwhelmed me and I fell asleep during First Day Meeting, causing concern and my first admonition.

As a child of Seekers I was entitled to attend the assembly and I wrote to Uncle Roger telling him of my good fortune, only for the meeting to receive a cool letter back which upset me so greatly I wept before the whole congregation and would not be comforted.

Rejoice Moorside, daughter of prisoners and sufferers, being nearly sixteen years of age and being without father or mother, was lately in the care of her kinsman Roger Windebank. She hath made profession of her faith in times past but hath shifted from place to place as her own instruction leads her which is contrary to Truth's order. It is hoped that within the care of Friends she will find a true calling and settlement of life.
     SIGNED: Roger Windebank. Edward Horton. John Swainson. Margery Windebank. Isabel Sampson

They were rightly angry because I had left the Hall without permission, and had word got out about me travelling with the Crankes? First Day should be the high point of my week but for weeks I sat at the back in bad humour. When it was our turn to host the meeting, there was food to prepare, a baby to nurse, the twins to dress in turn if I could catch them first. Then I had to help Tabitha dress before Zeph carried her down to receive her guests; but not before I scrubbed out every crevice, polished and scoured so that no one could say I shirked my duty. There was not a moment to myself to brood or enjoy the silence. Sometimes I fell asleep at kneeling prayers and I woke shivering on the floor.

Everywhere there were fleeces to be sorted. It took five stones of Yorkshire wool to make a dozen yards of tough, hardwearing kersey and fifteen people to make it: three to sort out the fleece, dye and dress the cloth, seven or eight carders and spinners to turn it into wool for the weavers and helpers and all of them chosen by Zephaniah from the fellowship for their skill and honesty.

It was my job to see that light ale and oatcakes were made to keep them fed. Sometimes there was a minute to chat and smile with the girls spinning as they walked back and forth. That's where I first met Ellinor Holt, working the great wheel with speed and skill.

We sometimes stood together at meeting if there was a crush and I tried not to yawn with exhaustion. Ellinor often gave testimony to her faith, speaking before her elders like a preacher. How I admired her quiet joy and gentleness. There was something in her brisk manner, her devotion that I knew I must follow if ever I was to be a worthy Friend.

She lived with her father in very humble circumstances, their cottage was little more than a hovel with thin walls and thatch and her father had a bad chesty cough that would not heal. I offered to make him snail juice, remembering every detail of how Dora Cranke had made the paste. Everyone laughed at my efforts, but I took no notice of the weavers' jibes.

It was in the giving of this remedy that I was rewarded a hundredfold, for John Holt had suffered in York gaol alongside my parents, recalling every detail of that terrible time to me. I clung onto his every word, with so many questions to ask him I think I made his chest ache with all the re-telling.

It was hard not to keep away from their door but Ellinor was patient with me and sometimes we took walks along the riverbank together. 'Have you a calling?' she asked me one day as we sat by the water.

'Calling where?' I replied and she laughed.

'Perhaps not yet, but women can be preachers too. You speak well when made to give answers. Your voice is strong and carries but it is the words we give that matter. One day I hope to cross the seas to the Colonies. I dream of a ship tossing on the sea.' She sighed. 'But it will have to wait until my father is in his glory.' She lay back, looking up at the sky. 'One day I will see the New World. Perhaps we will go together.'

I never had a special friend before, one who seemed to accept me just as I was, restless, a chatterbox, full of ideas about how we could go out preaching together as witnesses for the Truth. She smiled as she listened, her grey eyes looking into the distance as if she could see far beyond the horizon.

'It is the Lord who decides our path, Joy, not our own will.' She was the only person who said my name softly, the only person who seemed to use it without awkwardness. Every morning I looked forward to our chats. She never left off her spinning but stood at her work without complaint, feeding the wool and smiling as I prattled on about nothing.

As summer days opened into bright skies and spring blossoms floated on the water, I took to taking the children down to the riverbank to look for fish and birds, to tumble and play blind man's buff which turned into wild races and silliness that was observed by one of the tenters from the meeting. I was brought before the Women's Meeting in need of correction, to explain my conduct.

'Thou must curtail the urge to jump and play foolish games. That is what worldly children are about. We train our youth to sit in quietness, not foolishness. It hath also come to our notice that thee hath been dispensing potions to our friend Tabitha's leg without permission, and to John Holt,' said Martha Houldsworth, who seemed to take delight in ticking me off.

'I was just doing as I was taught to ease suffering,' I argued, cross that every action had to be accounted for.

'There thee goes, child, answering back to those who would seek to tame this boldness of speech. We are a community of the blessed set apart and there are rules as to your conduct in all things. How else can we distinguish ourselves from the world?'

I bowed my head and crept back to the house, steaming with indignation and resentment. Susanna and Tamsin took great delight in deceiving me as to who was whom, hiding so I couldn't catch them for punishment. For once I snapped and shouted so loud everyone was in tears and Tabitha was banging on the ceiling wanting to know what was going on. It was hard trying to be holy and patient and forbearing like Ellinor all the time.

As if reading my thoughts, sometimes Zeph would send me on little errands of mercy to let me wander into town, away from my tormentors. It was on one of those outings that I caught an unexpected glimpse of the Crankes about their business.

They did not recognise me at first in my new grey cloak and linen skirt. Part of me wanted to let them see how I had gone up in the world without their help, that obstinate pride that has kept pushing itself ever forward in my life. They were busy selling their potions from the stall and I thought I could see the children peering out of the flap, staring down the street.

There was Dora up to her old tricks with the stuffing at her belly, praising her latest tincture of raspberry leaf to ease the childbirth, pointing to the boys. 'When you have a wagon full of noise like me. Look yonder, Hedley and Rawden up to mischief as usual . . .'

Hedley and Rawden, not Holderness and Halifax; even Doctor Marvel could not grow children so fast. The boys looked like brothers with red-gold hair clipped short. These were not their children at all. I stepped back quickly, puzzled and confused but Dora spotted me at once and waved as if we were the best of friends. I nodded, meaning to go on my way but she hailed me again.

''Tis good to see you have come up in the world, Joy, back as a servant, I see,' she shouted. 'We've new children to mind, my cousin is sick. Come and meet Hedley and Rawden.'

The boys looked no more than three or four, silent and dull-eyed with sores on their chins and lips. Had they not returned for the other two as she promised, it being now high summer?

'But what of your other lads? Are they not with you too?' I asked her.

'They are settled with kin. This is no life for little ones.

These boys will soon be back home,' she said and busied herself with her customers.

I walked on some way but was puzzled enough to turn back, knowing I must have a better explanation about those scabby children. There was something about this that did not add together. I turned around the corner to confront them with my questions but in that short time she had upped sticks and left and their set was empty. The Crankes never left a fair until the last order to quit. What was the hurry?

Halifax, Holderness, Hedley and Rawden, what forenames were these; false ones, perhaps? I shivered with the enormity of my suspicions. None of these children were theirs. They were as sham as the stuffing cushion in Dora's belly. I had heard tales of gypsies who stole children in the night, of the pied piper who charmed away little ones to their death . . . but the Crankes as child-stealers? Surely not.

Yet once the idea was fixed I could not shift it from my mind. I scurried back past the Moot Hall towards the bridge, not even looking up at those dreadful pikes, bumping straight into a man hurrying in the opposite direction so that we collided and his sheaves of manuscript scattered in the mire. I scrabbled to catch them before the horses' hooves crushed them underfoot and found myself face to face with my old antagonist, Miles Foxup, a student no longer by the looks of him in his black gown and stock. It took but a second for him to recognise me.

'So we meet again, the Justice's little runaway,' he laughed, his eyes flashing with delight at my discomfort. 'So this is where you're hiding yourself. I had heard that you'd fled the chicken coop, but to hide in this den of industry and iniquity . . .'

My silly heart was thudding to be caught out with flushed

cheeks, cap awry and hair tumbling forth. What would the matrons of meeting say if I was caught talking to a young man not of our calling?'

'Miles Foxup!' I said, getting to my feet before his out-stretched hand could touch mine. 'And these are no student papers.'

'Alas! I did not stay the course. My heart was not in Divinity studies,' he replied.

'This is a lawyer's gown then?'

'Hardly. I am to be articled to one Abel Catherwood, if I can salvage these from the dirt. Not a good start on my first day, is it? So who has the pleasure of employing thee?' he said mockingly.

'I serve the Seeker family called Webster in the cloth district.'

'They treat you well, these Friends?'

'Aye, fair enough considering my past record.' I sighed.

'Is that a sigh I'm hearing?' he replied.

'Not really, 'tis another matter that troubles me,' I added, not sure if I should voice my suspicions, but seeing Miles brought it all back: Scarperton, the market and his distrust of Titus and Dora. I could not keep silent.

'You recall the doctor and his stall, the one you called a quack, the one who mended my ankle. I made the journey here with them and many a time I wished I hadn't, believe me.' I paused to see if he was listening. His eyes were fixed on mine, much to my unease. 'When we first met they had two boys by their side who they said were their own children. They told me the boys were farmed out in safety for the winter but now it is third month and there are two more boys in their cart and no sign of the others.'

'That was fast work,' he smiled but his eyes were not laughing.

'Exactly my thoughts, two red-haired boys called Hedley and Rawden, or so she told me when we met a few moments ago. I am concerned for their welfare.'

'And the others were called?'

'Halifax and Holderness, strange names even for Seekers,' I said. 'I thought they were true Puritans but I have seen them at work. Hedley could be Headingley and we passed through Rawden, I think. Is it possible they are trading in children, that somewhere there are mothers crying for their bairns?' My anxieties tumbled out, words spilling over themselves as I tried to explain my imaginings.

'I'm sure it's not unknown for children to be sold into slavery, but not in this country, surely?' said Miles. 'Are they still here?'

'No, I turned back to speak to them again and they were gone. I know their wagon and old mule, Moll. I have to go back now or my mistress will be wondering where I am. I don't know what to do.'

'Leave it with me, Joy. Have no fears. If there's something amiss, we will find it out,' he replied, putting a reassuring hand on my arm. Just at that moment of intimacy, as we were deep in conversation who should pass by but Martha Houldsworth's servant, Eliza. She pretended to delve into her basket but our eyes locked for a second. She nodded but I could see her frowning, reading everything wrong.

'I know what they look like and their mule. They can't go far with that old bag of bones. I'll set a watch on their doings even if I have to do it myself,' Miles continued, oblivious to our observer. 'You've a good heart in that grey garb you are wearing even if it does nothing for you. I have to say I preferred you in blue.'

'Mind your own business!' I snapped.

'We must talk of this again,' he added as he bowed.

'I think not, not in a public place.' What else could I say if he was to be my watch in this matter?

'What better than a public place, Joy? I shall walk early down the cloth market before the bell rings and if you should happen to be about your business at that hour we may bump into each other and pursue this matter further. Or are you not concerned?' He looked down on me with that quizzical expression and raised eyebrow that stirred something within.

'Of course I care what happens to those children,' I flushed. 'I will be there. I will not settle until there is a hue and cry. Good day to thee.'

'Until we meet again,' he smiled that broad grin that would always make my knees wobble and my heart tremble.

As I hurried back to the Websters' house I made a wager to myself how many hours it would take before my presence with a strange man on Briggate would be common knowledge among the women. Twelve at the most, I reckoned but I was two hours out. By nightfall I was summoned to Tabitha's bedpost for a full explanation and dressing down but this time I was prepared.

'It is such a burden to us to know thee prefer the company of unbelievers, Joy, talking closely as if he was privy to thy heart,' said my Mistress sitting up, her lips pursed in disapproval as she stitched a hem for Suzanna.

'Master Foxup is an old acquaintance, son of my uncle's servant, Widow Priscilla. He has left university for studies in Leeds. It was an accidental meeting on the Brigg and there was a matter of some urgency to discuss. I do assure you—'

'Be that as it may but I was informed that the young man was of uncommon comeliness, of high stature and bearing and wearing a lawyer's gown,' she replied, searching my face for any signs of untruthfulness.

'He is articled to one Abel Catherwood and newly appointed. We just bumped into each other, nothing more.'

'So what is so important that you take time from your errands to loiter together for all to observe?'

'The safety of stolen children, I fear, taken against their will.' Out came all the story of the Crankes and their evil schemes.

'Surely that is a matter to bring to the Elders,' she sighed.

'In truth it was such a relief to see a known face among the crowds, such a comfort when I was so troubled. Did I do wrong?'

'I have your word that there was no carnal talk between you, no attachment to this worldly man?'

'Not on my part, I assure you. Miles has promised to inform the constables that there is a witness to their deception. I have seen the children and the new ones. We have to find them. I fear for their safety.' I shivered at the thought of them being sold into slavery.

'Enough, child, your imagination is too violent. It is good you show concern for lost souls but let the authorities deal with the matter. The Lord punishes the wicked in due course. Let's hear no more on it. To your work,' she said, turning back to her stitching as I was dismissed.

'By the by,' she added. 'It pleases me you take time in Ellinor's company. She will be thy best guide. Don't take upon thee'sen to wander from her path. Sometimes we fear thee's an unbridled horse that needs a firm halter and discipline. I don't mean to be harsh but it is for your own good if we confine you to the household for the next sevennight; no gadding about on Zephaniah's errands. This restless spirit must be bridled before it leads thee into trouble.'

Thy name is Trouble: why did that word arise and assault

all my good intentions? What was so wrong in acting on the promptings within? Now I was confined to the yard and the household, but I must see Miles again. I had to go to the next cloth market and find out if the Crankes were discovered, no matter what.

13

As the morning of the cloth market drew near I was panicked at the thought of not seeing Miles to hear his news. Every day I went out of my way to be extra diligent, teaching Suzanna and Tamsin letters from their hornbooks, keeping Hiram and Hepzy out of everyone's hair and nursing little Will. I made sure I was up early and last to bed, that everything was done quietly, not running up the stairs or thundering about banging pots and pans; everything I could think of to earn a reprieve.

The thought of defying the Master and Mistress was fearsome, for I would bring them into disrepute with the meeting. I did not want to see the look of disappointment on their faces, for they were kind and loving in their own way.

It was to Ellinor that I took all my troubles. There was always a stillness to her manner, in her spinning and conversation, even the way she sipped from her cup that made me feel like a clodhopping cart horse beside her gentleness. I blurted out my dilemma and she sat in silent thought for a moment, looking me straight in the eye.

'Are the children thy main concern in this matter or the young man who sets your voice a-trembling and thy cheeks a-flushing?' Those pale grey eyes missed nothing, flashing like a torch, making me look away. It was as if she could read my very shame. 'There is something about him that troubles thee, sets a fire inside your chest?'

I bowed my head and said nothing. What was there to say?

'This is lust at work, not love's devotion. It will tear you apart with yearning for what can never satisfy. Hot love doesn't last,' she said, reaching out to reassure me but I pulled my hand away.

'When he looks at me I want to melt into those dark eyes. I don't understand . . . what shall I do?'

'If he has such a hold on you, stay away, Joy. Don't fall into temptation's net. Take another path. There is always a choice in these matters.'

'But I have to find out about those children, to know if they are rescued,' I argued.

'So you keep saying. Then write a letter to his place of work. There need be no connection between you, no carnal thoughts. Find peace in obedience to the inner truth that we preach.'

'Why is it so easy for you?' I snapped, turning from her in frustration. I had hoped she would be on my side and give me permission to see him again.

'Don't judge what you don't know. There are some things we cannot fight and must give in with grace. This man is not for you; believe me, I know how it can hurt. There was a weaver, a fine man, before I came here. He made promises to come to meeting. I had hopes of his convincement but he could not resist the lure of strong drink and worldly pastimes, playing cards and fiddle music. It was not to be, and the more we fight the harder it gets. We're not here to please ourselves but to bring others to the light of true understanding. All things pass, so will this,' she said, smiling.

'I'm sorry, I had no idea . . .' I replied, sure in my heart that

Miles would not be like her weaver. I didn't want this excitement to pass.

'Don't pity me, for I am glad that I am free to serve now. When I get permission to join the preachers I will put my trust where it never fails and you must do the same. There will be no contentment outside our community of believers, that I do know.'

Why was there no comfort in her words for me? If only I had her gift of quiet determination. If only I could be more like Ellinor and not be this tormented soul, turned this way and that. Why were the promptings of my inner heart so misguided? Did we not believe everyone had their own path to God? If only there was a sign like the milestones on the moors pointing a finger to the next destination. I heard the rightness of what she was saying with my head but not my heart. Those longings were pulling in the opposite direction altogether.

On the morning of the cloth market I was up before dawn at my duties, still struggling with the decision to go or stay at my post, for it was but six days since my admonition. I must not leave without permission.

Zeph was about his business, ordering which yards of cloth were to be rolled and carried to the market stalls. He was both a buyer and seller and knew the exact timings of this short journey, making sure Samuel the journeyman did not loiter around the alehouses until the first bell rang, sipping ale shots to keep himself warm.

Sometimes he carried a pack of small offcuts of irregular cloth to distribute among the poor families, lengths suitable for child's britches or jackets made from fents of rough wool, not perfectly finished off. There might be burls and flaws in a piece. Seeing the package on the floor gave me an idea and I kicked it out of sight under the table so it lay forgotten as I dished out some porridge and warm ale to see them on their way in the first light. The children were still abed and Tabitha had not yet banged for me to attend her.

I waited until they were out of sight and then made a great play of finding the sack and running after them as if there was some urgency. No one would begrudge me my absence on an errand of mercy. Zeph would be grateful and forget that I was not allowed to leave the houseplace until tomorrow. If I timed my arrival to the sound of the first bell then I would have every reason to saunter through the market unnoticed, along the side-lines while the merchants were about their business.

There was no time to examine how sly and cunning was my deceit or how there were wings on my feet at the thought of seeing Miles Foxup again. I hurried down to the stone bridge with the pack on my shoulder for it was heavier than I had first thought.

It was a fine market morning, the trestles were assembled before me with the long boards that acted like counters right along the wide bridge.

The seven o'clock bell was ringing and the clothiers suddenly appeared from all directions with their cloth, out of the inns and the side alleys off the Briggate, placing their wares at their appointed places, lined up side by side like long logs of every forest hue; rough kerseys, broadcloth, finer coloured woollens.

Everyone was standing to attention in silence as custom decreed, waiting for the merchants to saunter down the gangways in search of a good purchase at a fair cost, stopping to examine a piece with their fingers, nodding and leaning over to whisper what was the asking price; a shake of the hand and the deal was done without anyone in earshot knowing their business.

Zephaniah strolled down in his dark sombre jacket. He paused to acknowledge other men from the meeting but no one spoke. My eyes were flitting nervously through the crowd to see if Miles was among them. I was getting ever closer to Samuel and Zeph. I tapped him on the shoulder.

'You forgot the fents,' I panted. 'I thought you might need them today.'

Zeph turned, surprised to see me, putting a finger on his lips. 'Shush,' he whispered. 'That was a kind act but a wasted journey, Joy. Today there is no fent sale.'

Everything fell silent, not a cough or a laugh as the parade of merchants along the ranks of stalls continued; back and forth some of them went, not wanting to miss anything before the final bell rang.

Someone bought Samuel's cloth and pointed to where it must be delivered. Up and down like a silent dance they went and still no sign of Miles. Had he forgotten? Was all this deception for nothing? Then the bell rang for business to halt. Trading was over for the day. The merchants melted away as silently as they had come and Samuel set off to deliver the sale.

'I will go back now,' I whispered, still unsure of when to speak normally. 'I'm not supposed to be here.'

'Aye, lass, on thy way rejoicing but thee must take the fents back for another time. I want to catch Friend Houldsworth. There are matters to discuss.'

There was now a throng of clothiers and packmen with rolls of cloth on their shoulders bumping into each other, men busy taking down stalls and the sun was rising high; a bustle of people about their business, no one would notice if I lingered on the Brig a little longer. I tried to look busy strapping on the sack of offcuts whilst searching the crowd, my heart in my boots and then he was there, stepping out of a doorway.

'So you came then?' he smiled and my heart leapt to see him standing tall over me.

'I can't stay. I was forbidden to leave the house ... What news?' My voice was trembling with relief that he had come.

'Nothing much so far but there is an investigation going on. We hope to catch them at their trade,' he replied.

'That's good! I was worried in case there was trouble,' I replied, knowing I must keep only to this subject matter.

'Trouble?' His eyebrow raised in a query. There was something charming in that gesture that made me want to smile. 'Why the smile?' he asked me.

'Nothing,' I said, 'I feel uneasy, that's all. Your Master, does he know of this matter?'

'No, but Justice Moorside soon will for I wrote him a long letter explaining the search for the first boys in our township. I told him you are well served in your placement.'

'I doubt he'll be interested in me.' I had not thought that news would reach Scarperton so soon.

'He's an old man, you didn't make it easy for him to warm to you,' he said. 'You can be so icy and unbending.'

'I have taken a risk in coming here. The Websters don't hold with worldly conversations.'

'What are you talking about now?' he snapped.

'I am not free to mix with those not of our calling.'

'So why did you choose to meet me this morning?'

'To find out about the Crankes, that's all.'

'But I've told you nothing, so we'll have to meet again.'

'I will write to the Moot Hall, to your Master's office. We can keep in touch by letter. It is for the best.' I made to go but he stepped into my path.

'What have I done wrong now? Don't go. I would like to see you again.'

'I have to go. I'm sorry, this was not a good idea. We must keep within our own company or there'll be trouble.'

'There you go again, always trouble, trouble, just for talking together as old acquaintances. It's not as if I've come a-wooing,' he laughed. 'Don't take everything so seriously, Joy. We're far too young to think of anything else. Did you think I was after your hand?'

'I've got to go, please. When there's news let me know how I can help. That's all. Good day.'

'At least let me carry the sack, it looks heavy,' he offered.

'No, I can manage. I brought it here and I'll carry it unaided.' My cheeks were on fire with rage and frustration but most of all with disappointment.

He saw me only as a silly miss, a plaything to tease and taunt but he was not going to see my hurt. All this fuss and deceiving for a few minutes of pain and misunderstanding. I sighed, staggering under a burden far heavier than the cloth bits. Ellinor was right. There was only humiliation in continuing this torment.

My back was sore rushing over the bridge with my load and down towards Meadow Lane. I hurried, knowing there would be havoc awaiting me and lengthy explanations to endure but I was secure. Zeph would vouchsafe my errand and my honest intentions to Tabitha. No one knew about this meeting.

Lies have never sat easy on my soul. There was no reason to tell Ellinor about them either. I didn't want to see the look of sadness on her face when she found out that I was not taking her advice, sound as it was. Better she was ignorant of my wayward heart. It had a will of its own that would not be thwarted.

14

I have never been patient when waiting for news or for events to unfold. Every journey into town, I lingered around the Moot Hall hoping to catch a glimpse of Miles about his business. To my fevered mind it seemed he was keeping his distance from me as some punishment. The fact that he might have no news to bring was a mere bagatelle compared to the importance of seeing him again. There was nothing holy in my need to be by his side. I was like some famished dog ravenous for a feast, hungry to be under his gaze, breathing his very breath. Sometimes the very thought of meeting him sent me into a tizzy of desire and I would take the basket on any excuse to put myself in a place where by chance I might encounter him. Such a passion is hard to recall when bones are old and flesh is dry. It was as if I were under some witching spell that drew me against myself.

If Ellinor sensed my restless spirit, she said nothing. She was full of her own hopes to be given permission to go abroad preaching around the wider district. For this she would need the support of the meeting and the consent of her ailing father.

When she rose to speak on First Day, slowly and with modesty she addressed the assembly with gentle words that stung like whipcords into my disobedient heart.

'Let not duty and reason be at war within thee. There is no peace in worldly business, only in holy conversation. Beware of this infection, cut out the diseased flesh. Repent, for the day of judgement is nigh!' Her words were brief, not like some who liked the sound of their own voices.

It was then I knew however long I lived I would never have the contentment and peace of a true Friend like Ellinor. I was too wilful, too selfish in wanting my own way in all things. Always there was this restlessness in me when I tried to sit still, my mind flither-flathering across the room, wandering afar from the silence into a world of my own, thinking of the river that haunted my dreams, broad and blue, the river I had yet to find where I would meet the girl with long braids and give the glove tokens.

I had not thought of the gloves for weeks; not since I rescued them from Dora's clutches. They were packed away in my wooden box out of sight. I had not shown them to anyone else. There was something shameful in their extravagant detail that the Webster family would not understand. Friends did not possess such luxuries. They were unnecessary to our beliefs. Yet again, there was another disobedience in my hiding them. Out of sight, out of mind they were, until something happened to jolt their presence to the fore.

How can a day begin so fine and end so darkly? The heat of late summer shimmered, the meadow flowers were afire with colour and the tenterfields were flagged with a cloth rainbow of many hues flapping like banners. It was a joy to be out and about on such a fine morning, sweeping out, opening casements, helping the Mistress get ready for the day knowing that she could hobble on sticks and supervise my tasks with her eagle eye. Even little Will was stronger in the warm air, watching the noisy comings and goings of his brothers and sisters from his propped-up seat.

I was about my baking, elbow deep in flour paste when there was a commotion in the yard and suddenly a constable at arms stormed into the houseplace.

'Are you the servant, Rejoice Moorside?'

'Who is asking?' I replied, calmly scraping the paste from my fingers.

'Answer the question,' he snapped.

'What's all this about, Stephen Fletcher?' said Tabitha who was about her tidying up. 'Come to relieve us of another bolt of cloth for a fine?'

'Not this time, lass,' he said. 'I have a warrant for the servant, Rejoice to accompany me to the Magistrate. There are charges to be read.'

In my innocence I was not taking in his words or why he was addressing them to me.

'What is this to do with me? What have I done wrong?'

'That's for the courts to decide. Come along now, there's a good lass.' I was so stunned that I followed him meekly to the door. There had to be some mistake.

Tabitha hobbled behind him shouting for Hiram up the stairs. 'Fetch your father and sharp … She must not go unescorted!' Hiram dashed down the stairs and out into the yard.

'Aye, you Quakers should know the ways of justice enough by now. It's about time we called on you all,' he laughed. 'We've been a bit busy of late but watch your doors of a night. If there's more than five inside, it'll be another fine and the worse for you. I don't know why you don't just give up and go to church like the rest of us.'

'This girl has no moneys of her own. She is our responsibility.'

'I wouldn't be too sure of that, Tabitha Webster,' he said, eyeing me up and down as if I were a common criminal.

Zeph was blocking the entrance gate with Samuel. 'What's all this about? What can the child have done that is so amiss, other than be a Seeker of Light?'

'Ask her about a pair of gloves she stole from Scarperton Hall. Ask her why she made a sharp exit there without permission. Ask her what she keeps hidden in her box that has a value of many pounds and would keep this family in cloth for weeks. Go on, see what she has to say to that!' He was staring at me but still it did not register what was happening.

'Rejoice, is this true?' Zeph's pale blue eyes looked down at me, puzzled.

'Nay! Well yes ... I can explain. I never stole the gloves. They are mine,' I stuttered.

'That's what all thieves say,' said the constable. 'You are charged that on or after Yuletide you, being in service there, did wilfully steal from Scarperton Hall some lady's gloves to the value of ten pounds or thereabouts.'

'That's not true. There's some mistake. Who tells such lies?' I cried, suddenly very afraid.

'Are these gloves in thy possession, Rejoice?' asked Tabitha, stepping back to examine my response.

'Yes. You can find them wrapped in my box, away from moths.'

'They are hidden, I take it?'

'The gloves belonged to my grandmother, Millicent Moorside, wife of the Justice Elliot Moorside. They were given as a peace offering to my mother. How many times do I have to explain, my father was Matthew Moorside, the prisoner, and sufferer.'

'What's a Justice's granddaughter doing as a serving maid ... a likely yarn. It's what they said you would say. Come on, let's be having you and bring the gloves with you,' said the constable, impatient to be off.

Suzanna was sent into my closet to search my box and bring the package into the light for everyone to inspect. How they sparkled in the sunshine, the bright gold lace and the soft doeskin as fresh as the day they were given.

'Just as I expected, a pair of old wedding gloves, braided and cuffed, decorated with seed pearls and fancy work. Come on, you have some explaining to do. No one wants a liar and a thief in their house, not even a Quaker,' he laughed.

'In the name of all that's precious, they are my gloves. I'm telling the truth.'

'Then happen you'll have to swear an oath before the Magistrate to the very same; but we all know how you Quakers love to swear oaths, don't we? I'd take a cloak, lass, it's cold in them cells of a night.' His words were harsh and mean but I sensed some doubt creeping into his voice.

'I'll go with thee, child,' said Zeph, putting on his hat but his eyes looked hurt and unsure for a second. He was doing his duty but uncertain of the outcome. It was in such moments that you found your true friends. He had yet to be convinced.

We walked slowly and every step I was trying to figure out why this charge was laid on me. Was the Justice punishing me for disobedience? Was this his way of making me return the gloves? Did Miles Foxup's mother, Priscilla, know of these charges? I would soon find out who my accuser was, surely.

What I did know was that for such a theft there was only one outcome. I would be hanged from the gallows on the edge of the city and perhaps my head would be placed on an iron pike, like those poor men on the Moot Hall. My legs crumpled under me with fear at such a fate. There was only one man who could help me now.

'Sir, you must speak with Miles Foxup, late of Scarperton Hall. He can vouchsafe my kin to the Justice. I am no thief. These gloves are precious to me, being a gift to my mother. She would never have worn such worldly tokens, as I will never do, but they are a gift of love. You know Ellinor's father, Friend John Holt. He met with my mother and my father in York prison. There are others who knew of them both. Please speak to Miles . . .'

'Is this Foxup man a true Friend who attends a meeting?'

'No, no, but he's the son of the housekeeper at Scarperton Hall. She can explain my position there and why I left the household in haste. The Justice was angry with me. I offered him the gloves and he nearly threw them on the fire. I had to save them . . .'

'Calm thy voice, child,' Zeph replied. 'The truth will all come out in the end. We did not expect you to keep such stuff in a box. It could be sold to help the poor or keep our preachers on the road spreading the good news from town to town. Friends do not value such worldly decorations.' There was a stern admonition in his voice.

'I know, but they have a special meaning for me. I have a dream that one day they will be passed on . . . in a place I know not where . . .' I was sharing my deepest dream with him but to no avail.

'Thee talks such fancies, I have worried about you a long while, but no matter. We must find someone to speak on thy behalf.'

'Where are we going?' I asked, seeing we were passing the Moot Hall.

'To the cells where you can sit and think on your present situation and see if you can come up with an honest explanation,' said the constable, waving the gloves in my face. 'These will go into safe keeping until they go back to their rightful owners.'

I felt so sick and shivery as the lock-up gates came in sight. There was no time to waste if I was to convince Zeph of my honesty.

'I beg you, seek out Miles Foxup at the office of Abel Catherwood by the Briggate. He will explain everything. He will inform the Justice Moorside who knows I am in Leeds. Then there is my kinsman, Roger Windebank of the same district. He will explain why I was sent to the Justice. This is all a terrible mistake,' I cried as the gates shut behind me.

'Funny, that's what they all say,' sniggered the constable.

How can I describe the next few days of misery, confined in a stone cell with a drunken doxy with torn clothes and vile mouth full of cursings and oath-swearings. We were herded like cattle in stalls, some chained to the wall at times. The straw was foetid with the stench of piss and stools for there was no office of necessity, no fresh air to breathe and only the biting fleas and rats for company. Even our food must be paid for. Bread was passed through the grille so hard it almost broke my teeth to bite on it. Never had I felt so alone, so afeared that I was friendless and forgotten. How could such an accusation have been placed over me? As the days and nights pulled out into a week, I begged the jailer for news of my release and when I would face my accusers.

Had Zeph spoken to Miles? Were the children missing me? Was Ellinor praying for me? What if it was Miles himself who had brought this case? My mind was in turmoil.

I lay huddled in a ball with my face turned to the wall. I thought many times of my father and mother in York prison. How I lay confined in such a place within her, protected by her fortitude. Such comfort was meat and drink to me and I drew strength from knowing I shared their fate now. Alas, not for the same noble defiance as theirs. No one could touch those tender imaginings or steal the inner warmth they gave me. I would stay strong for their sake. I would not break down but pray for deliverance and hope.

But for hope and Ellinor's visit my heart would have broken and my faith been destroyed as I saw around me the filth and baseness of my fellow prisoners. I felt such pity for those who knew no better than to scrabble like animals, cursing each other over scraps of gristle. There must be a way out of this darkness and soon.

She brought me clean linen and a basket of cheese, pasties and boiled eggs. Just to see her calm smile and her eagerness to hug me when I must stink to high heaven with the stench of sweat and fear was a recipe for courage. She shoved a posy of herbs into my hand.

'Wear this round your neck to ward off the foul air, put it to your nose for comfort.'

I shut my eyes at the scents of rosemary, lavender and fresh sage and smelt the garden of Windebank. ''Tis all a pack of lies,' I cried. 'But no one believes me.'

'Your friends in Truth believe you. Zeph is doing what he can to secure your release but it will take time.' It was hard to part with her hand when it was time for the visitors to leave.

'Wait on the inward light, Joy. Sit within that light and no harm can crush thy spirit,' she whispered. 'Friends will visit. Thee's not alone.'

We were allowed to hobble around a small cobbled yard when our gaoler had a mind to throw us out into the rain. To feel the fresh water on a face caked in grime, to taste it on the tongue and breathe in the autumnal air was better than the cell.

As I reached out to catch the raindrops and lick my fingers I saw another familiar face staring at me.

For a moment our eyes met and she nodded.

'So this is what it comes to, Joy Moorside,' smiled Dora Cranke, her black hair matted, her bodice torn. 'Now we both know how it is to be wrongly accused.'

'Dora?' I frowned, not taking her meaning. 'What's happened?'

'As if you don't know! Someone accuses me of stealing children, babes in arms, would you believe! Someone laid a charge that my kin are not my kin. We've been watched and snooped on. It's all lies, lies and now my poor Titus has to prove that we are victims of some charlatan jealous of our remedies.'

I felt my cheeks flaming in the chill air. 'I must admit I wondered when I saw those other boys in your cart. Where are Hal and Ness now?' I faced her squarely but her eyes flashed at me and her tongue lashed me.

'You've no understanding of our circumstances or you would not be so quick to accuse us of child theft. We have committed no crime. But two can play at that game,' she sneered, giving me a strange, cunning look.

Dunce that I was, slow to catch on, only then did it strike me that perhaps it was Dora and Titus who were my accusers. 'So you charged me with the theft of what is mine own?' I cried out.

'I don't know what you are talking about. All I know is there is a law against false accusation. We have witnesses to prove our case before the Magistrates; all these vicious lies against us must be paid for. Don't go accusing where you've no proof, Miss Holier-than-thou.' She lurched forward to strike me but I was too quick and darted away. The warder grabbed her, pulling her back.

I leaned against the wall, shaken and confused. Miles had done his work. They were accosted and accused but only one of them had been arrested, and now it seemed she would be released and I was taking the blame for their fury. None of it was making sense.

It was natural they should guess that I was the one who'd been asking questions. So they had lost no time in attacking me in return. Had I accused them falsely as they had done me? Had I made a terrible mistake and caused them to lie and sin even more?

I paced the confines of my cell in terror that I had brought this on myself. I had set the constables on the wrong people and they had retaliated out of anger and frustration. How could I stand another night in this foul pit, drenched in sweat and filth and misery?

I lost count of the days after that until the door was opened and I was escorted before the Magistrates' bench. My eyes were misty with hunger and exhaustion, my skin crawling with sores and bites. I searched the room to see if my accusers were present but the faces around me were strange and stern.

The man in the wig read out from his script, barely looking in my direction. There was something about receiving letters on my behalf.

I heard the words 'Justice', 'Scarperton' and 'Rejoice'. My gloves were laid before the court but I dared not touch them.

'It appears that this maid is the true owner of the gloves and the charge against her is dismissed forthwith, on condition that the defendant swear the oath that she is indeed Rejoice Moorside, residing at Riverbank, servant of one Zephaniah Webster and these gloves are hers as stated in the letter. That is all.'

It would have been so easy to walk to the bench and swear on the Bible, take the gloves and let that be an end of the matter. My body cried out for a tub scrub and warm food, fresh linen and the welcome of familiar faces. For a second I was tempted but my boots, such as they were, rooted themselves to the flagstones.

'I cannot swear an oath though my word is true,' I whispered, holding my hands to stop them shaking.

'Why ever not? You have been falsely accused. Just swear and sign your name and be off with you!' said the man in the wig, peering over his spectacles.

'I cannot put my name to a sworn oath. It is against scripture ...'

'Oh no, not another of those trembling *Trementes*!' he laughed. 'Another Quaker earning her heavenly reward. Come on, 'tis a formality. I've other people to see to besides you.'

I shook my head, swallowing hard. No one in that room knew what this was costing me.

'Then you are fined for not swearing,' he ordered.

'I will not pay the fine.' I replied knowing now what was in store.

'Oh, put her away again for three months!' he said, exasperated, dismissing me without another glance. 'Let her stew down there until she comes to her senses.'

I sobbed all the way down the steps, my courage gone. Why was I so stubborn? What on earth was I doing back here? When would I ever see the light of day?

There was no one to witness my stand before the court, no Friends present to defend me but my heart was warmed by the thought that there were other eyes, not of this world, who were watching and praying that I would not let them down. My parents would know that I had been true to their memory. They would know what it had cost me. God had made this back for the burden.

I found myself in a quieter cell and to my joy there were Friends Norris from the Hunslet meeting, poor Seekers, a husband and wife who had chosen not to pay their tithes and dues and had no more beds or goods to be taken away.

In such company it was easier to bear the discomfort and filth. The old man coughed all through the night and kept us awake but it was no matter.

Then came a letter from Miles Foxup that brought no comfort.

I do not understand you. We have traced the Crankes, apprehended the woman but the man escaped. It was she who claimed you were a thief and unreliable witness. They have brought forth witnesses to swear that the children, Hedley and Rawden are kin; bribed liars, no doubt. There is no point in proceeding further if you will not swear on oath what you have seen in Scarperton. Unless the other boys are found, it is pointless going on. Dora Cranke will be set free. Webster is mightily impressed with your stand. I just think it a foolish, futile gesture. Miles Foxup

How dare he make such a judgement on this my testimony? It was galling that the Crankes would escape justice but perhaps that was for the best, since their story might be true after all. I was gladdened that Zeph had made contact with the young lawyer and he had approached the Justice yet again on my behalf. I must write and thank my grandfather. How sad it was that Miles would never understand that a Seeker must deal with every part of his life as if it were under a higher scrutiny than a mere court of law. There was such a gulf between us.

Ellinor would be proud that at last I had made a stand for the Truth against temptation. So why was there all this anger and frustration inside? Why did his words crush my spirit? I would never know if the Crankes were guilty or innocent. They would walk free and I would remain here, unwashed, cold, damp and hungry, a prey to prison fever.

How hard it was to stay dignified when you were forced to relieve yourself in full view of others in the corner. It was hard to watch Enoch Norris shivering and shaking, praising God as he struggled for every breath.

My spirit sank so low that I could scarce wake up to take exercise. There was no sign of the Cranke woman in the yard, much to my relief. At least one of us was free to go about our lives. Every day Ellinor brought food and comforts and news from the Webster.

Then one morning the grille was opened, the door flung wide and I was shoved out into the bright light, filthy, lousy and blinded by the sunshine. 'My time is up!' I cried with joy. I had been found a faithful witness.

'Nay, lass' said the warder. 'Someone has paid the fine so off you go and don't come back here in a hurry.'

This time I was given no choice as I was pushed to the door, confused by the news. Free at last but beholden. Had someone read my deepest darkest wish to be rescued from this hellhole? To make it easy for me, someone had taken my fate into their own hands. To be sure it would be no Seeker who had released me against my wish.

Oh no! There was only one person who could have done this for me in good faith and I was furious with him. Miles Foxup could go to hell!

15

My days at the Riverbank pulled out slowly, one after another like oxen at the plough. It was a relief to scrub away all the filth and stench of prison, rub my sores with elderflower liniment and wear fresh linen. The welcome home was warm and I sat at the back of the secret house meetings in silence, returned to the fold unharmed and secure that for once my place on the bench was earned. The issue of who had paid my fines was a mystery but the niggles of my own suspicions would not go away.

Sometimes the Friends took it upon themselves to shorten the sufferings of the elderly and sick for mercy's sake. This was frowned upon. I was young and strong, able to stomach a few more weeks but there was always the risk of gaol fever and the spread of sickness into the community. Enoch Norris was dead. His wife was so tormented in spirit that she needed constant visiting. No one questioned my early release especially as I was needed at the Websters' house.

Tabitha was crotchety and limping, her leg was swollen and she was with child again. Little Will was still not growing strong and could barely sit unaided. He sat by the hearth watching, rocking back and forth, his eyes flitting from one to another.

Even John Holt was confined to his bed and Ellinor would let no one in the house to visit.

Ellinor's strength was like a crutch for me to lean on. Her visits in prison had been my only comfort. I wished I could be a better friend to her but if I confided in her all my fears I knew she would be disappointed in my frail discipline and shilly-shallying over those feelings for Miles. I was cross her father was so sick and demanded all her time. How could she ever love such a selfish heart as mine?

The only joy was that it was harvest time and I took the children out with baskets to garner the fruits of the hedgerows: berries, nuts, seeds and wild fruits. Every moment we were out gathering in the fresh air. For the first time in my young life I realised how precious was the freedom to roam at will. There were elderberries and black spice to make juicy cordials, crab apples and rosehips, haws, mountain berries, beech masts and hazels and willow bark.

Nothing was wasted as we picked and squeezed, stripped and soaked, peeled and pounded into preserves and oils, drying herbs and flowers until the whole houseplace was scented with them. There was honey to collect, candles and rushlights to make, fresh matting to strew and bonfires of prunings where we could roast sweet chestnuts and root vegetables from the garden plot. With fresh cordial to drink, the children chased each other around the fire like wild things which got our mistress in a lather of vexation.

It was the season for harvest feasts and drinkings. There was a Bartle fair with stalls selling roasted honey apples, gingerbread men, pretty ribbons and dancing games that we must scuttle past and not watch for fear of being bad witnesses to our faith.

How my feet itched to tap to the fiddler's tunes but the

words of the songs were bawdy and unfit for children's ears so I must herd them past and not show any enthusiasm. My eyes roamed across the pretty scene with longing as they searched to see if Miles was among the crowd.

It made me think of Yuletide and my grandfather's house, the bonny blue brocade and the rustle of its skirt as it swished across the oak floor, the dancing and that first sighting of Miles Foxup. His smile flashed on my eyelids and I heard myself sigh. How far away now was that time, how cocooned in comfort and luxury was I then.

I had never even thanked any of them for saving me from the gallows. I must beg some paper from Zeph to write my thank you letters, show him the finished script for his approval and pay for it to be sent by the post boy back to Scarperton. Friends must be courteous in all things.

As for my gloves that were returned undamaged by the court, their fate was now to be laid before the women's meeting as public property. Tabitha didn't want them in the house.

'They must be sold for the poor, Joy, and that's an end of it,' she snapped when I raised the matter yet again, hoping to put them quietly back in my box. '*Lay not up for yourself treasures on earth, where moth and rust doth corrupt or where thieves break through and steal.* Don't put temptation in another's path, child. It burdens me that thou hankers after worldly treasure and wish to preserve such stuff.'

I bowed my head and said nothing, submitting to her nagging, knowing she was sick and queasy and much distracted but I slipped the gloves into my box when she wasn't looking. There was a stubborn resistance to yield them up at her command, but the forenoon came when I was summoned to bring them before the bench once more.

I sat as each one of the worthy women had their say on the matter as if they were some terrible affliction to be destroyed before they caused more havoc.

Three times I rose to defend them and three times the words froze in my throat and would not come out. I sat down trembling with such agitation that I felt faint. If I did not speak up then they would be whisked away, never to be seen again.

'See how she trembles and fusses. It is the Spirit battling within,' said Martha Houldsworth, who eyed me with suspicion. She had not forgotten that I had been seen in the company of a worldly young man. 'We are a people separated from the lusting after mere trifles and trinkets, objects of show; fol-de-rols and fripperies. Thee should know by now that we must show our contempt for outwards things.'

Friend Martha loves the sound of her own voice, I thought but bowed to her words with a meek countenance.

'Aye, aye, Friend.' There were nods of approval around the room at her admonition. How could I ever withstand their wish? Why did it matter so much to me to keep my grandmother's tokens? I sat back defeated, knowing I could not gainsay their united will but out of nowhere came a still small voice prompting me: 'Speak thy words in peace and love. Speak out now and hold not back what is in your heart.' I found myself on my feet in front of them.

'Friends of Truth,' I began as if the voice was coming from someone else in my head. 'I hear this loving concern for my spiritual welfare. I am truly grateful for such care of my eternal soul and the needs of the poor we must support.' I had no idea what was coming next or how I would deliver my argument; all I sensed was that I was about to make an utter fool of myself but still the words came clear.

'My weakness please forgive but in this twelvemonth I have

suffered many alterations to my living. Glad was the day when I was guided to the home of Friends Zephaniah and Tabitha Webster. Sad was the day when I was falsely accused and saw however mildly for myself how my own parents suffered in prison. As a daughter of Believers I am ever mindful of their precious sacrifices, but it comes to me now that I too must wait on the Lord's promptings to tell me when is the right time to yield up this family possession to His will.

'Are we not a people whose principles stand or fall by the Truth? Are we not guided by inner promptings of the Spirit? Do we not dwell together in love and harmony respecting that each one receives their guidance from the inner light?

'Therefore of all people thee will understand that until I am convinced of the rightness of this decision to give my gloves away, it would be wrong to release these tokens just because it is asked of me. As yet I don't feel or hear such a prompting myself. That time will come but it is not now. My heart is telling me that. That is all I am guided to say,' I said, sitting down, shaking with the effort of such boldness.

There was a deafening silence; a ripple of mutterings and other matters were raised for discussion. Soon the matter of my gloves was forgotten in the general morass of the women's affairs.

When the meeting was broken up and I rose to leave, one of the elders tapped my arm. 'There is a gift of preaching within, my dear. Thy words spoke to my heart in their plain sincerity and directness. Think on, lass. This is the most precious gift in thy possession. What will thee do with it?'

To my surprise she was not the only woman to comment on my delivery and the content of my argument, which puzzled me. I had no idea now what I had said and why some were so affected. In truth I could not recall a single word I had spoken.

Tabitha was quiet on the matter but Ellinor smiled with a sparkle in her eye as she pointed to the stool set out for someone to address the assembly.

'I want to see thee on that raised tub. There's always a place for a woman of Truth to raise her voice. Now I have found my travelling partner. We can go from place to place to preach the acceptable day of the Lord.' I didn't understand then what she was getting at.

Next First Day Meeting I was in my usual place at the back, hushing the twins and nursing Will. There were some glances to see if I would stand again but there was nothing to say and nothing would induce me to speak in mixed company.

'I like to see modesty in a preacher. My daughter tells me that thee is quite the little firebrand,' John Holt laughed. 'Don't expect the words to come at thy bidding, lass. The spirit of truth lists where it wills. We're never its masters, only its servant.

'Young Ellinor has spoken of your gift. She's eager for you both to be on the road but that is not our way. It has to be agreed by everyone that you can be released from present service into this service. It is not an easy path to tread. We might all find ourselves back in the jail ere long so we need every preacher that we can muster if this town is to be saved from the Day of Judgement.'

What could I do but smile and thank him. I had no calling to go bog trotting. I was not fit to wipe Ellinor's shoes when it came to holy conversation. She studied and prayed and attended every weekday meeting. She was obedient to her heavenly vision from dawn to dusk. My heart was always hankering after forbidden fruits: music and dancing and the arms of Miles Foxup around my waist. What use could I be to them in this condition?

Yet the thought of wandering abroad was tempting. It soothed my restless spirit to explore new places. How could I leave the household or live entirely from the gifts and sacrifices of other friends, dependent on the succour of strangers like our founder George Fox and his valiant preachers who never knew where they would lay their heads? Besides I had never given witness to my faith in public. With Ellinor by my side, though, I would come to no harm and it might be a great adventure to live as my father had done for a while.

Such thoughts were quickly countered by the prospect of leaving Leeds and missing the chance to bump into Miles again. It was exciting to know he was but a mile away. He was the link with the high dales and my grandfather. I sat down and wrote a long letter to my uncle Windebank telling them about the gloves and the jail and my first speaking at meeting. I wanted him to know that coming here was a true guided path and not an indulgence. I had forgiven him that he did not rec-ommend me to the meeting. I hoped now that he saw me in a different light. I waited and waited for his reply but none came. Soon there were more serious matters on my mind.

Friends make no secret of their meetings. Notice of the next gathering was nailed to the tree close to the lane for all to read and join. It was forbidden for more than five adults to meet for worship but the law was not enforced when the local constable was on duty. Then for some reason the raids began again.

For months there had been little interference but suddenly the silence was interrupted by loud bangings on the door of friend Proctor's barn. Everyone was hustled out by the con-stable's men and marched off to appear before the court on a charge of Riotous Assembly.

It would have been a peaceable assembly if the drunken louts from the Bear Pit tavern had not decided to join in the fun of pelting the prisoners with dung and shouting obscenities in the women's ears as they huddled past. One of the visiting preachers, Jacob Wrathall, started to protest at this behaviour and was kicked about the head for his trouble but not before he had dealt out a deal of punishment himself, so Ellinor told me later, being mightily impressed by his ardent spirit.

I was not present at that meeting, being needed at the Riverbank to nurse little Will who had a fever. Zeph was worried about Tabitha who was abed with sickness and for once our household was absent. It would now be up to us to visit and make provisions for nearly the whole meeting who were shoved into the lock-up with barely room to stand. For days I ordered Tamsin and Susanna, Hiram and Hepzy to help me find enough food and necessities for the prisoners. We took broth to John Holt and sat with him while Zeph summoned help to defend the Friends from another long sentence.

They were released in dribs and drabs, bedraggled and weary but strong in spirit, having kept themselves cheerful with singing praises. Ellinor was full of praise for the new preacher, Jacob Wrathall, who kept everyone enthralled with his stories of Sufferers in other counties who defied the priests and justices. I was looking forward to meeting such a valiant witness for our cause but aching with tiredness having kept the household going with all the havoc around us.

Perhaps now everyone was relieved of cloth and cows and cash, the constables would leave us alone but other tests of faith were on the way.

First came the sudden loss of little Will. He did not survive the crisis of his fever and slipped from us quietly early in the morning. Zeph and Tabby were silent in their grief. Samuel made the box and the children covered his shroud with rosemary and leaves. We buried him in the field by Meadow Lane that was laid aside for Friends and when I wept Zeph took my hand.

'Don't be sad, lass. Think of his great happiness. He's passed his sojourn here in such a little time and now he's safe in his Father's bosom where he's at peace forever more. Be sad for us who must trundle on this earthly road for a great while longer.'

How could I not be sad for a little lad who would never run in the poppy fields or splash in the River Aire, suck a toffee apple or climb a tree?

We prepared a special meal for the mourners. Tabitha was up early to oversee the preparations, struggling to stay on her feet but steel-eyed in her determination to greet her guests. By the evening we were relieved to see them all gone but Elders Houldsworth and Horner stayed on in the chamber, smoking pipes with Zeph while we cleared around the menfolk with a sigh wishing them gone too.

Suddenly there was noise in the yard and the kitchen door flew open. Ellinor and her father were shoved into our hall by the new constable, Caleb Black, and his men at arms.

'What have we here?' he laughed. 'Yet another illegal gathering of strangers. I want all your names on my list.'

'This is disgraceful,' Zeph stood tall. 'These are my friends come to comfort us. Be gone with you, we've done nothing wrong! Ellinor is part of our household. Her spinning wheel is across this wall. What do you want with us? Haven't you had enough? Can't you see Friend John here is a sick man and it is a cold night?'

'Just as we thought, crafty as ever, we knew you'd have an answer but we know your little tricks! Bring in the others!' he yelled. Through the door came Peg and Bryan Appleyard from down the lane. 'Now there's a funny thing. Five strangers and a houseful of servants all in their best clothes. If that's not a meeting then I'm a Turkey man!'

'This is a house of mourning,' said John Holt. 'Where is your heart, young man? They buried their child this morning. We were guests at his wake and departed soon after. Do not cause them more distress.'

'A likely pack of Quaker lies! I'll give you lot this much ... you're mighty quick on your feet to argue against the facts. The law is the law. Let's be having you! No more arguments or it will be the worse for you.'

They dragged the men down into the town. Ellinor ran after her father and took his arm to steady him. Zeph turned to me, his eyes blazing with fury. 'Write it all down, Rejoice. These sufferings must be recorded and sent to the Justice. We have witnesses to this trickery. Take care, my sweet,' he mouthed to his wife who was sat in shock on the bench unable to speak, breathless with fear. 'The Lord will have his vengeance.'

'Aye, Constable Blackheart,' I shouted down the lane. 'Before this winter is out, thee will freeze for this mighty coldness. It will lay thee so low the ravens will pick thy bones ...' My words came from somewhere deep. I could not stop them. The man turned on me with venom. 'And I'll have that wench for a witch. Watch thy step, Quakeress!'

'Why do they hate us so much?' I cried, suddenly shivery with fear. Tabitha was in tears and the children stood wide-eyed with fear watching their father removed from them by force yet again. Would this persecution ever stop? Once more our household was defiled by cruel men. How could we bring this trickery to light?

I had to be strong for Zeph's family and find someone to give me sound advice. There was only one name on my list and

I must ask him again for help in this matter. He was the only worldly man I could trust.

I penned a note next morning and sent Hiram running to the Briggate to deliver it to the lodgings of Abel Webster. Zeph would be pleased with my prompt action but I told no one else. I asked Miles to meet me on the bridge and I did not care who saw me this time.

He was standing in the midst of the throng with eyes scanning the thoroughfare for my arrival. I made to hurry past him just nodding briefly, hoping he would follow me down to the river path.

'What do you want of me now?' he bowed, raising his hat in a mocking gesture. 'I see neither hide nor hair of you for months and then I am summoned. Not a word of thanks for paying your fine but here I am at your beck and call once more. I think I've paid you back for all my Yuletide rudeness by now, don't you think?'

'I'm sorry. It was amiss of me not to thank you for the Justice's letter but never pay my fine again. It's not our way.' I stared up at him full on with no mock modesty as do carnal girls who flutter their eyelashes and lower their eyelids like fans.

'Don't worry. You can rot in jail next time, young lady. I'm finished with all that mullarkey. My Master says I must have no more dealings with Quakers. So what's it now?' I could see he was impatient to be off to his work. 'Did you want to languish in that smelly pit?'

'They would release me soon enough,' I replied defiant.

'Don't be so sure. People get forgotten in dungeons. What is it with you people?'

'Come to our meetings and you will see,' I said with a smile and some hope: How handsome he was, how sharp-eyed. I

liked the way he spoke as he found. He would make a good
Seeker once the edges were rubbed off him.

'No thank you, I'll refrain from that pleasure, if you don't
mind. Once a week at the Saint Peter's church is enough for
me. What's happened now? Spit it out . . .

I told him about the raids and Will's burial and the
trumped up charge. I told him about Ellinor and her sick
father, Zeph and Tabitha's troubles; all my woes tumbling out
like a ripped sack. 'They forced five people into the house to
catch us out. It's not fair! Why does Black do this? The other
constable would give us warning of a raid and time to hide
stuff away from them when they came to take goods for our
fines.'

'Ah hah! So Quakers are not above a little deceit themselves,'
he laughed. 'New broom sweeps clean, they say. Perhaps the
new man wants to rule his patch in a different way through
fear. Who knows what goes on in a man's head when there's
money and goods to be distrained and sold for a profit?'

'So how can I get justice,' I pleaded. fearing he was bored
with my request.

'I'll ask Abel for guidance but he deals with merchant law
and business not criminal affairs.'

'We're not criminals!' I argued.

'They see you as a threat to law and order, that's for sure.
But how are you, stranger?'

'I was content until all this happened. My mistress is with
child and now little Will is dead.' Tears filled the corners of my
eyes. 'I'm so worried for them.'

He stood over me, staring down with concern. I wanted to
reach out for his hand but knew I must not.

'You people breed like rabbits. I don't suppose there's anything else for you to do!' he laughed. The spell was broken.

'Miles Foxup, why must thee say such things?'

'Sorry but it is such a waste of a pretty face to see you trussed up in your black bonnet and plain stuff. I bet you miss that blue gown and the ringlets . . .'

'No I don't!' I snapped, not daring to look up at him for fear of blushing.

'What is it about you, Joy, that makes me run to your beck and call? Why should I bother with your sort? All for one brief glimpse of that pert chin and bright gaze flashing a cheese-paring of gratitude in my direction when all I want is to twirl you round and round and hang you on my arm at the dancing. The Justice is not a well man, living alone without kin. How could you leave the old man to be a servant in a weaver's cottage?'

'It's not just weaving and spinning at Riverbank. It's a cloth merchant's house with a parlour and upper chamber,' I replied, hoping to impress.

He shrugged his shoulders. 'So Quakers have proud ambitions too. You could be an heiress one day, Joy, free to choose your own path. Why must we skulk around as if it is forbidden to talk one with another?'

'I'm not here to dress up or be shown off like some vase of flowers. I need your help. I've no one else to turn to . . .'

'And if you did . . .Would you then summon me into your presence?' he snapped.

'I'm not sure. We live in different worlds. Our ways are not your ways. It does your prospects no good to be seen with the likes of me; Quaker rabble. I know what they call us.'

'If only you'd lighten your step and let me escort you. There's so much to do here, music and plays and dancing, walks in the park. It would be fun to share it with you.'

'Here we go again, it's what you want all the time. There

must be plenty of lasses happy to simper on your arm night and day,' I said, feeling cold inside.

'Of course, there are. Even Abel has a fine daughter called Melinda who plays the virginal and sings to me whenever I call.'

'Well take her then, 'I snapped, seeing in my mind's eyes a beautiful lass bedecked in pink ribbons and curls smiling at him from the keyboard. I hated even the very name.

'I do believe thee's jealous,' he mocked our speech, seeing the look on my face.

'Not at all,' I replied, trying not to look flustered. 'We just don't approve of such time-wasting.'

'Don't be so superior, it doesn't suit you.'

'Shut your mouth!' I was losing my temper and raising my voice.

'No, you listen to me. You can't have it both ways, Miss Sobersides Moorside; the Puritan prim way you tell me you prefer, or me dangling at your command every time there's a crisis. It's one or the other.'

'I came to ask for your help,' I pleaded, standing firm against such a strong temptation to burst into tears.

'I can see that, and I'll do what I can but you keep me on a short tether: good old Miles, he'll do the hard work and get no thanks for it.'

'What thanks do you want other than to see justice is done?' I said.

'I just want to see the light flashing in your eyes, a little desire in them that you want my company. That would do for now.'

'I can't be seen out with . . .'

'Someone like me. The same old story, isn't it? Am I not good enough for a Quaker lass?' His dark eyes were pleading with me and I shook my head.

'Come to our meeting. Judge us for thyself then and not on hearsay.'

'It's not that simple, is it? If I came they'd still not approve of me seeing you, unless I became one of them.'

'It's not like that . . .' My heart was sinking at his words, all the hope draining like water from a leaky boat.

'I've not got time for all this, Joy. You're only young the once and I don't intend to spend it wearing drab cloth and preaching on street corners. You're a pretty lass, but not that pretty that others can't rival your charms. It's up to you. I don't intend to stay in Leeds forever,' he said, his eyes staring ahead.

'Leaving for where?' I asked.

'Don't know, it depends. There's a whole world out there to explore, London, Bristol, the continent. Don't worry, I'll try and sort out your mess once more and then you can be shut of me.'

'Don't be bitter, please. I am trying to be true to the Truth as we see it.'

'And I to mine; pity they are so different. The choice is yours: Friends or this friend,' he whispered. I looked up and his eyes were glazing, already bored with our talk.

'This isn't fair,' I replied.

'Life isn't fair. I'll be seeing you or not. It's up to you. I think you've had your shilling's worth of me.' He raised his hat, bowed and swept out of view without a backward glance.

Why did I feel so sick to the stomach? We had met only a few times and danced a little, flirted a little. He had given me my first kiss on the lips. Why did all my senses cry out that on such stern choices would the course of my future life now hang?

If I ran after him to please his will I would be walking away from everything that had brought me to this place. If I stayed

rooted to this spot then he was out of my life forever and I'd
never know what a precious journey we two could have made
together or how his spark would have fired the flax within me;
the swagger of his walk, the flash of his smile, the strutting
cockiness of his youthful arrogance. He had it all and I was
letting him walk away into Melinda's welcoming arms, no
doubt. Why couldn't there be a middle way to walk together?

Even after all these years my heart winces at that memory.
It is still a raw wound easily opened but the truth is plain. I
had neither strength or courage to take my bed and walk his
way. Prison and suffering had weakened me, softened me to the
will of my precious beliefs. To betray their trust, kindness and
generosity never entered my head. It would be like betraying
my parents. I was wary of the world outside my community;
a country lass in a busy town still. I needed protection and
Friends needed my hands to help them survive another dose
of prison. I must be faithful to my chosen people, to the light
within which flickered for a moment with temptation and
blazed with certainty. How was I to know if it was a false dawn
or not.

My heart ached for all his compliments and smooth words.
He had made no firm promises. If I walked his way there
would be no surety of him honouring his intentions to court
me. He might woo me and then take Abel's daughter, leaving
me spoiled, ruined and without virtue. I might be left with
child, abandoned. I didn't know the man, only the raw youth
of my imaginings. We were little more than children and I
wanted a marriage of minds one day, not conflict. He was not
Providence's choice for me. I must stay faithful and await that
choice with patience; but why did loving hurt so much?

I stood on the Brig peering deep into the dark waters with
tears dripping on my nose. Once again this Seeker was bearing

public testimony to suffering of her own making. I brushed away the tears and sped on my way home. Thank God that there's always comfort in busyness and the thought of preparing baskets of food for the prisoners, broth for the children and Tabitha and taking up Ellinor's spinning.

No time to dwell on what might have been. It was time to step forward and trust that my future must lie elsewhere: perhaps beside the wide blue river of my dreams.

16

If I have skipped and jumped over events following that parting with Miles Foxup in my account, it is not from laziness or lightness of spirit. Far from it, for in turning my face away from him towards the busyness of Riverbank affairs, there was no time to dwell on what might have been between us.

Not an hour went by in those first weeks but I tortured myself with thoughts of him, turning each conversation over and over like butter that would not set in the churn. How I hankered to make some excuse to write and see if he could ease the sufferings of the Friends who filled the jail awaiting their hearing. It was not fair to make him work on our behalf without some warmth and recognition from me.

Such was the grief around me that there was no time for such temptations.

Tabitha's baby was born early and lived but a few hours, but worse was to follow when his mother caught the childbed fever and went to her Heavenly reward early. Zeph was still in prison but compassion was granted that he might attend to her funeral. He was in a maze like a walking skeleton and needed nourishment.

The children were bereft and clung to my skirts. I tried to

be motherly and run the household as she would have wished. How could I ever think of deserting them at such a time with vain and selfish lusts?

I thought our sadness would never end. John Holt was sick in prison and only the singing and encouragement of the other Friends kept his heart beating. Samuel did his best to keep the cloth rolling from the looms but the removal of his own loom was a blow.

One night there was a bang on the door and we thought the constable was up to his old tricks again. I lifted the latch with caution only to find dear Friends carrying in pieces of our loom that they had re-purchased on our behalf. What lanterns of hope on a dark, dark night they were. I was learning even then that he who is faithful in much is rewarded in much.

It worried me that Zeph took to sitting slumped by the fireside in a deep reverie. Sometimes his speech was slurred and his mind not on spiritual matters, which caused concern among the elders who took it in turns to visit him without warning to observe his behaviour. They say that an angry mind leads even a believer away from the fear of God. If that unruly spirit took hold it would lay waste all that was once in full bloom like the blight in our kale patch.

How cold a hearth can get when the mistress of the house has departed. I missed her presence giving me orders from her bedside, her quiet acceptance of bodily infirmity.

Ellinor was busy trying to coax her father back to health, nursing him through his final illness. She stood at her wheel without enthusiasm, pacing back and forth. Even the children's prattle could not lift her sadness. I wept at John's funeral for he was the last link to my parents. We were both truly orphaned now.

The silence of meeting was a great solace to me once I could settle into it and not be distracted by the hundred and one jobs I must attend to. Once or twice I felt moved to rise from the bench to bare my thought but I have no recollection of what I said that brought comfort to others in their trials.

The only time I do recall was asking for leave to become a travelling minister in the service of Truth. I was gently rebuked and told my duty as an indentured servant was to the Webster household until such time as I was free to be released.

'The time is not right for you to go wandering at your will, Rejoice,' said Martha Houldsworth with a glance that would wither a grape shoot on the vine.

However, events will take their own turn, I have found. The atmosphere at Riverbank changed as slowly Zeph's spirit started to rise like bread dough after a knock back. Just a cheerful glance at first, his hair combed back, a clean neck band, shoulders straightened, a heartier appetite.

He praised me for keeping the chambers tidy and freshly strewn, the rush lights ready and the linen pressed as Tabitha would have wished.

'Thee teaches my children better than any schoolmaster,' he smiled, examining their efforts to make letters and read texts. 'Thou art a talented vessel.' I blushed at his words, not used to such praise.

After supper we would sit awhile and I caught him glancing in my direction with a look that soon turned my pleasure to wormwood and gall.

'It was a good day when the Lord brought you to this door, Joy.' He had never used my familiar name before and I scuttled about my business blushing while Sam, who misses nothing, laughed.

'I think old Zeph has a hankering for a new wife. You'd better watch out for he's casting his net in thy direction.'

'Don't be daft!' I snapped but my hands were shaking at such a notion. He was old enough to have been my father, had he lived. His hair was almost white, his shoulders stooped. Surely he didn't think that I would be relieved to take the mistress's place?

Why ever not, some might say? I was young and full of vim about my chores. I knew his offspring as well as if I'd been their mother. The mistress's routines were now my own. If he took me as his wife there would be nothing to change. It would be as if Tabitha had never left us. In time I would bear him more children and his household would be secure.

The very thought of his embrace was making me shudder. I was not ready to be a substitute for his old wife or any other. I took comfort in the thought that before he might address me on the matter he would have to approach the meeting and the women's meeting first to ask their approval. If he dared declare feelings to me before then, his campaign would be lost before it began.

What if he got their consent? What if they expected my joy at such an arrangement, thinking I would be relieved to be raised in station to be a cloth merchant's bride? The very thought of such an outcome was enough to make me puke.

Matters flared up one evening when all the children were abed and Samuel was at his work, Ellinor was visiting old Widow Parry and we were alone once more. He was sipping his berry ale too quickly for my liking and muttering to himself.

'It is not good for a man to be without a wife too long ... Children need a mother, the house needs a keeper. It is well nigh seven months since poor Tabitha departed for her reward. She is happy now and at peace. She would surely want me to take another as a helpmeet and companion, methinks.' His eyes were shining, glassy with drink. There was no time to lose if I was to gain the advantage here.

'I'm sure the Lord will guide thee in the fullness of time in the right direction. You must pray to him for a sign,' I replied, burying my head in the darning patch of stocking.

'Perhaps he has already,' he smiled lurching forward as if to grab my hand but all he got was the stocking and the needle's edge.

'It's getting late.' I stood up to put distance between us. 'Ellinor and I must make an early start if we are to gather baskets of comforts for the last of the prisoners.'

'Thee's a good lass with a warm heart and fine stature. What if the Lord were guiding you in the same direction,' he sighed.

'Mercy me, see how the candle drips down! I must away to my bed. There must be many a widow who would look favourably in thy direction, given the nod,' I said in a brisk voice, hoping he would take the hint. 'Someone of your own age who knows what it is to lose a helpmeet; Widow Barker is lonely soul.'

'I'm not surprised, with a voice like a beast in labour,' he said, smiling at his little joke.

'Don't be uncharitable,' I replied coolly, knowing he was right but she was the best I could come up with on the spur of the moment.

'Then there's Friend Isaiah's daughter who has never wed . . .' No more faces would come to me in my panic.

'Perhaps it's time you were wed.'

'No, not at all,' I said, shaking my head. 'You know my heart is set on the travelling ministry with Ellinor Holt.'

'She's too skinny for my taste,' he said, still thinking about his own matter and not listening to mine. 'Like a willow reed, I fear. She would not survive a bairn in her belly.'

'Zephaniah Webster, shame for talking of my dearest friend in such a manner! I will not be party to such unruly talk. 'Tis the ale pot nonsense. It is unseemly to talk of such affairs without the meeting's approval,' I snapped, wanting to warn him.

'Stay awhile, Joy, I find company eases my sorrow.'

'Only the Lord can ease thy sorrow. Call on him for a sign or call on him to help you resist the temptation of strong drink. This is not holy conversation between good Friends.' I left him to stew on my harsh words.

For days afterwards I dare not so much as look in his direction for fear of a repeat performance of his silliness. It no longer felt right to stay under his roof for fear of being accosted with further intimacies. Yet I was reluctant to share the matter with the meeting. I owed Zeph some chance to redeem himself.

'What should I do?' I asked Ellinor, pouring out all my troubles into her lap as usual. She smiled and carried on her spinning, weighing her words before she spoke, waiting upon inner guidance to prompt her reply.

'Fret not and just go about your business as normal. Whatever they say about us Friends, we know how to conduct marital matters in a civil manner. Without your consent, he cannot prevail and from what's been said, he has already shot his bolt in the wrong direction in addressing you first.'

'How can I live under the same roof with him? I'm afeared for my honour. A new wife won't want me under her feet either.'

'Then come and stay with me and be unhindered until such matters are resolved.' She smiled to see my relief. 'There, all that worry biting for nothing. There's allus a way forward with faith,' she chided me for my lack of trust.

If I lived close by Riverbank there could be no argument. Perhaps I might grow to be more like her, given time and her constant example. Then perchance the idea of us both travelling in the ministry would be acceptable to our meeting.

'It would be a good venture for us both to travel side by side,' I confided to her. She sighed, nodding her head.

'The Lord hath laid on my heart that is time to work in his vineyard. Something draws my mind to a sea crossing and being of service in the wilderness colonies but something else tells me that can never be.'

'Now who's being faint-hearted?' I replied. 'I've always dreamt of this big broad river far away. Perhaps that means a sea crossing for me too. Together we could run errands, serve, teach, find work. I feel no call to warm Zeph Briggs' cold bed ... Oh, please don't let the women persuade me otherwise.'

'There must be a way forward in this for both of us since we're of the same mind. Let's lay the whole matter again before the elders and trust in Providence to soften their hearts towards the idea,' said she with a twinkle in her eye – the first I'd seen there for many a month.

17

Nothing is done amongst Friends without deep discussion. The matter is chewed over like cows at grass. There must be harmony and a unity towards the decision. All who feel moved to speak must have their say. Whether or not we would be granted certificates to become travelling ministers in the district was not ours to take. I was impatient for the matter to be resolved quickly in my favour, but nothing in my life has ever been won with ease.

'Here be two young women, not in bondage to the spirit of this frail world, not carried away by frothy doctrines and vanity; a spinster and a servant they may be but both were faithful children of believing parents and sufferers. Let it not be said in this meeting that we discourage our youth in the ways of service. They must spend their powers in service to the generation to come wheresoever they may be found. It is my hope that we will all agree in this matter,' said Friend Isaiah, speaking on our behalf before the assembly.

'But Friend Moorside is still beholden to her master and must work out her time in his service. She has wandered far from her first meeting. Who is to say she will take another fancy and gad abroad again? My wife and I see no evidence of quietness within,' replied Timothy Houldsworth, eyeing me closely to see how I would respond.

My heart was racing with fury at the unfairness of his comments but I sat in meekness, not even shaking my head. This was too important a matter to give way to emotion.

'But Friend, this is the girl who hath the gift of prophesy. Did she not warn the constable when he disturbed our meeting that he was in mortal danger for his cruel deed? Was not the very man then found buried deep in ice in the last great snows, his eyes picked clean by ravens and his flesh rotting after the melting? God brought down a righteous judgement on his evil ways. Hath she not stood in the silence and offered comfort in her words of late, making testimony of her faith? Who are we to deny her gifts and obstruct her willingness to commit her life in this way?'

I dare not turn round to see who was speaking on my behalf.

The hearing was so quick for Ellinor's permission. Who could deny that she had a true calling? But she was no longer indentured and free to travel. I would have to be released from my duties by Zeph and he was still hankering after finding a wife close to home. He might be in no mood to let me go.

'Beware of false humility,' Timothy Houldsworth argued. 'We know only too well that some have professed such gifts in times past, but walked only after the devices of their own hearts, to our sorrow and the discomfort of our purses. How can we be sure our sister here will walk in the Truth without wavering? Has she inner quiet or not, is my question. There has already been some intransigence over the matter of the gauntlets she refuses to abandon, so my wife tells me.

'If not restrained, might not her disobedient spirit lay waste any good intentions? Is she to be trusted? Are the walls of her faith strong enough to avoid temptation?'

How dare he, I seethed! Another who loved the sound of his own voice. He was provoking them to division not harmony. There had been a case of one young servant who had received a certificate to preach around the district and make a collection for the poor and needy. Sadly she had proved to be unreliable, tempted by a worldly man and together they had absconded, taking the purse of silver with them in order to be married by a priest in a steeple-church.

Her parents were sitting on the back bench of the meeting in disgrace and shame, trying to repay what was stolen from their own meagre wages. It was not for me to speak in their defence or in defiance but I felt the words forming in my throat, stirred up by an old memory, and I rose to my feet to take the floor.

'If I might just say a word on this matter: I am grateful to Friend Timothy for reminding me that on the day of my birth, on that sad day when my parents yielded up their own lives so I might live and gave me the name Rejoice, so bad was the storm that all the walls of the pastures fell down in protest. This event was taken by all who saw it, I am told, to be a sign, whether for good or ill.

'"She'll be trouble," warned one old sage but my uncle Windebank refuted them sternly saying, "Trouble she may cause but not to the faithful. She is destined to pull down old ways, bring others to truth and storm all obstacles in her way: a very Joshua in heart." That's all I have to say on the subject of walls,' I added, sitting down promptly as a titter of amusement rustled on the benches.

'May your words be ever as sharp a sword blade in His service, Friend. I see no reason to deny thee a chance to serve as other women have before. May thee be like a fenced city, a sturdy wall against all oppressors, a wall not to be prevailed against. Let no man despise the exhortations of youth. We need young women of plain apparel and lowly circumstance to speak out against all the temptations and foolish fashions of the world that so entrap our sons and daughters,' said Friend Horner in my defence. I could have hugged him, for his words would carry much weight amongst the wavering few left in the chamber.

It was agreed that under strict supervision the two of us would be knotted together within a band of ministers, prepared for the task by our elders and escorted around the district to visit weekday and First Day Meetings as a trial of our suitability; and that the matter would be raised again at a further meeting.

Zeph would say neither yea or nay on my behalf but within a few weeks I noticed a softening and shift in his manner with me. As if to prove that Providence was on my side, he began to cast his eyes around our assembly in hope of finding someone more enthusiastic. They alighted upon a young widow called Mary Allenby who was bringing up her children in straightened circumstances. She offered to serve in the household while I was away.

'Everything works out for them as love the Lord,' whispered Ellinor in my ear on hearing the news. 'Zeph's bed won't be cold for long!'

As children cut their teeth on hard rusks so we were sent about the district, from township to township, expected to visit and encourage the faithful, stand up against the priests and, witness to our beliefs, take the punishment: all those dung-peltings, pillories and whippings. No meeting was too small or too poor for us to make ourselves known. My boots were worn out tramping over rough tracks and sodden fords but we were given an allowance to cover such necessities.

We did not hide our purpose and nailed notices of meetings to doors and trees, knowing the constable and the angry priest would be hard on our heels. Sometimes we were greeted with courtesy and interest in the market place and church porch; other times staves were raised against us as warnings.

Had there been just the two of us I would have been afraid, especially for Ellinor, who was less sturdily built than me. Few outside our beliefs could stomach the idea of women preaching in the street. But there were always Friends by our side, taking the stone-throwing and rotten eggs and curses in good grace. From them I learned how to stay quiet within and not provoke anger in my stance and demeanour.

On travelling days we were at the mercy of the elements and reliant on Friends' hospitality for shelter. Sometimes we were pushed further up the dales of the West Riding to support those experiencing yet more persecution. In our sights sometimes was the great hill of Pendle where our guide and leader, George Fox, had received his first vision; but there was no time to climb the heights and see the view from the holy mountain, for there was a special rally towards Skipton way where travelling ministers would gather together in defiance of the authorities.

The Act of Toleration which had afforded us some leniency had lately been revoked and not in our favour. News came from all counties of raids and fierce fines, and of lengthy sentences. The constables and militia men were about their business in earnest, robbing Friends of every possession they could lay their hands on.

Yet my heart lifted at the sight of familiar hills and dales, the greenness of the spring grass and those lines of grey stone walls. The nearness of Scarperton troubled me for I was duty bound to call on my grandfather and pay my respects. I was not sure a visit would be welcome but Ellinor promised to accompany me, curious to see for herself the ogre I had made of Elliot Moorside.

I retraced the path I had taken with Nan all those years

ago, through the wide gate and the park and round to the side entrance, not wanting to make a fuss. Ellinor stared up at the house with wonder just as I had done. 'How can one man live in such a big dwelling? Do the Friends know you came from such splendour to live amongst us as a servant?' she asked.

'It was never home to me but a cold empty dwelling full of fine folk who talked of nothing. I was neither below stairs or above in their reckoning. My grandfather only wanted me for his own devices and when I refused to be obedient, I was dismissed, taking leave just as my father did. I come only to be respectful of the care he has taken on my behalf on that matter of my grandmother's gloves.'

My heart was beating as I looked up the window from which I had first seen Miles astride his horse. Ellinor did not know the power that weakness still held over me. In truth I hadn't thought of him for months but seeing those grey stones, the courthouse and the bustle brought it all back to me. We waited at the door while stable boys stared at us lewdly.

'I'll have the skinny one,' shouted one lad, mouthing kisses. We ignored them, being by now used to teasing and gestures. In our plain collars and grey cloaks and hoods we were taken for serving wenches looking for work. No one recognised me, for I had grown a little taller; my skin coarsened by wind and rain, my waving hair, bleached by the summer sun, drawn back tightly into my cap.

Suddenly the door opened and Mistress Priscilla stood before us unsmiling. 'There's no work nor begging here,' she said, 'away with you,' and she made to shut the door again in our faces.

'It is Rejoice Moorside, Mistress,' I replied, 'and this is my Friend in Truth, Ellinor Holt. We've come to pay our respects to my grandfather.' I got no further with my explanation.

'You've got a cheek after all these years, running away

without a please or thank you. So now you're back to beg for 'umble pie, is it? The Master's not at home, I'm glad to say. You were the cause of his great distemper for many weeks ...'

'I'm sorry. I wished to thank him for his courtesies towards me. Please let him know I did appreciate his concern, and taking time to write on my behalf.'

'I don't know what you're talking about. If I tell him you've turned up it will only upset him and he is not a well man.'

'I'm sorry, we'll pray for his recovery and return of strength. May I beg a pitcher of water for my friend then? We've been on our feet since dawn to make this visit,' I asked, seeing the look of exhaustion on Ellinor's face.

'Well I suppose you'd better come in, but not for long. I've a hundred and one things to attend to.'

We were shown into the familiar kitchen. Nothing had changed but the faces of the girls at their tasks. They looked us up and down with pity but said nothing.

'Is Master Miles well?' I offered in politeness. She turned on me quickly.

'Oh yes, very suited, betrothed to Melinda Catherwood. I gather you played fast and loose with him, using him as your unpaid lawyer by all accounts. Melinda is quite the young lady. It is good to know he has risen so well in the world.'

Priscilla slammed down a jug of water and two pots to drink from but nothing more. We sipped the cool water and made to take leave.

'I thank thee,' I said without bobbing a curtsey as she would expect.

'You haven't changed then, that bold stare and brazen manner. I hear Quaker women have no manners. They have done your looks no favours. Your grandfather would be sick at heart to see such a drab pair on his doorstep.'

'Then I will write to him in due course and tell him I called and you withheld my coming to him,' I snapped.

'Joy! That's uncalled for,' whispered Ellinor, shocked at my response.

'She can wear all the plain clothes she likes. She don't fool me with all that theeing and thouing. She's still a haughty baggage full of wind. You deserve a knock back, turning up here without an appointment and expecting a welcome. Be gone with you. Maybe I will tell the Master you called and how coarse mannered you've become.'

We scuttled out of the door without a word. It had all gone wrong and I was unnerved by the news that Miles would be wed. Why should he not, when I refused to even consider being seen in public alongside him? I had used him, she was right in that, but it had cost me hard to let him go.

Ellinor was quiet, too quiet. 'The news of the lawyer's betrothal. Did thee know? Do thee mind?

'No,' I snapped and promptly burst into tears. 'I knew I must take my leave of him but my heart has ached for the doing of it.' She held my hand as if to give me some of her own strength.

'I know how hard it is, but I've told you many a time, all things work for them that love the Lord. Be patient. It does not work for us to be yoked to an unbeliever. Only stay true to your beliefs and it will be rewarded. There'll be someone amongst us, someone for each of us who will make our hearts leap with joy, a fit companion for the tasks to come. Don't be discouraged,' she smiled.

I knew her words made sense but at that moment I would have given anything to be Miss Melinda Catherwood of Leeds.

*

In the months that followed that first foray into new districts our friendship grew apace. Sometimes we were sent just to give messages of support from one district meeting to another when there was persecution. Other times we were sent to make enquiries about new members. But there were gatherings where we listened to the rallying calls of visiting preachers who stirred up our hearts with their fervour and tales of the sufferings of others. Then we would report back all the news to our own gathering.

The meeting at which I first saw Ellinor's favourite preacher, Jacob Wrathall, was no different from many others I had attended, but there was something about this young man and his manner that made him stand out from other travelling preachers: something in his gestures, the deepness of his voice that commanded attention, those fiery sparks that flew from him, turning an ordinary First Day Meeting into a never to be forgotten encounter.

We both felt the tension in the air, the ripple of interest as he rose to address us.

'I am not here to give thee comfort but to call thee out from amidst thy congregation, hard pressed though they may be, for a greater task, a longer journey into danger. There has been a falling off of youthful attenders of late, but it gladdens my heart today to see so many young faces raised in eagerness to hear the word of the Lord as it is given me.'

It felt as if his eyes, that were roaming around the room, rested for a second on mine, drinking in my very person so that I flamed with his gaze.

'It gladdens me to see modest dress and not flesh on show. Only last week I saw a young Friend displaying her neck for all to see. I spoke to her in earnest. "Is this flesh for sale?" I chided, seeing her dressed like a common strumpet. She looked at me and blushed. "Nay, of course not." "Then shut up thy shop at once," I replied, giving her my neck band to hide her vanity.'

My hand flew to my neck. Was there something in my dress to cause such a comment? My clean collar was still tight and secure across my breasts, my hair out of sight as usual but I recalled how I had once worn that blue gown so loosely and enjoyed the compliments.

'Many of us, children of believers, have not been through the refining fires of sufferings as our parents did in times past,' he continued. 'I fear that time is coming again as those in authority try to trick us into swearing oaths and paying tithes. It will be a time of trial and scattering, a time of danger. So the Lord hath laid on my heart the burden of gathering a faithful remnant to go out into all the world and tell the truth. It is a time not for cosseting our young into little walking trips but of goading them into longer hikes in distant countries far from our shores.

'Dearest young Friends, you are but pilgrims called to labour in far-off vineyards, to spend and be spent in the service of His truth, wheresoever that may be. Let our message of peace and hope drop gently as morning dew, refreshing the earth and all that grows therein, so we can gather a fine harvest in the years to come.'

What was he asking of us, I wondered, raising my head, straining to glean another glimpse of his strong features and dark piercing eyes. As if reading my very thoughts he glanced once more in our direction.

'I had a dream the other night that the Lord was sending me forth like Noah upon the choppy waters, in a vessel full of servants, sending us out to unknown shores in answer to their call for Truth. Friends across the great oceans are calling out for young voices, young hands and feet to travel in His service in the footsteps of Friends Fox and Widders.

'Wildernesses call out for farmers and carpenters, families to set their cities on a hill for all to see. We must build a land not corrupted by false religion; men and women from Yorkshire to build a new York and Leeds, a new Bradford and Scarborough. Young men and women who will not shirk from menial work, servants and spinsters, bakers and shoemakers, all are needed, not just for their trade but for their faith.'

I felt Ellinor shaking, tears rolling down her face, her eyes aglow with emotion and worship. 'What have I been saying to you for many years and now the call is come!'

There was a stirring along the benches.

'It will cost many guineas to sail ships across the ocean, a lifetime's wages, so I've heard,' shouted a man from the back of the room. 'And there are savages ready to steal and kill. I don't want my daughters delivered into the hands of heathens!'

'I heard tell of my neighbour's kin who set sail and never arrived in Maryland. Their boat sank in the wild seas. There are enough heathen folk in this land without seeking others afar off,' said another preacher.

'I hear you, Brother Preston,' said our preacher, raising his hand. 'Not everyone is called to make such a sacrifice in yielding up the fruits of their loins. Not everyone is called to climb the ladder from this country to a far-off land. Those who are called know it in their hearts, for their dreams will be filled with such promptings as mine and with the Lord there is always a way. He never sends us new mouths but fresh meat, never a ship without sails and a fair wind. It is all a matter of trust,' he replied, looking once more in our direction, it seemed.

My heart was thudding with that dream of the broad river of endless water, a ship with sails bobbing up and down. Would I find my broad river only if I journeyed in faith and risked all?

'Amen to Jacob's ladder!' shouted Ellinor, grabbing my hand in excitement, her eyes sparkling. 'It's always been my wish to visit America. You know it?'

'I do,' I croaked. How easy to say: how terrifying to imagine.

'Then we shall both go.' She smiled as if it were as easy as floating leaves on the duck pond.

'How? Neither of us has got the price of one passage between us.' One of us had to be sensible. Was it fair for this man to stir us up?

'Then we will save until we have enough. You heard Friend Jacob. Coins will be found for our passage one way or another. They will want spinners and servants as well as weavers and farmers. They will want travelling ministers too,' she added.

'We're not learned folk,' I replied.

'Don't be false, Joy, your reading and numbering is better than most. Why should not the likes of us be useful in the vineyard?'

'We will have to get permission to go and I've only just had permission to travel abroad in our own country. Nothing can be done without a certificate of recommendation.' Someone had to throw cold water on all these flames.

'They have to allow our inner promptings.' I had never seen Ellinor so agitated. She kept glancing over at the preacher as if willing him in our direction. It was not the time to dampen her enthusiasm with such thoughts as how to survive once we got to our unknown destination. We must not be beholden to others to give us free passage, or could we?

Such was the consternation, the flood of ideas that I was parted from meat and sleep for many days afterwards. I ploughed up and down the same furrowed ridges trying to cost what we might need and how to convince our meeting that Jacob Wrathall's words had sewn such a seed of hope in our hearts.

I would like to say that once the idea of Jacob's ladder to the New World caught hold in our minds, the way forward was like the simple parting of the Red Sea before Moses. But once again I learned that nothing worth having is ever got without a deal of heart searching and hard work, patience and persistence. The heat of those first giddy weeks soon cooled in the harsh sharp winds of our everyday lives. There were rush lights to be dipped, broth and roasts to prepare, wool to be spun and cloth to be sold, meetings to attend and more and more prisoners to visit in the jail.

Jacob Wrathall came and went as he pleased on his mission to gather emigrants and visiting ministers. He often supped with us and the parlour was packed to hear his news. There were many across Yorkshire who felt this call to make the passage to the New World but it would take months of preparation at the right season for a ship to sail in safety.

I sat in the candlelight watching the hearth flame flickering across his face. His voice was deep and rich, his words both simple and learned, his lean body animated with enthusiasm. His eyes were like burning torches and when his glance turned in my direction I felt the heat of them burning my cheeks.

Then I glimpsed Ellinor sitting in rapture, her face aglow with worship. He was the object of her desire and my heart shrank back for a moment seeing her passion for him so plain, so raw.

How long she had waited in patience for the Lord to direct her path. Had he rewarded her with a vision of what might be between them? If I had any notions towards Jacob Wrathall it must be in friendship only. I was not worthy to wipe her shoes but my heart ached with a strange jealousy and envy to see them sitting together talking with such fervour. There was a furnace of agony within me until I tore myself from the room to prepare a supper for our guests.

Suddenly I was no longer sure that I wanted anything more to do with Jacob's ladder if this was to be the outcome. Two's company, three's a crowd in such matters, I sighed. I had imagined Ellinor and myself working alongside each other, good companions travelling together. My mind was racing ahead. If she went as his wife then I would be left to persuade the elders of my sincerity to travel on my own. Suddenly I felt very alone.

One by one as the year passed, we watched the first enthusiastic volunteers slink away, discouraged by family and friends and the cost of this enterprise. For a few days after Jacob's visit I resolved to abandon the whole idea of it myself but the dream came strongly in the night and I saw clearly the faces on the shore waving to me, beckoning me forward to join them. I woke refreshed and determined not to be a spoke in the wheel of Ellinor's hopes. If she was to be joined with Jacob in wedlock who was I to stand in the way?

I wrote to my uncle Windebank stating my intentions. He wrote back with loving concern that I would always be a wanderer but that I was giving in to fantastical notions. Time alone would tell if they were genuine. He suggested I returned to Windebank for a while to think all this over in the chill moorland air.

If he were to recommend my journey he must see for himself what had become of me over the years. There were still many persecutions in the district and my help was sorely needed on the farm.

I needed no persuasion to head back to my beloved hills. It would be a loving duty to see the family who had nurtured me from birth so I laid his letter before the meeting and obtained leave to make this visit, escorted as far as Scarperton on my journey by Friends attending a gathering there. We would travel by cart into the hills.

It was the first time Ellinor and I had been parted for many months and I would miss her company but the thought of seeing her with Jacob disturbed me. I am ashamed to say that I did not want to be a witness to their happiness. Uncle Roger would cheer my troubled heart. I had stayed away from them too long.

18

I have endured many harsh winters in my life, winters that began before leaf fall and lasted until the coming of the first or second month of the year. The autumn of my return to the hills was a strange twisted season of great winds and rainfall that battered down the leaves early, turning the tracks to a quagmire and the fording places impassable.

It was as if every hindrance was put in our path as we strove to make headway in the tempest, taking shelter where we could, afraid of falling branches and whirling thatch. It made that first journey south with the Crankes all that time ago seem so free of trouble as the three of us struggled on horseback, slithering and sliding along the treacherous bridleways.

My companions were travelling Friends, Ben Foster and his wife, Ann, guiding their horses through the lanes. They knew the terrain and suggested we took a higher track away from the flood plain of the River Aire. We followed the packmen and pedlars, humping packs strapped to their backs, who knew the hill routes and the most sheltered places to rest.

We talked over all the excitement of the past months and the call to go abroad which had stirred their hearts like mine but now they were wavering.

'Friend Wrathall has a way with words. It is easy for a single man to travel untrammelled by family cares and responsibilities. The cost of such a venture is beyond our means and now we have a child to consider soon,' said Ann as she bent her head into the wind.

'It will take wilder hearts than ours to leave this high country for good, I fear,' added Ben shaking his sodden hat so it sprayed water like a fountain. 'I would not like to take a young babby on board a ship bound for the wilderness countries. We have waited many a year for this blessing.'

How could I not agree with their doubts? They were only saying aloud what my heart had been thinking for months. Ellinor was strong in spirit but not in body. What if there was sickness aboard and foul weather? I had asked her.

She had laughed away my fears as if they were trifles. 'It's not like you to be cautious, Joy. There's danger in everything we do in this life. Maids can drown getting water from a well or a river. Children die from fever even in the grandest houses. Boys fall from trees and under cart wheels every day. The house could burn down over our heads. Don't fret thyself over such matters, they're in higher hands than ours.'

When it was almost dusk, Ben pointed to a lonely farmstead hidden in the lee of the hill far ahead. 'That's where we'll stop the night. They're distant kin to my owd mother, God rest her soul. Peggy Ackroyd won't turn us from her door and if she does there's allus her barn straw to kip down on.'

'Aye, they're not of our persuasion but Dales folk will not bar the door against us on such a terrible night as this,' said Ann.

Her words were drowned out by the wind moaning and groaning. The rain was stinging my cheeks like whipcords.. Many an old tree would not survive, nor loose stones in a swollen wall. It was a Joshua night and no mistake. I smiled, thinking of Uncle Roger's words. Was I really a Joshua girl or had he made that up for my comfort?

With every step northwards and westwards I was yearning to be back at Windebank once more just to see the faces I might never see in this life again; Aunt Margery, little Dilly and Mall who would be quite grown up now.

Enough years had passed for all the old business to be forgotten, I hoped. Having twenty summers behind me and almost a city girl, they would consider me old enough to know my mind and my place. I could still milk a cow and stir the porridge, card up wool rolls and spin a fleece.

There is a scent to high country, a scent of heather and peat bog, a chill damp air, the cackle of rooks and water rushing over rocks even in the storm that I can summon up at will to remind me of this blessed land as I write these words.

We were a sorry band of bedraggled travellers, mud-splattered and soaked through, whose presence the farm dogs barked out before we reached the yard. A storm lantern swung from a hook. The walls were thick and the roof low-thatched with twine and stones hung to hold the thatch against the wind. The shutters were closed and we had to bang hard on the studded door.

'Who goes there?' shouted a gruff Dales voice.

'It's Mason Ackroyd's grandson, Ben Foster, travelling on to Skipton in need of shelter for his wife and a young lass,' he bellowed. 'She's one of the Windebanks up Scarperton way!'

The door was unlatched slowly and a weathered face peered out from the darkness.

'I've never met thee, have I, lad but come in,' said the farmer. 'It's no night for honest men to be gadding about. 'I'd've thowt thee had more sense but sit thesen down, it's wild out there.' The man stared at us, scratching his head as we dripped pools of water onto his dry rushes. 'The wife'll give thee summat to warm thy bones, seeing as you're here now. And who might this be then, the wife or the maid?' he said nodding in my direction.

'Joy Moorside, late of Windebank, come to visit her kin before she goes abroad to America. This is Henry Ackroyd,' Ben said, taking delight in showing me off.

'I'd 'ave thowt a lass'd more sense than go tramping into savage lands. Whatever for? Has she done summat wrong?' the farmer replied, looking me up and down. 'Or has the Justice seen her off? I hear he's a right stickler for the law.'

'I'm answering a call,' I said with a little too much pride in my voice.

'Who's calling thee? It's a mighty far off way for someone to be calling out,' he laughed. 'Away with her, she's having me on, America indeed! I hear it's a wilderness.' With that he plonked himself by the fireside and sucked on his pipe as if drawing in all our words to make sense of them while his wife fussed over us taking our cloaks and hoods to dry them off.

Two young boys appeared dressed in thick leather jerkins and britches and were told to rub down the horses and take them to shelter and some oats.

'Mind and wrap up afore ye go!' shouted their father. They wrapped sacking hoods over their shoulders.

It was a small rough dwelling with wooden benches to sit on, an earth floor strewn with rush matting, a scrubbed table. The kettle pot was boiling and the hob irons sparkled in the firelight. Rush lights dripped their burning mutton fat and smoke, the draughts swirled around the chamber but this was a welcome shelter for weary travellers. The noise of the howling wind rattled above us.

'I'll go and see to the lads,' said the farmer rising up to follow his sons.

How lonely winter nights can be on upland farmsteadings cut off by snow and swollen tracks, I thought. Few strangers would knock on this door, perhaps chapmen and pedlars given a warm brew and a sit down and bog trotters sent packing with a crust. They would be grilled for fresh gossip and it would be chewed over for days afterwards and spread like muck across the fields to the next farmstead or market gathering.

At least there was always company down at Riverbank and among Friends.

This was not the place to talk of missions and ministry or advertise our chosen faith. Anyone could tell by our simple dress and our manner of talking with each other that we were Dissenters of some sort or another.

'I hope you've not come up here to cause trouble,' said Henry as if reading my thoughts. 'Market place is that thick with preachers you'd think the end of the word is nigh,' he laughed. 'There's this man from Settle who likes to bring curses down on the owd vicar. He spends most of the market day in the stocks pelted with horse muck. You'd think he'd nothing better to do, disturbing the peace.'

'Henry! Give over, you know our Mason was that way inclined . . . I expect Benjamin knows his own mind on these matters without you giving him your penny-worth of ranting,' shushed his wife, raising her eyebrows. 'Take no heed, he just likes to blether on.'

'We thank you for taking us in on such a wild night. It wasn't this bad in Leeds when we left, was it? I'd forgotten it's a cloak or two colder in these parts,' I said, changing the subject.

'Aye, there'll be a fair few bunking down in barns and byres for shelter tonight. Not a good sign is this, being so early in the season . . . Happen we'll be snowed up for months.'

'I expect you make good provisions,' I replied knowing how

farmer's wives hoarded away all the summer harvest needed to feed a hungry family in bad weather.

She laughed. 'Aye, lass, and with two bairns with hollow legs to fill. They'd eat the flesh off our milk cow's back given half the chance.'

The boys came in soaked and needed rubbing down by the fireside, sitting down to warm themselves by the hearth, boys of about eight or ten, one black-haired and the other a coppernob who stared at us wide-eyed.

'Say good evening to our visitors,' she prompted them. 'This is Hal and t'other is Holly. Show the ladies your manners, lads.' They stood up, bowed and promptly sat down again.

'You'll not get a peep out of them when we've company but out in the yard, 'tis another matter,' said their mother.

'Thank you for seeing to the horses,' said Ben, slipping them a coin each.

'We'll have none of that, son,' said Henry. 'They have their duties same as anyone else on this farm. I can see thee's gone soft in the city. Big place is it? I heard the houses are all stuck together there.'

Ann nodded, smiling, 'I hope when my time comes I'll have a son as strong as they. How did you manage, being so far from midwives and village women?'

Peggy put down her mug and leant towards us. 'I was spared that agony. The Lord never blessed me with bairns of my own.' There was an awkward silence.

'I'm sorry,' said Ann looking puzzled. 'I thought you said they were your boys.'

'Hal and Holly're as good as any I might have borned mesen, grand lads. I took them in when they were nobbut babbies, many years ago . . .'

Why was my heart throbbing in my ribs, banging so I

thought everyone could hear. Hal and Holly, surely not Halifax and Holderness, those names were carved into my memory. Was it possible these were the boys that the Crankes had brought to Scarperton?

'When was that?' I heard myself asking.

''Twere after the yon big flood and the great snow, you know I can't rightly recall. A friend told me how these poor babbies needed a home ... What's it to you?' she said, her blue eyes hardening. Did I see a flash of fear in them?

I had crossed a line of politeness in such personal questions and withdrew with a smile. 'It makes an interesting tale, that is all,' I replied.

'How's that?' she snapped.

'Oh, many years ago when I lived in Scarperton I heard tell of two little boys who disappeared overnight. Halifax and Holderness were the names given to me. As I recall they were sent to a farm for the winter ...'

'I hope you don't think my Henry and Oliver are owt to do with it. They've as good home here as any in the land,' she said rising up quickly, flushed in the face and I wished for once I could have bitten off my tongue.

'Remember, we're their guests!' whispered Ann, sensing the atmosphere.

'It was just a tale,' I shrugged my shoulders but the voice in my head was ringing. *It's them, I know it's them; the two boys I saw in the market place, the stolen children farmed out for a gold piece or two.*

Those Crankes had gathered young children like wool fleece from fence posts and scattered them far away: children who were too young to know their way back home, who soon forgot their real names. Surely they should know the truth?

'It's just a strange coincidence,' I replied, not wanting to let the matter go. 'I am curious, that's all.'

'It's not thy business to ask such questions,' Ann whispered, shaking her head.

We tossed and turned by the fireside on sheepskin rugs, glad of the warmth of the embers, lying in our dried off cloaks, tired and sated with kettle broth. Outside the wind roared and the stones banged against the walls. I felt the roof was going to blow away any moment. My mind was racing with the sight of the boys after all these years, convinced that Hal and Ness were found at long last but there was no comfort in the discovery.

In the morning we woke to the scent of salted bacon sizzling in the skillet, the porridge pot was warmed up topped with cream skimmings from the dairy at the back of the house place.

'It were a bad 'un all right,' said Henry. 'There's trees down all over. It's still blowin' hard. Best to stick to high road out of here, the valley bottoms'll be flooded out, I reckon.'

'They'll be anxious for us to be on our way,' said Ben, sipping his porridge with a slurp. Peggy Ackroyd never once looked me in the eye as she dished out some oatcakes and cheese for our snack. The boys were nowhere to be seen.

'How can we thank thee for thy kind hospitality to strangers in the night? Many would have barred the door against us,' said Ben, shaking their hands.

'Company is allus welcome in this house. If it were not for the kindness of strangers, there would be no family here to see to the farm and carry on after we're gone,' Henry replied in his gruff thick voice. 'It's grand to see kin.'

'Henry, let them get on their way,' snapped Peggy plucking at her apron. 'I'll not have that one thinking we've done wrong in this life by taking in a stranger's bairns. They've given us comfort and we them and hope for the future. No one can say as we've treated them ill.' There were tears in her eyes. 'These be my sons now, whatever thy lassie might think. We want no trouble.'

'Not another word will be said on the subject. Miss Moorside will apologise for giving you a night's worry, won't you?' Ben turned to me pleading with his eyes. 'She's young and you know how righteous youth can be in its opinions. She was curious and meant no harm.'

'I'm sorry if I have given offence in suggesting that these boys were the ones stolen by wrongdoers,' I said. 'I was mistaken. The matter will go no further. I owe you much for your kindness to us. Forgive my silly questions.'

'Then that is an end on it,' snapped Peggy her chin and jaw relaxing. 'And we can forget that we harboured Quakers in our midst. One good turn deserves another,' she waved us on our way.

Was there a veiled threat in her words? Did Ben and Ann not recognise it too? We gathered our sacks and went to find the stable. It would be a relief to be on our way with horses refreshed. I looked to see if the boys were in the yard when I found the little office of necessity but there was no sight of them. Perhaps it was better not to know if my suspicions were true or not.

Peggy was waiting for me, wrapped in her cloak and hood. 'Don't go plucking up roots that are doing well in these hills. Don't go stirring up trouble where it's not wanted, Miss Moorside. I know your sort are all for the truth. There's trouble enough in this world. Bairns are safe here from the wiles of the wicked world. One day the farm will be theirs to work,' she cried. 'Let it be.'

Who could not admit there was merit in any child living high up on pasture and moor? If they were indeed one of the Crankes' stolen band of children, then they had found a far better nest than being jostled in the back of their caravan at the mercy of bad weather and worse.

Hal and Holly thrived where they grew; any fool could see that they were well fed and watered. It was not my place to make claims I couldn't prove.

'What troubles me, Mistress, is the thought of Titus and Dora Cranke roaming the countryside about their wicked business, stealing other folk's children for profit, breaking the hearts of parents. There are many that will not know such loving comfort,' was all I could say to her. She had to know the truth of my suspicions. 'I meant no harm. You've been kind to us.'

'As God is my witness these bairns came to me as orphans and I have loved them as my own flesh and blood. When you've waited nigh on ten year with an empty belly that yearns for a bairn, when you've lived with the shame of being one who is called barren then you will know my pain and the joy in receiving an answer to prayer. I don't know who sent you here but may God in His mercy soften your heart towards us,' she wept.

'But it's a terrible thing to take a child from its parents,' I argued, trying to stay upright in the gale. 'That I do know.'

'Aye and there are plenty who're careless with them an' who beat and whip and are cruel slavemasters. Let us be. I know nothing of any stealing. I was told they were orphans. Don't tear them from the only home they know.'

I knew now how Solomon must have felt when faced with two mothers wanting the same child. Why had we stumbled on this farm out of all the others in the dale?

There was no one to answer me but that inner voice that sometimes springs into my ear, the voice I call the Truth within. 'Love is what matters most. Where there's Love and honour, there be God in his glory.' Was it not possible that the

Lord in his wisdom had other plans for these boys than to languish in some city cesspit?

'The beginning of all wisdom is knowing what you don't know,' came the voice again. I could not undo what was done by going to the Justice with unproven suspicions. Look where it had got me before. This matter was neither black or white but grey and murky with arguments on both sides: that I did know and it was beyond my poor judgement.

I smiled and held out my hand. ''Tis time to be on our way. Only God knows the truth of this matter and I commend you to His mercy. Many thanks for your kindness. We have many a mile yet to journey and the rain's not going to cease from the look of those clouds. I bid thee farewell.'

There was a smile of relief on her flushed cheeks. 'One day you'll know a mother's love in your heart and all the blessings and woes that comes alongside. However far off you are in savage lands, remember this parting and the wise thing you have done. Think on, when roots are disturbed and torn asunder they grow badly after that and are weakened, but left to themselves they grow tall and sturdy with many branches and all the fowls of the air shelter in them. Thank you.'

As I rode alone northwards towards my old home, I pondered over the lesson I was given in that farmstead. Sometime it's better perhaps to leave well alone and not sit in judgement on others' doings. My tongue is always quick to lash out with my own opinions, quick to condemn where I see a shortfall. In this I was no better than many of the worthies of the women's meeting. Having been at the receiving end of their disapproval I should know how that felt.

Perhaps a return to Windebank for a few months might help me curb this fault, teach me humility and patience once more. If I was to fulfil my dream and vision for the future, I would be needing their support in many practical things. Travelling to the New World must mean a fresh start, a renewal of my calling and a chance to put this old life behind me. I must not rely on the faith of Ellinor and her preacher but on my own spiritual strength. *I will lift up mine eyes unto the hills; from whence cometh my help.* Where better than in the high dales to find the courage and resolve to face the biggest challenge of my life?

JANUARY 2015

Hi Sam

Happy New Year! Hope you had a good holiday. Mine was quiet as I was struck down with the wretched flu. Not done much on Joy's life in Leeds but I spent a day in London at the Society of Friends HQ where I was able to browse into their records to see if I could find her court cases. I did find mention of Jacob Wrathall visiting outlying Dales villages preaching in their Meeting Houses. I also came across a fascinating book in the Settle Meeting House dated 1849 containing the letters from William Ellis of Airton who travelled across to America and walked up the Eastern seaboard visiting Friends. They made them tough in those days. The letters are nothing like as personal as Joy's account though.

One thing I was able to copy was the original Treatise written by William Penn for those intending to emigrate. It is a fascinating document full of specific details on what and how much to bring on the voyage and what to build on arrival. I have sent a copy by snail mail for you to peruse.

Looking forward to the next instalment.

I am reporting back to our local history group who are now on the trail of Joy's history with gusto.

Best
Rachel

19

Ellinor and I stood by the wharf alongside the Thames gazing up in awe at the forest of tall sailing masts and the large vessels bobbing on the grey water. I must admit to a great fear descending over me at the risk we were now about to undertake together. My dear friend's face was drained of all colour but she tried to assure me that all would be well.

'We're on the Lord's work. He will be our strength,' she added, seeing my lips tremble. 'And look, we're not alone in this trial.'

There was a horde of us travellers bunched together surrounded by baggage, bales, barrels of provisions along with children excited by the mighty port wanting to explore everything in sight. The sea journey down the Yorkshire coast was uneventful. We stopped to watch Friends from Hull boarding and it was here I was introduced to my new employers, Joseph and Mary Emsworth and their children, who would be my charge on the crossing.

This was by now a tried and trusted passage across the ocean. Lessons had been learned the hard way and nothing was left to chance. William Penn himself had published a Treatise for those inclined to go to America with lists of what must be supplied.

Jacob pored over it for months making sure all our group knew what we were supposed to bring with us in the way of clothes, food, practical tools. We must be ready to begin a new life in a new settlement.

It had taken nearly a year to gather together all the necessary certificates and permissions from our various meetings, to find enough moneys for a passage and expenses. We relied on the generosity of our fellow Friends to furnish the basic sums required for those like me of few means. Many enthusiasts fell by the wayside at the cost of such an undertaking.

Thanks to Uncle Roger, I did not go empty handed but with a great round of clothed cheese and a keg of salted butter. Aunt Margery offered some coarse linen and a strong woollen dress length, knitted stockings and a new shift to change into when I arrived at our destination. I should have sold my precious gloves to fund my journey but try as I might I could not bring myself to part with them. Already I knew I was falling into the devil's snare by coveting these fancy goods, hiding them in my sack with much shame.

That last visit to Windebank after the storm seemed many months away. It was the respite I needed to calm my troubled thoughts in hard farm work and family matters. The pieces of eight my uncle gifted me as I left were carefully sewn into my waistcoat to help us through the early weeks. Ellinor and I were now indentured as servants and preachers for four years in order to fund the rest of our passage and board and lodgings on our arrival.

In my absence in the Dales I imagined much lovemaking between the young preacher and my friend but there was no betrothal, only an understanding that if they felt as one on arrival in America, they would go before the selection committee and ask to be married. Jacob was supported by the Leeds meeting and taking bales of cloth to be sold in exchange for molasses, furs and fine timber.

'There it is!' shouted young George, who was nine, tugging at my hand and pointing the way to our ship. 'The *Good Hope*, the *Good Hope*! Do you think it knows the way?'

'I'm sure it has sailed across many times, trusting its name was a good omen.'

Staring up at the rigging with the breeze whipping my cheeks I tried to stay calm.

'Don't worry, we're travelling in summer. It will be pleasant,' added Mary Emsworth. 'Hold the babe, Joy, while I check that all our provisions are safe aboard and our barrels are labelled for our use. Not everyone on board will be of our persuasion, I fear. There may be thieves among the crew. I've heard they transport villains from our gaols to settle the colonies in Maryland.'

My new mistress was with child again and trusting that her stomach would not empty its contents with a rough crossing. If the journey down the coast was anything to go by, she would be confined to her cabin, unable to move with sea-sickness.

Already our clothes were crushed, soiled and our collars and caps grubby but this was no place for vanity. We would have no time to change garments. I was glad to be wearing my workday mulberry skirt and jacket over my waistcoat and shift. All my sewing threads and needles were carefully put in my sack ready to be of use. I hoped to knit socks with my knitting stick and mend anything that got torn.

I was trusting the Emsworths had provisioned well with barrels of oats, peas, salt beef and eggs sufficient to see us through the voyage without having to buy extra stuff from the Captain and his men.

There were crowds of other folk waiting to board, foreigners with dark skins and strange costumes, women in fancy outfits. 'We stay together at all times,' Jacob advised, gathering us up like sheep in a pen. 'If supplies get low we'll pool together, loaves and fishes,' he smiled. 'Loaves and fishes, remember.'

'We must make sure he eats with us,' Ellinor whispered. 'I don't think he has much in his purse. He's sold everything he has but his carpenter's tools. He's too proud to ask for extra assistance.' I noticed then how this passion was changing my friend like some fever taking hold of her body and soul. Only once in my twenty-two years on this earth had I known such brief amorous love, thwarted though it had to be. I could see it brought fire into her eyes and a softness to her preaching. I must learn to be patient and hope that the Lord would find a suitable helpmeet for me in the far-off land, a man who would bring fire into my belly.

Then came the moment of embarkation; a clatter of leather shoes and wooden clogs on the boarding planks, a rush to stay together in a group. There was hardly time to take my leave of the mighty city behind us. Who here would care that we were departing for a new way of living with freedom to worship as we thought truthful? Would I ever see these shores again except in my dreams?

The first thing that hit me was the smell. It was if the stench of years of sweat, vomit and excrement masked by oil and tobacco fumes had soaked into the very timbers of the ship. We were ushered down a ladder from the deck into the hold under the watchful eyes of seamen with walnut faces and grease-stained shirts.

That was when I realised that we were just another shipload, a human cargo to be transported alongside our goats, pigs, chickens, geese and livestock. For a second I wanted to turn back in disgust at what lay below but Ellinor was shoving me from behind and I had baby Liddy crying in my arms. It was too late now for second thoughts.

In our innocence we assumed we would be apportioned cabins, not herded like cattle into a narrow low-roofed between-deck. There was an open space along which were boards for bedding down. Were we to be living cheek by jowl in open view of strangers?

'Surely there will be women's quarters?' I was panicking, unused to being on display at all times.

'Give them time to fill the ship. Families will stay together so we can raise sheets to give us private spaces.'

'But where do we do the private necessaries?' I asked. Was there only a hole in the planking, or a bucket?

'We'll ask later. Don't fuss. It's only for a few weeks. The Lord will provide.' Ellinor as always stayed calm.

I was no longer sure about this in such a dark crush. The air was already thick with smoke and body fumes.

'Better keep to below deck and exercise with caution. If there's a swell there could be danger on wet decking. Let us sit in silence together and ask God's blessing on our venture. May we have a fair wind and a calm crossing so we start our new life refreshed in body and spirit.' Jacob was gathering his flock together.

The Emsworth boys were not for sitting still and neither was I. George was already tearing down the gangway looking for other children to play with. Passengers were still coming down the ladder with their bulky bundles so I charged after him in case he tripped and was trampled. Sam was clutching at my skirt, wanting to follow, when a seaman shouted, 'Women down the hatch to the far end with children and maids.'

Mary was protesting with some of the others who didn't want to be separated from their husbands but orders were orders. Better to separate and stay safe together. Liddy was still at the breast so needed her mother to be close by.

Aunt Margery would be horrified at these privations but those of us who had experienced the Leeds lock-up knew the conditions here in comparison would be bearable enough. Where bodies lie close and breathe over each other, would disease soon follow? What foulness was already waiting to pounce on us? I fingered the little leather-bound Herbal that Isabel Sampson had slipped into my hand at the last meeting. 'Study it well, my dear,' she added. 'Nature is the best doctor.' Little did I know then how precious its advice would be in the coming weeks.

We seemed to be stuck in the river for hours waiting for a favourable wind and tide to take us out into the open sea. Ellinor and I, once secure in our quarters, climbed up with others curious to catch a last view of England. The ship rocked gently and then as the sails unfurled we felt the chill of the wind and the *Good Hope* lurched forward on its outward course. I fell backwards in a heap, pulling Ellinor down with me.

A militia man in a scarlet uniform rushed forward to offer a hand which I gratefully accepted, my cheeks afire with embarrassment. 'I thank thee,' I muttered as he went to help Ellinor but she declined his hand, assuring him she could manage herself.

I was surprised to see soldiers on board this passenger ship but now the Colonies are filling up, there must be public law and order.

'Where are you two Quakers bound? Up the De La Warr to Pennsylvania, no doubt. Philadelphia's a fine new city by all accounts.' The young man was trying to make conversation with us but Ellinor took my arm and hurried us back down to the hold.

'We mustn't acquaint ourselves with those types. We have no truck with men who fire muskets and wield swords.'

'I think he was just being polite and curious,' I replied, turning to see who my helper had been.

'You mustn't encourage any intercourse unless it is of a spiritual nature. We were warned that intimacies on board ship are dangerous for young single women.'

'He only helped me up from the floor, not offered to lie with me,' I laughed.

'Don't be coarse, Joy.'

'Don't be so serious then,' I snapped and wished I hadn't when I saw the look of hurt on her face. Why could she not see the funny side of it all? Why must everything be either holy or sinful? What harm was there in smiling at a helpful stranger?

20

After those first balmy days when a fair wind took us along the Channel waters, I began to believe our journey would be without a hitch. As soon as we hit the open sea, matters took a sickly turn. Ellinor and I huddled together trying not to puke over our sleeping charges. For two nights and days a gale raged over us rocking and rolling the ship so that many cried out in fear and offered up prayers for our safety in their own foreign tongues. We whispered psalms to comfort each other as we lay prostrated by the urge to retch. Nothing I ate stayed down for more than an hour. My lips were parched for fresh rain water or thin beer but there was strict rationing of the clean stuff in favour of using up the brackish older water stored in the ship's barrels. It tasted salty and foul.

First the sickness and then the terrible stench of loose bowels and the flux that began to weaken older travellers and young children. A baby died and was carried up on deck. The mother howled and would not be comforted. It didn't help than none of us could speak her language but grief needs no words.

Ellinor soon recovered her sea legs, tirelessly visiting along the women lying down on the boards. She checked how Mary, Liddy and the boys were faring as I was too weak to stand.

When I felt suddenly strong again I played pick-up-sticks with Sam and George. We laughed when the ship lurched and all the sticks would scatter. Sam cried out that it wasn't fair, as he was winning.

I was desperate to go aloft and feel the fresh salty air on my cheeks but Mary was insistent that we obey Jacob's orders not to climb on deck in case a wave swept us into the sea.

Our legs were stiff and swollen, my throat was dry but the worst discovery was that already our bodies were flea-bitten and our clothes crawling with lice. You could spend hours just trawling the seams, scraping them off with a knife to no avail.

Filthy, itchy, hungry and sick, no one warned us that this was to be our lot for weeks to come. It was to be a test of courage indeed.

Mary chided my obvious frustration and impatience. 'Think of our Lord in the desert for forty days, Rejoice,' she admonished me. 'This is our wilderness trial.'

I had to admire all those who sat calmly around me. Only their eyes showed their fear when the waves crashed into the side and sent them flying in all directions.

'Are we nearly in America?' George asked in all innocence when he had only been on board just over a sevennight.

'Not yet, not yet but we're moving ever closer to it.'

That wasn't strictly the truth on those heavy days when we lay becalmed by a contrary wind that seemed to be turning us backwards. The ship bobbed up and down while the sun beat down on the timbers and the heat below deck was like a bread oven.

It was when Ellinor fainted with tiredness that I begged to take her up into the fresher air. No one objected as we staggered up the ladder almost crawling along with relief to be out of that stench. Suddenly there was a rushing of seamen along the decking and men hanging over the rail shouting 'Man overboard!'

We collapsed in a corner out of their way. I settled Ellinor in the shade and went to see what was happening. There was a crowd of passengers crying and waving. 'Come! Over here!'

Looking down into the water I could just make out a head bobbing, splashing, making his way towards us. 'The man went mad below, screaming he must leave the ship and go home. We couldn't stop him. He jumped into the water for a swim.'

They were trying to lower a rope to him but it was too short for him to grab the line. He was drifting further away from us until his head became a speck in the distance.

I couldn't bear to watch, knowing his thrashing would soon tire and that his fate was sealed.

'It's too late now. He's too far out to be saved,' said a voice behind me. I turned to see the same tall soldier who had helped me to my feet before.

'They didn't tell you the hazards of a sea voyage when you bought your ticket to freedom,' he continued. 'Only the strong survive this journey. Few children make shore except some of the babies born on the way and many of them . . .' He paused, shaking his head. 'I saw over thirty cast over the side on my last voyage. When sickness takes hold, they are the first to go.'

'How many times have you done this crossing,' I replied, curious.

'This is my fourth and the last, I hope. I have no intention of returning. There's only so much good fortune in a man's life and I fear I have used up most of mine,' he sighed.

I didn't reply. I disagreed with his words but had no handy riposte. Better not to engage in this conversation, knowing Ellinor would disapprove, but he was eager to walk with me back to where she was lying.

'Where are you from and why do you take such a risk upon yourself, Miss?'

'I am not alone in the mission to build a free settlement among Friends. The Lord will protect us in such a worthy undertaking.'

He stared at me. His eyes were very blue, I thought, forget-me-not blue and then he laughed. 'I never took you for a preacher, a tub thumper. Forgive me, I thought they were usually wild firebrands and old men.'

'In Christ there is no male or female, bond or free. We are all equals in this calling.'

'And your friend over there . . . is she of the same persuasion?'

'Oh, she is the best of us women ministers, with the sturdiest of hearts. I can't hold a candle to her when the spirit is upon her.'

'Pardon me, but from where I am standing she's in need of some good physicking. There is a doctor on board. You should let him bleed her.' He knelt down to examine her further but I put myself between them.

'I thank you but we take care of our own. It's nothing that a bit of cool breeze and salt air won't cure,' I replied, backing away from his attentions just as Jacob arrived.

'I gather Ellinor is unwell.'

'Get that young lass to a doctor,' the soldier refused to budge. 'She has spots on her cheek and her skin is as yellow as a quince.'

Jacob nodded and peered down at her. 'I'm afraid he's right. She has a bad humour about her and there's a rash.' He touched her hand. 'She's burning hot even in the shade. Perhaps we might have another opinion?'

I didn't like the look on his face as he spoke.

'Thank you for your concern, friend,' he acknowledged the soldier. He turned to me with a scowl on his face. 'You should have warned me how sick she was when we gathered for silent prayer.'

'I didn't see the rash. How can you see anything in that dark pit they've put us in?' I answered, suddenly afraid. 'I thought it was the heat.' I knew Ellinor was not strong in the flesh but in the spirit and will. We were going to minister around the farmstead meetings together. It was all planned.

'I will go and find the doctor for you,' offered the soldier.

'To whom are we indebted for this assistance?' Jacob replied.

'Captain Thane of the Dragoons. Captain Jordan Thane and you, sir . . . ?'

'Jacob Wrathall, and this is Rejoice Moorside and Ellinor Holt, my betrothed.' I heard the tremor of fear in his voice as he looked down on her.

'I'll stay by her side. I can nurse her fever.' Never for a moment did it cross my mind that we might be separated except on the day they were wed.

Shortly there arrived a man with a grizzled beard, spectacles and tobacco breath. He peered down at her, examining hands, neck, face, unwound her coverings to see her chest and shook his head.

'Another one with the pox. That's four already this day. She must be put aside from the rest of the passengers. Once this catches on who knows how many will be stricken. 'You,' he turned to me. 'Have you had cow pox on the skin?'

'Aye,' I nodded. 'I lived on a farm. I have the marks still.'

'Good, then come with her. There's a space at the end of the bows set apart for such but it is filling up fast.'

'But I have charges to attend, the Emsworth boys, and there is a baby. What if they . . .' I protested, fear surging through me.

The doctor shrugged his shoulders. 'It's in the Good Lord's hands who lives and who dies when you risk this voyage.'

'If it's only the cow pox, she'll recover, won't she?' I wanted to be reassured.

'This is the smallpox and when it takes hold there is no saying who survives and how pock-marked they might be.'

Jacob turned his back on me to talk to the doctor without me hearing, although I listened to them nonetheless. 'We are travelling as a group together. Is it certain all will become diseased?'

'Not if you keep the sick apart, but I fear it is too late now. Living in such a crush who knows what foul air and bad humours are on board even before we set sail. Keep well away, young man, if you want to arrive unmarked.' With that he left us staring down at Ellinor who opened her eyes, already glazing with fever. How much of this had she heard? 'Fret not, it's just the heat,' she croaked.

Jacob carried her down to the place set aside for the sick and turned to me with a look of desperation in his eyes. 'You must see to her. She is not to be left to die among strangers but be restored back to us in good health. How can she come all this way to fail at the last? I will warn the others. The Emsworths must look after their own children for the moment. Save her for me,' he pleaded.

I looked around at the stricken faces, the fevered bodies and their relatives and carers like me sitting helpless by their sides. I sat numb, afraid, trying to summon everything I knew about the smaller pox that could cover a body. There must be salves and remedies in my Herbal to bring her back to us but my own knowledge was scant. This was not how it was supposed to be.

21

My hands tremble still as I recall every hour of those agonising days spent by Ellinor's side, willing her to fight for life and breath. There was so little knowledge then to aid recovery. I forced infusions of feverfew, marigold leaves, willow-bark tea between her parched lips. She submitted to leeches and elderflower salves to soothe the terrible marks over her skin. I watched my dear friend fading before my eyes, the light flickering out of hers, knowing all we could do was pray for a miracle, but none came.

'Look after Jacob for me,' she whispered. 'He's not so strong as he would have us believe. Let nothing hinder his ministry in the promised land ...'

To the end she thought of others. I was ashamed that my thoughts were all of despair, knowing that I would be travelling on alone.

There was no comfort in her last hours lying among the other dying passengers, struggling to breathe in the foetid air. I watched her to the end and wrapped her within her woven cloak for the last time, blind with tears and weariness. They bound her body with cords and carried her above to be cast over the side.

There were other bodies to be buried at sea. A young soldier that Captain Thane had often visited in the sick bay lay beside her. Jacob then insisted that no Prayer Book ceremonies took place over Ellinor. 'It is not our way,' he said, so the group of us stood in silence, the wind whipping our clothing, beating our cheeks as we made our silent farewells.

My heart was sick with rage. Why did she leave us, the best of the whole bunch of settlers, when I was in need of her rocklike strength, her convincement that 'All will be well'? How could I carry on? And how could we part with her without some words of recognition? If no one would speak then I must.

'My dearest friend was a faithful servant of Truth and gave herself to spend and be spent in its service. She was an able speaker, her words dropping soft as dew or rain on tender grass, never harsh even in admonition. Her company was pleasant to all. Much can be said in praise of Ellinor Holt. She may not have reached the promised land we seek but now she has passed into a far better reward, relieved of all the trials and sufferings of this weary world.'

The words spun from my tongue like silken threads but my heart seethed with selfish confusion. How would I survive without my friend and guide?

'Spoken well, Friend.' Jacob nodded. 'It is good to honour her sacrifice. She was never strong in body. Perhaps in His wisdom, the Lord saw fit to gather her home before she failed.'

'But she was to be thy life's companion,' I replied.

'All things happen for a reason. Perhaps He has other plans in that regard. It was an arrangement made in ignorance of what we are undertaking in making this passage.' He was staring at me, examining me as if for the first time, those coal-black eyes looking over my person like a farmer inspecting cattle for strengths and defects. 'There's the makings of a good preacher within you. I see the sturdiness of your constitution and a toughness, if a tending to obstinacy at times.'

Was this some sort of compliment? I did not reply at first, staring out into the cold grey water, shivering. 'I will be glad to be off this doom-laden ship onto dry land. There'll be much to do before winter comes. My obligation now is to the Emsworth family as their indentured servant. They'll have to give permission for me to preach abroad so it is good that I am not burdened by any amorous binding to another.'

'Friend, we Seekers do not look for that sort of attachment but only the sober sort of love among men and women that is sensible and worthy.'

'No servant can bind themselves to another until they have served their time. Ellinor's circumstances were different to mine, but now I'm nothing without her guidance,' I sighed.

'Then let me guide you further as she would have done.' He moved closer, with a look on his face that puzzled me.

'I thank thee but I think I am meant to plough my furrow alone, learn to stand square now and wait for the right path to open up to me.'

'Suit yourself. The log that leaves the fire soon cools. Be not too proud to take advice when it is offered in sincerity.' He looked hurt by my rebuff but I was too weary to care. How could a man who had just seen the body of his betrothed consigned to the deep be making suggestions to another so soon?

How eagerly had I once sought his approval and envied Ellinor winning his special favour. I felt nothing for him now, nor for anyone else, lost in my own sadness. There was only one way to address this despondency and that was to throw myself into busyness, to find ways to endure the rest of the journey.

As we turned away I saw Captain Thane hovering as if to pass on his condolences. Jacob brushed past him but I nodded in his direction, knowing he had just buried one of his men.

'I wonder if I could have a word of warning,' he offered. 'If the sickness spreads as I've seen on other vessels, keep apart as best you can. Some say it is better to stay upon deck and let the rain water soak over you. I am sorry for your loss. I saw you by her side to the end.'

I was too upset to speak but bowed my head as he continued. 'This is no paradise you are coming to, believe me. The shores are infested with biting flies that bring another kind of sickness so make sure you settle further inland by a river or fresh springs. The town of Philadelphia is growing fast and we're going there to train militia men.'

'Why? Is it not a peaceful place?'

'It was, but lately there are unruly rogues and drifters who upset the native Indians and cause raids on isolated farmsteads. You must know how to defend yourself should danger suddenly appear in the night.'

'We do not hold with violence,' I replied with sharpness.

'Then I pity you, for you will be in peril through ignorance.'

'We look to a Higher power for protection, but I thank you for thy concern.'

'What concern might that be?' Jacob was tugging at my sleeve, ushering me back down below with the others. 'Come along. We don't want you talked about any more than is necessary.'

'What have I done now?'

'Some of the elders think you take it upon thyself to speak without permission and some are afraid that you may now carry the contagion on your person.'

'How can they say that when all of us are crushed together

like animals in a pen? It's a miracle of Grace that more aren't sick already.'

'Enough of this talking out of turn, tempting Providence. Who knows what lies in store for us before this terrible voyage is over?'

'Captain Thane is concerned for our welfare when we make shore. It might be good for our elders to talk with him and take advice.'

'That's not necessary since we have correspondence from other settlers telling us what to expect on arrival. We don't talk with unbelievers, however well meant.'

'He said there might be danger from attack,' I continued.

'Our future's in higher hands than our own,' Jacob repeated, impatient for us to be out of sight of the soldier party.

'That's what I told him.'

'Good, so no more ungodly discourse with a man of the sword.'

We clambered down the ladder to be met with the Yorkshire group beckoning Jacob to their side and pointing at me. Joseph Emsworth was among them.

'She can't stay with us, not with the sickness,' he said out loud. 'It won't do, Friend. Happen she must be kept apart until the voyage is over and after that, I'm not rightly sure.'

Jacob turned in my direction, shaking his head. 'Our sister is clean, unmarked and she is bound in service to thy family. It was agreed.'

'What's done can be undone,' Joseph continued. 'It is but a bit of paper. My wife no longer wants her around our children. I heard as how her last mistress died in childbirth. She's known for trouble. We can't take the risk.'

Everyone was looking at me, arguing in low voices. To his credit, Jacob was right to warn me of this change of heart. If

I lost my post how would I then pay my passage? The gold hidden in my waistcoat would hardly cover it. Who would take me into their service? Suddenly I felt sick with panic. Was I to be set adrift on this cruel sea to fend for myself? Who among them cared if I lived or perished?

22

There is a common saying amongst us that often when one door is slammed in our faces, another opens elsewhere and so it was for me on that bitter night. I sat huddled in a corner out of sight knowing that my presence in the women's bay was no longer welcome. It felt an unfair punishment, like the shunning given to unruly Friends who disobey the teachings of our Society, who drink to excess or fornicate with the ungodly. I had done nothing but nurse my friend in her last hours.

But they were afraid and rightly so, for the sickness raged through the hold. You could smell death in the vomit, flux and sweat of deadly fevers. My head understood their caution but my heart ached with this rejection, cut off from those I thought were my friends.

Between my sobs I was aware of another woman crying, rocking herself in an agony of tears. Her evident grief needed no translating. She was one of the passengers from the Low Countries I had seen walking above deck with her child. They were a group of Protestant Dissenters who joined ship in London. Like us they kept separate but on stormy nights they sang psalms in rich harmonies to comfort us all.

I edged towards her, moved by the woman's wailing, tears I

knew meant only one thing: 'Rachel weeping for her children'. I reached out with my hand to touch her. I couldn't converse with her but I felt her pain as she felt mine.

She looked into my face. 'Thank you. You are one of the English.'

'Aye,' I nodded.' My name is Joy.'

'Sabine Boyer,' she whispered in broken English. '*Mon petit enfant* is gone . . .' I noticed she was clutching a little linen cap in her palm.

'My friend is dead.' I replied, hoping she would understand as I banged my fist into my chest. We hugged each other in the darkness and spoke no more, just sat holding hands. In the morning there was no sign of her when I woke stiff, red-eyed and wondering if the encounter had been a dream.

It was when I walked on deck that I saw her coming towards me with a limping man with white hair and beard, leaning on a stick. He raised his hat.

'My daughter is grateful for your kindness in the night. She would like you to walk with us. We have heard that you are being kept from your Friends but surely the contagion is passing now. Alas too late for our precious little Paul who has been taken from us. Sabine says you have lost a sister. Come, we can console each other. My name is Henri Boyer. We are merchants travelling to Philadelphia. My son is out there preparing for our arrival but it be sad news we must bring to him.'

'You speak so well in English,' I smiled in awe.

'It is nothing. We settled in London for a while selling cloth to dressmakers. Sabine speaks a little but would like to learn more. Speak slowly and I will share your words with her.

I spent the morning in their company. After terrible persecutions in France when his wife was murdered by the dreaded Dragonades militia, they fled to Leyden and then on to London to start a new life. Now they were bound for America as we were, Sabine's husband having gone ahead. I told them about Ellinor and how we had sought permission to travel as servants. 'Now the family no longer want me so I shall have to stay on board until someone hires my services, I am told.'

'They may change their minds.' Sabine smiled, her green eyes flashing with concern.

'It is fear that makes them wary,' Henri added. 'Your leader will find work for you. I have met Brother Jacob, the firebrand preacher. He has already bent my ear about the heresy of our beliefs,' he added with a twinkle in his eye. 'But he is a sincere soul.'

'He was to marry my friend Ellinor who died but now I fear that he ...' How could I express my fears to strangers? But Henri was quick to see my hesitancy for what it was.

'You fear you will be expected to take her place, am I right?'

I blushed and looked away. 'It is too soon for such thoughts, but if it is my duty ...'

'We have a saying in our country, that he who weds only for duty or money may have pleasant enough days but endure nights of sorrow. Better to be sure and wait upon the Lord's good mercy. He will provide in due course.'

His words were kind enough but I felt disloyal to Jacob in sharing my misgivings. Yet a morning in their company and I felt refreshed and strangely hopeful.

Then Jacob himself came striding down on us. He took his leave of them politely and drew me aside to talk privately.

'They've had a meeting to discuss your position. The Emsworths have released you from their service. I think they are being too hasty but they agreed to fund thy passage, to be repaid in full when you have found another position. Once we establish our town, you will be indentured there.'

'So now am I free to visit and speak at meeting houses unhindered by household duties?'

'All in good time, there's practical work for all of us to do raising homesteads before winter comes. Everyone will be needed in our new township, Good Hope.'

'Named after this ship of doom, is that a good omen?'

He ignored my doubts. 'The ship's captain says we are doing well and it won't be long now until we see land.'

Much as I had been longing for the voyage to be over, I was too caught up in his news to be thankful. 'If I am taken by another family I will be beholden to them for years of service, as well as indebted to the Emsworths until I can repay my dues. How then will I ever be free to make my own life out here as a free woman or to minister to women's meetings as was agreed?'

'Be not so hasty. Serve in obedience with good humour and the years will go quickly enough. Happen it will tame thy restless spirit so that in time you make a dutiful wife and mother.'

'I'll be an old crone before that happens,' I snapped. 'I think I prefer to take my chance and wait to be hired from the ship.'

'That is not our way and well you know it. Wait upon the Lord in silence. He will direct thy path. Have patience, young woman.' With that he stormed off, leaving me sulking at his words. They were as welcome as water in a leaking ship.

I spent many hours in the company of these Huguenots, learning how badly they had been treated in their own country and how they had been forced out by the revocation of an Act of Tolerance. Many were bribed back into the old faith, or else banned from holding office, their children forced into baptism, their property forfeited just as had happened to us at Windebank. 'Why can't we all live in peace? We do no harm to anyone,' I complained.

Henri smiled and sighed. 'It is a tenet of our faith to endure blows and not to deal them out, but given time we're an anvil that has worn out many a hammer.'

The mood on board was lifting as rumours of land ahead spurred us forward in hope. It could not come too soon since our barrels of pickled herring and oats were long gone. We were down to meagre ship's rations tasting of foul mouldy peas and hard biscuits. There was no nourishment in those bowls of potage. All the poultry and edible animals were long slaughtered. Hunger was making us all tired and our skin erupted in boils.

Thank goodness our Yorkshire group had heeded William Penn's advice, making enough sensible provision for us all, keeping most in good health. Now it was sad to see strong men withering, women fainting with hunger. It is my opinion that they should give everyone gold coins to travel in such discomfort, not make the voyagers pay for the privilege. The price has been too high for so many of us.

'They've told us it will be a land of plenty, with rivers full of fish, grapes hanging off the vine, deer and cattle for our table,' I said, trusting this was true.

Sabine raised her hands in horror. '*Peut-être* ... Jerome, he writes me outside the city, wild animals living in forests as tall as the sky.' She was pointing upwards '*C'est terrible* ... full of savages, a wilderness to be tamed by sweat.'

Henri saw the alarm flit across my face and smiled. 'You are young and the men are strong. After what we have suffered, there is nothing to fear from hard work. There is a question Sabine and I would like to ask. Now you are no longer indentured within your group perhaps you might consider working alongside us. We will be in need of domestic help and someone to help us in our new premises in the city. We have brought much stock. I only hope it is not ruined in the hold. `

My heart leapt at this unexpected offer. If I went with them I would be free to work out my passage away from the strictures of Jacob's followers. If they didn't want me then I could cut loose the ties that bound me. Why shouldn't I do as I pleased with people I liked. I would be among fabrics, sewing and making clothes.

But suddenly there was excitement spreading through the ship like wildfire. 'Land ahead, land in view!' We are saved!'

There was a rush of bodies pushing to clamber on deck so unruly the crew men shoved us all into line. 'Hours away yet, calm down.'

Sabine and I gazed across the horizon picking out the thin shore line that would change everything. By the mercy of Goodness our ship had found safe passage. The worst was over and the smiles of relief on faces around us told us that we had but another day or two on board.

It was then the cold realisation hit me that Ellinor would not see this promised land. Her body was fathoms deep in the ocean behind us, while an unknown path lay before me with strangers. The joy and relief I first felt at the Boyers' offer melted into uncertainty.

Ellinor may not have survived but our joint mission still stood. I could not just abandon her vision by going where I pleased. Would she mind me leaving the Yorkshire Friends? In a few days we would be put ashore to fend for ourselves. I could leave knowing Henri and Sabine had a community waiting to receive them close to Philadelphia. There would be a place for me there with kind masters whose beliefs were not that different to my own. Perhaps I could slip away and no one would be any the wiser. The temptation grew but it didn't sit easy on me.

If I went with them I would be living up to everything that

was said of me in the past when I fled Scarperton: wilful, disobedient, unreliable, weak in spirit and, if I left others to pay the rest of my passage, dishonest. But oh, how I longed to say yea, not nay.

It was then I noticed Mary Emsworth approaching slowly, holding Liddy on her hip. 'Joy, a word please,' she said softly. I stepped aside from Sabine to let her have her say.

'It has troubled my soul that I sent you away for no good cause but fear. The example you set in nursing Ellinor has shamed us. Joseph and I are burdened by the thought we caused you great sorrow at a time when you were in dire need of friendship and support. Please accept our apologies and continue with us in our new venture. Sam and George will give me no peace if you're not with us. It was unthinkable for you to be left alone. It was not what was agreed in London. I fear the lack of good sustenance and weariness has addled my judgement. Are we now of one mind?' She held out her hand in friendship and I grasped it with relief. Thus was the decision taken from me and the temptation avoided.

Much as my heart would prefer to have the company of Sabine, my duty lay with my own sort wherever they settled so I smiled at Mary. 'All forgotten, Friend, we must stick together to make Good Hope a fine dwelling place.'

She took my arm and together we took a closer look at the approaching shore.

That night there was much singing and jigging between deck and above. A fiddler played merry tunes, the sailors danced a hornpipe and my feet were tapping at the beat, watching fellow travellers circling round to the music. It was a still and starry night, lanterns flickering in the darkness.

'Come and join us,' beckoned Captain Thane. I shook my

head, reluctant to refuse but knowing it was not our way. I should be down below sitting in thanksgiving, not standing brazenly watching the excited dancers. How I ached to join them but then I would have a foot in two places and it would be misconstrued. Yet my feet tapped as I was drawn to them despite my wavering resolve.

'Go and dance with the handsome young soldier. He has his eye on you.' Henri teased, seeing me watching the soldier. Sabine poked me in the back as if to shove me forward. 'To dance is good?'

Could she sense from my flushed cheeks that I was tempted to swish my skirts alongside the jolly group? Music has always stirred me.

'No,' I replied with a firmness I didn't feel. 'It must not be.' It was then I told Henri I could not go with them when we left the ship. They sighed. '*Tant pis* . . . Pity, I think you would prosper well amongst us. But we respect your duty to your friends.'

Duty, there was that word again. It lay cold as ice on my chest. What was duty without love?

23

How can I describe those first hours of discovery as we sailed up the De La Warr river towards the City of Brotherly Love! The vessel crept so slowly towards the landing station that we were able to gaze at leisure on the vast forests, the sandy shore-lines and coves while hawks soared above us. Suddenly I knew this was the wide river of my dreams at last. Men with painted faces stared back at us from their tiny boats and naked children scampered away at the sight of us waving to them.

'Savages!' cried Mary, clutching Liddy to her hip.

'I have it on good authority that they are peaceful people if treated fairly. William Penn has signed a treaty with them.'

Mary was not convinced. 'But are we not taking their land?' she asked.

'It's been bought, not stolen. They will keep to their own territories and many are eager to work alongside us, I am told.' Jacob was trying to reassure us with hearsay.

My eye was taken by a bare-chested girl covered with beads, in a skin skirt fringed at the hem, her black hair braided tightly and decorated with feathers. I waved but she darted back out of sight.

There was so much to see as we slowly edged towards the

landing stop of the new city. It was a bustle of ships and cargo hauled by men with black faces and arms. Here we would be lodged with Friends for some nights. First was the weary wait to collect baggage, barrels and what was left of our poultry stock. I kept my hand on the boys for fear of them getting lost among the crowds milling around waving letters and kerchiefs. I saw Sabine enveloped in the arms of her husband. We had promised to keep in touch somehow as we made our sad farewells. I felt I was losing a kindred spirit, regretting my decision to stay with Jacob's group but accepting I had no real choice in the matter.

We were escorted by Friends down a long street to a small dwelling where we would be housed until Joseph and the group could verify where our settlement was to be located and claim the acres of land that went with it. I would have liked to explore all the new buildings and the shops but my duty was first to the children and my employer. We were all exhausted from the travelling and in no fit state to be seen abroad.

The memory of those first days on dry land is hazy to me now. I recall that the city was most civilised to the eye with streets laid out in a pattern of orderly lines. There were elegant houses with gentle folk walking the pavements in fancy clothes edged with lace and ruffles, with silver-buckled shoes and silken hose. To my relief there were also many plainer citizens with familiar tall hats and sombre clothes.

How wonderful it was to receive fresh fish and fruit, cool beer and clean water and to change our linen at last. I would have liked to jump into the river and swim away the grime of the voyage but it was not allowed.

Soon it was time for this brief respite to end as we were summoned to a meeting to discuss the whereabouts of our new township. Once again it was stressed there must be shelter and land cleared before winter, food conserved and bought in. Each of the purchasing families would have a hundred acres to clear and fence in the fullness of time. But first they must build a house from wood and my duty was to help in any way I could to safeguard the children and the supplies. We were to start a small school. Education of both boys and girls is a necessity in our community.

As we set forth on that first trek into the wilderness our hearts were lifted by the farewells of Friends. There were carts lent for the journey but they were filled with baggage, supplies and the elderly. I walked behind with George and Sam.

As we passed a stockade I caught a brief glimpse of Captain Thane exercising his men. He stopped on seeing me and took off his cocked hat and bowed. My cheeks flamed with embarrassment as the other women noticed this singling out and tutted amongst themselves, giving me looks of disapproval. I would have to explain this at the women's meeting. What was remiss in acknowledging his kindness to me during the voyage and Ellinor's last hours? I had done nothing wrong, nor encouraged his attentions to warrant the reproach that would surely come. I bent my head low and turned towards the children, pretending he was nothing to do with me. My discourtesy to him did not sit easy.

As we trudged on Jacob stopped back to chivvy our weary legs into walking another mile along the rutted track that passed for a road.

'Where do we lodge tonight?' I asked, hoping it would not be far.

'Where the Good Lord directs us to shelter among the trees where we can find sticks to make a fire,' came his answer.

Why did I find his pious comments so irritating, when once I had hung on his every word?

Lately I caught him staring at me as if to question me further, but then he hesitated as if fighting some inner battle and retreated. Even Mary had noticed this and teased me. 'I think the Lord has charged him to love thee and make thee his helpmeet.'

I laughed away her comments, aware that as one of the few single women not spoken for, I would be subject to this sort of scrutiny until I was safely betrothed to one among the community. I will freely admit I gave none of the single servants a second glance. I was here to fulfil my mission to teach children. I had no thought of marriage with Jacob. He was a little too fond of his own opinions for my liking.

There was nothing holy about that first night under the stars, sheltering in a makeshift tent of twigs and blankets, huddled under cloaks nipped by ants, the strange forest noises calling in the dark with only a fire to guard us.

We kept the big river to the right of us as we headed upstream through a vast wilderness of shrubs and trees. Our meals were little more than bread and cheese, cool water and sips of milk from one of the surviving goats. There were three such nights before we reached a bend in the river with a marker on a tree that Jacob insisted was the beginning of our township. 'Look around at the supply of timber, fresh water, fish, deer and forest fruits. Everything is at hand for our convenience.'

I looked around with dismay at the unclaimed land that must be hacked from the forest. This is what we had crossed an ocean for, this piece of God's earth that must be forever home.

'Let's just wait on the Lord in silence,' Jacob added, seeing the weary faces of the group stunned by the tasks ahead. 'Here we can build a new Jerusalem, a fortress of holiness and fruitfulness.'

No one spoke, too overawed to offer an opinion as we bowed

our heads and tried to hide our fear. How would we build a proper town from a forest of thick oak and scrub? How could we keep our children safe?

On that first night Mary wept tears of despair. 'I thought there would be houses ready for us,' she sighed, 'or at least some decent shelter.'

'Now lass, none of that,' Joseph encouraged her flagging spirits. 'Take heed of Jacob's words. We have everything we need around us. Tonight will be but a makeshift tent but tomorrow we'll chop down enough wood for a frame. Amos the carpenter will guide us all.'

Morning broke to the sound of axes and crashing trees; stumps were gouged out of the ground and all the kindling stored to be dried in the sun. My hands were soon blistered, my body sweltered in the heat but every able body must lend their weight to make the first clearing. We reread William Penn's Treatise for guidance again: *'Four hands in four months' time may easily clear five and twenty Acres for the plow.'*

His instructions were so precise that there was no excuse not to follow them but for the heat and the weariness. Some were still weak from the voyage and splitting staves of wood for planking was beyond their strength. But I look back on those first days with a warm glow. We battled together against the terrain as one. It was only later that things turned to bitterness and we battled each other; but I digress.

Within days there was a temporary dwelling erected for the old folk and the younger women and children to rest in shade even if it felt as if we were back between decks on ship again cloistered together in harmony. Many of the men slept in foxholes. The tent served as our meeting house. As I looked around I wondered how many of us would survive the coming winter. This was no place for the feeble and old bones.

Within weeks Joseph and his friends secured a fence around his patch and cleared the earth enough for us to plant turnips and roots. We were also encouraged to plant Indian corn as we would barley and oats in the old country. We were lucky enough to arrive in the warm season but were plagued by biting insects that caused great weals on arms and legs that itched to high heaven. Gideon Smith, the apothecary, made salves of herbs and grease to soothe the worst sores.

Each family was responsible for their own acres but if help was needed they would leave their own work to guide and advise another. Jacob turned his hands to anything required. I had to admire his stamina and determination that Good Hope would be ready to face the onslaught of winter. This meant Amos and another Yorkshire craftsman, Caleb Gibbons, building a boat to take people downstream to Philadelphia to purchase hay, seed and whatever was needed to complete the building work before the river froze over, as we were warned it would.

My task was to help wash and dry all the soiled linens and clothing at the river's edge with a cake of lye soap and a good rock to thrash them against. It was good to scrub away all the stench of the voyage but the very smell reminded me of Ellinor's terrible dying hours. How her weaving skills would be missed but more than that, her absence left a great gap in my spiritual life. Who would sustain my faltering faith and purpose?

I found my mind wandering on First Day as we sat in silence, wondering if the patches on my clothing could be mended and stockings darned neatly enough not to show too much. At least the company assembled on the benches didn't reek of stale body odour but of linen and wool dried in the fresh air. I thought about Sabine and her fine lacework collar, the cut of her garment and the life she would now be living close to the city. She too would be mourning the loss of her son. Perhaps I might be allowed to take a journey to visit her one day. Then Captain Thane's handsome smile flashed into my mind and I felt my cheeks flushing at the thought of him wanting to dance with me. What was wrong with dancing and singing? There was not a spiritual thought in my head and I was glad no one could read all this muddle.

Picture if you will how Good Hope grew from that first clearing into the prosperous township it is today. The elders decided to build one main street at right angles to the river and then another broad track along the riverbank that led to some of the smaller houses built closer to the water's edge. Farms and homesteads pushed further out into the forest but down town were a cluster of little trading posts, a forge, a weaving shed and a baking oven. This took years of toil and determination that we would live independent of others except in relation to Friends in neighbouring townships. The temporary shelter became the spot on which the present meeting house stands with a field set by as a burial ground. I am describing this to explain that what happened over the years was confined to our community, though I reckon we were not alone in having troubles.

Caleb Gibbons, who had charge of the river boat, bought barrels of molasses spirit shipped in from Barbados on his trips to the city; a firewater he sold to native men, making them noisy and quarrelsome. The issue was raised at a monthly meeting, where Jacob argued that this was not the best use of Caleb's time. But he shrugged off the criticism, saying that the profit he could make could benefit the poor within our community, the widows and the old people dependent now on others to survive.

Two weeks later Caleb returned with four black-faced men whom he had purchased on the dock to help with heavy work.

He said they were Christian men and willing to work, but Jacob suggested they were slaves and we did not hold with such transactions. Because of this dispute, Caleb and his family left, taking his men with him, and he refused to return the river boat.

Without river transport we would be sorely tested as the track south through the forest took so long. So the meeting decided to approach the local natives to secure another boat. But to do this a gathering must be prepared so that the tribe closest to us would feel honoured by our request and feel suitably rewarded.

'I don't want my bairns mixing with savages,' Mary whispered. 'Better to live apart and not have dealings with them. How do we know they can be trusted?'

What could I reply about our tawny-skinned neighbours who drifted in and out of sight when we were at our chores? Surely it was better to treat them with courtesy. After all, we were the strangers here, newly encroaching on their terrain and I was curious to meet them face to face. If Jacob's assurances were true we had nothing to fear, but much to learn from them if we were to survive the harshness of the coming months.

24

One afternoon Mary sent me out with the boys to collect as many nuts and berries as we could find, acorns, beech nuts, huckleberries, raspberries, anything that could be dried or stored for the pot. By now I knew the path into the forest and as we ventured further in I always left markers to find our way out again. Sam and George loved these expeditions, stuffing themselves with far more berries that I ever brought home in my basket.

It was peaceful walking along the now flattened path, listening to the bird calls high up in the canopy. The leaves were beginning to turn from dull green to the most magnificent spectacle of flame colours so we wandered further than I might have done on my own. We came to a clearing of light and berry bushes and dived into our task with relish. It was then I had a feeling we were not alone and were being watched from the shadows and my heart thudded with fear.

We had heard terrible tales of settlers being taken captive, scalped or tortured, of children being led away never to be seen again so I shouted to Sam and George to stay in sight. I was ready to retrace our steps but there were so many luscious clumps and we had hardly done justice to them. I was their guardian first and foremost so I shouted 'Time to go!'

They were picking raspberries with scarlet lips and cheeks. Then Sam pointed to a drupe of red berries as deep as holly berries and darted to grab them for himself.

Suddenly a woman's voice yelled '*Mata. Mata!*' Out of the shadows a half-naked woman was pointing at the berries, shaking her head and rubbing her stomach. The sight of her stopped Sam in his tracks.

We were all staring at her tawny skin, her exposed breasts half hidden behind rows of brightly coloured shell beads. Around her loins she wore a skirt fringed and beaded but on her back cradled in a stiff board was a chubby baby who grinned at us.

'We must thank the lady,' I said bowing my head. She had saved Sam from sickness or worse. We stood staring at each other unsure what to do next. She was the first of the Lenni-Lenape women I had encountered close enough to read her dark eyes. 'We thank thee.' I offered her some of the berries we had collected but she held up her hand and pointed to another patch hidden from our sight at first. '*Min, Min.*'

There was a cluster of purple huckleberries that we had missed. I smiled and bowed again. I pointed to my chest. 'I am Joy' and held out my hand. I gestured to the boys. 'Sam and George.' I think she understood because she nodded and with her hand pointed to her own breasts. 'Apatooquay.' It was a mouthful to repeat but I managed 'Tookay?'. She laughed at my effort.

Together we picked in silence. The boys were stunned by her presence especially when she hung the cradle board by its straps onto a branch of a tree so the baby could inspect all that was going on before it fell asleep. What a sensible way of carrying it, I thought.

When we had finished gathering she pulled out some corn from her bag and sprinkled it around the bushes as if to make an offering for all we had collected. Then she was gone as silently as she came and we sauntered home with a basket full of berries. Sam rushed ahead of us to spill the beans of our strange meeting.

'What's this about you and some squaw?' Mary was waiting for an explanation, her eyes wide with fear.

'She saved Sam from eating some poisonous berries. She had her baby strapped to her back and her name is Tookay, I think.'

'Sam says she were naked. I can't have him seeing such things at his age.'

'Her breasts were loose to feed the baby. She wore beads and a skirt made of fine skin. Her hair was braided and looped back with a shell pin. We owe her thanks.'

'Be that as it may, in future, you keep clear of Indian camps. If I'd known there'd be danger.'

'We were the danger ourselves in not knowing what is safe to pick and what is not. It's an easy mistake for anyone to make, especially a child. Our children must be taught to recognise safe berries and mushrooms and roots. I shall bring it up at meeting, happen. I'm glad she came to our rescue.'

'The Lord looks after his own. He has not sent us this far to poison ourselves. The less we have to do with them savages, the better.'

I knew Mary had had a scare but it irked me that her mind was so shuttered from the light of new knowledge.

I spoke to Jacob after First Day Meeting the following week and told him about the dangers of gathering berries in ignorance. I suggested we be given instruction on native plants and their uses. I told him of Tookay's kindness and how we couldn't share our thoughts.

'It's all in hand,' he smiled 'We have invited the local chief and his elders to come and sit with us in peace. There's a Swedish settler who can converse with them and he will interpret for us. We want to know how they make those dug-out boats on the river. We have gifts to offer in return.'

The gathering took place in the clearing down by the river's edge. Our township lined up as if it were First Day in bonnets and tall hats to greet the guests who were rowing towards us in a line of boats.

A tall man emerged from the first boat dressed in skins, no longer bare-chested as the weather was chilly and the wind whipped our skirts. He wore a cloak decorated with quills and feathers and his clothes were decorated with beads of all the colours of the rainbow. Behind him came other men and boys with shaven heads and feathers in a band. The women followed behind. To my relief the women also wore shirts and cloaks and I soon spotted Tookay who caught my eye and nodded.

Sven Aldersen stepped forward to greet the chief and take him to meet the elders waiting in their tall hats. There was an exchange of gifts and a lot of nodding while Sven explained what the citizens of Good Hope wanted from the tribe.

I wanted Mary to meet Tookay to see how wrong she was about her but Mary hung back with the other women, fussing around the food bench and not catching my eye.

What a contrast we must make in our drab-coloured clothes against their decorated fancy work. All the colours of the forest were in their dyes and patterns, the sea in the shells around their necks and the sky in the eagle feathers and plumes. They were wearing their finery in honour of the occasion. What must they think of our sombre apparel?

I was curious to know more of their customs and way of

living. They had lived on this land for a thousand years or more. Now we were making demands, needing to know how to survive in this territory. Our houses were half-built, the land hardly cleared enough to sustain us. We had transplanted ourselves halfway across the world and our own roots were fragile and barely planted. How would we prosper? Not for the first time did I wonder just what purpose our coming had served; but then I recalled my schoolteacher's death at the hands of our persecutors and the trials of my own parents. Here we would be free to live in our own way.

Yet I sensed we would not always live by the river's edge. As families grew and settled and demanded more acres to farm and build, we would push these peoples further into the forest and wilderness. How would they respond to this invasion?

When the formalities were ended, platters of pies and meat were handed round. I noticed the Lenape ate little of our offerings. I made my way with a huckleberry pie to Tookay. '*Min, Min*' I said and she replied through Sven when I offered my thanks for her kind action in the forest.'

'They were only moon berries. The boy would have gripes in his belly. Perhaps Miss Joy would like to bring her boys to see their village one day.' I nodded but explained that they were not my sons. 'I would love to visit your family. I would be honoured.'

'She says come soon before the snows cut off the trails.' Sven added.

'I'll try,' I replied, knowing I would need permission to make this journey from the elders and ask leave from the farm. I would not be allowed to go alone.

Jacob called a week later to inform the Emsworths that there was to be a return friendship visit to the Lenape camp and would they give me leave to accompany them with gifts from the women's meeting. There was talk of starting up a school for the Indian children so they might mix more with the settlers and learn English. The purchase of a dug-out boat was almost complete in order to carry trading goods back and forth to the city.

I offered some of my woollen cloth to encourage the native women to cover themselves in our presence. The basket of gifts we garnered was mostly cast off linen caps and baby rings and rattles, nothing of any value but it was a gesture of friendship.

The party set off one bright autumn morning along the river path admiring the spectacle of gold and flame-coloured leaves. We trudged up the trail for a few miles until we saw smoke rising and smelt fish grilling on a fire and realised we were close.

Along the path were rows of gardens filled with vegetables and roots. Women bent over their hoes standing up to stare at our white faces and strange clothes. There were round huts dotted at intervals around the edge of the settlement with smoke coming out of the roof. We were now gathering a crowd of curious onlookers as we entered a clearing of open land with larger squarer huts built on three sides. In the middle was one hall-like building covered in bark and thatch. This was their meeting place and we were ushered forward into the hall.

It was smoky and dark but there was a pleasant scent of tobacco spice in the air. The fire burned in the middle but along three sides was a raised platform on which a row of elderly men with pipes and much feathered finery sat cross-legged. I recognised the chief who had visited us. A brave stepped forward, handsome, straight-backed and light skinned, who had a good understanding of English. I found out he was Tookay's brother and he introduced us to each man in turn.

Then he pointed me to the door where a young girl beckoned me towards an oblong hut where Tookay was waiting at the door with a shy smile, holding her baby on her hip. 'My sister,' he added as we greeted one another. It was not going to be easy to share our thoughts in words neither of us could understand.

Her house had the same raised platform on which were scattered thick skin rugs and walls lined with tightly woven grass mats. All her utensils were stored under the platform in a neat array of bowls and pots. Everything was strange to my eyes and the scent of pine needles and cedar shavings cleansed the air far better than in our cabin in the town.

I offered the basket of gifts and tried to mime what each was for. She fingered the cloth with interest examining how it was woven with approval. I showed her it would make a skirt or shirt but she shook her head. '*Mata.*' She pointed to the bed of rugs.

'Ah, a blanket?' I asked

She nodded and smiled. '*Wanishi.*' That was a thank-you word I did know. It was a start, but a slow one and tiring trying to concentrate without an interpreter, being watched by a series of her friends who came to view the strange white woman in her cloak.

Then to my relief, her brother spoke English and came to help me out. Tookay had so many questions. 'Did I have a man and if not, why not . . . as I was old?'

I tried to explain how Seekers did not marry so young but waited for permission to marry one of their Lord's choosing. She roared with laughter and told the blushing young interpreter: 'We choose who we have by our side and if he is lazy or does not hunt well and provide then we put his belongings out of the hut and he must leave.'

I asked about her baby's name.

'Baby has no name yet for he is still in the hands of the Creator and may be taken from me as He wishes. We wait until he is four or five and know he is destined for this life before we give him his true name in a ceremony. It is a name chosen by those who know him. My name means White Deer. The deer is my special animal that guides me and I can run as fast as the wind.'

How could I explain we had no namegiving ceremony and perhaps it was a discourtesy to the Giver of Life not to do so. I hated Rejoice, it being such a challenging name, hard to live up to every day. It spoke of being ever joyful and the giving of thanks. A plain Bible name would have suited me well.

'*Alakwi,*' she sighed, getting the gist of some of this. We lived in two different worlds but there was something even then that bound us together in friendship. I decided to learn as many Lenape words as I could so we could talk a little more.

We returned to the square where there was a feast of vegetables and fish in a stewpot and a corn dish laced with tree syrup that was like honey to the tongue. When it was time to leave I wanted to invite White Deer to my cabin but knew it wasn't mine to offer. I was an indentured servant for four years and Mary did not want any mixing between us. All this I confided to Jacob on our trek back to Good Hope.

'It is better to leave them to their own ways, Joy. They have strange beliefs in so far as men are subjected to the women of their clan. On marriage he takes her tribe as his own and the older women select the chief from among their own. The word of the womenfolk is law, I gather. This is not what our Bible teaches us.'

'More's the pity,' I quipped but he didn't see the humour. 'Are we not all equal in the sight of the Lord? We believe we are guided by the inner light but they call it the Creator Spirit in all things.'

'That's not the same and can be misunderstood. We must teach them to read and write in our language. Then our trading and meetings will be more profitable. I fear most of the time we do not understand each other at all, especially on the subject of owning land.'

'How's that?' I asked.

'They think that land belongs to no one but the Creator who gave it to us. It makes negotiations difficult.'

'But we bought land. There are deeds to prove it,' I added, puzzled.

'They signed away the deeds but not the right to roam over our territory to hunt and fish and that's not going to go down well once farmers are established. No one wants Lenape chasing deer over their crops. I see a whole heap of trouble ahead. All the fences and barriers we put up will be misunderstood unless we can sit down and thrash things out.'

We walked in silence after this debate. I knew the Emsworths had the right to a hundred acres of cleared land with a chance to buy more later. Mary would be afeared by men tramping over her fields in search of game or harvesting on their own patches. Sharing this new land was going to be more complicated than any of us thought and I hoped it would not lead to trouble as Jacob feared.

25

Nothing prepared me for that first winter. It was like the worst Yorkshire winter on the moors and then a whole heap more; such a cruel time for man and beast when the branches of the trees snapped with the weight of the snow and icicles hung like daggers from the roof of the cabin. The driving blizzard blew through the cracks in the clapboard walls even though we had plastered them over with mud and straw. Our supply of dry wood dwindled, for the fire grate was our only warmth. How I wished we had a supply of White Deer's bearskin rugs. Our quilts did not give enough warmth as I shivered close to the children of a night to give them some of my body heat. We were cut off from our neighbours by feet of snow and drifts that towered up like steeples.

Mary was near her time and lumbered about knowing that I alone might be there to help her in the birthing. At least I knew what would happen, but we prayed that Joseph would reach Rebecca Hindley, our neighbour, when the pains began, leaving me free to see to the children; but alas it was not to be.

Mary woke as her waters broke and began her labour as Joseph tried to dig his way out across the yard to summon help.

Soon he was exhausted with tunnelling through the drifts and returned. We all had to endure her suffering as she struggled to bring new life into the world. It seemed like hour upon hour before she was delivered but sadly to no avail for the baby was born asleep, cold and lifeless. It took not one breath however hard I slapped it. I thought then of White Deer's words on that first visit about how the Creator often took the weaker children to himself. Joseph wept at the loss of another son. 'He is with the Lord' was all he could tell the children. I held the tiny mite in my arms so Mary could see how beautiful he looked but she howled and howled until her throat was dry and I spooned berry cordial into her lips to revive her. Joseph removed his son out of the cabin, I know not where but out of danger from wolves and coyotes.

Mary needed to rest but Liddy mithered for attention, sensing the bitter disappointment and grief. 'Let Mother sleep,' I chided her knowing it was up to me to keep the children occupied. 'Fetch my wooden kist,' I offered, sitting them round in a circle. We began to take things out of my little wooden chest. Each object was a memory of my past life.

'Here are the certificates of permission to come to America. Look at all those signatures', for everyone present in the Leeds meeting had signed. I could see each name in my mind's eye: Zeph, Jacob, Ellinor. 'Now here is a piece of hanky edged with lace given to me one Christmas by my grandfather, the Judge.' This was not strictly true, of course. It was just a leftover purchase I had made in Scarperton market. All my treasures were scented with sprigs of rosemary, which took me back to my parents and their burial ground at Windebank farm. Then Liddy picked up the bright ribbons I had worn.

'Me, me!' She grabbed them. 'Pretty, pretty me,' she laughed.

'You can play with them and put them on your dolly.' The

bright red sateen caught the firelight and Liddy had other ideas. 'Put them here,' she demanded, pointing to her hair.

'I don't think we should, not just now,' I cautioned.

'Yes, me, me want them now.' She tried to tie them into her hair and darted off to show her mother who was lying listless on the mattress, her breasts bound tight to stop the milk oozing from them.

The sight of the little girl posing in her finery was too much for Mary. 'Take them off at once,' she said.

'No!' Liddy stamped her foot in protest.

'Take them off this minute or else ...'

'No, no,' Liddy ran back to me clinging to my skirt. 'Joy gave them to me. Mine!'

'No, child, I did not give them. We were just playing in my box in order to be quiet and let Mother rest.'

Mary was not accepting of my explanation. 'Now look what you've done. How it burdens me to see you clinging on to such worldly stuff.'

It was then that George pulled out the linen bag in which I kept my golden gloves and waved them in the air. 'Look at these!'

Mary stared at them in disbelief. She rose from her bed and snatched them from him. 'What's the meaning of these? I never expected to see such fripperies in a servant's box. Are they stolen goods?'

Why did everyone think I would steal? 'They are not,' I protested, knowing I must retell my sad history and convince her of their personal value. 'They belonged to my grandmother and were passed down to my mother as a token of reconciliation. She was a glovemaker, not of fancy pairs but plain ones made of leather and wool. She died unaware of them and they were given as a parting gift to me. How can I part from them?'

Mary fingered the gold lace and the pearls stitched into the gauntlet cuff. She rubbed her fingers over the beautiful doeskin. 'I gather then you would see us all starve and not sell them?'

'It is but a token of remembrance, that's all.' I replied but Mary shook them like a goose feather duster and for one moment I thought she might cast them into the fire.

'Poof! No true Friend would desire to keep these, mother or not. They reek of wealth and rank. You must let them go.' She paused, looking me up and down. 'Why am I not surprised at this disobedience? Put them away and when the snows melt we will take them to Philadelphia to be sold. Are our elders aware of thy vanity?'

'They're mine to keep. I have received no charge to part with them yet. When that time comes I will know.'

'Do as I say and put them out of sight and the ribbons too.' Liddy was kicking and screaming in protest. 'Look what these things have wrought. Is it not bad enough to have lost my bairn and now for you to stir up the household even more. Out of my sight, all of you!'

I knew Mary was distraught with grief and I was in tears of frustration. There was no place to get away from each other in the cabin. We were cooped up like chickens in a pen. I was only trying to help but had now made matters worse.

Then Joseph returned with a chicken under his arm. 'I found it frozen. We'll pluck it for the pot and have a feast.' He was met with silence. Then he produced three small icicles for the children to suck on. 'Look what I found.' Still no one spoke, for the air inside our little cabin was far frostier than the world outside.

I lost count of the weeks we were confined within these four walls. Every ounce of fleece was carded with brushes by the boys and spun into yarn by me. Mary mended and patched every garment and we had to burn good timber for firewood. The chickens died, the goat's milk dried and the starving cows bellowed for hay in the barn. Night time was worse for we had no rush lights or candles left and sat by the flicker of firelight. You can get mighty sick of the same company day in and out.

How I yearned for city streets, stone houses with thick walls, shops and social visits. In daylight I taught Sam and George their letters and script on the slate. We read the Bible and told the famous stories of David and Goliath.

I tried to do what White Deer would be doing in her hut. How had they survived the ice storm? I knew the men would go fishing on the frozen river. On my last visit she had said it would soon be the season of the 'clacking stones' and I had asked the interpreter to explain. It was the time for sharpening tools by the fire as the old men told stories of the great spirits and hunts. When I tried to share all this with the Emsworths, Mary held up her hand. 'We don't want to hear about the ungodly.'

'But they believe in the God of all things,' I assured her. I had seen how carefully they gave thanks for everything they took from the earth and the forest, making offerings back into the soil.

'You see too much of that young woman.'

'But they know so much about how to survive and grow. If you could see how they use animal skins for clothing, shoes, blankets. They will not be as cold as we are. I helped her tan some fur.'

'We have a good tanner here,' Joseph added in support of his wife.

'I know but he is used to cow hides and sheep. There's so many other skins to use. Our fur clothing could be so much warmer.'

'And live like savages? We are here to civilise them. If you want fur, there's a heap of rotting raccoon skins out back. The tanner won't touch them dirty things.'

How could anyone guess that this passing rebuke was to change my life in so many ways? Had I not watched the Lenape at work, tanning skins from the piss pot, stretching them out on frames to dry, scraping the insides, working the leather and softening it before stitching furs together to make slippers, leggings and gloves?

'Let me have a go then. The boys can help me prepare them. I shall make us all warm mittens.'

'No one will want to wear such dirty things.' Mary sniffed. Nothing I did lately was welcome or praised. Her spirit was laid low with sadness.

'Wait and see. I think I know how to make them soft and clean but I will need to use the chamber pot.'

'Aagh! I'll believe this when I see it,' was all the encouragement I got for my new venture. Perhaps I would never make gloves as fine as my mother's or those in my box but they wouldn't last five minutes in this harsh terrain. No, I smiled, I would start with the lowly raccoon and see if I could remember all the processes. Better to be busy than staring at four walls until spring came. I was pleased with the result of my efforts. Surely, someone would be happy to purchase them when this winter was over? But the Lord tempers the wind to the shorn lamb. Little did we know that with the first melt of snow there would be far more of a challenge ahead.

We were like bullocks let out onto fresh grass when the first greening of spring appeared; thinner, weary of each other but grateful to have survived the winter storms. The first meeting when almost all the township gathered was a noisy affair of much greeting and few silences. The sap was rising within us and it was so good to catch up with others and meet the strangers who had taken shelter amongst our neighbours. Jacob had taken in a man and woman from the frozen river boat on their journey towards the Jerseys. They came to First Day Meeting to share their gratitude for the refuge given.

'Come and meet Thomas and his sister here,' Jacob called over the room to me. He was eager to show off his guests. 'They have a great story to tell of God's merciful rescue.'

I was too busy with Liddy and the other children to take much notice of the strangers in their dark cloaks and tall hats, their faces half hidden by wide brims.

It was only in the quiet of the meeting that I had a chance to examine them from across the room. I saw nothing remarkable about them until the man stood up to give thanks for the kindness of his host. It was his voice that jolted me out of my daydreaming, a deep resonant tone with an accent common to us all. Where had I heard that voice before? I stared at them now with interest, aware that he reminded me of Titus Cranke, who with his wife Dora was my adversary in Leeds all those years ago.

How could this white-haired man with the snowy beard and stooped shoulders draped in a jacket that hung from his bony frame be the trickster I once knew? Surely it was not possible that he should be in America? Yet the resemblance was marked. Curious, I turned to the woman beside him. She bore no likeness to that blowsy gypsy rover with whom I once shared a van. These two were shadows of that flamboyant couple. I was mistaken. But when the service was ended I was eager to take a closer look. When I found time from my duties to greet them, they had vanished from sight.

'Who are those two strangers?' I asked Jacob.

'Brother Thomas Black and his sister, Tamar, sent out from the meeting in Hull but caught in the winter storm. They had a terrible journey across and many perished when their rowing boat left the ship and capsized in the Bay. They clung to the wreckage and were saved. Why do you ask?'

'I thought I recognised them as a couple I once knew in Leeds who did me a great wrong, but they were man and wife. When he got up to speak, his voice took me back to those days. How long are they staying with us?'

'I am persuading them to stay put and make a home in the district. He is an apothecary and now that Gideon Smith has departed this life he might be useful to us.'

'Then I look forward to making their acquaintance at next meeting. How good it is to see so many faces after such a long confinement,' I added. 'But I've not been idle and made good use of the skills I learned with the Lenape women. Next winter there will be lots of fur mittens to share around so no one's fingers go black in the frost.' I was proud of the pile of mittens I had scraped out of the raccoon skins.

'We shall have to make better provisions now we know what must be endured. Penn's Treatise did not warn us how bad it would be.' Jacob sighed. He looked weary and drawn. He gave me one of those soulful looks intended to soften my heart towards him but I felt nothing of that nature.

'Did those two bring their certificates to travel with them?

He looked at me in surprise. 'When you're swimming for thy life, there's no time to bother with belongings. They have relied on the kindness of Friends from Maryland to Delaware but it has taken a toll on their health. The sister hardly utters a word, such is the shock on her, and he never leaves her side. They are such a devoted couple and good company for me in the long nights we shared together. Thomas has travelled all over England and has many stories to tell. How he was once a blackguard having fallen far from Grace but found salvation at a meeting where George Fox preached. I do believe the Lord has sent them to us for a purpose.'

I thought no more of the strangers for life on the homestead was a round of sowing seed, clearing land, baking, sewing and minding the children. Now the river was flowing again there was the promise of a boat down to Philadelphia soon to look forward to. I could not wait to see real civilisation once more and besides, I had a letter to post.

26

The letter to Roger Windebank was long overdue but I had taken pains to find parchment and now it lay sealed and ready to be posted in the Blue Anchor Tavern where some kind soul heading back to England would see that it got passed among Friends until it reached the farm. We landed at the docking station for Philadelphia, excited to be among the throng of sailors and merchantmen who crowded the little port. Joseph would not allow me to walk unescorted into the tavern with my letter, the street being full of women who plied a different trade among the fishermen, but in my sombre cloak and tall hat there was no mistaking I was not of their kind.

It had taken me hours of thought to compose a suitable letter which might be read out many times before it reached its destination: I filled it with news and praise for the Friends of Good Hope.

Seven days ago we raised a new barn with the help of Friends.
It has three bays and I thought it would be better built of
stone as the one of yours that I see in my mind's eye but stone
building is for the future. Everything here is hewn from the
forest wood and will ensure safe fodder and shelter animals. Our

meeting house is modest and built for shelter as well as worship. Good Hope grows in size apace and with new houses raised in days with the help of neighbours.

It was a long hard winter but I have not been idle, making use of skills I learned from native women in the camp close by. Please remember me to our dear Friends, to Margery, Mall and Dilly and your good self . . .

Yours in Christ

I gave them all the news that would interest them and warned about the hardship of our crossing, the death of dear Ellinor and the sicknesses which plagued us. How could I write of another sickness that filled my mind with longing for those hills of home, the lambs in the pasture and those familiar faces I had once been so eager to leave. Now as a bondswoman I did not have the freedoms I once enjoyed so carelessly but today would be different. Here among the thronging streets I was just myself, free to explore the city's new buildings and the tree-lined blocks of houses away from the smell of the brickmakers, the tan pits and the iron-smelting furnaces.

Mary made straight for the open market hall where the bell overhead clanged to say there was fresh produce to sell and buy. There were barrels of fresh and salted fish, racks of strange vegetables, slabs of meat in the shambles, millers selling bags of flour and grain and crowds jostling for provisions. I strapped Liddy to my hand in fear she might get snatched as Mary went rushing off to find linen cloth. We all dawdled along, gazing into the narrow alley of shops with their pretty window panes through which I could see fancy goods, hats, gloves, periwigs and mantles: so much to see and admire but safe in the knowledge I had but a few coins to spend.

Suddenly I felt such loneliness among the throng. I had been so looking forward to this change of scene, recalling how I had once strode the streets of Leeds in youthful ignorance. I don't know what made me look up at the sign overhead but the name BOYER took my eye. Could it be the very family that I met on the ship?

'Friend Mary, a moment please. I have to see if this is where Sabine is living.'

Mary retraced her steps hearing my plea as I released Liddy into her charge. 'If you must, Joy, but don't be long. I have a day's worth of business to do in hours without loitering around these worldly shop fronts.'

I opened the door of the little shop where the shelves were full of beautiful fabrics, silks, brocades in a rainbow of colours. A young man stepped forward.

'Jerome Boyer?' I asked and he smiled and nodded. 'How can I help you?'

'I met your wife, Sabine, on the *Good Hope*. Is she well?'

'Ask her yourself . . . Sabine!' Out of the workshop to the rear of the shop came my friend and we fell into each other's arms.

'Joy, *ma petite amie*. It has been a long time. How are you?'

'I can't stay long, my mistress waits. I just wanted to know it was you.' There was so much to say and so little time. Here was a known face who had shared some terrible moments with me on the ship. I no longer felt so alone, seeing her face.

'Come again, come and stay. I was hoping you might come to the city and we know someone who will be pleased to hear you are safe.' She laughed. 'The handsome Capitaine Thane has asked after you when he came in for some shirting. I will tell him you called.'

Just his very name made me flush. 'Oh, really? I must go.'

'*Tant pis*, Joy. Come again, promise?'

I smiled. 'I will try but my time is not my own.'

'Then we can choose some material and make you a pretty dress so you can walk out with *le capitaine*.'

'No, Sabine, thank you. It's not our way.' We kissed on the cheek as is their fashion and I fled, flustered at the suggestion I might meet the Captain again.

Mary was hovering in her grey cloak with a face like thunder. 'I don't know why you want to make acquaintance with that French woman. Now I'm late so take the boys for a walk while I carry on. Be back at the landing dock when the hour bell strikes.'

George and Sam were happy enough to chase each other as I strolled behind them wool-gathering, still smiling from meeting Sabine. She looked so much prettier now she was away from the dreadful memories of our journey. Her neat blue gown with its wide collar edged in lace was just what I would like, but of course without the lace. I had noticed that Friends in the city dressed a little more freely than we were permitted to do. I was dreaming of the day when there would be proper cart roads that would allow us to reach the city without having to use the river ferries. I would take tea with Sabine and perhaps purchase some materials. The bale of woollen cloth Margery had given me had made my simple skirt and jacket but gave no pleasure.

I did not notice how far out of the centre we had walked. Here the red brick and timber buildings were half built with wooden scaffolds to reach to the roof tops and the boys were darting around the site playing tag.

'Be careful and no climbing,' I yelled but the boys were too intent on their play to listen to me. They were like puppies let loose, egging each other on to further disobedience and I sensed trouble ahead if I did not discipline them.

There were no builders in view to curb their antics and when they began to mount the scaffolding I grew afraid and screamed at them to come down. George made a rude gesture for which he would be beaten later if I had anything to do with it. He began to swing upside down from a ledge little more than a plank, his legs jerking as he was showing off to his brother. Then the flimsy plank buckled at the force of his jerks and suddenly gave way, sending him head first onto the ground.

Sam watched in horror as his brother lay in a stupor and I was running to help him, dreading he was already dead. 'Stupid lad! How dare you disobey me? Now look what you've done.' His face was ashen and he didn't move but I saw his chest rising. I had to find help and fast but the place was deserted. I flung my cloak over him and made Sam sit by his side calling him back to us. I have never felt such terror, knowing I needed help to carry him. How I prayed to our Lord for guidance and he answered my pleas with the sound of a pipe and drumbeat in the distance.

'Help!' I cried as I ran towards the sound of the music, praying that I was in the right direction. Turning a corner there was a troop of soldiers marching to a drumbeat, drilling in the sunshine, so without a second's thought I dashed in front of their path, waving my arms. 'Help, please stop. There's a child who needs thee!'

They almost collapsed into me and an officer came bounding up to see me sobbing on the ground. 'The boy is sorely wounded,' I said. 'Please come.'

He helped me up and with relief I saw those blue eyes and tawny hair. 'Captain Thane, it is you?'

I could hardly speak for the terror I felt, still shaking as I pointed in the direction of the building. 'Hurry, it's little George. He fell and can't move. I fear the worst.'

The Captain ordered his men to continue the march but

brought two other soldiers along with him. Sam was sitting by his brother, his eyes wide with fear. 'He won't wake up, Joy.'

Thane knelt down to examine him. 'He's breathing and there's one hell of a crack on his head. He's in the deep sleep that comes with such wounds, I fear. We need to find a doctor.'

Just at that moment George opened his eyes. 'Where am I?' He tried to sit up but fainted again.

'We have to get him back to the river boat and I'm late already. We are only here for the day. It is all my fault.'

'Let me carry the boy and you go ahead to warn the others of his coming. What in God's name were they doing up there?' He was giving me such a stern look. I wanted to weep but refused to show him my weakness. 'They raced ahead. I called them back but they refused to obey.'

'Lads will be lads, Miss Moorside.'

'Aye, more's the pity and now look at the state of him.' I was full of the anger that comes with relief and embarrassment. 'What will I say to his mother?' I stormed ahead, dragging poor Sam by the hand while Thane carried George tenderly in his arms.

We made a sorry party returning through the streets. Crowds parted to make way for the injured child with an escort of red-coats. When we reached the landing I saw the look of horror on Mary's face. 'You'd better explain yourself,' she snapped but it was Sam who came to my rescue.

'We ran off. Joy tried to stop him climbing up. He was naughty and the soldiers came to help us.'

'Did they indeed?'

'No, Ma'am. Miss Moorside did everything to save him. It is her prompt action that has gotten him here.'

Joseph stepped forward holding out his hand. 'We have our Good Samaritan here to thank as well. I recognise thee, soldier from the ship. Our boy looks no worse for his lesson.'

I wasn't so sure, for George was very groggy and his eyes fluttered. 'Perhaps we should stay and let a doctor see him?' I ventured.

'Later. When we return, Friend Thomas will check him over.'

There was no time to thank Thane as I would have wished. Once more he had come to my rescue. 'We thank thee, Captain' was all that was said, for the passengers were anxious to be out onto the river. As the boat rowed out into the busy harbour I stood to wave a farewell to him as he watched us depart.

'Don't be forward, Joy,' Mary whispered.

'Why not, he helped rescue thy son. He deserves our sincere thanks.'

'If you had kept a weather eye on my boys this never would have happened,' she chided me.

'It was not my intent,' I replied, suddenly so weary, trying to stay calm whilst choking with rage. How I wished I could linger in the city, among the bustle of the streets with Captain Thane by my side. If only I had chosen to go with the Boyers when I had the chance, instead of returning upriver to an uncertain future.

27

The journey back was fraught with concern for the sick boy as he fainted back into another sleep and a swelling rose up on his forehead. We sat in silent prayer for his wellbeing. No one looked in my direction but I felt their blame. Now we must rely on the medications of the new apothecary, Thomas Black, whom I had yet to examine more closely. Was my strange sense of recognition correct?

It was pitch black on our return as we made our way to Jacob's lodging with George but I was bid to take Liddy and Sam back to our own cabin and was no party to their meeting. I swallowed back tears at this rejection, knowing I must have failed the lad in some way. All the pleasure of our day's outing, the discovery of Sabine and her shop, exploring the city and that sudden meeting with the Captain, had long faded.

'Is our Georgie going to die?' Sam asked as I tucked him into the bed, seeing the dent in the pillow where George's head usually lay.

'Of course not,' I snapped. 'We won't let him, will we?' I paced the cabin floor praying for some cure that would restore the boy back to us whole. If all we were depending on was Titus Cranke in disguise, convert or not, I knew his potions were not worthy of the name. Suddenly White Deer came into my mind from nowhere.

The wise men of her village had many medicines from the forest that healed their sick. Perhaps they had something we could use. I had not seen her since before winter set in; yet I felt sure they might know how to cure the boy.

Mary would never let a native into the house but I could get a recipe or some knowledge to share from them.

Mary and Joseph returned late in the night with George's head bound to reduce the swelling. He still did not stir from his deep sleep. His father's face was white with worry.

'Did Friend Thomas have a cure-all?' I whispered.

'He says it is too early for potions. We must wait until he wakes. He must rest and sleep on and let the swelling down.'

I could have told them that. At least this would give me time to seek answers from the Lenape tribe. It was only this hope that allowed me to sleep a little and then take my watch over him while the others wept and prayed.

At dawn's first light I rose to walk the well-trodden path to the Lenape village, carrying a little bundle of gifts for my friend. I did not stop to ask permission from my master. They must punish me later.

Walking alone into the forest held no fear for me for I knew our neighbours were peace-loving people and bore us no ill will as yet. But I was not sure if I would be welcomed, having stayed away so long. I prayed someone with English on their tongue would be around to help me get the advice I felt sure would help us.

Who should be the first person I saw working in the field but White Deer. She looked up and smiled shyly. We greeted each other with nods of the head and gestures of friendship. The baby carried on the cradle board had grown round with chubby cheeks and a cheeky smile as he stared at my white face. We walked back to her hut. 'Come,' she said.

'English?' I grinned in surprise.

'Yes,' she said proudly. 'My brother, Little Bear has more words.' He sat out in the square and came to join us. I presented my gifts as is the custom and praised his new leather britches. Then I began to mime and tell about George's wound. 'He will not wake up.'

'Ask the medicine man. He will know but first we must ask if he will see you.'

White Deer boiled water on the fire and gave me a strange herb tea that I found refreshing and some bread made from ground corn. Then I was summoned to a hut at the far end of the village where an old man with a face like cracked leather sat smoking his pipe, surrounded by baskets of dried herbs. The hut reeked of tobacco and I bowed and presented a gift of tobacco that White Deer said I must offer before I asked a favour. Little Bear explained my visit and waited to be my interpreter.

'How long since the boy fell?' The old man pointed at me.

'Yesterday,' I replied.

'Do his eyes roll? Has he been sick?'

I nodded.

'Has he swelling and where?'

I pointed to the place on my own face.

'Then you must set the swelling free or it will be bad for him.'

But how? I looked to Little Bear. I didn't understand. They talked at length before he gave me his answer.

'When a warrior is wounded by a fall, we scrape off the hair and scalp to make a hole in the bone so all the badness can be released. Leave the swelling too long and the head cannot contain its contents. He will die.'

'Scalp him, are you saying?' I knew this was what angry warriors did to their victims.

'No,' he said pointing to his own shaven scalp. 'Medicine man says it must be done with a special tool to bore into the skull and remove an opening. A medicine man will know how to do this.'

'Can he do this?'

Little Bear shook his head. 'No, not for your boy, seek one of your own medicine men, but he will give you special herbs to soothe any pain.'

The old man dipped his hand into a basket and pulled out a little bag. 'Use only a little for it has big power and make many prayers to his Guardian spirit.'

'*Wanishi, thank you.*' I bowed and held my hands together in greeting, knowing it would be difficult to explain all this to George's parents.

I ran back to Good Hope along the river path hoping I hadn't been missed, but of course I had and got another telling off from Mary.

This was not the time to alarm her with my news so I got on with my daily chores, determined to take this remedy further. Who better than the new apothecary to share this cure? It would give me an excuse to meet him at close quarters. Thank goodness I had many messages to take in the town and sped down the track for there was no time to lose if Georgie was to be saved.

I came upon Thomas's sister, Tamar, by the well and realised at once that this was not Dora Cranke but a tall thin woman who jumped when I spoke. 'Friend Tamar, we have not met before. I am Joy from Emsworth's Farm. Is Friend Thomas at his work?'

She nodded, pointing to the cabin, not uttering a word of

greeting, contrary to our custom. Her dark eyes were glassy and dull. It was as if she moved in a dream but it was a relief not to be faced with my old enemy, Dora. I slipped silently through the door, half expecting Jacob to be inside, but relieved to discover that he would not be party to my strange mission.

The man in the black doublet and britches was about his business clearing shelves and pots, whistling, and then as he looked up I saw a flicker of recognition on his face.

'So, Titus,' I smiled. 'It is you then.' There was no doubt in my mind.

'Thee's mistaken, young lady. I am Thomas Black. How can I help, a love potion perhaps?' Titus Cranke was older, thinner and up to the same tricks. I was not going to be fooled by his banter.

'But you know me from way back in Leeds. Where is Dora, thy wife?'

'Nay lass, thee's mistaken. I know you not, never clapped eyes on you afore. Now scarper ...' That was not how true Friends greeted each other. I stood firm.

'I've come about Georgie Emsworth. I am their bondswoman, Joy Moorside, as you well know, but no matter. I think the boy needs greater physic than we first thought.'

'Aye, so you're the careless wench that was the cause of the injury, I hear.' There was steel in his eyes. He knew me and I knew him but it would be my word against his and at the moment all that mattered was getting my charge well again. Was he playing a cat and mouse game with me? 'And a doctor as well as a maid?' he sneered.

'I saw a medicine man from the Lenape village this morning, a wise old man who suggests that George may need a surgeon's knife to release the swelling by removing a bit of skull bone.'

'Ah, trepanning,' he nodded. 'Yes, that can be done to release venom from a brain but it is a dangerous operation. You are not suggesting we let a savage loose on a Christian boy's head to scalp him?' he roared. 'You have the strangest notions, girl. Are you expecting me to risk my reputation in such actions? Off you go. Tamar will see you out.' In his anger he had reverted to the 'you' rather than 'thee', I noted.

The woman stood in silent witness to all our conversation but said nothing. I turned to her for help. 'I am trying to help a sick child. There has to be someone who can perform this in safety.'

'Aye, in Philadelphia for a bonny penny, I don't think your master can pay their fee,' he sneered. She said nothing.

That was true enough but that did not stop us holding one of our regular collections within the meeting house to help those in need. If we all pooled together there would be enough to pay for his treatment and I must make my own contribution.

I set off back up the track in turmoil. Was it really Titus before me or was I mistaken? Had I not shared a journey with him for many weeks? All I could think of was if the boy had woken yet. How could we let him sleep unto death for the want of a few pieces of silver?

Mary was waiting for me at the door, her face aged with worry. 'Where've you been? Why when I call, are you never around? Joseph has gone to a special meeting. Liddy's been fretting all day.'

We sat at our knitting until Joseph returned in a better spirit. 'Friend Jacob did us a mighty favour when he lodged the healer Black. They have come up with a wondrous idea to save our son. Thomas suggests we take him to a surgeon in Philadelphia to open his skull to release the swelling. This is an ancient cure for such injuries, we are told on good authority. There will be a collection to pay for this service. All the elders agreed after hearing his fine words. Praise the Lord for such a welcome addition to our township.'

I sighed. Trust Titus to take my idea and claim it as his own. Only that crook knew how to charm his way into everyone's favour. In fairness, if the idea had come from me it would not have been so well received. Better for George if it came from him but it rankled just the same.

Mary swooned at the thought of such treatment. 'Mercy on my poor boy, how can we let them do this to him?'

'It's our only chance to bring him back to us whole,' I answered. She turned on me with scorn.

'What does you know about owt? He's not your bairn.'

'Now then, Mary, the girl means well. Be thankful that Friend Thomas can organise the travel and take his sister.'

'Then let me go with them,' I pleaded. 'Georgie must not awake with strangers or he will be frightened. Besides I have something to sell to help pay for all this, seeing as it is partly my fault.'

'Nay, lass, the boy himself was laiking about and disobeyed thee,' Joseph came to my rescue. 'Happen she's right, mother.'

'It is me he will want, not her,' Mary argued.

'But the other children need their mother for comfort at this time. Let Joy do her bit to help.'

How good it was that Joseph was on my side in this. I wanted to make sure Titus did nothing to jeopardise the outcome. I recalled those stolen children and I didn't trust him but now was not the time to denounce him as a fraud. When the opportunity presented itself I would speak out at meeting about my dealings with the man who could do no wrong at present. Georgie's life must come first however, no matter what the cost.

28

They carried George onto the boat, his mother wrapping blankets around him, weeping and kissing his hand. I didn't like the size of that swelling on his forehead. The Blacks came on board, not looking at me. I knew Titus would not be happy to see me there. I was so sure it was him and yet once more doubts crept in, for he was much aged.

In my leather bag I carried my grandmother's gloves for it was the only thing of value I possessed to sell towards the boy's treatment fee. He was to lodge at the surgeon's house recommended to our elders by none other than Doctor Thomas Wynne, William Penn's personal physician. Word had got round Friends in the city about the boy's injury and help was offered freely. We were to be lodged with a Yorkshire family nearby and it would give me a chance to observe Titus more closely. I wanted to catch him off guard.

It was this sister who puzzled me and I asked Jacob her story. 'She was thrown overboard in the shipwreck and watched many Friends drown. Thomas rescued her and kept her afloat but the shock has made her dumb.'

Why did I did not believe this story? Yet there was such a look of fear in her eyes. She sat like a wooden doll slumped against the boat, staring with a fixed expression bereft of any sign of life. Was this journey on water reminding her of the dreadful wrecking she had endured? Who was I to sit in judgement on her terror?

I was determined not to leave Georgie's side, hoping the fresh river breeze would rouse him but he slept on. After landing he was conveyed by carriage to the doctor's fine brick house where he was placed in an upper room for examination.

I was dismissed to get on with the other business in hand, knowing it was time to let those precious gloves go: my grandmother's gift that my mother, Alice, had never gotten to hold. She would never have made gloves as fine as these, for Seekers did not hold with fancy trappings as I know only too well. I had clung onto them for so long as a link to my old life in England. They must fetch a fair price and I wanted no trickster cheating me of their full value. I knew there was only one shop where there would be honest advice.

'Joy, *ma Cherie!* Two visits in one week, *c'est bon.*' Sabine kissed me on the cheek in greeting but then she saw the look on my face. 'What is wrong? Come sit down ... Jerome, fetch some wine.'

Out poured all that had happened after our last visit, the accident, Captain Thane, the medicine man and even Titus. I'm not sure my friend understood everything but Jerome assured me that the former ship's surgeon, Doctor Wallace, was a reputable physician who had saved many lives. The treatment he was undertaking was used even in France.

'Nevertheless it will cost and I have only these gloves to sell towards the fee.' I pulled out the linen bag containing them, giving a garbled history of how they came into my possession.

Sabine fingered them with a loving touch. 'Such beautiful work of the finest quality and very old. Look at the gold lace,

the little pearls. Your family must be of great wealth to own
these. You can't sell them.'

'I must, I have a debt to honour. George was in my charge.
Please, how much will I get for them?'

Jerome also examined them, shaking his head. 'I am not sure
there is a call for such fancy work, the cuffs are of a bygone
fashion but Mr Coats, the haberdasher would price them better
than I can, my dear.'

'Will you take them to him on my behalf and get the best
price you can? I must get back to George in case he wakes. He
must know I am there.'

Sabine hugged me. 'Hurry along, you must do what is best
for the boy. The gauntlets will be safe with us and you are welcome to stay here. Come and eat with us tonight. You look as if
a good meal is a stranger to your stomach. Come back later and
let us put some colour back in those white cheeks.'

How could my mind rest, wondering how the boy would
fare in the hands of the surgeon? To cut a hole in a skull with
instruments I could only imagine made me shiver. I prayed for
the surgeon's guiding hand not to tremble at this task. I was
received by a servant into a lower room and Tamar was there
staring listlessly at the door when I entered. I wished I could
break down the invisible wall she had built around her.

'How goes it up stairs?' I asked her. She shrugged her shoulders. 'What's wrong, Friend Tamar?' I added gently. 'Are you
afraid of someone?'

She shook her head, all the while looking to the ceiling not
at me. We could hear movements overhead. What if the little
boy screamed in fear? He must still be asleep. The pain would
come when he awoke from the surgery, I feared. But I had the
medicine man's herbs in a safe place to dose him should the
need arise.

'Where is your brother?' I continued but she ignored me and I wanted to shake her out of this dreamlike state. Now was not the time to press further the mystery that was Tamar Black, if indeed that was her real name. Thus we sat it seemed for hours before Doctor Wallace came down wiping his hands on a bloody apron. 'The boy lives, the blood and venom is released. Now it is up to his own healing powers to restore the wound. The boy must not be moved until we are sure it is healing.'

'We thank thee,' I croaked.

'Nay, young lady, thank the man who had the sense to bring him to my door before it was too late. Come back on the morrow.'

Once again Titus must take the credit for my own initiative, but if George lived it was a small price to pay. There was no sign of him in the waiting room or outside, I noticed. Was he not bothered about the outcome? Why should I sit with this mute woman when I had good friends waiting only a few streets away? Their cheery company would take my mind off the coming hours of danger. I left Tamar to stew in her own juice, which was not good Friend behaviour and a poor example of my faith; but I had my own selfish need of comfort that day.

Through the open door of the Boyers' shop I could smell such rich aromas and when Jerome showed me upstairs to their living quarters my mouth watered at the sights before me. The table was set just as it was once in Scarperton Hall. There were fine pewter dishes and linen napkins, glasses of such delicate crystal, a fire in the grate for the nights were still chilly. In the panelled room overlooking the paved street below, candles flickered over the walls. It was such a relief to be among friends to whom I could relate all that had happened. Henri, Jerome's father, came from his room to greet me. He looked frailer and leant heavily on his stick. We talked ourselves hoarse about the sea voyage and the sad times we endured. We lifted a glass to Ellinor and to baby Paul.

Soon the rich red wine went to my head so I could hardly stand with fatigue when it was time to leave and return to my lodgings. They begged me to stay with them. 'You mustn't walk alone in the dark streets. They are not safe these days for a woman so we have taken the liberty to find you an escort,' Sabine smiled at Jerome and I knew there was mischief afoot. When I reached the bottom of the stairs I saw through the window the outline of a soldier in uniform waiting like a sentry at his post.

'How is the boy?' were Captain Thane's first words to put me at my ease. It was a safe topic of discussion for us, knowing I must not be accused of familiarity with a militia man how-ever kind he had been. In the distance we could hear shouting and drunkards revelling with oaths and curses ringing in the air. Captain Thane took me right to the door of the lodgings. He seemed reluctant to leave me there. 'May I see you before you leave? I must know how the boy fares,' he asked with such a look of concern on his face. How could I refuse this kind inquiry?

'I will leave a message at the Frenchman's shop. I have busi-ness with them. I must go in now but many thanks ...' The door was opened and Friend Betsy Barnes stared down the street in disapproval at the soldier's presence. I tried to explain how the Captain had helped us save George's life but she shook her head. 'It is not good for a maid to consort with an unbeliever, whatever the reason.' I knew this would not be the last comment on my escort but nodded politely and made my way to the chamber set aside for Tamar and me.

She was not asleep but lay, eyes open, staring up at the ceiling, but I received no greeting. We were all woken in the night by a crashing noise in the room below. Someone was stumbling about and shouting. Wrapping my shawl around my shift I crept down to investigate to find Will Barnes mopping Titus's bloody brow.

'He's been attacked by villains and robbed.'

His cheek was bruised and his lip burst as if he had been in a fight but I also smelled strong Jamaican spirit on his breath and gave our host a look of disbelief.

'What was stolen? Why out so late? Have you been to see the child? Is he worse?' I wanted to shake him.

'I was on my way when I was waylaid. They sprang on me from behind. I had no chance to defend myself. They took my purse. The fee I was about to give the doctor, most of it is gone.'

'What do you mean ... all the collection money?' How could I believe this story? I recalled the roistering drunks that Thane and I heard. Had he spent the proceeds or gambled it away? 'Your breath stinks of devil's brew,' I snapped, offering no sympathy.

'They knocked me to the ground and someone gave me spirit to restore my senses. It happened so quickly.'

'Has all our money gone?'

'Not everything. Tamar has kept some aside for expenses as was agreed.'

'Then we will have to use that. How could you be so careless to carry it on your person in darkness?'

'Nay, lass, don't be harsh on brother Thomas,' Will Barnes interrupted. 'He's been sorely treated. Don't fret about the shortfall, the Friends here can help with that. It is the least we can do. This city is becoming unruly. We are glad the militia are in their fortress. Get thee both to bed. It has been a right bad night.'

I could not sleep for the fury burning in my chest. Titus was lying but he had a plausible answer for everything. I guessed he had been down the rough streets filling his belly with rum, spending the surgeon's fee. Now he had a cock-and-bull story making him a victim but I had no proof of my suspicions. The old Titus had not changed his soul. He was not convinced of the Truth in my eyes but he could spout lies like sermons when he was challenged.

Tamar must know the real truth of his deceiving heart but if she would not speak, there was nothing I could do but pray that one day I would catch him unawares and shine a light on his shadowy deeds.

29

When I woke late next morning, Tamar's bed was empty and the apothecary was gone. Betsy Barnes, our hostess, said they had left early to check on the boy before heading back to Good Hope to give their news. I was to stay on until further notice and there was no mention of the stolen money or the replacement of funds that Tamar had held on her person. Will assured me that local Friends would not see us short but I felt uneasy at this turn of events, fearing the two of them had disappeared for good.

It was with a heavy heart I retraced my steps back to the surgeon's house but on arrival, to my surprise, their maidservant told me that Master Emsworth was stirring from his deep sleep and I could go and sit with him for a while.

At first George wasn't aware of me, his head was bandaged and he looked so small. I held his hand and whispered. 'It's Joy. Can you hear me?' I squeezed his fingers. 'Squeeze me back if you can.' I felt a flicker of tightness and found myself crying with relief. 'The Lord be praised.'

George's eyes opened and flickered in my direction. 'Where's Mam?'

'Waiting for you back home but you must rest awhile longer here.'

'Where am I?' I saw the bewilderment in his eyes at the fine four poster bed and curtains. 'My head hurts.'

'The doctor will bleed thee and give a potion to soothe it.'

'Don't go.'

'Of course not. When you're a little stronger I will read us a book.' My presence gave him the familiar face he needed. He shut his eyes and went back to sleep but I sensed in that moment that he would be restored to us almost whole. I slipped out of the chamber when he was deeply asleep and took it upon myself to go to the haberdasher's store, the one whose fine windows were filled with fancy goods and trimmings. Had Mr Coats bought my gloves yet? I didn't want to enter the shop and be disappointed so scurried back to the Boyers' house to ask Jerome but the shop was closed up for the day. Suddenly I felt cast adrift among the crowded streets, feeling guilty that I had left the boy. I rushed back to the surgeon's house, asking if I could stay with the boy until he awoke.

They gave me pen and paper to write a note of good cheer to Mary and Joseph which could be ferried up river to them. Their servant accompanied me down to the landing station fearing I might be accosted walking alone among the wharves and taverns. We lingered to find a ferryman going in that direction and then returned back to George who was still asleep. I made my way back to my lodgings, feeling restless.

I couldn't wait to make another visit to little George, taking a book of sermons that Betsy lent me to read. They made very dull reading so I made up stories about our Lenape neighbours, the medicine man who had first helped me save his life and given me herbs to make a tea to soothe his headache. It was good to see him awake and already bored. I gave him the sleeping draught, which seemed to work.

When Doctor Wallace returned from his visits, he was

pleased with his patient's progress. 'We left open a gap in his skull which should close up once healed,' he told me. 'He's a lucky laddie to have recovered his senses so quickly but there is always risk after such a treatment. He must not exert himself in boy's play. Two more days' rest and he will be fit for travel, but be sure to change his dressings to protect the wound.'

I stayed to bathe George and give him his broth, waiting until he was sleeping soundly before returning to Sabine's shop with my good news, but still the shop was shuttered and I was worried. Just as I turned to leave I saw the three of them strolling down in my direction dressed in their sober finery. Sabine was wearing a wonderful headdress with black feathers. Her elegance showed up my grubby travel clothes and stained collar.

'We've been to a wedding in the German church,' she greeted me. 'A couple who met on Jerome's ship have joined together.'

I told them George was recovering and that in two days' time we would be leaving for Good Hope. 'Did you sell my gloves?' I asked Jerome.

'Come inside,' he insisted. 'Let's discuss this further.'

My heart sank, sensing his hesitancy. When we were settled upstairs supping a rich dark brew which they called coffee, he brought out my gloves still in their bag.

'I have shown them to Thomas Coats and we both agreed a price but we also agreed they should not be sold by you, not to be ripped apart and stripped of valuables. They belong to you, so we did a little deal between ourselves under the circumstances. Here,' he said, thrusting them back into my hand along with some silver coins. 'This is a gift towards the surgeon's fee.'

I was mortified. 'I can't accept this as well as my gloves. Keep the gloves, please.'

'Why? They have no meaning for me but they mean everything to you. One day you will part with them, but not this time. We are glad to contribute, dear Joy. Don't be proud. It is a gift.'

What could I say? How blessed I was to have found such friends. They had made the past few days bearable and now there was the delicate matter of Captain Thane.

'Has there been any message for me? I blushed as I spoke.

'Do you mean this?' Sabine removed a packet from the mantelpiece. 'It came first thing this morning.'

'*Merci*,' I said in their tongue. 'The Captain wanted news of the boy. I promised to speak with him again.'

'Of course you did.' They were laughing at me as I went puce with shame. 'Open it then!'

I read his note and closed it quickly. 'He will call later this evening. I am to wait here if that is acceptable.'

It was Henri who teased me. 'I think there could be another shipboard romance brewing.'

'No, no, that's not how it must be. Seekers do not engage themselves to those not of our persuasion. We are but good friends.'

'We understand. It's always difficult when people of different faiths find themselves attracted to each other. It can cause great conflicts. Protestant and Catholic ... but Captain Thane is surely a Protestant?'

'But not of our Assembly. Rules are strict. Like must join with like and it must be approved by all at the meeting. Worldly friendships are discouraged.'

'So you should not in fact be friendly with us, then? We are Protestants but not Quakers.'

'Oh no, that's different. You are my true friends, but we are not joined in wedlock.'

'Ah well, Joy, perhaps you may have to make some hard choices should the occasion arise,' Henri added. 'Remember what I said on board. Marry for duty and have comfortable days but lonely nights.'

'Papa, that's enough, the poor girl is confused. You must do what you think is right. No point in starting what you can't finish.'

'I'd better go then,' I said, jumping up from the chair.

'No, you have to stay and see this through. That young man deserves an explanation. Don't run away, it will make matters worse for both you.'

'I ought to go now.'

'Why? Do you not want to see him?' Sabine challenged me with her dark eyes.

'No, yes, I would like to see him one more time.'

'Then follow your heart, not your head.'

'But it is forbidden.'

'By whom?'

'By the meeting. I have not received permission to look in his direction.'

'So are they the final authority? I thought that belonged to God and your inner conviction, or am I mistaken?'

'Yes, but ... oh, it is so confusing.'

'It's time to think for yourself, Joy. Trust the inner promptings of the heart and gut. They never lie.'

There was no fight left in me after this discussion so I sank back into the chair and waited for the knock on the door.

When I look back on that far-off evening I sense that was when my great disobedience was born, in the candlelight of their upper room as I sat opposite the young officer with his tawny hair and bright blue eyes. We made polite conversation under the watchful eye of the Boyers, revisiting the perils of our ship's voyage. I gave a full report on my little charge. He offered to escort us back to Good Hope, but I said that was unnecessary. I explained about the apothecary losing our collection, but I had no proof of any wrongdoing, only my inner conviction, so I made no direct charge against them.

We relaxed by the fireside as Jordan told us about his family in Northumberland. He was the youngest son of landowners, trained from an early age for military service. He hoped one day to settle and buy his own land here. I told him my strange history and how we had suffered for being Dissenters. 'The short time I lived with my grandfather Moorside in Scarperton, I could not make that life my own and ran away. In Leeds I found a good position and that's where I met Ellinor Holt. We had such plans and dreams, but alas . . .'

Jerome smiled sadly, shaking his head. 'Nothing is certain, for the road of life is full of twists and turns. We did not expect to lose our home, my mother and our business in Nantes, flee to Leyden and find ourselves beginning again, and then lose our precious baby.' He sighed. 'But we all must make the best of what we've got now, especially as there is new life to come.' He turned to Sabine.

'There's a child on the way soon, I hope,' she confirmed.

'That is the best news of all,' I said, reaching out my hand to hers.

The evening passed quickly and it was time to return to the Friends' house. The opportunity to be alone with Jordan was slipping away to just a short walk to another street. How we spun out that journey with short pauses and lingering looks that meant more to me than any open professions of love. Under a torch-lit corner we stared at each other, unsure how to proceed. 'I have to go now or there will be talk,' I said.

He seized my hand and kissed it. 'Stay here in the city. Don't go back. The Boyers will take you in. I don't want to lose you.'

I pulled back my hand. 'Would it were so simple. You forget I am indentured for four years to the Emsworths to pay for my passage. I am bound by the faith of my father to be of service to Friends. Too many saints have perished in the crossing. I am not free to make choices, not yet and when I am I must look to my own persuasion or be cast out.'

Jordan sighed, 'I don't understand any of that. I'm just a simple soldier. All I know is that each day without the chance of seeing you is dreary and long. From our first meeting on the ship I knew there was something about you that captured my attention.'

'Yet we've only seen each other but four times since the ship,' I replied, my heart leaping at his words.

'So you have counted them too.' Jordan smiled with such warmth. 'We're young. Everything is before us in this new country. I have nothing to offer you yet but hope for the future.'

'No, no,' I pulled away. 'It can't be like that for us. I'm sorry, I must go.' I ran towards the lodgings. He did not follow but yelled across the street for all to hear.

'You are for me, Joy Moorside, and I will wait . . .'

30

I was sustained by Jordan Thane's plea for many a long day in the months that followed George's return to us. Mary did not wait for us to make the journey home but had sailed downriver to see him for herself. We were contented passengers with the boy safe by our side until I told her how the apothecary had lost our collection. 'How it happened I have no proof but he was in drink that night.'

'That's enough, Joy. If you've nothing good to say then hold thy tongue. If it weren't for that man our George would be dead.' Mary was having none of it.

'But I am just saying, he may not be all he seems, or his sister.' Perhaps I should have spoken out then but the moment passed in acrimony.

'Did you not hear a word I said? I fear too much time with worldly folk has coarsened thee. Don't think your own conduct with yon soldier had not gone unnoticed.'

So the gossips had been at work again, spying on my conversations however innocent and making mischief. I was in a bad humour as we landed at the little jetty. George was carried into the waiting arms of his father Joseph and Jacob stood by his side ready to greet us. He held my hand as I disembarked. 'Well done Joy, you've kept your charge safe from harm.'

It felt as if I had been away for months, not days, but in no time it was back to the daily grind with a troubled heart. My thoughts were still downriver, reliving those precious hours in Philadelphia with Jordan Thane and the Boyers. My discontent was like bile at the back of my throat, burning and spoiling the taste of everything I swallowed. I lost interest in glovemaking and the leather jerkins I was sewing for the boys against the winter chills to come. Liddy was jealous of her brother getting attention and had fits of temper, so it was my duty to appease her with trips to pick wild flowers and to paddle by the shore, watching the native boys fishing. We picked shells and pretty pebbles.

My life was no longer my own, I sighed, feeling sorry I had made the decision to leave England for this harsh land. Yet walking through the forest full of flaming leaves under a glorious canopy of tall trees, how could I not admire our achievement in surviving in a town made out of wilderness? If only I felt I belonged amongst them, but I still felt an outsider. Being a servant did not sit easy on my pride. Had I not once been a Justice's granddaughter? Now I was at everyone's beck and call and what had happened to my faith?

All this changed at First Day Meeting when we were joined by a travelling band of preachers who had newly arrived from Chesapeake Bay and were heading north to Boston, holding meetings of encouragement wherever they found hospitality among clusters of Friends.

Among the visitors was one James Hartley from York who belonged to a network of Friends across the county and he brought to me the most welcome of letters from my uncle, Roger Windebank. Such unexpected news warmed my heart as I pored over the tightly written page, savouring every word.

Greetings Beloved Friend and Sister.
It was with joy and relief we received thy letter from America
knowing thee's settled well and safe from shipwreck . . .

There was news of all I knew in the village, the passing to
Glory of my old schoolteacher's wife, Isobel Sampson. Cousin
Mallory was to be wed and Dilly in service in a farm close by.
I closed my eyes to imagine them all together under those open
grey moors and that stretch of starlit sky, looking at the same
moon's face that lit our path. To be so far apart and yet so linked
by love and kinship brought me to tears.

It was Jacob who caught me in my sorrow and gave me
comfort. 'Home is always where the heart dwells. This is thy
dwelling place now; but all who share our Light are never far
away.'

Later that evening we all gathered to listen to our visitors
who stood in turn to exhort us to deeper faith and trust in
God's will for this settlement. Only by holding our beliefs
would we prosper. There was a woman in their company whose
name I recall as Susanna. Her words seemed to speak to me
alone.

'Great truths such as ours are dearly bought, not found by
chance on the highway or wafted in on a gentle breeze but
grasped in the great struggle of the soul when buffeted by a
contrary wind and harsh currents. We sail with the lantern of
Truth to guide us against temptation's rocks that will wreck us
and strand us on a desert shore. We are a peculiar people set
apart. Now is the seed time. God alone knows the end harvest
of our efforts. It is hidden from us. Our duty is to sew and scatter, nurture new growth, not seeking any reward other than
doing His will.'

Who could not say 'Amen' to these stirring words? I felt

my spirit lifted, my resolve stiffened to be in the presence of holy missioners who had suffered much to give us hope for the future. When I came out of the meeting it was with a lighter heart than of late. Here was where I was meant to be, among people of my own kind, saved for a purpose to be an instrument of God's will. I was on fire with good intentions and it was Jacob, seeing me flushed with excitement, who leapt to my side.

'Wonderful words, sister Joy. Just what was wanted to fire us with fresh zeal. We have been lukewarm of late, lacking the drive to plough forwards. Now is the time to teach the children of the Lenape labourers to read and write and learn our language. Time for deeds, not words.'

'Aye, Friend,' I answered him. 'We have held off long enough on many things. Now our edge is sharpened once more.'

Jacob's black eyes flashed with new interest at my response. 'My thoughts, sister, my thoughts too.' Now he was looking at me in such a way that I sensed what was coming next.

'I was concerned that I might never find a helpmeet as would love and serve the truth as Ellinor Holt. For our hearts can only open to such as we can really trust and I trust thee, Joy Moorside.' He held out his hand to me.

In the first flush of enthusiasm for all that had happened that evening, it seemed as if all my doubtings were resolved. In taking Jacob's hand in intimate friendship, I would no longer be an onlooker here but be drawn ever deeper into the life of Good Hope through his work and good standing. I would continue the work that Ellinor had so wanted to promote alongside him.

With Jacob by my side there would be no wavering, no more temptation. We would support each other on our spiritual journey. I had been led to this moment of decision, all resistance subdued, so I took the hand offered, looking at him directly. 'This must be approved by others,' I cautioned.

'Of course, but I see no obstacle to us joining together, do you?'

'I'm still indentured to the Emsworths.'

'That may cause a delay but nothing more.'

Why did I feel as if we were discussing a piece of land at a price to be bargained for? But there was such relief, too. Of all the single men, Jacob was the most worthy, being both educated and passionate for his faith. I could not do better, and yet . . .

When I lay on my mattress hugging this secret, I could hear Jordan Thane's voice ringing in my ears: 'Joy, you are for me.' I buried my head in the pillow but there was no hiding place from the promises I had just made or the feeling that I was making a terrible error of judgement. At least there would be no haste in the matter of a wedding.

When a man wants to wed a woman in our community there are certain protocols that must be observed. Everything must be set before committees, searches of ancestry must be held, records must be consulted but our family credentials were excellent. I was still bound in service and there would be no rush to link us together in matrimony, but there was an understanding that would allow us time to walk out together and make preparations for our new life and home.

There was still the matter of Titus Cranke to address with Jacob and since they were still in lodgings together I was reluctant to speak of my suspicions. I still hoped to steer Tamar into trusting me enough to speak out against him but she avoided me at every turn.

After that first burst of enthusiasm for revival, attendances at meeting slumped again as people prepared for their second winter older and wiser as to what must be done.

Joseph busied himself repairing our thatched roof and adding layers of clay to the inner walls to seal us from the wet. The boys took a cart to collect kindle for the fire and there was much chopping and repairing the clapboard walls. Now we had a barn for hay and livestock perhaps we might be less stretched for fodder and food.

It was the time for gathering, pickling and sealing up vegetables, drying beans and storing roots. I made visits to the Lenape camp first to thank the medicine man for his suggestion and then to buy more animal skins to use as blankets. I brought wampum shells that came from the sea shore and were much valued. White Deer was busy re-stocking her herbs and showed me all the useful medicines and oils they used when sickness struck.

Our families learned that corn, squashes and beans would eke out our stews and meats but it was the special wild plants that held so many secret remedies I wanted to know; willow bark, cherry tree, juniper and the seeds that made dull food flavoursome. I watched them tapping the sap from the maple tree and tasted its amber sweetness.

Many native men now worked alongside us, boat-building, hunting and learning our metalwork skills. They didn't work in the fields as that was work for women but they did want their children to speak our language, so the promise to hold lessons in the meeting house began and for a short while my little school prospered.

Then a new family arrived from England who were relatives of the carpenter, Amos. There was a stir of excitement as letters were passed around with news of a new king and battles in foreign countries.

The family had three children and were eager for them to meet others of their own ages so Patience and Charity came to play with Liddy and joined in the little sampler-making lesson I held. Patience was attentive but Charity kept scratching her arm and was restless. I took them all into the autumn sunshine to play games and encouraged some of the Lenape children who were standing shyly on the sidelines to join in a game of tag. I gave no thought to the matter until Liddy started to scratch and complain about spots.

'Look at her covered from head to toe in flea bites,' Mary complained but both of us knew these were pox marks, not bites. Most of us had suffered from this ailment as children as had Georgie and Sam so I gave it no mind. Her fever was short lived and the scars soon faded but it was with horror that I learned that the whole Lenape village was laid low with the disease. Both children who played with us died as did many more and the chief forbade any contact between us. No Lenape children came to school after this outbreak and when I saw Little Bear on the river he told me that White Deer had also suffered much from the outbreak too. I prayed her child had been spared.

'How could such a mild skin affliction cause such devastation?' I asked Jacob on our evening walk down to the river.

'The children brought the pox from the ship. It is a setback to our plans but all will be well. Don't take the blame on thyself. Thomas assures me that once the pox is caught it doesn't bite again.'

'Has Tamar Black spoken yet?' I changed the subject, knowing it was time to address my fears out loud.

'Not that I've noticed. Why do you ask?'

I took in a deep breath and began my rehearsed speech. 'The man we call Thomas I once knew as Titus Cranke. Although much changed and aged, it is surely him, and he was more a conjuror and mountebank than an apothecary. He had a wife called Dora and they were cruel people, believe me.'

I was waiting for a tirade of disbelief but Jacob just smiled and patted my hand. 'Ah, so you know his story, then?'

'Only that he stole when he could and snatched children from their true families. Why, what has he told you?'

'Many things in confidence which are between him and his Maker. His wife betrayed him with another man and caused him to be cast in prison. It was there in Hull that Friends came to his aid and brought him to the light, so that when he was convinced of our beliefs he took on a new name for his new life. Coming to America was all part of the new beginning.'

I was taken aback by this confession but still unconvinced. 'But Tamar is not his real sister, is she?'

'Only in Christ, as we all are to each other. He befriended her after the shipwreck to protect her from harm. Her wits are addled and confused. You must pity the poor woman, not condemn her. See the best in people, not the worst.'

'Did he mention he knew me in Leeds, though?'

'No, why should he, the old world is past and all things connected to it.'

'But he lost our collection and was in drink. I saw it for myself.'

He gave me a look of pity as if talking to a child. 'We all have weaknesses to fight. The upset of the robbery turned him to the ale pot, no doubt. Don't judge until you know your own frailties.'

Was Jacob preaching at me when all I wanted to know was the truth about his lodgers? Titus had spun some story but it did not sit right with me. The fear in Tamar's eyes told me of other less savoury doings that weighed heavy on the woman. It looked as if I was alone in this search to find out the real reason behind their coming. Jacob might be easily satisfied but I was not.

31

It is wearisome now to recount all the afflictions of the following winter season, cut off as we were from neighbours and
city, thrown once more on our own resources but our survival
assured by better preparations. Mary and I spent many hours re-
lining our petticoats and jackets with a layer of sheep fleece. We
padded the boys' clothes and Liddy's dress so she waddled like
a duck but was kept warm. The only danger was her getting
too close to the fire grate. At night we heated bricks and stones
in the fire and then wrapped them in rags, taking them to bed
to warm the new feather mattresses that softened our sleep and
kept us from scratchy straw.

My glovemaking efforts were renewed with a supply of raccoon skins. No one had frostbitten fingers but our toes were
chapped with chilblains and we ran barefoot into the snow to
relieve the itching. But winter held us in its treacherous grip and
two neighbours were lost in the snowdrifts looking for stock.
Their bodies were only found when the ice melted.

Jacob came on his snowshoes to visit us and it was common
knowledge that we had an understanding. His lodgers continued to stay, Titus providing what remedies he knew from his
decreasing store of salves and pastilles. I had never seen him out

gathering wild herbs in the woods as would be sensible. Tamar helped silently in the preparation and cooked their meals but I never felt comfortable in their presence. Two women in the keeping room did not ease the tensions between us. It was hard for me to accept that Titus had a new life here, as did we all; but the unease I felt about him never left me, making our few conversations stilted and brief.

On the finer days when we walked back after First Day Meeting, Jacob escorted me, discussing who had spoken in the Spirit, who had said too much or too little. Why must he dissect our worship piece by piece until I had heard everything twice over? He never caught my hand as sweethearts do. It was if I was his sounding board, not a treasured companion. Sometimes we went the whole way back in silence. First Day especially in dreary weather is always a strain, there being no playing out for the children or sewing or field work that might take advantage of a dry spell. But boredom was relieved when we fed visiting preachers and visiting Friends who brought welcome news of the world outside our township.

I tried to put all thoughts of Philadelphia behind me, praying that Sabine was safely delivered of her baby. I couldn't wait for the river to melt and the tracks to open up. Surely we would make a river trip down to the city to restock our provisions and I would be freed to visit the Boyers?

A determination to embrace my life in Good Hope with a less judgemental spirit and more submissive acceptance was the tight girdle that kept me looking forward to my life with Jacob. No matter what irritations life with the Emsworths could bring at times, I bridled my unruly tongue and prided myself on doing as many acts of charity among our poor as I could fit in during the long days. I tried to keep the children out of danger and mischief, playing games, doing lessons.

Leah Fleming

How I longed for the sun to rise high and the greening of the shoots and leaves to begin. The wild geese flying overhead from their winter in the south lifted my spirits with new hope, but with them came news of a disturbing nature that would affect us all.

The Governor of our Province sent round a public notice to warn of unprovoked raids on isolated settlements further into the wilderness. There was tribal warfare among the native men for guns, rum and stock. The Lenape had suffered at the hands of marauding Susquehanna in the past. It was his ruling that all townships should be prepared to make defences and give musket training to all males as a precaution against an attack. This notice was duly discussed and recorded among the elders at their next preparative meeting.

'We hold no truck with militia training,' Jacob explained. 'Guns, we use for hunting in season. What need have we for stakes around our town? Our neighbours are peaceful. There's never been trouble between us nor do I expect any. We did not come here to be soldiers or take up arms. God alone is our Protector.'

'But the men spend all day in their fields,' I said. 'What if we are caught unaware, just women and children alone, what then?' I had not the first idea how to defend the family.

'It won't come to that,' he snapped back, surprised at my question. 'There are always men around by the river, in the workshops and tannery.'

'But surely we need a plan, if only to put people at their ease?' I was not convinced by his argument. Jacob's eyebrows lowered and he gave me the stare given to a naughty child.

'She's right, tha'knows,' said Mary. 'I might not know how to use a firearm but I would wield an axe if them savages came near my bairns.'

Suddenly the atmosphere chilled in the keeping room as Mary and I stared at each other in dismay.

'It was my uncle who did the shooting at Windebank,' I added. 'So I would like to know if I can pot a jackrabbit or a coon. We could practise our aim on them. Where's the harm in that?'

'Joy, you don't understand how it goes against our principles. We will never take up arms, ever.'

'So you will let thy families die at the hands of raiders and not raise a finger to protect them? Is that faith or fear?' I could not hold back my anger. 'I watched how innocent men were beaten down to the ground and killed because of their beliefs and how they were mocked for not fighting back. No good came of that act of witness or none that I ever saw. Jacob, how could you forget how it was in Leeds when the meeting house was attacked?'

There was silence at my defiance. There I went again, challenging authority, stepping out of line in my indignation, but for once Mary stood by my side.

'The girl talks some sense. Thee wouldn't let thy bairns be carried away and scalped, Joseph Emsworth?'

'Fret not, there are other ways to defend ourselves than with guns. We can make safe the cellars and find hiding places or thee can flee to pits in the woods. Our doors are stout and we have shutters. Better still to parlay with the enemy to prevent bloodshed, hear their grievances and find some meeting point and treaty like they did in the old war in England.'

'And live in fear and dread as our grandfathers in Cromwell's time, not knowing who would stampede through the fields and demand quartering? Have you forgotten how Cromwell's army demanded someone go in his place to join them in combat? His yard boy, Perkins went with them and never returned.'

'Enough, that was a long time ago,' Joseph snapped back. Our sniping and bickering went on for days after that. Joseph was in two minds about the matter but Jacob never wavered that there should be no palisade built around us. Thankfully there were some Dutch and Swedish neighbours who held no such convictions, eager to billet the militia when they arrived. Their coming divided Good Hope into two camps and as usual I tried to straddle the both of them.

At the town meeting all of us attended to hear the officer of the militia explaining how we must strengthen our defences.

'This is a precautionary measure but the fact of having a firm wall shows that you are prepared to sit out a siege or stand and fight back. It takes away the element of surprise. These natives in war paint are not your Lenape river folk but savages from the north and south who burn houses and kill every white face, causing great fear. Those who trade in guns and rum have much to answer for.

'We have grown soft in the middle lands. Peace has made prosperity but it causes jealousy and a demand for the shipped–in goods we enjoy. I can't stress enough how important it is for you to have a plan, should danger come. We can't patrol the whole of Delaware and the wilderness beyond. We have good native scouts who can warn us and track their path, so who among you will volunteer?'

I saw the Dormundsens and Hautmanns raise their hands and a few I did not recognise but our elders rose as one and walked out of the chamber. Other Friends followed, though I did not leave but hung back to hear what was going to happen.

'Bring your arms to the river field for drill and exercises,' the officer continued. 'My men will advise you further. Have no fear, they are well trained and experienced under the leadership of Captain Thane here.'

Jordan Thane stepped out of the shadows. How had he been hidden from my view? Had he seen me lurking at the back? Our eyes met briefly and then I knew just the sight of him standing tall was too much to bear. If I stayed on there would be a temptation to converse with him; that one glance was enough to know I must speak with him again, if only to explain that I was now engaged to another man.

Jacob was hovering in the lane with a face like thunder. 'You were the only Friend left in the hall. Why do you linger so long with such people? I was beginning to think you would never come out.'

'The officer is talking sense and not all soldiers are wicked unbelievers. He has our best interests at heart,' I argued.

Jacob sighed. 'I despair of thy faith sometimes. Is the convincement of Truth so weak within you? I hear from the women's meeting that you are inclined to stubbornness in many matters of discipline. I know you can never be as compliant as Ellinor was but I need thy support if I am to sit among the elders. Do not draw attention to thyself with contrary opinions that go against our teachings. I see you rush about where others walk calmly. I see you fidget when others sit still in silence. I had hoped together we might subdue thy restless spirit. I must speak the hard truth in love if we are to walk together in life.'

This was the moment to have spoken of my own doubtings, the moment to disengage from any future promises and vows but I let that moment of honesty pass and walked on in silence at his rebuke.

Jacob Wrathall was a good man, sincere and fair, forthright in his judgement of others as many Friends tend to be but kind in many other ways. If any man could tame my wildness it would be him, I mused. It was still early days in our understanding of each other. His faith was like a steady lantern in the darkness. For a time in Yorkshire mine own was like a blazing torch of certitude but now it felt like a firework that exploded high with sparks that lately had fallen to earth and faded. What was left was a flickering pinprick of light and not much comfort at all. Were we mismatched in every way?

For all his firebrand opinions and certainties, Jacob was a good shepherd, tender at the sick bed, playful with the school children, dutiful in his preparations and record-keeping but there was as yet something missing between us. I thought of Henri Boyer teasing me about the nightly joys of lovemaking. In almost two years since our arrival and before that in those travelling years in Leeds, not once had Jacob attempted any touch or kiss to express his physical need of me or Ellinor. Theirs was the most chaste of courtships, as I recall. That night I lay pondering my feebleness in not withdrawing from our arrangement. What was is it about me that made him wary of any physical approach?

No palisades were built around Good Hope. That was the compromise made but farmers and citizens did their target practice, had their muskets and powder checked and ammunition stored safely. One morning after the town meeting I walked along the river field to view the training and I saw Jordan Thane watching me from a distance. Nothing was said but a sign was passed between us none the less. I had brought Liddy along as my chaperone knowing if I so much as spoke to a redcoat she would report it back to Mary.

'Why do we have to walk on this path?' she asked, staring at the troops marching up and down. 'Are they fighting?'

'No, just practising with their firearms.'

'Have you got one?'

'Of course not,' I said.

'Don't ladies have them then?'

'Perhaps among the gentry folk there are some hand pistols.'

'Why?'

'To arm themselves against highwaymen and robbers.'

'Will you buy us one? Then you can save us from the Indians.'

'Who told you that?' All our talk of unrest had gotten to the ears of this child.

'Sam says the Indians cut your hands and heads off and stick them on a pike.'

'What rot! Wait till I see that boy. The Lenape are our friends. There's nothing to fear. Come along.' I hurried her away, regretting this detour.

The thought of owning a hand pistol troubled me. Where did the children dream up such schemes? This was what came of meddling in warfare and rumours of war. Suddenly, though, Good Hope didn't feel quite so safe. Could tribes from the north canoe down and attack us by night, plunder our barns and fields, burn our wooden houses and barns and carry us off as prisoners for ransom or worse?

'You've had a visitor,' Mary sniffed the next day. 'Yon soldier as helped Georgie, he called with this.' She shoved a package into my hand. 'Said as how he wanted to see how the lad was faring but I told him you were all up the fields and doing fine. I don't want Friend Simpson seeing a redcoat at our door but it were kind of him to ask.' She eyed my letter with interest. I was miffed to have missed his visit. To be so near and yet so far and with a genuine reason to call that no one could take fault with.

'Good news,' I said, reading the contents of the letter. 'Sabine has been safely delivered of a girl child called Marianne after

Henri's wife. She was murdered by the king's men in Nantes when the Huguenots were attacked.'

'Mercy me!' Mary said. 'Is there no peace to be found in this world?'

'I must send some gift for the newborn. What do you think, a rattle, a shawl or cap. No, something special.'

'Don't ask me,' Mary replied, her curiosity sated. The last bit of the letter I did not read out to her:

We look forward to hearing all your news and Captain Thane has promised to deliver it in person to us from your hand.

What could I send with him . . . ? And then I remembered the tiny moccasin shoes worn by White Deer's baby, lined with soft fur for winter. They were little slippers decorated with beads and embroidery. I knew Sabine would appreciate the fine workmanship. I would make a trip to the camp and barter for them. Of Thane's return I made no mention. 'Sufficient unto the day . . .' I quoted from the Bible under my breath. Yet I could not help my heart leaping at the thought of meeting with him again, even if it would have to be our last.

32

I did not have long to wait before Jordan Thane found me scurrying along the town track to Good Hope with a basket of fresh pies for some old Friends in need of support.

'Joy,' he called, stepping out from the copse and making me jump. 'Why have you been avoiding me?' It was a hot afternoon and he wore only a shirt and breeches, not his redcoat jacket.

'I must go,' I replied, hurrying on. 'I can't be seen talking to a soldier.'

'Is that all I am now, a redcoat?'

'Of course not, but Friends are suspicious if the likes of me are seen consorting with a worldly man.' I was too flustered to look him in the eye. 'Thanks for delivering the letter. I am so pleased for the Boyers.'

'I was hoping you would send word to me through them.' He was not to be put off by my sharp answers.

'How could I when the river was frozen?'

'There are other ways to send packages.'

That was the point at which I stopped stock still and faced him head on. 'I can't walk with you. I am no longer free. I have pledged myself to another Friend. It would not be seemly.'

'Not the preacher, Wrathall?' He saw the look on my face.

'Oh, I see ...' The silence between us grew painful and I picked up my pace to flee from him but he caught my hand to halt me.

'That is your choice but that's not why I am here, at least not the only reason,' he answered hesitant. 'You have to persuade them to take up arms should there be a raid. Have they no idea what danger you may be exposed to? I wanted to give you this.' Jordan darted back from where he had met me and brought out a package, pressing it into my hand.

'What's this?' The parcel wrapped in cloth felt hard and metallic.

'It's a pistol, the smallest I could find for your defence should you need it. You must aim and shoot straight. I can show you how to load it and charge it.'

Suddenly it felt white hot in my hand. 'I can't accept this.'

'You must, for the children if not for yourself. Did we go to all that trouble to save George's life only to see him scalped or worse for want of a firearm? Think about it. If the Emsworths won't defend their family that is for them to decide but to let innocent children suffer ... that is diabolical.'

I could see the flinty determination in his eye as he put the gun into my palm. 'Take it, Joy. Pray God you'll never have to use it but I will sleep easier knowing you will be the safer for having it.'

It was in that look of concern that I knew this man loved me and cared what happened to me and mine. It was all I could do not to fling my arms around him in gratitude but I held back at first, all my resolve weakening.

'You will have to show me how to use it,' I whispered.

'Gladly, but it must be tonight. We leave soon. I will call at the farm on some pretext; excuse yourself after I have gone and meet me at the lane end.' He clicked his heels in salute and sauntered ahead of me, leaving me to hold this dreadful weapon in my hand.

It was only as I made my own way that I heard a rustling in the leaves, thinking he had darted back, but there was Tamar standing behind a great oak tree staring at me with a look that chilled. Had she heard and seen everything that had passed between us? Did she know what was hiding in the basket among the mutton pies?

'How fares thee, Friend Tamar?' I smiled, all sweetness and light, pretending that I was not shaking with fear. The woman said nothing as usual but her eyes went to the basket. Had she seen the exchange, heard our conversation? She raised her eyebrows, but I couldn't read her silence. Then her smile made me shiver as her lips curled into a sneer. She held out her hand, looking to the basket, so I opened the linen cloth and gave her one of the pies, thinking to satisfy her need. She pushed my hand away, trying to thrust hers into the basket but I shook it away hard.

'Nay, nay, Friend . . . not for you. Go away!' and I turned and ran, hearing a strange calling noise in my ears. So Tamar was not dumb as we all thought but biding her time. A chilling fear all but froze me to the spot, creeping like ice over the river. How much had she really seen and how long would she keep silent?

That night I sat down to compose a brief letter to Sabine.

. . . *The Captain will call to collect this as they leave tomorrow back to their quarters in the city. Their presence has caused much concern. He fears for our safety but we are assured from the local natives that what threats there be are not for us but for them.*

> *I have some news of my own regarding Jacob Wrathall and myself. We hope to be joined in matrimony as soon as I am free to do so and with the Friends' permission.*
>
> *We hope to acquire all the land due to us and build a farmstead as close to Good Hope so he can continue in his educational work among the Lenape children. I shall be his assistant in all of this. Wish us well in our new venture.*
>
> *We rejoice in your safe delivery and hope to visit with you on our next river trip down to the market. I long to see Marianne for myself and Liddy is making a little dolly to give to her . . .*

I rushed home after visiting the sick women with our pies, hiding the little pistol carefully under a pile of stones by the kale patch. It could not be concealed within the house in my wooden chest alongside the gloves and certificates and indenture papers. Liddy was too curious a child, rooting round my few possessions in case I had ribbons for her. It was also better to forewarn Mary of the Captain's return. I tried to make light of it. 'They leave tomorrow, so I hear, so no more redcoats to disturb our peace.'

'Too right,' Mary said, her arms deep in the flour trough. 'I suppose we can spare him a bit of pie, seeing as how kind he was to George. Shall you ask Jacob to join us in fellowship?'

'Not tonight, we don't want more arguments. The elders have discussed and asked everyone's opinion. The decision is made. Better to leave things unsaid.' I didn't want Jacob as my chaperone. I wanted Jordan to myself.

How I longed to pin up my hair without the stiff linen cap I must wear to conceal its glory. I must appear indifferent to his visit and not show how confused I felt when in his presence. The hands of the precious timepiece that hung on the wall seemed to creep so slowly towards dusk. Joseph and the boys came in from the fields dusty and sweaty. Liddy was fast asleep in the truckle bed in the alcove that served now as the Emsworths' private chamber. The boys slept aloft up a ladder. I must wait until all were abed before lying on the mattress behind a curtain that was my only hiding place.

'I saw Friend Tamar on the road. She acted most strange and I heard her calling out. Her voice must be loosening,' I said, trying not to make it sound like gossip. Someone had to know what I had witnessed.

'Poor lass has suffered much. They say her wits are addled. She's not been the same since you and Jacob declared your intentions. I reckon she has grown sweet on him.'

This was all news to me but it would explain why she was so cold around me.

We were at evening prayer when Jordan called, standing hat in hand in silence as Joseph led us in silent worship. Then Mary pointed him to the table.

'Sit thee down, lad, and share some pie and ale with us.'

I found my hands shaking at the nearness of him across the board. We made polite conversation about the harvest, the continuing warm weather, new settlers into the township, skirting round any mention of the recent militia training or Indian raids.

I spoke not a word but dutifully cleared away the best pewter dishes and wooden trenchers, trying not to catch his eye.

He looked at the clock on the wall and made to leave, having slipped pennies into the hand of Sam and George, leaving one for Liddy. I held back until I knew he would be down the track and then jumped up. 'Would you believe it, he's gone without my letter, the very thing he came for.' This had to be a deliberate ploy and worked as planned.

I chased after him, stopping only to pick up the firearm on the way. 'Wait, Captain Thane,' I shouted. 'The letter!'

'Aye, the letter,' he laughed. 'Did you bring the other . . . ?'

I nodded. 'This must take only a few minutes before I am missed, so show me how to charge it.'

He showed me how it worked, how to load the lead balls and charge of gunpowder into the barrel. 'Just unscrew the barrel, place the shot and powder and then screw it back and charge up the flintlock. This has two barrels for two shots. That's all the time you will have. Be careful with the powder and keep the whole thing dry and clean. I have some shot here for you to practice on a target.'

'This is too much to take in. How can I keep it safe outside?'

'Then make a hiding place, put it in a box and bury it in the wood wrapped and dry, but hide it under your skirt in a secret pocket if you feel uneasy. Let's just hope the situation never demands it.'

'You're so kind. I don't deserve it. It must have cost a lot to find such a one as this. How can I return the favour?'

'You know what I want from you but that, you say, can't be given now.'

'Would that I could, Jordan Thane, but I made my decision to stay within the fellowship.'

'Do you love this Jacob?'

'It will grow as we grow together in faith.'

'That's no answer.' He held out his hand to me. 'Think again, dearest Joy. Don't give your life away to please others. Think for yourself. Life is too short to waste.'

Why did men not of our faith think this way? I remembered having this very argument with Miles Foxup all those years ago. I had walked away from him just as I must walk away from Captain Thane. 'You will never understand what I owe these people.'

'You owe them nothing but the service you signed up for, a duty to serve out your time with honour. Then you are free to take up your due.'

'Without Jacob and Ellinor I wouldn't be standing here now. I owe them this new life.'

'You are not Ellinor, God rest her soul. You are yourself to do with as you please.'

'Those may be the words of someone who is not a Friend of Truth, nor a seeker of enlightenment.'

'Maybe so, but it is my thinking, and am I not allowed an opinion of my own, or have we all to think as one on every matter?' he challenged me.

'Oh don't you be confusing me with fine arguments. I must go.'

'Not before you grant me one wish, Miss Moorside.'

'What wish is that?'

He pulled me into his arms and kissed me hard. I did not struggle, but drank in his lips.

'Joy, where are you, girl?' I could hear Mary calling me from the house. It was with reluctance that I withdrew from his arms.

'Coming, Mary, just tidying away,' I lied. 'Go, please and may God find you happiness in life and keep you safe,' I whispered, choked with such feelings of regret as our hands parted.

Jordan turned and smiled. 'Never forget. You are for me.' And then he disappeared into the night, but I could hear him whistling as he went.

I crept back to the door trying not to cry, knowing I would have to explain my tardiness, ducking down to shove the pistol and charger back under the stones.

'What on earth are thee up to at this time of night? Not with that man, I hope?' Mary stood arms folded as I hurried past.

'I went to check the chicken pen was secure. We don't want to lose any more birds. Never miss the opportunity to be watchful, the preacher said.'

'Against unbelievers and worldly temptations, not fowls of the air.' Mary laughed. 'What a funny girl you are and no mistake.'

That night I lay in the darkness with the taste of Jordan's lips, salty and tobacco-fumed, wanting to relive every moment of our embrace. There would be no nights of sorrow with him by my side, but the price was too high to pay. I had neither the courage nor the will to break from all that I knew. To accept his loving was to betray all that my martyred parents had died for. How could I do that to them?

33

My pen has travelled far and fast in this account but now I must recall a time which is still painful for me to share. Some might say it was my own disobedience which snared me in a trap born of carelessness, but I know otherwise. It was a time of trial such that, in the course of a long life, many have to endure in some form or other.

It began one morning in late Fall after the Governor's warning of incursions by rebellious Indian tribes which we had no reason to heed, being among peaceful people. I visited White Deer to purchase pretty baby slippers for Marianne, travelling often along portage trails with no fear of danger. This gave me time to practise with the pistol, now concealed within the hollow of an old pine tree stump, out of sight of prying fingers.

There was no proof that Tamar had seen it in my basket or given notice to Jacob or Titus. She could have written a letter condemning me but no censure was given at the next meeting.

We were a motley band of forest harvesters who set out that autumn morning to pick berries, nuts and mushrooms to dry for the winter store cupboard. Mary and Liddy joined me and somehow we drifted deeper into the trees than we had done

before. Liddy kicked leaves that crackled dusty and dry underfoot. Then she skipped ahead chasing birds.

I always took the precaution of marking trees with a cross
to be sure of finding our route back should we go astray. As
I looked back I saw the familiar tall figure of Tamar following behind us with her own basket and my first feeling was
of annoyance at her unwelcome presence. Her silence always
unsettled me. Why did she choose not to speak? Was it a game
she was playing?

Mary beckoned her to join us, pointing to a tree which was
laden with nuts. 'Better shake them down afore the squirrels
do.'

Tamar smiled and glided in our direction. Then we all split
into separate thickets, lost in our own thoughts until I noticed
how late it was and the sun had shifted direction, torching a
path through the canopy above. It was then I heard a crackling
of leaves that startled me. Had we disturbed a bear from its
foraging? Was there a snake lying hidden waiting to strike? I
sensed danger and shouted. 'Watch out for Liddy. Call her back
at once.'

Mary yelled for her child but she didn't come. 'This is no
time for laikin about. There's a bear on the loose. Come here
at once!' Still there was no sight of her. 'Mercy on us, has she
gone astray and can't hear us?'

I could hear the panic in Mary's voice as she dropped her
basket and started to search.

'Better you stay put in case she comes. Tamar can come
with me and watch my back.' This she did, sensing our fear. I
reckoned we were a mile or two from the nearest farm that I
knew of. 'Lydia!' I called. 'Where're you hiding?' I heard a muffled cry and darted towards the sound with Tamar following.
There was a clearing and an eerie silence at first but I sensed

movement and a presence. 'Liddy, come here.' Don't hide from us. This is not a game.'

Out of the bushes stepped a fierce native of great height covered in face paint and carrying the terrified child who was wriggling to get down.

'Oh there you are, child,' I smiled. 'Thank you for finding her. Come here to Joy.' I thought he had rescued her from some dangerous beast.

'Howdy'do,' he said in a gruff voice, his eyes glinting like a hawk's. 'Come, me.'

'No, give us the child, she's frightened.' I replied. In response he pulled his tomahawk from his belt and raised it above her head to split her skull.

'*Mata*! Oh, please, no!' I cried knowing there was nothing of value to give him for her release. 'Tamar, can we spring him and free her?' I muttered under my breath. She shook her head.

'You come me.' I knew that he wanted all of us or he would kill the girl.

'Me come, girl, no come.' I hoped he understood this bargain. 'Please.'

Suddenly he was not alone as out of the bushes where they lay silent came four more of his men. They were waiting for his word to pounce on us. Now my wits were razor sharpened by fear. There was no going back. Tamar began to shake. 'Don't show your fear. We will pretend to go with them but Liddy must be set free.'

I sat down on the ground and pulled Tamar down beside me, showing we were being obedient. I opened my arms. 'Give girl,' I pleaded and I prayed to our Saviour to give me the courage to stay calm and find a way out of this predicament.

The very act of sitting made them relax and Liddy was let

down, running into my arms and clinging to me for the protection I could no longer give.

'What do we do now?' I turned to Tamar as a last resort, not
expecting any answer but to my astonishment she whispered
back. 'Pray out loud. Bow thy head in submission.'

We placed our hands together in prayer and began to recite
familiar words of comfort. Liddy followed us as if it was a game.
Pretending that I was still praying, I whispered in her ear. 'When
I tell you, you must run. Run back to Mother. Tell her there's a
firearm in the hollow of the pine stump, third from the gate, run
like the wind and stay low. Go back the way you came.'

'You come too?' she pleaded. 'Not yet. I will come back to
you.' I could not risk her being put into captivity. We heard
stories of little fair-haired girls put into camps to be brides or
sold to slavers. How had we stepped into this nightmare? How
could we have woken up this morning in freedom and now be
at the mercy of savages?

They were curious and closed in on us, tearing off our caps,
pulling down our hair and touching our locks, laughing as they
raised their tomahawks as if to scalp us. Liddy buried her head
in my lap as we waited for the blows to fall. I gave myself to the
mercy of the Almighty, asking for a swift end to this suffering.

Then strong arms dragged us upright and a leather cord
bound us to each other as helpless prisoners. Such was the fear
that my bladder lost its grip and hot piss trickled down my legs.

It was then that anger fuelled my limbs and I could not stay
silent. '*Saa Saa,*' I said as I stood before the chief warrior in all
his black and red face-painted glory. 'Shame on you to take
child. Only coward take little child. Brave warrior let child
go. Show the Great Spirit that child can live.' I prayed he had
enough English to get my meaning. 'Lenape no hit child.
Lenape love children.'

'No Lenni-Lenape.' He spat on the ground. 'Susquehanna.'

'You must not anger Great Spirit. *Saa. Saa!*'

The other braves were listening and watching. 'We will come with you and be your slaves but child go back.' Not once did I flinch from his hard gaze but held my ground, tied as I was. For a moment nothing happened but then he took his knife and cut Liddy's wrist bindings, pushing her away from us.

'Run, Liddy, run home and God go with thee. *Wanishi. Thank you.* Thank you.' My legs buckled with relief. Tamar managed to touch my hand in support as we walked along in silence. Onwards down a trail we walked for hours until my legs ached and my tongue was parched with thirst.

Had Liddy found her way home? Were there raiders already in Good Hope or lurking in the forest ready to attack isolated farms? Our capture would give warning to others of danger if nothing else. How relieved I was not to be alone, even if my fellow prisoner was a woman I hardly knew and didn't much care for. There would be plenty of time to talk when we were permitted to rest.

Why had he relented and let her go? Had my few words of their language earned some respect? I no longer felt the risk of death to be nigh. They could have scalped us in the forest; but perhaps they thought there was not much honour in killing a feeble white woman. Reason told me we would be more useful alive as slaves, wives or as bait for ransom.

With each mile we were leaving all we knew and loved behind to a fate unknown as yet. I tried not to stumble and quake at what would befall us, trusting we were in the hands of higher powers. It was Tamar who lifted my flagging spirit by quoting a psalm under her breath: '*Hide not thy face from me in the day when I am in trouble, incline thine ear unto me . . . in the day when I call answer me speedily.*'

How far we walked into the night I have no recollection, but by the direction of the moss on the trees we must be travelling northwards. I had blisters on my heels and slipped off my shoes for comfort but that was a mistake for the pine needles and sharp stones and stinging insects pinched me. Tamar stumbled, crying out as we jerked each other. I pushed her on. 'To stop is to invite punishment. Stay strong. They will halt for the night soon,' I promised.

To our relief we reached clear water and a fire was lit to scare away scavengers. All I wanted to do was lie down but being tied to each other it was not easy. Pieces of dried meat were thrust into our mouths to chew on. My thirst was raging and I begged '*Mpi, mpi* . . . water.'

'Go,' the chief said, pointing to the lakeside. I thought at first they were going to drown us but then it dawned on me we were their amusement and must lap the water like dogs. Struggling and shuffling we edged ourselves down, our hands still tied, and took it in turns to lap the cool water with our tongues while the men roared with laughter.

I did not care what they thought, knowing only the relief of gulping in fresh water. No point in showing my contempt for their cruelty. These men only responded to strength. We sat together as best we could, our dresses soaked. 'Try to rest,' I whispered to Tamar. She smiled back and rolled her eyes. We must distract each other from this present condition. 'Why did you never speak to us?'

It was dark and she could speak into the night without looking at me. 'I had nothing to say that anyone would care to hear. Mr Black had enough words for the two of us. How could I tell my true story without him contradicting every word.'

'What do you mean?' Now I was curious. What would she say next?

'My husband farmed near Bridlington and was much taken with news of settlements in Delaware. I came aboard with Erasmus and our daughter, Faith, to start this new life. The ship was overcrowded and my husband fell ill with the fever and died midway, one of many. It was a ship of doom from the moment we set sail. Mr Black and his sister befriended us, being much taken with Faith. There was something about the woman I did not trust as she was often in drink.'

'That would be Dora. I knew them both.'

'You did?'

'Yes,' I said. 'I'll tell you after. Carry on.'

'I think Black believed me to be not without means to secure land and property. Who told him that I'll never know, but he went out of his way to make sure we were kept apart from any disease and given the best provisions. This annoyed his sister and they argued loud and hard until one of the elders took them aside. They were no example to others on the ship.

'No sooner had we sighted land than a storm blew up and the ship was driven onto rocks and foundered. There was no time to do anything but scramble over board.' Tamar hesitated. 'I never saw Faith again. It was Black who pulled me out of danger and guided me to the floating wreckage that saved us. I thought Faith was with me but she must have slipped away. I called until I was hoarse. There were heads bobbing in the water, voices crying to God for rescue and I saw Black's sister clinging to a plank and calling, "Titus! Titus!"'

Much as I despised Dora Cranke I would not have wished such a pitiful end as this. 'She did not reach safety then?'

Tamar was weeping quietly. 'I will never know. Sometimes I think I must have imagined what happened, but in my dreams I see Thomas pushing her away. He had her hand, and then he cast her off , saying she would drown us all. But my remembrance is clouded. I know I was crying for Faith. So many died for the want of a helping hand. Somehow we were rescued by fishermen, shivering half mad with grief and thirst. I don't recall much after that but Thomas sitting by my side with strangers, saying to them, "This is my sister, Tamar Black", and I was too confused to say otherwise. The words stuck like pebbles in my throat. I was afeared that if what I thought I had seen was real and I spoke out, he would find a way to silence me too. I am so ashamed to have acted like a half-wit, but I was terrified, as I am now.

'All my belongings were lost at sea. Everything I held dear was gone and I knew I needed protection. Thomas still seemed at first to have some regard for me. "You will be my new sister in Christ," he said. He must have known by then I had no wealth to offer; just the clothes I stood up in. The Friends who helped to feed and clothe us wanted us to join their township but Thomas was eager to move on. News came that a few more survivors had been rescued lower down the coast. I prayed Faith would be among them, and would have stayed behind to wait for her, but then I heard there were no children saved. That was a bitter blow.'

Tamar sank back in her distress, pulling me down with her. I could hear her ragged breathing as I fell across her chest.

'What a brave heart you must have to suffer so in silence.' I felt for her sadness.

'What do we do now?' she asked me when she was calmer. 'I can see no means to escape.'

'Perhaps not yet. There are too many of them. But we will not be defeated by ignorant men. We have not endured all we have to live in peace with our neighbours to end up in the roasting pot.'

'Lord have mercy, they eat human flesh?' Tamar cried in horror.

'That will not be our fate. Take heart and trust in Providence that we'll make our way home.' What else could I say to her? We would need all our strength and hope if we were to continue on this trail of tears.

34

We crossed the lake in a birch-bark canoe which was hidden by
the shore. We passed bushes, stuffing cranberries in our mouths
using our loosened hands to tease them out. Another day's
walking followed. My feet were bleeding, my belly pinched
with hunger but I refused to beg from these savages. I took note
of every signpost of trees and trail in case we could escape but
it was a forlorn hope.

As we approached their camp, the men let out whoops and
yells to herald they had prisoners to view. We were surrounded
by women and children fingering our skirts and pinching our
skin, pulling off our collars and caps and fighting over them.
It was then I knew real fear for the women seemed more fierce
than their men.

The camp bore no resemblance to the tidy clean dwellings of
White Deer and her kin but was a temporary huddle of makeshift, skin-covered tents which were easy to take down when
they moved on. Out of one such, two white faces appeared,
a man and a younger boy with ginger hair who stared at us
with eyes wide with fear. In heavily accented English the older
man – a Dutchman by birth, whose name was Wim – warned
us of what was to come.

'They have a game to welcome us, a custom none of us can avoid. When they line up opposite each other you must run between them from start to finish. If you stumble or stop you may not rise again. Watch for the squaws with staves.'

'But who are these people?' Tamar asked.

'Rogues, scavengers the lot of them. They will sell us on to other tribes for a good price. Do not try to escape or they will kill us all in revenge. Watch for the big fellow, he's a very devil in cruelty and shows no mercy to the weak.'

We stood together, sharing our names and stories. It was good not to be alone but then as Wim had warned, the whole camp gathered clutching stones and sticks, laughing and chanting, their eyes on us, waiting for their game to begin.

The chief turned and spoke through an interpreter. 'The spirits of our dead warriors cry out for vengeance against their killers. Now we must show their anger at you, white face murderers who steal our land.'

I made to protest but Wim stopped me with his hand. This ordeal must be faced if we were to survive. First the lad, Jan, made his dash between the lines; young and nimble, he dodged and darted, bending low, avoiding most of the blows until he reached the end of the race track.

Seeing what was to come Tamar began to weep. 'I can't do this.'

'Yes, you can. God will guide thy step,' Wim encouraged her as he began his own trial. He was slower than the boy and the blows rained down on his back and head until he stumbled and was beaten but he struggled to his feet, blood streaming down his face as he crawled across the line.

I pulled Tamar to the start but she drew back, shaking her head. 'I can't . . . You go and leave me.'

'Just do it! Bunch up thy skirts and run like the wind, set

your feet on fire and show no fear. They will not defeat us.' The poor lass did her best but being tall she was an easy target and the squaws took delight in hitting her hard until she could only crawl. How she got to the finish line I will never know but then it was my turn and I was fuelled by such fury at this cruel treatment of exhausted captives. I fixed my eye on a post at the far end and forgot my bleeding feet. I thought of Jordan Thane and Sabine, Mary and the children of Good Hope. I was not ready to be murdered for their sport. I hitched up my own skirts and ran as never before, chest out, eyes on the finishing line. Sticks came down but I did not feel them. Never in my life had I been so swift or determined and to my astonishment I cheated them of much sport with only bruises to show for this ordeal.

We were shoved together in a tent, guarded by young braves, given water and some corn stew to eat. The boy asked for water to wash our wounds but none came. We lay down as best we could, tied to each other by the neck at first, too exhausted to talk. I was relieved to be away from those dark curious hawk eyes. We stank with bodily waste, sweat and fear, a ragged bunch of captives whose fate was unknown. I knew the women would want our skirts and shirts. To relieve ourselves we pissed where we sat but we were not defeated.

Tamar led us in the Lord's prayer and then we shared our stories together and talked about those we had left behind. Were they out in the forest searching for us? Did Liddy reach her mother in safety?

Jan and Wim were carpenters, ambushed on a trail further north, their horses stolen, and then passed on to work as slaves. This cruel welcome ritual was a trial of strength to test our fitness to work. They would not feed us for long without expecting us to earn our keep.

In those first days of captivity no one showed us any kindness until a young brave entered our tent bringing a bowl of nuts and berries. We counted them carefully and divided them into four portions, picking at them as if they were some rare delicacy, savouring each moist mouthful on our parched tongues.

'We have to get out of here,' Tamar said under her breath .

'We must bide our time,' Wim cautioned. 'It is too soon. They will wait for us to try and then there will be another game.'

'What's that?' I asked.

'They will make a cage or tie each of us to a pole. They set the stakes alight and prod the poor victim with burning torches. I saw it once, or what remained of the man who suffered this torture.'

The rest of us fell silent at his words.

I kept track of the days since we were taken by gathering little sticks: three for the trail to the lake and seven since. The nights were chilly and we huddled in flea-bitten skins waiting for our fate to be decided by the chieftain who was out fighting. His council would make tobacco offerings to their spirit guides. Our fate lay in their hands. Until then we were penned up like stray dogs in a pound, beginning to scratch at each other's fears.

When you struggle to find a straight place to sleep tied by feet and neck there is plenty of time to go over the life that once was and the existence endured now. When I thought of Good Hope I gave no mind to Jacob but to Tamar's chilling account of Titus's threats. Why could he not be scalped instead of us? He must be exposed for the charlatan he was. Then I tried to remember everything I had learned from White Deer about their customs and skills. How different was her tribe to this bunch of renegade scalp-lockers. What did I know that might help us survive, other than not to show weakness or fear?

We had only our bodies to offer, nothing of material value to please their eye, not even a wedding ring or trinket. To be at the mercy of such as these filled me with foreboding. Surely they would not burn women and boys?

But we burned them if they were found guilty of witchcraft. This most cruel of deaths was not exclusive to savages. It was even there in our Scriptures. '*Suffer not a witch to live.*'

How I wished I had taken Jordan Thane's advice and hidden the pistol on my person. There it was stuck down a tree trunk, of no use to anyone unless little Liddy had told her mother where to find it.

How I wished to have the faith and fortitude of my parents in their captivity. Fear made liquid of my bowels but I was not alone in that. Whatever plan we made to escape, we would have to be all together and it had to succeed or the punishment would be unbearable.

In the weeks that followed I watched the tribe preparing for winter. The men constructed a bark-clad hut, bringing fresh skins to line the inside. When the snows came there would be no chance for us to make a run for freedom. Footprints in the snow would soon be tracked.

As I suspected, our English garments were taken, replaced by greasy skin tunics fringed at the edges, well-worn leggings and fur-lined leather boots to cover our feet. At least that was a good sign. We had a clay pot between us and some old sacks of corn meal, pots of bear grease and some strips of dried meat; but that we were four extra mouths to feed worried me. They would want to get rid of us one way or another, a sale or slaughter, perhaps? I thought it wise to hide my fears from the others, suggesting instead we make plans to escape ere long.

'How can we run with ropes round our necks and braves guarding our door,' Tamar cried. It was Wim who voiced the best idea. 'It will soon be their special feast with much drinking.'

'But they always leave two or three sober so as not to be caught unawares.' That was something we had observed.

'They think we are safe enough so we can ask for liquor for ourselves to honour the coming of their chief and pray our guards are greedy enough to drink our measure. When they sleep then is our chance.'

'But we have nothing to cut ourselves free.'

'I've thought of that. If they give us a little fire, allow us to get close enough to it, one of us might burn his bonds and then release the others.'

Our spirits rose at the thought of such a possibility, though I knew we needed many things to be stacked in our favour. The return of the warrior chief was one of them.

He arrived on his horse with a band of painted warriors who carried many dried scalps of their victims on their bandoleers. The colours of the hair were both black and fair. My eyes could not see them without wanting to weep but we stood in line for inspection and I refused to bow my head in submission. We were paraded before him like animals in the cattle market. The man was handsome and muscular with a proud stance but his eyes were cold as he spoke to us in broken English.

'You white faces are thieves, you steal our fishing, hunt our deer, cut down sacred trees. You come among us and smoke pipe of welcome but your tribe is full of bad spirits, build big forts and turn big guns on our people. There is no friendship with you. When all of you are put into the earth then we will roam free over the lands of our ancestors.'

No one spoke but hung their heads at this accusation. Yet I felt moved to defend us and stepped forward as best I could to make my plea.

'I have met with Lenni-Lenape in great friendship. They say that land belongs only to Great Spirit and no tribe white or red. It is the Great Spirit who decides who lives and who dies. We are all pebbles on the sea shore, small but many. This land is large. There must be room for all without taking those things from women and children.' I pointed to the scalps. 'We have done you no harm.' I stepped back, keeping my eyes upon him.

'You speak mighty big words for small squaw. There is eagle spirit in you. If you work, you live. We fetch good price for young white face boy and white face woman make wife for warrior.' His eyes roamed over me with interest and I sensed danger in them for me. 'We speak again, Eagle woman.'

This was my chance. 'Let us share in your feasting, sir?' I asked. There was no reply but I sensed a shift towards us. That evening we were brought better food and drink. Perhaps the plan might work after all.

Two nights later the feasting began in earnest as the venison roasted on the spitfires, drums beat over the camp and the dancers thundered around the sparking fire. We sat in our usual tent hoping for a fire to warm us but none was given close enough for us to use.

'What can we do now?' Tamar cried with frustration.

'Pray for a miracle,' I snapped, being just as disappointed as she was.

The chanting and dancing went on all night. Shadowy figures leapt around the firelight in a frenzy as we sat sunk in gloom.

Then our guards rolled back staggering and laughing. 'Dance, whiteface.' They pulled up Jan, trying to making him join in, tied as he was to us. He hung back but Wim whispered. 'Just do it, boy.'

As they fooled around, their belts jangling, something fell onto the earth floor, something shiny and sharp in the darkness. It was the warrior's knife. Quick as a flash Tamar pulled it with her foot and hid it under her tunic, shuffling out of view.

Holding our breath, we knew it had gone unnoticed. The dance went on and the guards drank their fill and soon were snoring fast and hard.

Leaning forward Wim grasped the knife with his foot and somehow got it into his hands, loosening his legs from the thongs and doing each of us in turn. The neck ties we did for each other. Now came the most dangerous time. Were the dogs alert to our movement and were other braves on guard close by?

In the past weeks we were allowed to exercise our limbs around the clearing and recognised the direction from which we had entered but to creep away under cover of darkness unheard would be a miracle of grace.

Slowly we opened the tent and crawled on our bellies, the last of us trying to scuff away traces of our exit. The earth was damp and I felt soil in my mouth as we edged ever slowly towards the forest, hardly daring to breathe.

Once out in the wilderness we would be easily tracked down but we had a head start enough to scatter into the trail. We had no provisions, just one knife between us but our Indian clothing was enough to protect us from the worst of the elements.

Those last agonising yards to freedom exhausted us. Luck was on our side if we stuck together for protection.

Without light the path through the dark canopy was treacherous. We knew not what lurked to attack us but as first light rose from the east, Tamar and I headed in the direction of the lake that divided us from the trail home. Jan and Wim wanted to head north.

'Come with us,' I begged. 'We will see you are returned. Divided we may fail,' I said, sensing I was now in charge. Wim was breathless with the speed of our walking. Jan scouted about for something we might cook, for hunger was making us dizzy.

At night we sought safety in trees out of the way of night prowlers. When it rained we gathered precious puddles of water in our leathers and sucked the liquid into our parched lips. With the rain the leaves lost their crackle and silenced our footsteps on the forest floor.

The afternoon when Jan snared a rabbit, he wanted to eat it raw but Wim showed us how to raise fire with tinder and sticks.

'Smoke will give us away,' I cautioned.

'Wait until dark then,' was his answer. All day I thought of the warmth of a fire and meat juices. It would be the most delicious meal of my life but the carcass was lean and gave up little flesh. I skinned the fur, knowing it might give comfort to blistered feet. Wim was finding walking painful. He had never recovered from his beating.

We scavenged what we could from shrubs until our stomachs heaved at the sight of crushed acorns. Our guts were loose and limbs weakened from the scouring but we pushed ever forward, following the sun, trusting we might find the lake.

'They will know we will head for the water,' Tamar pointed out. 'What if they go straight there?'

'Then we will skirt round the sides. If it is a lake we can walk round it. I have no skill to swim.' It was with relief we saw a glimpse of water shimmering in the distance from the steep slopes of a bank. We left the trail and turned east to creep under cover of foliage, wading through the marshy edges, pushing our way through scratchy undergrowth.

'We're losing time this way,' Tamar complained, being tired, hungry and frightened at the thought of recapture.

'Better than walking straight into a trap,' I countered.

'What if it's not a lake but a wide river?' she continued to moan and I wanted to throttle her doubting spirit.

'Then we'll walk down it until we come out at the sea or it joins another. If we come to the De La Warr we are almost home.' It was like trying to cajole a child.

'How can you be so cheerful? I see only danger lurking behind every rock.'

It was Jan who tried to chivvy her along. 'There'll be fish in the river. My cousin taught me how to tickle trout. I can find eels and we won't starve.'

He was right; with water alongside us we would not starve, I thought, feeling hope surging through me.

Jan was giddy with his idea and dashed off to try his luck. That first meal of roasted fish we saved until darkness covered our little camp. The spare fish we gutted to carry for later. Then disaster struck when Jan was playing the fool waving the knife in the air. He toppled backwards, slipping on a stone, and lost his grip. Our precious knife spun into the air and disappeared into the deep.

'Now look what you've done!' I yelled. It was like losing a friend and the one piece of security we owned.

Wim pulled the sodden boy out of the water shaking his head. 'We carry staves from now on,' he sighed. 'Better than naught.'

'But how are we to cut them with no axe?' I cried with frustration.

Wim was not daunted by this difficulty. 'Find a branch and hang until you snap it off or hit it with a sharp stone like our ancestors did. Everything we need to survive is here, if you know how to find it: shelter, food. There's still fire to warm us.'

The nights were so cold, the wind cutting through our clothing so we clung together under a shelter of woven branches covered with anything we could find. Wim's cough was getting worse and I found willow bark to boil in a broken clay pot we found by the lakeside. It helped him rest but his colour was grey and I feared he must slow us down.

The worst thing was knowing we had no idea where we were when the clouds were heavy, hiding the sun and the north star at night. Jan was silent and full of shame at losing the knife but all of us were afraid of losing our Dutch friend. Tamar sat with him and searched for anything we could boil, leaves, grasses, anything to fill our bellies with fodder. I had lost count of the days since our escape and with it the chance to work out how far we were from known territory.

Next morning we walked to the head of the lake and saw a stream. 'Follow the stream,' I called out with relief. By the weak sun I knew we were heading east and south. Such was our raging hunger we snapped and complained each step of the way. There were few fish to ensnare and our little store had been quickly used. Jan took to throwing stones at birds and we roasted them, eating bones and all.

Wim wasn't hungry, being in a fever, but we couldn't let him lie down and give up the ghost. We were the four escapees; without his wisdom and kindness, how could we have ever left captivity? 'You go ahead,' he croaked. 'I am finished.'

'No,' I insisted. 'We all go together or not at all.'

The others agreed, taking it in turns to sit with him. Jan found enough strong branches to weave into a sled tied together with the rope-like forest vines and we dragged him along as best we could.

My heart was heavy knowing Wim was not going to finish this journey with us. He slept and his breathing was laboured.

That night we made a fire as he taught us and sat round watching for the slightest change in his breathing. He was rambling now in his own language as Jan held his hand. I noticed his feet were like ice and knew death would call him home soon.

'Ya. Ya, I will tell them.' Jan nodded as if hearing some last request.

Tamar sat with her head in her hands. 'What will become of us now?'

'We go on as we have done until we find help.'

'But there's snow on the wind. We'll freeze in this rocky dungeon.'

'If it be the Lord's will, then so be it. Better to die in the attempt than to be spit-roasted on some savage's fire.' I was cruel to be kind. My fear was as great as hers but I was determined not to show it.

35

We buried Wim as best we could between two rocks and covered him with stones. Jan wept and needed comforting, being just a young lad who had suffered much in his short life. The wind turned icy now and we were glad of Wim's skins to share out but I felt real fear for us. Our bellies were empty and our minds began to wander from keeping eyes on the rocks in case we fell. My flesh hung loose, my tongue was parched and foul tasting but I kept them walking. When the first snowflakes began to fall I knew we must build shelter or perish. 'Look for a hollowed-out tree. We can creep into it and hide.'

'But bears live in trees,' Jan warned. 'Keep going.'

'I can't go another step,' Tamar cried. 'There is no more hope for us. We're lost and here will we die. There is no way out.'

'Shut up! If we follow the stream it will lead us out. In the Dales streams lead to becks and then to rivers. There may be caves to hide in among the rocks. Don't give in now. Look how far we've come,' I pleaded with her.

'With only a dead man to show for all our effort, better to

have stayed safe in the camp, warm and fed. Why did we listen to you?' Tamar was trying my patience to the limit.

'That's hunger talking. Where's thy faith, woman? There has to be a way.'

That night it snowed hard as we clung together in the lee of a larger boulder. My spirits sank with despair and Jan cried with the cold. Had I led them to die in this barren spot? The snow was gentle but treacherous for it froze with a crust on the top. How could we find a path and why must I now make decisions for all of us?

I tried to imagine Jordan leading his men. They would look to him to keep them safe and encourage them forward into danger. How I longed to see his face again. That night he came to me in a dream. 'You are for me,' he shouted and I woke with tears frozen to my face. I was not going to lie in the snow and give in to the sleep of death.

As if to lighten our path next morning there was a quick thaw. Jan found a dead fish but we were too hungry to make a fire and ate it raw with green leaves and the last rotting berries we could spy. It was a race against the seasons now for should the storms come from the north, there would be no hope of us living through them.

Suddenly the stream widened into another small lake with swampy undergrowth that soaked us up to the waist. If the water had frozen over we could have crossed quickly but it was too early for such good fortune.

'What now?' Jan paused, looking to me. 'We swim?'

'No, we will drown,' said Tamar. 'It is too cold.'

For once she was right. 'We'll walk all around it again like before,' I said.

'Not again, I'm sick of walking and getting nowhere.' Tamar sat down and refused to budge.

'Get up! What else can we do? We still are heading east and south. Perhaps there are trappers or homesteads within a day's march. Sulking will get us nowhere fast.'

'You go then,' she muttered. 'I'm too tired to move.'

'We all go or none of us do. We're missing precious daylight. Don't you want to see thy home again?'

'What home? My husband and child are dead and the man I live with is a charlatan. Who will care if I return or not?'

'Jacob will be worrying about you,' I offered, hoping it would shift her stubborn spirit.

'Friend Jacob is thy intended. It's you he wants, not me.'

'Who knows what that man desires in his wife. Perhaps I am not the right choice for him.'

'But you've got an understanding.' Tamar looked up, suddenly alert.

'Aye, but no vows have been taken, no date fixed, nothing that can't be undone. Besides my mind is not set on matrimony,' I added. 'You would make him a better helpmeet than I.'

I saw her eyes light up with hope at this suggestion. 'Of all the men in Good Hope he has been the kindest to me. Is it possible?'

'All things are possible if it is the Lord's will. Now rise and shift thy arse,' I smiled, knowing I had sewn seeds that might keep her travelling on.

It was a long wearisome journey around the edge of this lake. Then I noticed something about the alignment of the trees and rocks that seemed familiar. When we reached the south side, there was the slope into the water where the men had hidden a canoe. 'Isn't this where we crossed in their boat? I'm sure we're back on the right trail, the one where we lapped the water by the fire. We're almost home,' I cried with excitement.

'How can you be sure?' Jan said. 'There is no canoe.'

'They carried it back on their heads to the camp. If I am right there will be signs of a fire and score marks on the trees as we passed. I lost my shoes somewhere close to here.' I searched around for evidence but there was none.

That was weeks ago. The snow and wind may have moved everything, I thought to myself. Was it too good to be true? My spirits rose with the thought we might only be a few more days from the settlement. 'Let's camp here, catch as much fish as we can and warm ourselves with fire and wash our faces, make ourselves ready. There's little water on the way back so we must drink our fill.'

This discovery spurred us all on into a frenzy of shelter-making and gathering dried tinder for kindling. Jan made a dam of stones to ensnare a fish. Tamar foraged for yet more greens to boil. We sat round our fire with no thought now of danger as dusk fell, finishing off the skin and bones of the little fish with relish. Who knew when we would eat again? The sleep of exhaustion and relief came to us all that night as we huddled together for warmth.

At first light I woke feeling a draught on my left side where Jan slept. Thinking him out fishing, I lay back content but as I peered out from our shelter I could not see him out by the water's edge. 'Jan, Jan Vries?' I called as loudly as I dared but he did not call back. 'Wake up, Tamar, Jan's gone. Something is wrong.' We brushed ourselves down and went in search of him. Had something snatched him in the night? There were no signs of a struggle, no scuff marks or blood to suggest an attack.

'What shall we do now?' Tamar cried, as upset as I was at losing our brave companion.

'We wait in case he's wandered out of earshot. He may have gone into the forest hunting.'

'But what if they have caught him? What if even now they're waiting and watching on us?'

'They would not wait but take us all back together and kill us for escaping.' It was hard to sit and wait all day until the sun slid down behind the hills but there was only silence and the usual sounds of the forest. Frozen with fear and chill, lying in our den like abandoned puppies, unsure of how to make sense of Jan's loss, we waited on.

'Perhaps he decided to make his way north.' Tamar's suggestion, although reasonable, did not ring true. Jan could have left with Wim weeks ago but they chose to stay together with us in a pack. He needed us as much as we needed him. In my heart I knew he had been snatched and made captive again. I couldn't bear to think what might be his fate in the hands of those savages.

Fear and disappointment choked me. We would have to retrace the trail from memory but what if we were being watched? Were they playing a cruel game of hide and seek, snatching us one by one at their leisure?

To be so near and yet far was the worst trial. It took all the courage I could muster to continue without Jan. Hand in hand we left the comfort of our lakeside shelter, searching to find that special narrow trail that had brought us here. Every minute I feared our enemy would leap from the shrubs to silence us forever.

The ground was sodden with no crackle of dry leaves to warn us. We dare not speak for fear of giving ourselves away but crept like forest animals, hiding, alert to every sound.

How long we walked that night I cannot recall but one step at a time we edged away and no one came to take us. Native men knew every inch of this terrain, every nook and cranny while we were strangers unused to fending for ourselves; but the past weeks had changed us from farm hands to forest folk with new respect for this wondrous land with its ridges and valleys. We had known fear, hunger and desolation that many others would never experience. There was a cunning animal manner to our progress, acting like savages, sniffing the wind, creeping out of sight. Starvation made us desperate. There were dead carcasses that we dare not touch. We were no longer the innocent women who had been dragged from their homestead helpless and ignorant. We had seen terrible things and this knowledge could never be wiped from my mind. Yet in all of this there had been some shifts. Mine enemy had become my friend. Tamar regained her voice, her hope and for all her trembling she was a stalwart companion. I thanked God for the comfort of her friendship.

There was no snow that night and the forest floor made a dry enough bed to lie on. We were now bitten, covered in red weals, our skin filthy and black, our hair matted and lice-ridden. No one in Good Hope would recognise us but a good wash would quickly change our outward appearance if we found our way home. I thought of the pistol hidden in the tree trunk and wondered if it would be there to protect us. Had Good Hope been raided? Had the militia come in search of us? Had they given us up for dead?

I was drifting slowly into my dreams when I heard the thud of traffic on the trail; the sound of hooves pounding the ground. We were no longer alone. Sensing danger I shook Tamar awake and we crawled on our bellies under cover to hide. Surely not now, so close to home, they had tracked us down? Had they tortured poor Jan into telling them where we were heading? How I cursed Heaven for this cruel turn of events. A dog sniffed us out, barking at our hiding place. There was no use in trying to escape. We were surrounded by horses and the smell of tobacco leaves. There was nothing to do but pray for a merciful end to all our sufferings.

36

'Missy, Missy.' I looked up from my hiding place at a young brave, his cheeks painted in a familiar shade, his head shaven with feathers and quills in the tufts at his crown. 'You come.' He gave a loud whoop to announce our discovery. My legs could not move for the terror but he didn't look like the savage who had taken us. Tamar clung to me weeping. 'It's all been for nowt.'

We surrounded by other men staring at us and I noticed they had no scalp locks dangling from their belts. 'Howdy do, Missy ... Come.'

Were these kind gestures a trap? We must have looked the most wretched of white-faced squaws stumbling out of our hiding place filthy and scabby, our faces fearful, not knowing our fate.

'Water,' I begged and we drank from their water pouches, long deep gulps. Then a young boy gave us something soft and sweet from his sack. I ate it too quickly and brought it straight back. Tamar supped slower and hers stayed down. There was nothing now but to follow them, in silent gloom.

I was certain we were on the homeward trail and I looked for crosses on the trees and for my shoes. We were heading south and that gave me hope that soon we would be back in Delaware country. We came to the clearing we spent that first terrible night of captivity but then we turned off the trail taking a path through dense undergrowth and my heart sank that we were travelling away from the direction of Good Hope.

We rested by a stream and I realised no attempt had been made to tie us together. Perhaps there was a chance to escape. I glanced at the head warrior on his horse in a beaver-skin cloak and round his neck I spied the sign of the Turtle Clan. I had seen these neck pieces many times in White Deer's village. Were these men of her tribe? Were we among friends? Was it possible we would be safe?

It was dusk when we came to another clearing of huts in the familiar shape I recognised from my visits to my Indian friend.

'*Yuhu!*' the men yelled and faces appeared and suddenly there was Jan grinning and waving. 'They found you?'

We ran to him with relief. 'Where were you? Why did you leave us?'

'I went to find some meat in the forest but I got lost, going round in circles until these men found me while they were out hunting and brought me back, gave me food and drink. I told them where you were resting and they said they would find you. Praise God! We are safe here among these people.'

'Who are they?' Tamar asked, shaking her head in disbelief at this good fortune.

'Lenni-Lenape of the Delaware tribe.'

'The same as my friend Running Deer and Little Bear. Do you know what this means? We are safe, Tamar.'

Tamar was already asleep where she sat.

The next morning the squaws came with clean skins and took us to the women's sweat lodge where we sweltered naked beside a steaming fire as they showed us how to scrape off the dirt with a special scraper. They tended our sores and soaked our hair in sassafras oil before washing it by the stream. To feel clean is to feel human. How can I express the tenderness of those women on seeing our fear and frailty. Kindness knows no race or faith. Love belongs to no one belief, for where love is God resides, I reckon.

We were summoned to the chief's hut and with an interpreter we told our sad story to the elders who listened with interest. The chief sucked his pipe and then spoke.

'There are good and bad among all tribes in this world. You have been on a strange quest and will want to return to your own people but one word of warning. They have not walked in your steps and I fear they will not want to hear of your sufferings, for shame they were not there to protect you.'

It was Tamar who spoke on our behalf thanking them for all their kindness. 'Our Friends, the Seekers will want to repay your kindnesses.'

The chief waved his hand. 'Will they come to greet us as Christians or to make us Christians? We of the Turtle Clan are men of our word. We follow the Great Spirit. It is enough for us to follow our own ways, but we have sent out runners to spread word of your return.'

'How can we truly thank thee?' I repeated.

'Be people who also keep your word and open the door with kindness to all who need it. Keep your eye sharp so you can guide others to keep theirs. Then there will always be peace among us.'

In those few precious days of rest and recovery, we felt a friendship that knew no barrier of language. They helped us prepare for our journey home. Winter was now upon us and soon the snow would blanket us with high drifts and ice. All I could think of was seeing the faces of Friends when they discovered we were safely returned unharmed and that Tamar had recovered her speech. They would be lined up to greet us not with sticks and cudgels like our enemies but would gather us back into the arms of our community.

Most of all I imagined Jordan Thane waiting with arms outstretched to hold me close; but first there would be Jacob to disappoint, Titus to challenge and all that that might entail. The women who had left the township on that bright afternoon in autumn were not the same women who would be returning with terrible tales. Was the chief right to warn us that our coming might not be welcome? Surely not.

We were escorted on horseback down a river trail until we reached the village where White Deer lived. They came out to greet us and begged us to stay for their special deer Feast that heralded the change of season. Desperate as we were to reach home I knew we must honour this gesture of welcome and enter into their ceremonies with an open heart.

White Deer brought us out fine fur-lined boots to wear. 'You come back to us,' she whispered. 'I said many prayers.'

Tamar tried her best to join in but everything was new to her and she struggled to make sense of their rituals. Jan danced and smoked and spoke in the Algonquian language as best he could. His cheeks were filling out again and there was the start of a beard on his chin. He was no longer a gawky youth but growing into his manhood. He wore a breech cloth and leggings and drew admiring glances from some of the younger girls who kept touching his long ginger curls.

Over the past weeks we had become a little family and it would be hard to let him go north as he must to join his own Dutch kinfolk.

Word had been sent of our return and a party would come

to escort us back to Good Hope. What would they make of our native clothing, bony bodies and ragged hair? Would they bring us proper dresses to wear?

How I longed to see the familiar faces of the children and Mary, Joseph and Jacob. Who would be coming to greet us?

There was one person neither of us wanted to meet and that was Titus, alias Thomas Black. There would be danger for Tamar if she opened her mouth to condemn him.

Courage almost failed me when I saw those tall black hats appearing down the track. There were two men on a cart who dismounted to greet us, handing over gifts of shells and tobacco leaves. I saw that one was Jacob.

'It looks like they are buying our freedom,' I whispered to Tamar. The formal thanksgiving took some time but not once did they look in our direction or even acknowledge our presence. Perhaps they didn't recognise us in our native clothes.

We stepped forward to meet them, smiling, but they barely glanced at us. 'Did you bring us clothing?' I asked.

Jacob shook his head. 'We thought you dead so Mary gave your apparel to a poor widow. Fresh outfits will be found: better for everyone to see you as you have been.' He did not look me in the eye as he spoke, which puzzled me.

It was time to say farewell to our rescuers. There were embraces and promises to visit again. They gave us gifts of beaded necklaces and animal skins. I was ashamed that we had little to give in return but I would find some way to thank them soon.

'Are thee well, Friends?' Jacob sat alongside me.

'The Lord has been merciful to us and taught us much,' I replied. 'Tamar will speak for herself. She has found her voice at long last.'

'Joy kept us alive and gave us hope when all was lost. I owe her my life,' she added, making me blush. 'We have prayed for this homecoming.'

Jacob did not reply, looking ahead. He turned his attention to Jan, ignoring us. As we drew near to Good Hope, I felt a stone in the pit of my stomach. Something was wrong. This was not the welcome I expected from the man who was supposed to be my intended husband. It was then I feared the worst, for no mention of Mary or the children was made. As we rode through Main Street there was no line of welcoming citizens eager to hear our story. What was the reason for this stony silence? Why did I fear that some heavy judgement was to fall upon our heads?

APRIL 2015

Hi Rachel

I guess you have read the account of her capture by now. There are many written accounts of how captives lived to tell the tale. I have read quite a few. These two were lucky to survive.

We have talked to many Lenape descendants and learned much about their way of life that fits with Joy's account. Haven't we travelled far and wide in following her story?

I would like to know about this Titus Cranke character. He sounds a right trickster. Is there any record of him your side of the pond?

We're nearly at the end of her Journal and are planning to have it published in the Fall. Would you be willing to come over as our guest? It would make the event even more special to have one of her direct descendants present.

Think about it.

I will ring you later.

Sam

37

As I alighted from the cart, Jacob turned to me. 'There's to be a meeting this night and you must attend to give testimony of your sufferings.' Tamar rose with me but he turned to her. 'You will reside with Widow Harris.' He pointed to a small cottage in a clearing. 'You must abide there.'

'But I need to speak with Thomas,' she said.

'We will deal with that matter at the meeting. Everyone now knows you're not his sister nor his wife. It is not proper for you to be under my roof.'

'I don't understand,' Tamar turned to me for support.

'What have we done to be treated so coldly after we have endured? What has happened?' I snapped.

'It will be discussed at the meeting. There have been events of a serious nature.'

'Are Mary and Liddy safe?'

'Aye, your conduct in that matter was exemplary. Joseph will speak on thy behalf.'

Tamar was deposited by the cottage door and I made my weary way up the farm track. I took comfort in the sight of golden leaves still on the branch, the corn stubble, smoke coming from the hearth. After so many weeks away I longed

to see the children running to greet me but no one was waiting
at the gate.

'So you're back at last.' Mary looked up from her sewing as if
I had just been down to the store on an errand. 'Skin and bone
you are and dressed like a savage.'

'Where are the children?'

'With a neighbour for the night. I don't want them to witness
all that must be said.'

'Please tell me what's wrong. I sense a cold coming. Tamar is
bewildered. She has so much to tell.'

'It can all be said at the meeting. There's some broth in the
pot. You look half starved.' It was the first kind thing anyone
had said and I burst into tears as I thanked her.

'I've set aside some of my old clothes but I doubt they'll
hang on you proper. Take those skins off. I don't want them
frightening the bairns. Liddy has bad dreams and cries out of
a night.'

'But she is safe and found you. How far were you from us?'

'Too far away to be of any use, but she ran with the devil
at her heels straight into my arms, poor little mite. We never
thowt to see you again.'

'Aye, so I gather and not pleased at our return by all accounts.'
I was weary and sickened by this unexpected coldness.

'There's reasons but you'll hear them at the meeting. Not
that I'm ungrateful for saving Liddy. I've told them but I have
to ask,' she put down her sewing and looked straight at me. 'Did
them savages dishonour you in anyway? Is there a half breed in
thy belly that must be seen to?'

'No, we are both as we were. Plenty of beatings and cruelty,
starvings and shame but we were never touched in that way.
Many braves treat white faces as we treat them and would not
wish to lie with one. We were to be sold on as slaves, ransomed

or married off but we escaped before that happened. There were two Dutch men captured. One of them died while we escaped. Jan was found by Lenape and we were shown much charity. Without them we would have perished. Now I am thinking perhaps better to have died than to face all your stony faces.'

I hid my tears in the corner of the room. After the freedom of loose skin clothing, it was hard to be laced up in Mary's old jacket and skirt that still retained a hint of vomit from the ship's hold all those years ago. My feet found it hard to be forced into heavy leather.

'Where's my chest?' I couldn't see it in its usual place.

'Liddy wanted to play with it so we gave it to her.'

'And my gloves, have you sold them?'

'Not yet. I was planning to take them to the city.'

'That won't be necessary. I have made other plans for them now.' My words came out like ice. How could they scatter my few precious possessions?

'All in good time, lass, hardly through the door and thee's mithering about gloves. You need a clean cap and collar. Your hair's a mess of coils and stinks of lice oil. We need you to look presentable.'

'Why? When have I not been clean and tidy?'

'It helps to stand before Friends looking your best.'

'Am I on trial?'

'No, there's just a lot of talking over things. Matters to set to rights,' she said while continuing on with her sewing. Mary was talking in riddles to me and I was tired and ready to curl up in a ball in my own space to sleep. Now I had to go before the meeting to make an account of myself.

There was a forest of black hats and bonnets bobbing along the benches of the meeting house. It felt like First Day worship but without the usual silence. Tamar arrived in a grey cloak and cap, sitting beside me shaking. I feared she would lose her voice again. 'Don't be afraid. Tell them the truth of your story. If this is about Titus, it will be your word against his.'

'Thomas has gone,' she replied, bowing her head .

'Gone where?' Yet I was not surprised at this news.

'Fled from the township and they think I helped him.'

'But you were with me. What's he done?'

'No one will tell me. They think I already know.'

We were sitting in a half circle, our bench set a little apart from the elders who sat in a line with a table before them. The room went quiet and all eyes were on us. Why did I fear we were in a court of judgement?

Elder Mathews rose. 'We are assembled to address the welcome arrival of Friend Tamar and Friend Rejoice. We rejoice at their safe return after many trials and hardships. We are grateful to the native tribesmen who like the Good Samaritan offered them shelter.' He paused and turned to us. 'But in thy absence situations occurred that have burdened us with doubts. We must have explanation from these our Friends before we continue with our regular business. Friend Moorside, how did thee come in possession of this?' Elder Matthews produced Jordan's pistol from a sack and held it for all to see. 'What purpose did this disobedience serve?'

I shot to my feet. 'It was given to me for protection at a time when danger threatened us all.'

'But we do not hold using firearms in a conflict.'

'I know, but my friend felt it was necessary for my personal safety.'

'So thee is above our rulings on discipline?'

'In this matter I felt I must search my conscience in the light of our teachings and other opinions.'

'What Friend among us would lead you into such disobedience? He looked around the room but no one spoke.

'He is not of our persuasion and was concerned that the town should be protected.'

'I take this to mean it was a military man who tempted thee with this ... thing?'

I nodded. 'His name is Captain Thane, who came among you to advise better safeguards. He was the man who helped save George Emsworth's life. He is a man with a good heart.'

'Why then in seeking thine own conscience did thee choose to hide this firearm out of sight?'

'In case of sudden attack, it would give me chance to protect the children.'

'And were thee attacked?'

'Yes, Friend.' I replied knowing where this was leading.

'And did thee seize thy weapon?'

'No, it was too far away to be of use to us.'

'So the firearm did not protect you or bring you back to us unharmed?'

'No, that was down to God's mercy alone.'

'What firearms did you see in your captivity?'

'Axes and Tomahawks that put many scalps on the belts of our captors. They wanted to exchange us for guns and rum, I was told.'

'Indeed. So why did you encourage a little child to run and find this weapon?'

'I thought if Mary and family could defend themselves, it would save their lives.'

'Or did you promise the gun in favour of the child's release?'

'Never!' Tamar shot up in my defence. 'Liddy was released solely by Friend Joy challenging the honour of our main captor. She asked him to show mercy on the child and take her in her place. She was so brave and showed no fear. His respect for her saved all our lives.'

'Be that as it may. Thy turn will come. Be seated,' he continued. 'So words alone were your best defence?'

'In this case, yes, but—'

'Let me continue. It has troubled us much that you consort with a worldly man, not of our beliefs, choosing to take his offering knowing the military among us deny our peaceful ways.'

'I did as you say.' I had no heart to fight his arguments.

'And would thee do so again?' His eyes fixed on me with concern.

'Aye, I would.' There was a gasp around the room. 'We have witnessed at close quarters the savagery of our enemies. Tied neck and foot, beaten and fearing a burning death at the stake. Should that happen again I would want to end the suffering of all around me by shooting all first.'

The room was in an uproar of disapproval.

'Silence!' Elder Matthews boomed out. 'Friend, you are in dire need of reflection on these words of yours. Sadly we cannot have among us one who undermines our principles and consorts with unbelievers. You show no signs of remorse.' He sat down to discuss with his elders and then delivered the judgement of the whole room I feared.

'We shall take it upon ourselves to visit with you to ascertain what is thy decision. For be it known, we cannot harbour one who consorts with a man such as Thane. We are a loving and merciful people. Come before us in humility to confess thy mistaken judgement and no more will be said on this matter.'

'But—'

'No more. It is now time to turn to Friend Tamar in order to obtain all she knows about the disappearance of Thomas Black and why she chose to come among us as his alleged sister acting as one who was dumb of speech. Miraculously she now finds her voice restored. You have also much to explain, Sister.'

Tamar remained sitting and muttered. 'What is it thou wants to know?'

'How came you to be his consort in deception.'

'That is not how it was. I came with him in fear and trembling. I was struck dumb with what I had witnessed when our ship was wrecked. I lost my husband and child. Thomas Black, as I knew him to be called, promised to protect me. I was easily led, I confess, but knowing what I knew . . .' Her voice failed.

'Speak up. What did you know?'

'Firstly my name is Tamar Wilson, widow of Erasmus Wilson late of Hull. We travelled in the *Warrior* in the company of Thomas Black and his sister Dora, or wife, I know not which. They argued much. When the ship sank and my family were lost to me and likewise Dora was also drowning, Thomas kept me afloat. When his sister approached the raft he did not help her and I fear she drowned with the others. I think he thought I had property and means but when he saw I had witnessed his treachery, he silenced me never to speak of it. I was weak and grief-struck. I thought him kindly at first. When he realised I had little to offer in worldly goods, his manner became cold and critical. He said if we were to continue to together then I must become his sister.'

'So you had no knowledge of his schemes?'

'What schemes? I did fear the loss of the collection for George Emsworth was no accident, seeing him often in drink. He consulted me on nothing and I kept in his shadow. Where is this man now?'

'That is something all of us would want to know. Three weeks ago a woman dressed in scarlet arrived claiming to be

his wife. She had come from Chesapeake Bay in search of her
erstwhile husband, Titus Cranke, both having assumed new
names on entering into the fellowship of Seekers. She claimed
he was seduced away by the charms of a married woman on
board. They tried to drown her when the ship sank. However
this woman survived the wreck and has reverted to ungodly
ways. She came seeking vengeance on her husband.

'Thomas was summoned to explain himself and there was an
unholy scene of violent altercation between them. The woman
had to be restrained from assaulting him. It was then we saw
the true colours of his heart in his cursings and threats. The
constable came to put him in the lock-up to cool down his fury
but in the morning by some foul means he had escaped with her
connivance, we are sure. There has been no sighting of them
since that day.'

'But none of this I knew. How could I, being in mortal
danger myself.' Tamar jumped to her feet. 'I am entirely innocent of any of this.'

'But if you had spoken out and told the truth . . .' The questions continued.

'Hold fast,' I rose by her side. 'I told Jacob Wrathall that I
recognised this man as the charlatan Titus Cranke but I was
assured he had changed his ways as well as his name for a good
reason.' I paused to take a breath, looking round the room for
support. 'And when the collection was lost, I warned again that
it was suspicious but none of you believed me. Do not blame
my friend here. She has suffered such losses as to render any
person speechless but is now restored to health. Her only fault
was to let us think them related, but a poor woman without
means needs protection in a strange land. I think I might have
done the same.'

'Thy opinion so readily given was not asked for. Sit down.

It appears Friend Tamar has been much maligned by our suspicions but we had to hear the truth from her own lips. I think we are satisfied by her explanation.' He looked around the benches to see everyone nodding. 'There will be no recorded note of this unfortunate happening. Now we can proceed with the business of the meeting and thank everyone for thy attendance and consent.'

I looked at Tamar, seeing relief flooding over her face. I watched Jacob make his way to offer her an apology, I hoped. It was time to exit this stuffy room full of coughs and sneezes to drink in fresh night air, collect my thoughts and cool my own fury.

I was to be chastised like a naughty child, not with a rod but with endless words of admonishment and arguments that I no longer wanted to hear.

It was Joseph who came out to stand by me seeing my distress. 'Have no mind, lass. They're doing it for thy own good. Better to stay within the meeting than be shunned for marrying unlawfully.'

'I have no promise of matrimony,' I replied.

'Just as well then that yon soldier thinks you're dead.'

My ears were suddenly alert to this news. 'How so?'

'None of us expected to see you again in this life. We have heard such stories of slaughter. A search party was sent and the Captain, give him his due, spent days in the forest tracking your path. They found a shoe and feared the worst. Better he thinks you gone. No point in being pestered by his attentions. It would sadden Jacob's heart to see you shunned.'

How could I tell Joseph that his words had frozen my heart with fear? I didn't want Jordan Thane thinking me dead, taking comfort in the arms of another perhaps. It was then I knew that he alone was for me.

As for Jacob, there was no space within my heart for him to reside. As we walked home in the darkness, there was a chill wind heralding the long winter to come.

With each step towards the farmstead I felt a spurt of defiance growing within. Tamar and I came close to death, so close to despair, but the thought of returning to Good Hope – and back to the man I now knew to be mine own – had pushed me forward. How could I survive the winter without seeing him again?

38

Once the formal meeting was ended, life was expected to resume its normal pattern for me. I was allowed to mind the children, to serve out my duties and chores as before. Mary was pleasant enough. I was even given a new brown jacket and skirt as compensation for all that was lost. I still wore White Deer's comfortable fur-lined boots, kept my head down and spoke little. The public embarrassment still rankled. Better to keep my own counsel as I scrubbed and washed but my mind was racing with defiant thoughts. There was only one thing that mattered to me now and that was to see Jordan Thane. I wanted him to know my change of heart but with winter upon us this decision was urgent.

After the first visitation of the women's committee to instruct me in more compliant behaviour, I felt my hackles rise at the worthy words poured over my head like cold water. To return to the fold would take courage and humility and a certainty of faith. None of which could I find within me.

For many months I had been a stranger in their midst, unruly, proud, questioning the rules of discipline. It was hard to sit and take their pious suggestions, well meant as they were, knowing I no longer wanted to be part of their tribe.

We were no different from our neighbours in the Lenape village. We had our distinctive dress rules, our spiritual pow wows and rituals and manner of speech that set us apart from others.

We had come across the ocean to protect these precious ways of worshipping, and to keep faith, people like me must bend not break. There could be no picking off the ripest fruits from this basket of beliefs. I would obey this but not that. A woman who chose to marry outside the ordinance no longer belonged within. The choice was stark. If I were to leave without permission of our congregation, that would be final. If only it were that simple. But how could I betray the very parents who had stood firm in their imprisonment by my desertion? Their memory was sacred to me.

'Joy, you are no longer a child but a woman who has crossed the ocean, forged a new life and friendships in a world they never knew,' a voice was whispering in my inner ear. 'Your choices must be your own and any price you pay for them.' Why was I using 'you' instead of 'thee'? Had I already trespassed into the other world out there, the one that contained the man I loved?

Early on the morning of the women's second visitation, I asked leave to visit White Deer with a few gifts and treats for the children in the little school. I wore my new outfit and cloak and carried the biggest basket I could find, hidden in which were my indenture papers, my gloves and personal toiletries. I kissed Liddy's golden curls and waved to the boys, walking away from Emsworth's farm hiding my tears.

I had vowed never to shirk my duty and to see out my servitude but needs must. Once more I was running towards a new life, not away from anything. It was the only way I knew to get myself to Philadelphia before the tracks were frozen over. It was a cowardly way but there was a note by my pillow thanking

Joseph and Mary for their kindness and asking forgiveness for making a choice of which they would never approve.

As Good Hope faded from view, the seriousness of what I was doing hit hard. I had told no one of this plan, not even Tamar. I did not want her involved in my deception and if she did have strong feelings for Jacob I wanted to clear the path for her to make them known in due course. Perhaps one day she would also forgive me for not saying goodbye. Jacob had not come near me since the day of the meeting. I owed him no explanation.

At the Lenape village, I was greeted as always in friendship. I gave White Deer some of my rough wool stockings made last winter and asked if anyone was able to ferry me down to the nearest landing stage where I could catch a boat to the city. I offered a little silver and tobacco leaves to one of Little Bear's friends who was going fishing.

'You go market?' White Deer asked.

'I go to see my friend Sabine. I will come back to see you.' It was all I could say that she might understand.

'Go well, *k'neXa'sin* ... Take care.' She waved me down the path. In my heart I guessed we would not meet again. With each beat of the paddle, the canoe carried me from the forest clearing down the fast-flowing river to the landing stage where the boats bobbed on the water. I did not look back for fear of wanting to turn back.

On the ferry I had time to dwell on what must be done in the city. First I would put myself in the hands of the Boyers once more. What if there was no room? How would I earn a living? I felt for my fancy gloves. I must sell them to pay my way.

Dear gloves, now was the time to let them go, for this glove-maker's daughter was not worthy of them. They belonged to my mother. Once again a small voice whispered. 'No, they never were hers but your grandmother's. She gave them in good faith. Now they are yours to do with as you like. Don't make an idol of them. They are just skin and baubles after all.'

Soon Philadelphia grew large on the horizon: smoking chimneys, ships with tall sails, all life bustling along the shoreline. I would miss the peace of green pastures and forest glades but this must be my hiding place for now.

Wrapping my cloak and hood around me, I scurried away from the noisy harbour and rough taverns towards familiar streets, my head bent into the wind.

The compass of my life was shifting. Here I trusted I would find my true north.

I hurried down the cobbled street towards the Boyers' shop but then I saw the sign above the door was no longer there. It was a shop selling liquor and groceries. For one awful moment I wondered if they had gone back to France. My legs almost buckled with fear as I opened the door. 'I am looking for the Boyers.' My voice trembled with uncertainty.

'They moved up the hill to a bigger place. Just make towards the Town Hall and you'll see the sign.'

How relieved I was to know they were still trading, but my body was tense as I trundled uphill recalling the terror of when George had his accident.

The shop had two fine windows of displays and a smart wooden door with panes of glass to peer through. I was not the sort of person to make purchases here. The fabrics on display were of the finest quality: sateens, brocades, silks and velvets with braids and trimmings in a rainbow of lush colours. I waited, hesitant, as the assistant came to attend me. 'Can I help you?'

'Is Mistress Boyer at home?'

'Who is asking?'

'Miss Moorside, late of Good Hope. I am a friend.'

'I will see if she is free to receive you,' he said with caution, unsure of my poor clothes and faded bonnet. He ran upstairs and then down the fine wooden staircase dressed in deepest black came Sabine, her sleeves edged with black lace.

'Joy, *ma cherie*. *Mon Dieu*! Come in. I can't believe it is you.'

'I came to see Marianne and to ask a favour,' I blurted out.

'You ask nothing until you have a dish of hot tea. You look so cold and pinched. We thought you dead but you have survived. Praise God! Who rescued you? We were all praying for your safe return but as the weeks went by . . .'

In the warmth of her embrace, I felt hot tears flowing, tears of relief to be among friends who would make no judgement on me.

'There's so much to say but first I must confess, I have run away, renounced my membership of meeting, abandoned my fiancé. Perhaps you will prefer not to give me tea or sympathy.'

'Sit down, sit down. Louie will bring us cordial and when baby wakes we will play with her while a bed is made for you.'

The luxury of spiced cordial with toasted muffins and fruit conserve was brought to the table in the upstairs drawing room.

'How is Henri?' I asked, smiling at his portrait on the wall.

'He departed this life only a month ago. It is his room we can give you.'

In my selfish need I'd not observed her mourning clothes. 'I am so sorry to hear this . . . But your baby is well?'

'Marianne is full of life. She was her grandfather's delight to the very end.'

It was like old times sitting by a fire talking as the light faded and the lamps were lit. I recounted all that had happened in the past months.

'You have left your church?'

'There was no choice. It is a strict and narrow way. Their judgements are harsh on any who fall below expectation. I no longer see my faith in that light and yet I know I have betrayed all those who had faith in me.'

'I don't understand. You were always so dedicated to the Seeker way.' Sabine looked concerned.

'When we were rescued by the local tribe and returned to the township, all that mattered to them was the anxiety we had given them about certain matters. No one seemed to care about our suffering. There is a phrase in the Bible: *Though I speak with the tongues of men and of angels and have not charity, I am become as sounding brass or a tinkling cymbal.*

'Sometimes the faithful observe the letter of the law but not its spirit. They cannot bend and I cannot make a bridge to meet them any more.

'*Tant pis* . . . 'tis a pity for it is no little thing to cut oneself off from your fellowship. They have lost a great worker in you.'

'Alas that's another matter, I have not finished my duty of service. No one will want to give me work knowing this.'

'We heard you saved their child from captivity. I would count that as service indeed. You owe them nothing now, Joy. Come, enough gloom. Marianne will cheer you with her prattling. Jerome is busy measuring for fabric drapes. All the new town houses want curtains to draw against draughts and to hide their shutters.'

'Can you use another pair of hands below stairs?' I had nothing else to offer them.

'Of course not, you are family now and besides I think there's another reason you hastened in this direction, *n'est-ce pas?*'

I found myself blushing. 'Have you heard from Captain Thane?'

'What do you think? We were the first to hear of your capture. He searched and searched.'

'He thinks I'm dead. I couldn't have him thinking that. I have to see him again.'

'He may be on the move. The war continues against the French in the north and some of the militia are summoned to join in the battles.'

'He has left then?' My heart sank at this news.

'Not yet. But we must let him know you are here at once.'

'Perhaps he has forgotten me by now.' I was being coy.

'I think not. We will give him a wonderful surprise with perhaps a little extra toilette for your hair and a pretty dress and cap to delight the eye. If you mean to cross over into more colourful clothes, it will be my delight to help you,' Sabine laughed and I knew under her skilful hands, Huguenot as she was, there would be a transformation. Then sense prevailed.

'No, not yet, the Captain must see me as I am and in sombre hues. I too must mourn Henri. He was a fine gentleman who gave me courage at a dark time. Colour can wait.'

39

My pen trembles as I recall that first sight of Jordan racing up the stairs two at a time, thinking there was something serious and his services were needed. I peered out of the shadowy corner by the gallery waiting to make my entrance, still in my drab browns but with my hair piled up in the current fashion with loose tendrils framing my pale face. I heard them chattering in the sitting place, offering him wine and ringing the bell for a servant. This was my cue to appear and bob a curtsey. 'You rang, Mistress?'

Jordan turned and I saw such a look of surprise and delight in his reaction that it has stayed with me all my life. 'Joy, is it really you? We heard rumours that some settlers had escaped but I dared not hope . . .'

I couldn't speak for the joy of seeing such pleasure on his face at my appearance.

'I'm staying here for a while until I settle myself.' I was trying to stay calm but Jerome and Sabine smiled as they tiptoed out of the room leaving us alone.

It took all of a second for us to rush together in an embrace. He kissed away all the sorrows of the past months. His loving touch was all that was needed to still my questioning heart. This was where I belonged.

'I searched for you for days and days. We followed your signs in the hope of catching up but the trail went cold on the other side of the lake. I had to turn back for we were needed to guard from further raids. The fighting in the northern Provinces has unsettled tribes down as far as Virginia. We may have to leave at short notice to give support.'

'Sabine told me as much. But not yet, surely? We have so much to share and so little time.' I clung to the tobacco scent of his jacket, the coolness of his brass buttons on my cheek, the warmth of his hands on my body.

'Then let us wed and live as one for as long as we can. Will you need permission?'

I shook my head. 'I left the community. I am of age and have waited too long dithering. The ties that bound me are cut. They will make no claim on me for I am an outsider now, having forfeited all rights owing to me by abandoning my post.'

I was sitting on his knee when Sabine and Paul returned with a tray of fine glasses. We shared our news and my heart was bursting with excitement that all would be well.

'You will be married from this house but where do you choose for the ceremony?' Sabine asked.

'Not in the new meeting house here. Will your own church accept us?' I ventured knowing it was not the roof over our heads that mattered but the love in our hearts as we plighted our troth to each other.

'You are both Protestants. I see no barrier but we will make inquiry of our pastor. We will invite friends to be witnesses and to join us for a wedding breakfast. First though, thee and me must do a little dress making.' Sabine laughed and it felt as if the room was filled with light.

*

There has been so much sadness in my life's journey that it delights me to pause awhile over one of the happiest of times in my long life. Starting afresh in the big city as wife of an officer of rank would mean some changes to my speech and dress, and after years of speaking thee and thou, to address men of rank only as equals was not easy to unlearn. I fear I have never quite mastered the finer courtesies of deference.

My eye faltered at the choice of fabrics Sabine suggested when it came to making up a bridal gown. She brought out golds and russets and greens to compliment my colouring but they felt bold and awkward to my plain eye. I settled on a cheerful deep forest green to offset my sandy hair. The design was modest but she insisted I wore a pretty golden collar edged with lace.

We made a visit to what I had always called a steeple-house. It was the first time since that attack in Windebank when village men killed my schoolteacher. How could I not feel ashamed to now be entering this place? Was I letting all my family down? The pastor was welcoming. His church was plain and unadorned. I was sure the Almighty heard the prayers of those who worshipped here as the Great Spirit listened to the prayers of the Lenape people. What mattered was the sincerity of a loving generous heart.

On the morning of our wedding, I stared at myself in a long mirror for the first time. We had no mirrors but caught glimpses of our reflection only in glass and water. I was still dressed plain. The habit would be hard to shift. My collar lifted the wool but something was missing and I knew in an instant just what was needed.

In the cabinet drawer where I kept my papers, I fished out the linen bag to pull out those beautiful skin gloves. They were a little faded but the seams were intact even if the lace was dull.

I slipped them on to my hands with such tenderness, pulling them gently down each finger, thinking of my grandmother, the bride who had worn them so long ago on her wedding day. They were old-fashioned relics of a bygone age but to me they were the perfect link from my past to brighten my future. I would wear them this once and then let them go.

I gazed again at my dress enlivened by those fine gauntlets, the lace cuffs linking to the lace on the collar. That was enough adornment for this ceremony.

I would remove them when I accepted the Captain's gold ring. Seekers wore no rings but I was no longer one of them and I chose to wear this symbol to proclaim my love for him. In Henri's room I smiled, recalling how he had warned me not to marry for duty or comfort alone but to give myself body and soul to a passionate man no matter how poor he might be. These be wise words, I reckon.

On my head for once I wore no plain cap but a wide-brimmed hat with feathers like a cockade and a little veil to protect my face and hide any tears.

It was the season of Christ's birth which they call Christmas. I had only known this celebration years ago in the Justice's house. Sabine brought greenery into the house from the hedge-rows and flowers for the wedding breakfast table. How could I repay their generosity? We had met in the darkest of hours on board the vessel but now we were joined in a friendship I hoped would never end. Her respect was wealth indeed.

In contrast I must record the difficult meeting I had when Tamar came into the city to seek me out and suggest I return to explain myself. 'Thee can't just walk away from thy obligations, giving no reason to Jacob or the family who supported you. It is badly done, a selfish act of indulgence,' she said with a sniff.

'Are these your words or Jacob's?' I asked, refusing to rise to her accusations. 'Do you begrudge me a chance of happiness with the man I love after all we suffered together? I thought you were my friend. We are taught to follow the inner path of conscience, those gentle whisperings that speak of love and truth and honesty. I have made my choice with my heart not my head, Tamar. There is no going back. Wish me well in my new life as I wish you joy of your own with Jacob. Seekers are loving and forgiving people, we are told many times, so now let me see some of that in practice. Words without deeds are shallow empty noises.'

I could see her torn by my reply so I tested her even further. 'It would be a joy to me if you would attend my wedding.'

'Thee knows I can't. It would not be approved.'

'Not even for friendship's sake?' I took her hand. 'But I understand how it is. No matter what separate paths we now tread, I would like to think we would still keep the bridge of friendship open between us. You and I are more than our beliefs and differences. We sheltered each other when all was lost. I owe you much and will bear no ill will if you can't attend. Give me your blessing if nothing else.'

Tamar did not reply. How could she, torn as she was between friendship and the pull of her community? She hugged me hard and then left. I did not expect to see her again.

When the moment came to leave in the carriage for the wedding on that day so long ago, I was ready to meet Jordan in his scarlet tunic looking so handsome in my eyes. The service was simple, but I smiled when I saw his men standing guard outside holding swords over our heads in honour of the day.

I lifted my veil to see a little crowd of well wishers and to my surprise I think I caught a glimpse of a white cap and tall bonnet, a grey cloak, a tall figure hanging back out of sight. I often wonder if I imagined this, such was my hope that Tamar was still my friend. I will never know if it was her own small act of defiance in witnessing my wedding or just a curious bystander who paused en route to her daily chores to see if the bride was known to her.

40

My heart warms to recall the merry party that completed our nuptials. We shared a fine meal of capon with fresh pies made of squashes and tree syrup with syllabub covered in forest berries soaked in brandy. There was a bride cake to share among the servants and guests, cordials to toast and a fiddler came to set feet tapping. For the first time in my life, I allowed myself to lift skirt and petticoat and dance a jig around the room. It released within me such joy as I joined the circle of merry folk. If dancing be of the devil, as I was told, why did it bring such laughter and pleasure? Singing and dancing released my body and mind from its tight restraint.

Soon it was time for leave-taking but Sabine had gone ahead to prepare the bridal bed as is the custom here. We were staying close to the fort in quarters set aside for us. There was much ribaldry that made me blush and clanging of pots to alert the town that a bride and groom were off to their chamber. I wished them all gone but customs must be observed and there was much shouting when we entered the bed chamber from the street outside. To my delight the bed was adorned with a quilted counterpane full of flowers and strewn with herbs.

I trembled as I shed my fine new dress and jacket to be left only with my shift. My hair unfurled from its prison of pins fell down my back. I had dreamed of such a night in my darkest hours and waited for the Captain of my heart to join me. I felt shy at this new intimacy, knowing full well what we were about to do. I snuffed out the candle so he would not see my red face.

'What are you thinking?' he whispered in my ear.

'I don't want this day to end. It has been so full of richness and friendship,' I sighed.

'But the night has only just begun and it is a long time till dawn,' Jordan laughed holding me close so I could taste his skin. His hands roamed over my body. I sank into the feather mattress with a secret smile knowing I had made the best of choices in this man. Was Henri Boyer laughing in heaven knowing I had exchanged days of sorrow and duty for many nights of joy? I was not disappointed.

Still my hand lingers lovingly over recollections of those early days of our marriage when the whole world outside our chamber faded from view as we lay in each other's arms to find pleasure in our bodies. We were one flesh indeed and I longed that this union would soon bear fruit but as the months went by there was no sign of a child. At first we were wholly occupied with each other but the threat of Jordan's departure still loomed large.

How quickly I came to live the life of an officer's wife, preparing suppers for guests, helping younger wives in their domestic troubles, shopping and visiting friends but there was at the back of my mind a lingering guilt that without a child, my life was without purpose. I envied Sabine and Tamar who called to announce she was now the wife of Jacob and was with child.

She did not desert me as I feared but slipped in quietly to give me news of Good Hope and of the school for Indian children that Jacob established among the Lenape, the school I had hoped would be mine too one day.

On hearing this, next morning I took my gauntlets to the haberdashers to see if they were of value. Mr Cook examined them with interest. 'I've seen these afore: nice work, good quality, more of a keepsake than practical but I can give you two guineas for them, Mistress Thane.'

I nodded and passed them over without regret. All these years they had been a talisman to me but I had no need of such now that I knew they could be put to better use.

When Tamar called a few weeks later, I presented her with the guineas and some extra I had saved to be spent on their school.

'Are you sure? This is most generous,' she smiled with those dark serious eyes. 'It will help us feed some of the orphans.'

We did not talk of meeting business. I sensed her testing to see if I had regrets. I had yet to find a regular place of worship on First Day which I now called Sunday. I dressed plainly even though we were not without means to dress me in finer clothes. Our town house was well appointed and I had a maid to help me with daily chores. I had the use of a carriage should I need it but I preferred to walk to where there was green wilderness or a park. It helped me sort out the muddled thoughts in my mind that my life was now empty of purpose, my spirit restless and in need of consolation.

I have been examined many times by doctors, treated with potions that did not open my womb. Was this a punishment, this barrenness? Had I forfeited the right to this special joy when I chose to leave Good Hope? If so it was a bitter pill to swallow, but over the years I have become accustomed to this loss.

It was Jordan who suggested I might like to mother on someone else's bairn, an orphan child in need of a good home but I
was still hoping that all would come right in the end if I prayed
and found some use for my few talents.

As those months turned into years I found myself with slate
in hand and a room full of soldiers' offspring to teach to read
and write as I was taught by the Sampsons in Windebank. At
last I found a distraction that gave me reason to rise early to
greet the day. Pupils come and go which can be annoying when
children are removed by families to take up land or travel back
to England at short notice but I leap ahead here.

We have been at war for years with France and I dreaded the
day Jordan would get his own marching orders. We got plenty
of news when ships came into harbour but I heard nothing from
Yorkshire. That bridge was truly broken and beyond repair. I
could hardly recall the hills and dales of my birth place. When
they heard through that strange link of kin within the Seekers
of my desertion, I knew there would be no more contact with
me.

It was the summer of 1694 that Jordan was ordered to take
his troop to join a command further north. I waved my husband
off not knowing if I would see him again in this life. There
were no nights of joy after that but long empty days when even
lifting my head from the bolster was an effort of will.

The evenings when the shutters closed for the night were
the worst. I had some sewing and mending but little to occupy
my time except to visit my dear friends and listen to their news.
Sometimes I stayed to mind Marianne while they were out.
I stared at their pianoforte, wishing I could play like Sabine.
Instead, I did some crewel work and dressmaking for the
orphan children, adding little skin gloves to their outfits. Yet
my mind was restless, going over all that happened to bring me

to this city. Then the idea of writing down my thoughts on parchment came to me one morning.

Seekers were trained early to read and write, to study scripture and a little learning for both boys and girls. We often would debate and argue for nothing was ever done in meeting without the consensus of all. This strengthened the use of our native tongue in its infinite variety. I have always used words and phrases that do not habitually flow from a servant's lips: now I could put them to good use.

I went to the bookbinder to buy myself a leather-bound journal which had at first the smell of musty Bibles in its pages but soon became my faithful companion of a night. With quill and ink I set down all that had happened on the journey that brought me to the City of Brotherly Love from my beginning in the West Riding. It has been a slow and steady labour of love to recall as much of the detail of those early days.

Strange as it may be, as I wrote from my heart long forgotten scenes opened up as I relived them: those precious years on a Yorkshire farm, the months I spent in my grandfather's house and those first heart flutterings over Miles Foxup. I could see his mother, Priscilla, as if it were yesterday, when I can scarce remember what I need going from one chamber to the other. Soon I had filled every page and bought two more. My stay-at-home nights were no longer lonely knowing there was so much to record.

I have had many experiences that might be of interest should I ever share my words but not in my lifetime. How can I say what needs spoken onto a page of the intimate happenings in a woman's life or describe folk for whom I have little sympathy?

Speak the truth in love I was taught so I have tried to be charitable but sometimes my own pride and mistaken loyalties get between the lines. With a cup of warm cordial by my side, I spent many hours revisiting my past history.

I had hardly begun the journey by ship from Hull before a rumour came to my ears that chilled my heart. Our militia had been in some skirmish close to the frontier and many men were missing and taken prisoner. By the time more news reached us it was already stale so I spent hours with Sabine trying to comfort myself that Jordan would not be among the lost but no dispatches arrived or letters and this silence made me fear the worst.

I found no comfort in my journal pages and set it aside. I had a duty to other young wives who were as fractious as I was in waiting for news. Then one forenoon we were summoned with fresh news. The prisoners had been taken to Canada to a place called Mont Real by Indian tribesmen loyal to the Frenchies in the hope of a ransom. Jordan was among them. There was however to be an exchange of prisoners and he would be returning with the remnants of his men by ship. We were to make preparations for their return.

How could I sleep, pacing the floor in a fever of plans and lists to make his homecoming welcome and comfortable. I longed for a letter but none came. News like wildfire swept through the city and I knew months of anxious waiting would soon be over.

We stood on the landing dock for hours before the sighting of their vessel was possible. There was a stiff breeze and I was glad of my fur-lined hood and cloak to stop myself from shaking. Slowly the great sails appeared and we saw the deck crowded with soldiers waving and cheering. My eyes were pinned on each one but in uniform they were hard to pick out.

When the gang plank went down and the able bodied men disembarked, their women rushed to greet them. I hung back, jealous of these joyful reunions, impatient for my own to come. The ship was almost emptied of travellers before I saw a man being led out slowly, held up by others. There was something in his height and gait that set my heart thudding. I walked forward hoping it was my husband. I saw him stumble at the sight of me and I rushed to help him with tears flowing.

'Careful Mistress, he's much wounded in the head. He is unsteady on his feet.'

'Oh Jordan, you are home at last. Why did you not write to me?' I cried as I held his hand. He did not reply and only then did I realise that one eye flickered unseeing but his smile was as always. 'Joy' he whispered as he trembled and was given over to my care. In that moment I knew our lives had changed forever. We took a slow painful walk back to our house and within the privacy of our four walls did he remove his tricorn hat. I saw with horror the scars, the bare wounded flesh at the back of his head. My beautiful man had suffered a scalping, not enough to kill him but to leave him maimed. Only then did I weep for this loss. 'How did this happen?' I cried.

He waved away my pity. 'I survived; so many good men did not. Some were roasted in cages before my eyes. No more tears, Joy. I am alive but very tired.'

He slept for two whole days and nights. All my plans were abandoned in the nursing of him. He was home and we were at one again. Whatever the future held we would face it together. Of one thing I was certain, my husband would never lift a musket again.

41

I want no pity from any who read these my words and wonder how a man and woman survive such disasters to find each other again. In due course Jordan set down an account of his terrible captivity for the Governor to read and spared them no horrific detail in order that other soldiers might know what could befall them in enemy hands. It makes grim reading. Yet in the midst of all this misery there was one little snippet that gave me much amusement when he told me his story.

'We were kept prisoner in a Canadian fort close to the border and those who had anything to sell were able to buy extra food and comforts for themselves. I became aware of an English man, a debtor who tried to ally himself with the Frenchies, a rough sort who was not above begging from us and who for some reason I thought I recognised from Philadelphia. He was friendly enough in his way but there was something about his ingratiating manner that set my teeth on edge. I did not trust him.

'I challenged him why he was not fighting on the British side and he replied he owed the old country nothing. He said he was an apothecary with powers to heal the sick for a fee so we gave him money for potions for our wounded. I asked him to treat my own open scar which in fairness he did his best to protect

by making me a skull cap to cover the skin. He called himself
Tom Smith but I guessed it wasn't his true name for his eyes
had a shifty look that never kept your gaze. He then suggested
we club together to bribe a guard to help us escape but by then
few of us had anything left of value to give him. The other prisoners thought him a grand fellow and somehow found enough
hidden rings and their boots to help him along. His French was
poor. He said he was running from his whoring wife who had
robbed him of all his trade but then he was arrested for cheating
at cards. They had travelled across America through the Jerseys
and Boston, coming from Yorkshire on a ship that was wrecked.
It was then I suspected that he was the same apothecary who
helped George Emsworth and then lost the goodwill collection.

'"Perhaps you'll know my wife," I asked to test this out.
"She's from that county. Joy Moorside, captured by Indians
from Good Hope. I'm sure I've seen thee in Philadelphia and
Good Hope." He looked at me for a moment and I swear he
went white. He shook his head and told me, "Nay, sir, never
been down that way. I know of no such person. America is a
mighty large country." He removed himself from my side and
never conversed with me again.

'I warned the others of my suspicions but they would have
none of it, thinking he would help them make a run out of the
fortress. He said he knew a door that was often opened and a
man who would row them away to freedom.'

It was my turn to smile, sure in my mind he had indeed
met Titus Cranke up to his old tricks again. Why is it that the
wicked flourish and prosper? 'And did they succeed?' I asked.

He laughed. 'He did, the rogue, took their silver and scar-
pered. God help him if any of them meet him again in this life.'

Surely if the law does not catch up with Titus, a higher Judge
will call him to account when his life ends and yet for all his

trickery, he had given me a safe haven once and kept Jordan's scalp wound clean. There is good and bad in all of us, I mused.

There were other stories that my husband would never discuss with me, wounds that were invisible to the eye, nightmares when he woke in a sweat crying out for long lost comrades. There were days when he fell into the slough of despond, saying, 'What use am I to you now with only a pension to tide us over? Better I were dead.'

'Stop that,' I cried. 'For better, for worse: that's what we promised each other. There will be a way forward for us,' I told him, more in hope than expectation.

The walls of the busy city seemed to be closing in on our spirits. There were fights and drunkenness and former slaves wandering looking for work. It was no longer safe to walk some streets of an evening. What we needed was a fresh start away from all the smoke and fumes, an open space to breathe freely. What we needed was land.

I had forfeited any right to purchase land after four years by my desertion from my employers. We were not afraid of hard work for I knew what must be done to raise a dwelling and a barn, to grow enough to keep us. It would be a better future than sitting idle in the city. Once the idea fixed in my head, there was no shifting it.

We discussed it late into the night when sleep would not come. I could see Jordan's spirit rise at such a possibility. He would write to his family in Northumberland for assistance with our new venture. His eyesight was weak but he wasn't blind. His strength was restored by regular meals but we had, as yet, few capital assets to exchange into acres.

I talked to anyone who would listen. Had I still been within the Fellowship of Seekers, doors would have opened but I could no longer ask in that quarter.

Sometimes, however, answers to silent prayer come from the strangest of coincidences. I had kept my little Dame school in our living space. The fees it brought in were useful. Jordan was not yet discharged from his duties so along with soldiers' children, other children of tradesmen joined my group. There were enlightened men who wanted some education for their girls as well as boys. Word spread that I was thorough but a kindly instructor whose husband had been wounded in battle. Soon I took on an assistant called Hetty Prentiss who proved herself more than able and eager to take children aside who were slow to grasp their letters.

Hetty came from one of the earliest English families to settle here and her father had several shops. They supplied seed corn and farming tackle into the Delaware district and up the Schylkill River. I don't know why I confided in this young girl as we were clearing away the slates and hornbooks sitting together discussing the day.

'How we'd love to find somewhere out of the city to live for a while,' I said. 'Jordan might grow stronger in a greener place. The smoke catches his chest so.'

'My uncle has a farmstead up towards the German district. He is always looking for help,' she offered. 'But you can't leave this school. It's the best of its kind for little ones.'

'That's kind of thee.' The odd thee still found its way into my speech. 'You have learned all there is to know in these past months, perhaps I could lease these rooms for your use.' Was I being too bold? 'Does your uncle want a yard boy or a couple?'

'I will ask,' she replied. 'I know Uncle Adam would prefer to come closer into the city. He is over fifty and not in the best of health when we last saw him. His wife died of the yellow fever when it raged over us.'

How is it that when a thing is right sometimes everything

falls into place? We travelled upriver to the part where many German families were settled to see if he was willing to let us work his land and we found to our delight a kindred spirit who welcomed us and showed us to a small cottage with a wooden barn and acres of land turned to sheep and cattle. It was to us a piece of paradise.

'You come highly commended,' Adam Prentiss shook our hands with a firm grip. 'As you see I have let things slide. There is a boy who can do heavy work but he needs pointing to chores.'

I roamed over his land with a good eye on what was in decent repair and what fences were loose. The soil had a good tilth fed from the riverbank. There were fruit bushes and trees and a decent well. Jordan walked around in a daze. 'I don't know the first thing about farming.'

'You'll soon learn. I know enough for the two of us. What do you think? Could you make a life here away from everything you've ever known?'

He pulled me into his arms. '*Whither thou goest, there go I*,' he said. 'Together we will make Adam Prentiss proud. This will be our home.'

It is many a year now since we first set eyes on this blessed earth and the homestead we call The Paradise. We tilled and ploughed, sewed and harvested, gathered in together and when Adam passed away we had enough put by to make this place our own. The years that followed were indeed golden but nothing in life lasts forever.

42

The winter of 1724 was hard and long. Jordan caught a chill in his bones that no potions would shift. I sat up many a night praying that he would not desert me for we were entwined together like gnarled roots in the deep earth. How could I let my beloved go? I lay by his side to warm him but his legs grew cold and his breathing rasped and then was no more. I kept vigil by his side unwilling to be parted from my dear Captain. The ground was frozen hard and there was no chance to bury him. He lay there for days until our near neighbours insisted they hack out a grave in the field.

People were kind and help was offered as I struggled on. Without children to pass on the farm I knew I would not stay to see all we had done fade as I was fading. The Paradise needed young bodies and eager hearts and there were plenty willing to take it over. How can you leave a place that smiles on you, a place where you have shared such good and bad times together? There was no future for me here.

My dearest friend, Sabine, was also widowed and suggested I should come back to Philly to join her and help in their shop. It seemed the right move for I have learned many times over to let go of one life to start another. Once more my dusty journal was taken up to record all that happened since Jordan returned from the wars.

Tamar still called there to ask after me, another dear faithful friend, still hoping I would return to the fold. It was from her that I heard the meeting house was to be pulled down and rebuilt in stone. Good Hope was now a prosperous town. I took a notion, for old time's sake, to make a visit. Not many living would remember me. Joseph and Mary Emsworth had long departed this life and Jacob too from a fever in the brain. All their children grew plump, flushed with success, some with children of their own.

Sabine offered to come along too out of curiosity but I preferred to make this pilgrimage alone. It had long been my hope that a copy of my early writings on the settlement of the township might be of interest to this new generation of Seekers. There was much in that story that would echo that of their parents' journey to the New World. It was with this intention that I carried my heavy journal bound together to present to the elders for them to read and keep in their records.

I knew there was much that might appear ungodly and hurtful but I wanted them to acknowledge their part in why I left when I did. Tamar arranged a meeting in which I would present my offering as of historical interest rather than a spiritual document of faith.

How the township had changed in over twenty years of absence, I noted, as I stepped away from the river. Stone replaced wood, slate replaced thatched roofs. The forest trails were now cart roads and the Main Street paved with sidewalks, lined with elegant brick houses. There was a church with a steeple for not everyone was of the Seeker persuasion. There were shops with provisions for all trades and a fine Town Hall. I paused by the lane leading to the Emsworths' farm but had no breath left in my lungs to make the uphill journey.

Tamar's town house was close to the new building works that rose up two storeys high with large upper windows to let in light and air. It wasn't quite finished and sparsely furnished. There was a porch to shelter the door and stabling for horses. It was a pity Jacob did not live to see all his plans come to fruition. It was Ethan, his eldest son, dark haired and dark eyed like his mother, who greeted me and offered me refreshment as I lay down my offering on the table, the red leather binding gleaming in the dusty sunlight.

Suddenly I feared that my visit might be misconstrued or misunderstood. It had been too long a separation. I was no longer one of them. Perhaps they thought me presumptuous, since I had shown little interest in Good Hope since the day I shook its dust off my feet. They did not know I had supported the Lenape school with secret donations to Tamar for years. I owed those lovely people my life and had tried to return their gift with one of my own.

Three men in tall black hats and stern faces sat across from my seat in silence. I had forgotten how powerful silence can be. I felt an old familiar flush of guilt like a woman's flash of heat. This was a mistake. I was not welcome. Ethan made a wan smile and coughed.

'I'm afraid thee is misguided to think thy account would be of value to us. There is a record in the minutes of 1692 that thee was *"obstinate, wayward, going thine own gait in defiance of our discipline and that with sadness thee were given up to the will of the Lord and put from us."*

'There will be nothing in these pages that will be edifying to the spirit and might in some cases encourage weaker brethren in defiance. Thee made thy choice when thee stepped away from us into a worldly marriage. Now being a widow, it is a hope that thee might once more be ready to submit to our ordinance in the light of humility.'

He paused looking round to the others for support and continued.

'We bear thee no ill will but see no reason to continue to consort with you. Should you wish to be re-examined and restored to grace, we would, of course welcome thee back into fellowship among us. I can say no more but pray thee will see the error of thy ways. May the Lord grant thee peace and salvation.'

They did not even open my journal. It lay like a coffin on a slab as they filtered out of the room leaving the two of us alone. Thus were we both dismissed. Nothing had changed here as I had changed. The spirit of the place was still chilly, not even lukewarm.

There was no anger on my part at first. I felt numb and sad as I lifted my journal and saw behind it there was a pen and quill with ink still in place on the table, so I sat down to write in these closing words: '*I have no strength nor the will to lug this account of my life's journey all the way back to the city.*'

For all their careful records of Seeker life here I know in my deepest core that my own account will be acceptable in the eyes of One who alone is our Judge. This book must be preserved and where better than within the walls of the new building, wrapped as it is in a leather sack. I have already noted a hiding place safe from wind and sun and rain where I might lay down this little part of me, so it only remains to write:

Perhaps someone one day will read these my words and hear my voice across the oceans of time. Then all shall be well and all manner of thing shall be well . . .

GOOD HOPE

October 2015

'It was right here where Dean found the package.' Sam was pointing to a stone low down in the wall. 'The gap has been filled in now, of course.'

Rachel stared down, shaking her head. She then looked up at the tall guy towering over her, with his tanned face and warm smile. 'I can't believe I'm here in Good Hope at the very spot where Joy hid her book. I feel as if I've got to know her over these past months better than any of my closer relatives. She was ahead of her time in so many respects. How could she have ever fitted into their narrow ways?'

'It's not like that now, believe me. The Friends here are lovely people and very forward thinking. They would never have refused to read her story. They're very proud to call her one of their own.'

'It's been such a lovely visit, I can't thank you enough. The launch of the book was so special. Here's me thinking retirement would be one day after another and you set me on a journey that has opened so many new interests.'

'But it's not over yet, Rachel. There's so much of this

beautiful area to see and trails where we can walk in the steps of our mutual friend. Please stay on a little longer.'

Rachel smiled, sensing Sam Storer was a loner like herself. She would like to know him better. And there was no pressure on her time. 'In return I hope you're going to visit Yorkshire for yourself and see all Joy's places in person.'

Sam nodded. 'Sure, I'd love to come over. There's so much I want to see there.'

Rachel smiled, hoping he meant what he said. 'There's just one thing missing,' she added. 'I would like to have seen a portrait of Joy. Perhaps there's a resemblance in our genes. They said she was a Moorside in looks.'

'Oh there is . . . I only saw her once,' Sam whispered.

'You what?' Rachel said. 'You're having me on.'

'Promise you won't laugh, but I once saw her here by the wall. I now think she was waiting for someone to find her story. I've gone back many times but she's never appeared again.'

'Oh do tell me more, Sam.'

Sam took her arm and led her down the path to the bench in the old burial field to share more of his secret, knowing it would be safe with this new friend. Why did he wonder if this meeting was all Joy's doing and that it was she who had brought them together . . . but that would be fanciful, wouldn't it?

ACKNOWLEDGEMENTS

I was inspired to write this story by a visit to the Quaker Tapestry on display in Kendal's Meeting House, Cumbria. It tells the history of the movement in wonderful stitchery. One panel stood out for me where children sat in silence defying the authority that forbade them to worship in their own way. This made the starting point of Joy's own journey.

This is a fictional story about the founding of religious colonies in Pennsylvania and not based on any one town but an amalgam of many. The persecution of Quaker families in Britain in the late seventeenth century is well recorded in Joseph Besse's *A collection of the Sufferings of the people called Quakers.*

I would like to thank the Settle Society of Friends for the loan of relevant books from their library, especially Jean and John Asher for pointing me in the direction of letters from William Ellis of Airton during his travels to America in the 1690s.

The journey of this book has taken me across the pond in search of the Lenni-Lenape people, to the National Museum of the American Indian in Washington DC and The Museum of Indian Culture near Allentown. I also acknowledge information from *The Indians of New Jersey* by M R Harrington.

Once again many thanks to my son, Josh, for transporting us far and wide in search of locations and to our friends, Lorraine and John Chilton of Coopersburg, for their warm hospitality and more, making this visit so memorable.

I thank my editor, Joanne Dickinson and copy editor Sally Partington for some useful suggestions and corrections to my text, also my writing friends, Trisha Ashley and Elizabeth Gill for their continuing encouragement.

Finally to David and our family: much love for all your support.

Leah Fleming, 2017.